RISE OF AHRIK

RISE OF AHRIK

Nathan W. Toronto

TORONTO INTERNATIONAL MEDIA

This novel is entirely a work of fiction. The names, characters and incidents portrayed in it are the product of the author's imagination. Any resemblance to actual persons, living or dead, or events or localities is entirely coincidental.

Electronic Edition July 25, 2021
ISBN 978-0-9976550-1-8
© Nathan W. Toronto. All rights reserved.

The Arabic block *noon* colophon is a trademark of Toronto International Media.

Cover design by Nancy Wride. Cover © Nathan W. Toronto as a collective work. "Haenau Golau Seiniog ar hyd y Gwastatiroedd Wrth Ymyl Hafn Juventae" by NASA/JPL/University of Arizona (public domain). The cover model is Timo Kohlenberg. Book trailer created by Nathan W. Toronto and Aaron R. Toronto. Trailer © Nathan W. Toronto as a collective work, with attribution specified in the trailer description.

Other editions: ISBN 978-0-9976550-2-5 (ebook)—
ISBN 978-0-9976550-3-2 (hardcover)

For those who hunger
For those who thirst

Typset using LaTeX.

There is a great deal of ruin in a planet. The War taught this to Man. For all his malice and for all his power and for all his desire to destroy, Man failed to see that no annihilation could truly be final. It is true that much was lost—much of love and knowledge and much of filth and hate—but Man lived on. Nothing, even Man himself, could destroy life.

It was life, but it was not living. What remained of civilization settled into the dust of memory. The War sheared families asunder. It drove Man deep into the mountains. It wasted all that grew green. It killed all who loved science, all who desired a better world, and all who fought to control that world. Life—pitiful, cruel, thankless life—stumbled on.

And so Woman rose. The heart of Man failed, so she ruled Dom. She disdained the ancient weapons, the weapons that ravaged the planet during The War. She hunted down these weapons and destroyed them. None killed anymore with aught but her own strength, nor did she wage a war of such destructive magnitude again. Seven generations of destruction had changed life forever, but so had it done for war also.

Introduction to "Life after War," Part 2 of *Origin of the Emerald Moon*, by Zharek Jeber-li, in the sixth recorded generation after The War

CONTENTS

1 | Day of Decision

Boys are betrothed before birth into the family of young girls, to ensure the wife is always older and wiser. If a woman is to bear twin boys, the girl who is betrothed will choose between them on the twins' *qer'ish*, midsummer's eve of their eighteenth year.

Law of the Mothers, Article IV, Clause 13

A HRIK commanded ten thousand secret clones, and he refused to feel guilty about it. Whispers of war hung on the air. Lazy, contented civilians complained about women's rule. Rebels armed themselves for war cross-planet. He didn't have time to feel special.

He didn't have the luxury to question his duty.

He pounded a run up Meran Mountain at dawn on his *qer'ish* instead. He had to be faster, stronger, and smarter than his sons, even though all ten thousand were genetically enhanced. Every second of training prepared him for the day that he would lead his sons in battle. He would be ready. To kill. To die. For women's rule.

He slowed to a trot at the crest of Meran Mountain and let the crisp, early morning air of midsummer refresh his lungs before it lost its knife edge. Yes, he was ready to step onto the pages of history and take his place beside the fathers and mothers who preceded him to the eternal realms.

Ahrik was ready for war, but today he needed a plan to keep Zharla from choosing his brother as her husband. In the entire history of the Eshel, no match made less sense. If Zharla chose his weakling little brother instead of Ahrik, the future held only fear and uncertainty. Peace would elude them.

The sun cleared the horizon and warmed the morning. The sun would soon bathe the bay in bright orange light, and fill the air with warmth. He needed a plan. He adjusted the *qasfin* at his side and drew a centering breath from the calm midsummer air, then focused his thoughts on the tendril link, his connection to his sons. *Ayen,* he cast to his aide, *report.*

Father, preparations for deployment almost complete, Ayen cast. *Morale high.*

Ahrik's smile grew at the thought of his ten thousand. *Training in space is a great honor. The Eshel can count on the Ketel of Ahrik to help defeat the rebels.*

Check, Father.

Ahrik cocked his head. He sensed hesitation on his aide's end. *What is it?*

Father, received credible report of planned rebel attack vicinity in-mountain Meran today.

Ahrik couldn't believe his good fortune. This might be the spark they needed to unleash the *ketela* on the rebels. Finally. *Where in-mountain?*

Unclear, Father, but your brother and betrothed...

At the social hall near Shtera Umqi? I know.

We could extract them quietly, Father.

That was risky. Ahrik growled and flexed his hand against the metal band at his wrist, the reminder of the secret that he would carry to his grave. He shifted his feet on the rocky ground. This match with Zharla was almost important enough to ignore fifteen centuries of orders and oaths and secret executions. He eyed the steel bracelet with the Oath of the Ketel engraved on it.

Ahrik had to be Zharla's choice, not Shahl. He kicked at the ground, then the beginning of a plan suggested itself, like the fiery sunrise creeping over the bay. Either the attack would happen, or it wouldn't. It was a dangerous game, playing with the lives of his brother and his intended, but if the attack went on it would sway Zharla's decision in Ahrik's favor.

It took Ahrik another breath to calm his excitement. *Under no circumstances will you dishonor the oath. We will not risk the secret of the ketela.*

Father, everything rides on this match. Your betrothed and your brother. They could die.

Ahrik didn't respond, only sent a mental warning to his aide.

A pause. Ever so slight. Contrition. *Check, Father.*

Ahrik shook out his legs and started down the mountain. He looked around, as if someone or something on this empty mountain peak might perceive his thoughts. Might see the plan forming in his mind. He would have to change into his ready uniform, maybe even his combat uniform, depending on what kind of impression he wanted to make.

Ayen, he cast, *send me coordinates for the Matron Tamer-li.*

Check, Father.

Shahl breathed in the sweet tang of the in-mountain leather market, in an effort to keep the coins from clinking together in his trembling hand. He counted them and gave the shopkeeper a painful shrug. He didn't have nearly enough for the gift he wanted, but he had to make a good impression this morning.

He had to.

Even at this early hour, in-mountain Meranis pulsed in and out of Shtera Umqi, the market at the heart of the mountain. Callers sang the news, and vendors named their wares. A transporter rushed by in its *kall* field, and the lively cacophony of the leather market droned in the background as he searched for the perfect gift for Zharla.

Farther down the leather market he spied a trinket at a stall. Its merchandise hung in precarious rows, on flimsy racks. Shahl nodded in the direction of the trinket and asked the shopkeeper, "How much?"

The shopkeeper rose from her little stone stool with the reluctance of someone whose first customer looked too poor to afford anything in her inventory. Her black robe whispered with movement and her eyes ran him up and down before she cocked a surly bottom lip and spread all her fingers. *"Tun."*

Shahl made a show of counting out his coins, even though he already knew he was short. He had to save some money to buy cinnamon later, to bake some of his special biscuits for Zharla, to give to her before the decision ceremony. He drew in deep breaths to calm the fluttering in his core. He cast an assessing glance in the direction of the trinket. It wasn't perfect, but it would make a good impression. He raised an eyebrow at the shopkeeper. "Wou... would you take fifteen *keina* for two?"

Before she could answer, someone bumped into Shahl from behind, and he had to catch himself on the shopkeeper's rickety table. The merchandise rattled.

"Ho, surry."

Shahl raised a hand and turned. "It's ok—"

He saw who bumped him. A soldier, his presence overbearing, matched only by the wide, half-tooth grin on his pale, in-mountain face. The bump wasn't an accident. The soldier nodded toward the trinket. "Have 'nough?"

The soldier produced a coin from somewhere and extended it toward Shahl's still-open hand. Shahl's panic flared. He knew what it would mean if the soldier's meaty fingers pressed cool metal onto the flesh of Shahl's palm. With trouble brewing over in the Kereu, the army was on the hunt for fresh recruits, and no one down here would give even a moment's thought to an out-mountainer like him, pressed into service amid the bustle of the leather market.

The shopkeeper would probably cheer.

Shahl snapped his hand shut just before the soldier's coin made contact, and his face blanched at the lie that came to his head. "I'm not old enough."

The soldier placed a hand on Shahl's shoulder, light enough to feign kindness, but firm enough to intimate the threat of force, if it came to that. With his other hand, the soldier held up a palm scanner. He set his jaw in a challenge. "Scun yer han'. It'll tull me when yur *qer'ish* is."

Shahl's eyes grew as wide as the out-mountain sky. He couldn't give the real reason for his reluctance, that he was a pacifist, that he despised everything about the military, that even the thought of violence made him sick. War or no war, his brother was as close to the army as Shahl wanted to get.

Shahl inched his palm toward the scanner, lowering the shoulder with the soldier's hand on it at the same time. Just before his hand made contact with the scanner, he ducked, spun, and ran.

"Ho, there," said the soldier, his voice jerky with surprise.

Shahl darted through the crowd, hoping that his smaller size would help him elude capture. He slipped into an alley and chanced a look behind him. The recruiter, such as he was, did not give chase, but continued to wend his way through the market, on the prowl for other, more gullible prey.

Shahl moved in the opposite direction, and brightened when he found something that would work. After pocketing his find and making sure he still had enough for cinnamon, he looked around to get his bearings. He saw the back entrance to the social hall and a wide smile crept onto his face.

Time to make a good impression.

Zharla brushed a strand of hair away from her face and pursed her lips. She was not the type of woman this was supposed to happen to, withered by flights of teenage fancy, fluttered with infatuation.

She certainly had grown to care for Shahl more than Ahrik over the years, but if it were up to her she'd marry neither.

It wasn't up to her, apparently, but that didn't mean she had to like it.

She paused to catch her breath, one hip resting on the counter, her serving smock splattered after ladling soup into bread bowls for over two hours. Shahl had asked her to come serve the poor and unemployed at the social hall that morning, but it was only supposed to last an hour. Now her feet ached, her back stung, but she had actually enjoyed being with Shahl more than she thought she would.

She resisted the encroach of these feelings. Today, on Shahl's and Ahrik's *qer'ish*, the Law of the Mothers gave her the right to decide which twin to marry, but Zharla's own mother thought she'd already made the decision for her. Zharla had to push back, to reassert her right, so she relished mingling with the people her mother disdained, the disadvantaged and downtrodden, that Shahl, in his generous way, cared for so well.

Shahl seemed content to work in silence, but it drove her crazy. She needed something to fill the air between them, some action. "The line just keeps coming, doesn't it?" she asked. She pursed her lips. *What a stupid thing to say.*

Shahl stopped mid-cut, his knife stuck in the bread, now halfway between a loaf and a bowl. "That's the thing about the disadvantaged, Zharla." He looked at her with his tender eyes, eyes that looked at her like no others ever did. "They never really go away."

She reached for a newly carved bread bowl and continued ladling. She smiled at the next man in line. She'd stopped cringing at their missing teeth and pale skin. It wasn't their fault their lives were confined to in-mountain Meran. Two thousand years after The War, too much of humanity was still trapped inside mountains. "Shahl, I didn't mean—"

He stopped her with a raised eyebrow. "Zharla, most women of your station don't even realize these people exist." He smiled at her. "I'm thrilled you're here."

She shoved down the warmth pounding in her breast.

They kept carving and ladling. Zharla found a rhythm, keeping time with the ebb and flow of conversation in the social hall, the clink of utensils on plates. The din reverberated off the stone walls. Men, and a few women, kept coming through the front door of the social hall to the serving line.

Zharla glanced down the line at Renla, her faithful personal servant and friend. Renla's eyes had shifted this way and that ever since coming down here, in-mountain, where she'd spent her abusive early years, before becoming Zharla's personal bondswoman. Despite trembling hands and nervous glances at the in-mountainers in line, Renla was loyal, preserving propriety while Zharla was with Shahl, insurance against ridiculous accusations of Zharla damaging the clan's honor.

Renla served vegetables, so her smock wasn't as spattered as Zharla's. Her stubborn curls snuck out from under her servant's cap, but Zharla saw the false calm in her stance. She kept her face pleasant, but her eyes scanned the line with perspicacity, ready for the flash of an edged weapon, ready for a fight, as always.

Such was the life of those who survived in-mountain.

The social hall was almost full, yet veterans, laborers, and the unemployed kept coming. The stone walls of the cavern had long ago been smoothed down, as had the stalactites on the ceiling. No evidence of stalagmites remained on the floor after thousands of years of feet passing through. They said that during The War humanity had fled to the mountains to escape the destruction scouring the planet's surface, but now in-mountain Meran, their fair city, housed the uneducated and hopeless.

Zharla considered what taking Shahl as a husband would be like. He worked hard to serve these people, his ideals stronger than his sense of self-preservation. He had a singular soul, which was why she would rather choose him over his twin brother at the decision ceremony that day.

Zharla cared not a whit for the whispers and rumors she heard in the family. The clan elders wanted her to choose Ahrik. Old hags. Let them wed Ahrik's precious fame to some witless cousin of hers.

These disadvantaged men here, and making sure their rights were preserved, that was the future. She would gladly give up this marriage decision and her inheritance, if she thought she could make a difference without them. "The family will fall into ruin if you're not leading it when I'm gone, Zharla," her mother always said.

The implication, or threat, was that she would inherit nothing from her mother if she made the wrong choice today.

Zharla had considered this often in recent weeks. Ahrik's presence taxed her sanity. His self-righteous commitment to women's rule blinded him to its more insipid qualities, and his puckish devotion to himself made everyone around him feel less human.

And he never looked at her like Shahl did. She could get used to Shahl's positive attention in her life.

The soup line began to dwindle, as did the supply of soup. She heaved a sigh after the last man left the line, then lifted the soup pan from the warmer and turned to Renla. "I'm taking this back to the kitchen."

When she emerged once again from the clamor of the kitchen, she froze at what she saw. Or, who. "Mother," said Zharla, "how nice of you to come by."

Renla stood rigid, gaze fixed on the spoon she held. The murmur in the hall bore a new, nervous quality. Shahl stood as taut as a bow string, and he exchanged pleasantries with her mother on the other side of the counter, his hands fidgeting behind his back. The discomfort in his voice wrenched at Zharla's heart. She clenched her teeth.

Her mother was covered from neck to toe in white silk, her visage stony, hair pulled into an austere bun. The grizzled house guard, Ahjoz, stood back a pace, eyes seeing everything, his white stubble a testament to years of service to the Tameri clan, the distiller weapon at his side evidence of his privilege and power.

Her mother leveled a fierce glare at her. "Leave this den of sedition at once. No daughter of mine will consort with bandits and traitors."

"Mother." Zharla spoke the warning loud enough for the patrons seated closest to them to hear. She steadied herself on the counter, fingers pressed white against cool, polished stone. The murmuring of those in the social hall died down, and heads turned toward the tension at the serving counter. Zharla reached for another pan, breathing out to calm herself. "Some of these men and women served in the last war."

Across the hall, a veteran stood up. His old army uniform jangled with decorations. With military purpose, he moved toward the speaker's niche carved into the cavern wall opposite, then turned to address those in the hall. Zharla groaned within herself.

Even though he stood on the other side of the hall, the acoustics of the cavern made his voice clear. "Friends, I led a company in the War of Unification ten years ago. Did it end war on our planet, like it was supposed to? No."

A smattering of applause went up. Zharla cast her eyes down, embarrassed.

"War is starting in the Kereu again." He stomped a prosthetic foot.

Her mother grunted and stared at Zharla, arms folded across her chest. "Just because they serve does not mean they are loyal."

The veteran coughed and held his side, wincing. "Friends, why should we fight another war over there?" More applause, and the veteran raised his voice. "Haven't we left too many of our dead in the Kereu already?" Clusters of men, and the smattering of women, shouted their assent. The veteran beat his fist against the air. "End this war!"

The social hall erupted with cheering and applause, curiosity at the conflict brewing between Zharla and her mother forgotten.

Zharla's mother glided around the counter. She brushed Renla aside to stand before Shahl, sizing him up with a severe stare. Before her mother could say anything, Zharla stepped between her and Shahl.

Her mother's nostrils flared. "Zharla," she whispered, "the clan council has chosen Ahrik. He will be your husband. Leave his brother. Come with me."

Zharla slammed the pan down and jabbed her finger into her own chest. "My husband. My life. My choice." Anger glimmered in her eyes. She leaned her head in Shahl's direction. "At least he stands for something besides money and power."

Her mother's airy chuckle conceded nothing. "Someday you'll thank me for this, dear. Most women with as much power as you don't even get to choose."

Zharla perturbed the soup with her ladle. A false calm swirled within her. "I'm so powerful that I don't know what's good for me." She looked over her shoulder to be sure Shahl was close. "Here's something I do know, Mother: women's rule can't survive without giving men more rights."

Her mother's glare grew even more chill. She leaned close. Only Zharla, and possibly Shahl, could hear her. "You'll be on the Council soon enough, dear, but not if you choose him." She sneered an eyebrow in Shahl's direction. "Shall I ask Ahjoz to escort you, or will you come quietly?"

At an almost imperceptible nod from her mother, Ahjoz slid around the counter.

Zharla's insides churned with tension. She fought to keep the tremor out of her voice. This was her moment of freedom, when the course of her life would be set. Her day of decision. If a gaggle of crones from the clan thought they could decide her fate, they had another think coming. "My place is here, Mother, with Shahl, not with Ahrik."

Behind her mother, Renla tensed, staring toward the door of the social hall, over Zharla's shoulder.

Zharla followed her gaze. Ahrik strode up, his superciliousness leaking from every step.

Shahl trembled. "How did you. . . ?"

Ahrik's uniform gleamed. His blade dangled from his hip. He wore the smirk that Zharla had grown to hate.

Zharla pointed at Ahrik and glared at her mother. "I want nothing to do with him."

"Good morning to you too, Zharla," Ahrik said, sounding almost amused. He raised his hands in surrender, then motioned at Shahl. "I'm not here to fight. I'm here for him."

"Zharla." Her mother's voice held menace, and she reached out to place a hand on Zharla's arm. "Little time remains before the ceremony." Her touch was light, but Zharla felt her mother's fingers coil, ready to spring and snatch like the fangs of a snake.

Zharla gripped her mother's wrist and wrenched her arm free. Shooting her mother a defiant glance, she turned to Shahl. "I will choose Shahl for my husband today. He will be father to my children."

Zharla glared at Ahrik, leaned toward Shahl, held his shoulders, and kissed him. The kiss was not salacious, a mere peck on the cheek, but Zharla had broken social norms, had shredded them apart, in fact. No unmarried woman could display affection toward a man in public, especially a woman like Zharla, heiress to the largest mining conglomerate in the western Eshel, and a candidate for the Council of Elders. But if this was to be her moment of truth, she would make it one to remember.

Her face close to Shahl's, she whispered, "No matter what, meet me at the tea shop at midnight."

He beamed, then blushed. So innocent. He had no idea what role he played.

Zharla courted a scandal, and loved every second of it.

But then her mother's hand closed on her arm in a vice grip and whipped her around. Zharla froze in shock. Her mother's hand sailed toward her face. Tears sprang to Zharla's eyes when her mother's palm made contact. Finely buffed nails glanced across Zharla's face. Too late, Zharla's hand flew up to parry the blow. A wave of humiliation washed over her, and she recalled with blistering clarity the first time her mother had struck her, years ago, after her father disappeared. Zharla had asked after her father and her mother had backhanded her across the face, forbidding her ever to ask again.

The sound of the slap echoed from the cavern walls. Renla sucked in her breath, bit her lip, and moved toward Zharla's side, but Zharla held her back with a hasty shake of her head. Ahrik stared, as if even he, the military officer, did not expect violence. Zharla kept Shahl behind her. If her mother lashed out at him, Zharla would fight back, because she knew he would not. She widened her stance, ready to defend him.

Then Zharla felt the silence, the utter stillness in the cavernous hall. She blinked back tears and saw that all eyes stood riveted on them. Why? Were they shocked that her mother had hit her? Were they shocked that she had kissed a man in public? How could her actions possibly be worse than her mother's?

Her mother gave a silken toss of her head. "Ahjoz, escort my daughter out the back. Renla, see to your mistress."

Her mother swept toward the kitchen and the back exit.

Renla rushed to Zharla, fear covering her face. "Zhe'le—"

"I'm fine," Zharla cut her off. She pushed down Renla's probing hands and fixed her friend with a steely gaze. "Am I bleeding, Re'le?" she asked, using the familiar form of her name, for emphasis.

Renla shook her head, eyes awash with a mix of anger and concern, but Zharla wiped her cheek with her sleeve anyway.

"Collect my things, please, Re'le," Zharla whispered.

Renla bit her lip again and looked down. "Yes, Zhe'le."

The old guard Ahjoz cleared his throat with mild distress. He didn't touch her, nor would he dare. Instead, he showed the way out the back exit with one hand. His tone and body language were quiet, almost apologetic. Ahjoz was loyal to the family, but Zharla sensed he felt a wrong had been done, so she turned to Shahl for a goodbye. "She'le, I'll see you at the decision ceremony?"

"I...I can't wait, Zhe'le." He glowed, the smile covering his face, except for the worry he showed when he glanced at her red cheek. She twinged at the thought that she could have him as her husband instead of Ahrik. He might not have Ahrik's political and military connections, but he stood for something, and men's rights were an idea whose time had come. Let her mother and her aunts from the clan rot in their collective idiocy, in their regressive thinking, and let them watch her as she rose to power and influence anyway, with Shahl at her side. Zharla would win, no matter what the old hags thought.

Suddenly Shahl's hand was in hers, and a surge of excitement filled Zharla's core. He slipped his fingertips away, and she realized that something remained nestled in her palm. She opened her hand and saw a simple leather necklace with a small metal amulet shaped like a flame.

"It's the symbol of peace," he said. "I've got one myself." He opened his other hand to reveal his own necklace. "I wanted to give it to you later, after we were done here, but—"

Ahrik laughed on the other side of the counter. "Really, Shahl?" he asked. He shook his head and made a face. "You're trying too hard."

Zharla froze Ahrik with a glare, then Ahjoz cleared his throat again and looked at Zharla and Renla, expectant, arm extended. His face bore a look verging on shame.

"I'll wear it close to my heart, She'le," Zharla said as she nodded to Ahjoz. Zharla slipped the necklace over her head and let the metal slide under her tunic, where she felt it cool against her skin.

Zharla's mother waited for her, shadowed by a merchant stall, posture erect, eyes like a wolf hunting for weakness. The masses of dark-clad humanity eddied to and fro over the cobbled street, the dimness of in-mountain Meran swirling around her white-clad dress in mute solemnity, a reverence born of resentment for someone with much more than them. A caller, voice tired, sang out the news from a niche just down the street, the subtle hum of commerce ebbing whenever he called out.

The grainy smell of the leather market lay thick on the air. This must have been where Shahl got the necklaces.

Her mother's eyes found her. Zharla gathered strength for yet another fight. She guarded the pleasing thoughts of Shahl, of progress, of some bold future, in a special part of her mind, ready to be recalled when her mother's predations created the need.

Her mother stalked toward her, focused on Zharla's cheek. Her eyes softened. A handkerchief emerged from somewhere, and a look of worry overcame her face. "Dear, I'm so sorry it had to happen this way."

Zharla wanted to shy away, but she knew this would only make it worse. She cringed within as her mother dabbed at her face while Ahjoz glared at any passersby who stopped to gawk.

"A mother's touch is always so tender," Zharla said, lying to avoid provocation. As she had so often done before, Zharla wondered how her mother could be so blind to her own hypocrisy, monstrous as it was.

Her mother's flowing white dress swished. She reached up a hand to graze the good side of Zharla's face. "You are so young, so beautiful."

For a split second Zharla wanted to believe this caress.

"Mother." She paused to let a weary headline pass from the caller down the street. "About my decision..."

Her mother pressed a finger to Zharla's lips. "Now is not the time." She smiled and brushed the back of her hand against Zharla's face, the same hand that had struck her only moments before. Zharla suppressed a shudder.

"Mother," Zharla said. She took her mother's hand and kissed it before clutching it to her chest. Zharla's performance had to be just as convincing as her mother's. A swirl of thoughts coursed through her. *Mother, I think you're a monster, but you're the only mother I have. Mother, I hope you burn in sunfire, but please teach me your wiles before you do. Mother, how did I come out of you?* "Mother, I know you love me."

Calm settled over her mother's face. "Will you repeat the mantra with me, please?"

Renla moved to recite alongside Zharla, as she always did, but Zharla's mother shooed her away with a flick of her lip, then bore eyes of incisive judgment into Zharla's visage. "An Esheli woman…"

"…serves the Eshel, because it gives life," Zharla said. She hid her confusion. Every Esheli woman, man, and child knew the mantra and recited it every day as part of the prayer to the Lady of the Emerald Moon, but repeating it in the middle of the day felt awkward.

"An Esheli man…"

"…defends women's rule, because it gives order." She hoped for a time when men and women would govern the Eshel as equals, but the only thing that exceeded the clan's dedication to the decrepit, backwards-thinking social order was its wealth. When her mother finally relinquished control over the family mining conglomerate, then she and Shahl might have a chance to do something about the challenge of men's rights. Until then, if Zharla was to take over the business, then she had to play the game, bide her time.

Her mother continued. "We desire order…"

"…because it is safety from The War, when all life ceased." Her performance threatened to crack. Every Esheli learned from infancy that nothing is worth a return to the unbridled violence of The War, but she could not bring herself to believe it. The War had happened over two thousand years ago, or so they guessed. Many wars had been fought since. None ended life like The War. The ancient weapons remained in the past, but if the War of Unification ten years earlier hadn't brought about a global cataclysm, she doubted anything would. The War was nothing but a trite story to scare the weak-minded.

Her mother smiled as the recitation faded. Her voice hushed, almost at a whisper. "Why, Zharla, did life cease during The War?"

Zharla strained to hear her over the market hum rippling over the dim street. She concentrated on not rolling her eyes. Her mother wanted to give her a history lesson, right there, in-mountain, at midday. "Because of the ancient weapons, Mother. Because our

Esheli Mothers had not yet discovered the power of the *ketel*." The taboos against discussing the ancient weapons and the *ketela* were so strong that Zharla had only a vague idea of what they were. Soldiers like Ahrik and powerful women like the Chief Elders were entrusted with giving these words meaning, not her. She questioned many things, but not this. Not yet. In time, though, and with Shahl at her side...

"And why, dear Zharla, are the *ketela* powerful?"

"Because they are loyal," Zharla whispered, trying to match her mother's fervency.

"Yes, Zharla, the *ketela* are loyal. You are a Tameri woman, and a Tameri woman..."

"...is loyal," said Zharla. Her heart sank. She could not challenge this. Saying anything else would embroil them in some new fight, and Zharla did not need that now. The quickest way to start her new life with Shahl, her choice, was to get to the end of the conversation.

"Now, Zharla." Her mother squeezed Zharla's shoulders, a bit too hard to be loving. She drew close, close enough for Zharla to feel the sting of her mother's breath on her wounded face. "How will you choose this afternoon?"

Zharla couldn't avoid confrontation now. She could make her mother think she would actually choose Ahrik, which would avoid her anger now, but risk an explosion when she lied to her later. Her heartbeat quickened. The backs of her eyes trembled to think what might happen, especially if her mother lashed out at Shahl. Honesty now would give her less flexibility later. She felt so helpless as she considered her terrible choice, laying her case before such a heartless judge. "Mother, I...I can be just as loyal with Shahl as with Ahrik."

Her mother's face twisted in anger. She dug her fingers into Zharla's shoulders and put her mouth next to Zharla's ear. "Lies." She paused, as if to let the threat in her voice sink in. "This is a marriage of families." She sighed and cast a forlorn face, with eyes Zharla trusted not a whit.

"Mother—"

Her mother patted her neck. "I tried, I really did, but the clan council said that if you chose Shahl"—she choked back a deceiving sob—"he'd be dead by morning."

Zharla's head swam. Shahl dead? Hot tears clouded her vision. The old crones wouldn't dare stoop so low. Allowing her tears to tumble was all Zharla could do to keep from striking, from remedying betrayal with violence. Her fists quivered at her side. Zharla knew that her mother had engineered all this. Zharla's fury rose.

She drew in a long, slow breath. If Shahl had taught her anything, it was forbearance. Violence would not diminish the threat on Shahl's life, nor would it erase her mother's deception. Maybe, if she played the loyal daughter, she could run away with him before the ceremony. She had to talk to Shahl, somehow. She cast her eyes down in feigned submission. "I will choose Ahrik."

Her mother slipped an arm around Zharla's shoulder. "Let's go home."

"No, Mother...I mean, there's something I need to take care of before I get ready for the ceremony." She tried to make her voice sound as calm as possible, but she did not even convince herself, her voice trembled so. She slid away from her mother's arm and made for the social hall once again.

Her mother's voice broke in, and a few passersby flinched at the tone of command. "Ahjoz."

Ahjoz's lithe form darted between Zharla and the door, separating her from Renla at the same time. Zharla stopped short. For an old man, his body moved fluid and quick. His face bore a stern expression, no hint of the apology it had shown before. Was this performance for her mother's benefit, or was the previous performance a benefit for Zharla? Her mother touched Zharla's shoulder with a finger. She laughed. "I'll hold you to your word. That boy means nothing to me, but he means more than nothing to you, does he not?"

The warning in her voice confirmed what Zharla dreaded, that her mother never had cared for her. Zharla's life, from then on, would be a game of lies, of stealth and a sideways glance. She may be forced to marry Ahrik, but she would still have Shahl's companionship, even a child by him, if possible.

Zharla scoffed, her innocence gone, her life newly born into a knowledge of her own capacity to deceive, the truest evidence yet that she was her mother's daughter. She began to walk toward home with her mother and offered a smile. "You act, Mother, as if love is choice. Is it any more a choice than war or hate or violence? Our lives play themselves out on someone else's stage, do they not?"

The crowds parted for them, aided by Ahjoz' scowl and his nonchalant hand resting on his distiller. Her mother inclined her head and beamed, as if proud that a lesson had sunk in. "You still have much to learn." Her mother waded through the crowded cavern at the heart of Shtera Umqi, pulling Zharla along. She squeezed Zharla's hand. "You always have a choice."

Ahjoz padded along in front, watchful.

Zharla pled at Renla with her eyes. Zharla brushed her fingers over the scratches on her face. She did not like who she had become.

Shahl closed his eyes, branding the moment onto his memory, the thrill of Zharla's hands holding his shoulders and her lips brushing his cheek, her towering declaration that she would choose him as her husband later that day. She had used the familiar form of his name. More veterans would rise to denounce this new war and other men and women in the social hall would raise the call for men's rights, but all that made no more difference than a mild breeze at sunrise, when a fervent moon stood high, to overawe the senses. He, Shahl Jeber-li, was going to be the husband of Zharla Tamer-li. Nothing else mattered at all.

Ahrik chuckled, an intrusion on Shahl's reverie. He shook his head. "Are you done playing idealist, little brother?"

Shahl sighed and considered his fraternal twin. "Being born five minutes ahead of me doesn't make you my big brother, Ahrik. Make yourself useful. Clean up."

Shahl used a free hand to hang his necklace on a hook next to the sink, to keep it free from sully and grime. Another man stepped up to the niche at the opposite side of the social hall and began speaking. His voice was softer, too young to be a veteran, probably a *melmezi* student like Shahl.

Ahrik raised an eyebrow. "I don't think so. This show is too interesting."

Shahl lifted a container out of its warming bay. He knew a lie when he heard one. "Why do I get the impression that your arrival with the Matron Tamer-li wasn't a coincidence?"

Ahrik grunted. "You're a grown man today, little brother. Midsummer's eve of our eighteenth year. Did you really think that getting Zharla to come here would make her choose you?" He placed a hand on his chest. "Over me?"

Shahl clenched his teeth and carried the container to the kitchen. His brother's words hung especially vile today. Shahl returned from the kitchen and picked up a damp rag. "Give me a moment's peace." Shahl had learned well enough over the years that Ahrik had more regard for his precious *ketel* than for his own brother. "Don't you have a war to train for or something?"

"Now that you mention it, little brother, I have a bit of news that should make you respect me more."

"You doubt that I respect you?" Shahl asked. He suppressed a wicked smile.

Ahrik's eyes narrowed to slits, but he shrugged off the question. "Read this."

Shahl sighed and wiped his hands on his smock, then took the square of stiff cardstock that Ahrik held out. It bore today's date and a curt message:

Shadhir Ahrik Jeber-li:

Deploy with *ketel* tomorrow at sunset. Preparation for space training.

Aanin Sheresh Shehur-li

Shahl raised an eyebrow. Even he knew that not everyone in the military was put through space training. He grunted in begrudging respect. "May the Lady guard you," Shahl said, using the traditional well wishing and handing the message back. He picked up the rag and wiped at the counter, hoping that the subject of the conversation would change, or that Ahrik would leave.

Ahrik shifted his weight, and his weapon clanged against the counter. Ahrik's hand darted down to steady it, but he knocked a dish of salt off the counter instead. The dish shattered on the ground, and Shahl heard salt skitter across the polished stone floor on the other side of the counter. Ahrik gave a detached look at the clay fragments and the scattered salt, as if he had had nothing to do with the mess.

Shahl stopped his cleaning and gripped the counter, his frustration brimming. That blade should have been a symbol of peace, not a symbol of his brother's conceit. The law allowed an officer to wear his blade anywhere, but Ahrik should not have worn it to the social hall, where so many spoke out for men's rights and against war. Ahrik just couldn't resist displaying his entitlement and superiority to the world.

With a peeved look at Ahrik, Shahl grabbed a vacuum pack and sucked up the salt and shattered dish. He called back to the kitchen, "Can you handle it from here?" At the muffled affirmative, Shahl stuffed the vacuum pack back in its place. He would not stand to see his brother flout the social hall's norms. "Weapons aren't allowed in here, Ahrik."

War was an evil thing, but Ahrik couldn't see it. Shahl rounded the counter and saw the crescent-shaped *keteli* blade gleam in its sheath at Ahrik's thigh. In Shahl's earliest memory, their father had given that blade to Ahrik. Their father called it Biriq, or Lightning, for how fast it flew. It was the last time Shahl had seen his father alive. "My boys," he'd said, "I fight so you don't have to." When his father hadn't come back from the War of Unification, Shahl had learned that war and killing held no glory at all. But war and killing were all Ahrik talked about.

Ahrik snickered as he followed Shahl to the front door of the social hall. "It's my right to carry Biriq, little brother."

Another veteran hobbled up to the niche, metal bars gleaming on his chest, and cleared his throat to gain the crowd's attention.

Shahl pressed his palm to the reader to open the door. The mechanism clicked. The door dissolved. Shahl glanced at Ahrik. "Father wouldn't have carried his weapon in the open like that."

"Pacifist." He spat the word, like a curse. "What do you really know of Father?" His tone sounded even more triumphant than normal.

Shahl stepped through the door and called over his shoulder, "His death pained me as much as it did you." Slicing through the vigorous foot traffic of the spice market, he turned back to see Ahrik weaving behind him. The sharp smells of saffron and thyme lilted on the air. Shahl grimaced. "Why are you following me?"

The clamor of merchants hawking their wares rose over the midday bustle. Shahl would have preferred to go out the back way, via the leather market, since it would have gotten him home quicker, but he thought better of risking another encounter with the Matron Tamer-li.

"Pain?" asked Ahrik, drawing level with him. "What caused you pain gave me great pride. One day soon, I will carry father's noble legacy into battle, and I pray to the Lady of the Emerald Moon that I will fulfill my duty with honor."

"Who's the idealist now, Ahrik? That's the kind of mindless devotion that got us into this mess in the first place, fighting legitimate opposition cross-planet and the men's rights movement at home."

"Traitor," Ahrik said with a sneer. "If we don't fight the rebels over there in the Kereu, we'll have to fight them here. The honor of those that fight keeps us safe." He pulled Shahl into a gap between two stalls and stuck a finger into his own chest. "My military honor is the reason that Zharla will choose me over you. Imagine it: the wealth of the Tameri mining conglomerate combined with our Jeberi military courage. Can there be a more powerful union? We will be the envy of the region, maybe even the entire Eshel."

Shahl slid past Ahrik and into the foot traffic once again. "You're wrong." Zharla despised Ahrik. She'd told Shahl as much, but he didn't dare tell Ahrik that. He saw no need to provoke Ahrik's ire without a very good reason. Shahl stopped at a stall to buy the cinnamon. "I know Zharla better than you do. She will choose with her heart."

Ahrik scoffed. "You may know her heart. I know her family."

"Thank you," Shahl said to the spice merchant, taking the bag of cinnamon and slipping it into a chest pocket. "I haven't lost yet, Ahrik."

Ahrik patted Shahl's shoulder. "Shahl, Shahl. Maybe she likes you more than me, but your obsession with men's rights is almost as dangerous as your opposition to the war."

"Dangerous?" asked Shahl. "Granting men equal rights is the natural concomitant of a modern society, Ahrik. And if we honestly pondered the kind of peace we're creating, we'd stop this war in the Kereu before it starts."

"There you go again, using your big words. Do you really believe them, like you believe Zharla will actually keep that necklace on, once she's out of your sight?"

The necklace. Shahl had forgotten it by the sink. He slapped his forehead. *Curse my academic's memory!* "Go home, Ahrik. I forgot something."

▫

Ahrik watched his brother scamper through the spice market and back toward the social hall, thirty meters away. Too late to stop him. He'd be back soon enough.

The spice market filled the wide passageway carved out of Meran Mountain as a refuge during The War. The dim artificial light strained Ahrik's out-mountain eyes. The stone walls, smoothed by generations of erosion and wear, still bore a few divots from that hasty work of long ago. He smiled with pride to think on the civilization their maternal forebearers built. Ahrik saw loyalty and purpose in women's rule. He saw no reason why Shahl should want to change anything.

Ahrik scanned about for a place to wait. He wanted to be sure his brother came home, where Ahrik could keep an eye on him. Where they could learn about the attack in safety. A wizened woman shuffled up the middle of the passageway. The traffic curled around her as she worked her way up the gentle slope that ran from the beginning of the spice market to the social hall. The load she carried forced an awkward gait, but Ahrik knew it would be nothing for him.

"Let me help you with that," he told her. He swung her pack onto his shoulder.

She clutched his arm and patted his chest. Her eyes smiled at his uniform. "Thank you," she said. Her voice rose little above a croak. "The army turns out good boys."

She craned her head, turning sideways to compensate for her hunched back. When she beamed, Ahrik saw gaps in her teeth and smelled cardamom on her breath. This woman was the product of a hard, in-mountain life, but she was a woman all the same. Any Esheli woman, no matter how poor, was greater than any Esheli man.

Ahrik lived to serve the women of the Eshel. He would sacrifice every last one of his ten thousand sons to preserve women's rule. His sons swore an oath to him. He swore an oath to an idea. This oath was more powerful than anyone outside the *ketel* would understand, especially his weakling brother and Zharla, who seemed to believe that order and peace simply created themselves. Men like Ahrik stood in the breach to defend women's rule, to bring peace to all.

Especially to women like the one whose bag he carried. Her bony fingers dug into his arm as he escorted her through the spice market.

Besides, escorting the old woman brought him closer to surprising Shahl once he came back out of the social hall, so they could get out-mountain and back to the light of day. To safety. The real point of this day was Zharla choosing her husband, not Ahrik chasing Shahl. The Jeberi family was betrothed to Zharla's clan when he and Shahl were still in their mother's womb, even before the family knew she carried twins. Now that he and Shahl were grown, his silly little brother actually thought Zharla would choose him. Ahrik stifled a snicker at the thought.

His plan was working.

Ahrik and the old woman continued their slow shuffle. Ahrik shielded her from people pushing past them. Only ten meters left before the social hall entrance. Men filed in and out, traitors all.

They knew nothing of what Ahrik really was. Twenty-one generations earlier, Ahrik's ancestor Zharek founded the *ketela*, the elite military class of which Ahrik was part. Only those within the *ketela* knew they were composed of clones. Civilians like Shahl and Zharla thought the *ketela* were made up of *hayla*, volunteers, like the rest of the army, but the secret of the clones was the key to the *ketela's* success. The clones lived and trained and fought together for their whole lives, and no one except their comrades mourned when they died. Commanders like Ahrik lived with the secret of the *ketel*, and held this secret close to their hearts, on pain of death.

Ahrik flexed against the steel bracelet at his wrist. The burden of this oath gave his life meaning. His secret, and the power of the *ketel*, ensured the survival of women's rule.

And his weakling brother wanted to go read books for the rest of his life. Become an academic. Useless. Somewhere in those books, Shahl learned that men had the same rights as women. Ahrik scoffed. Women had guided Esheli society to peace and prosperity for hundreds of years. They even built a republic that spanned the entire planet. The unrest in the Kereu was temporary, yet Shahl acted like the very soul of the Eshel was on trial. This war would be a little flare-up that the Chief Elders would deal with. Ahrik saw no reason to mess with success.

The old woman tugged at Ahrik's arm and patted his chest with her knobby hands once again. They'd almost reached the entrance to the social hall. "Here, give that back," she said. "I need some shoes."

Confused, Ahrik cast his gaze about and only then noticed a dim side passage that led to the next passageway over. Probably the shoe market. The old woman's flowing black robe swished as she pulled him close. Ahrik bent down so far that their eyes were nearly level. She placed a meatless hand on his head, in blessing. She recited, "An Esheli woman serves the Eshel."

"An Esheli man defends women's rule," Ahrik answered.

In unison, they both recited, "This is safety from The War." Good women like this were the reason Ahrik kept the secret of the *ketel*. These women were the reason he trained with his *ketel* all his life, and why he would deploy for space training tomorrow. He and his sons would fight to protect women's rule, even if it meant that weaklings and traitors like Shahl were also kept safe. The old woman turned and shuffled off down the side passage.

Ahrik smiled with pride.

Someone shouted inside the closed door of the social hall.

Ahrik tensed.

A loud boom consumed the world. The door to the social hall disintegrated in a shower of splintered rock and dust. A concussion of air made Ahrik check his balance. His adrenaline spiked. Vibrations coursed through the rock at his feet. Earthquake? No, couldn't be. The sirens would've gone off. Shoppers froze. Ahrik's senses sharpened. Confusion swirled through the spice market.

A man stumbled out of the ruined doorway to the social hall. His face and hands dripped blood. He wobbled and crunched over ragged rocks, body caked in pale dust, and held his head. He steadied himself on a nearby stall. He wheezed, then collapsed.

Ahrik sprang into action while the crowd scattered. "You!" He pointed to the nearest shopkeeper. "Help him!"

Not like this. It wasn't supposed to be like this.

He had to get Shahl out.

Ahrik slid to a stop at the rubbled doorway to the social hall. His eyes widened in dismay. The ragged opening showed more ghostly forms staggering toward the exit, covered in the same pale dust, many with clothes partially torn from their bodies. An eerie silence reigned. In the fraction of a second before the nameless shapes got to the opening, Ahrik slipped in. He coughed. Most of the victims clutched their ears or bellies. Many were covered in blood. Ahrik had never seen a weapon do anything like this, and he'd witnessed every weapon in the modern arsenal, at least at the range.

A swirl of fear attacked his gut. Could it be that the ancient weapons had been used once again? Weapons not seen for over two thousand years. He refused to believe what his eyes saw. He never imagined the rebels would do something like this.

The cries of the wounded broke the silence of the social hall. They grew. Ahrik peered through the murky dust. He searched for some sign of his brother. The epicenter of the blast was just a few meters inside the door. Stone tables were blown apart. Bodies were strewn over the ground. Some writhed and moaned in pain. Many lay still. Ahrik saw gaping, mortal wounds. He saw a human head with no body. A fine gray tint covered everything. All the forms looked the same. He peered at gaunt, haunted faces through the haze. Could Shahl have walked out without Ahrik seeing?

"She'le!" he called out. Only weak cries for help answered. In vain, Ahrik waved away the dust. He coughed back the taste of dust.

Ahrik didn't want to believe that the ancient weapons could be reborn, but if this is what they did, then he knew why the Mothers condemned them after The War.

This could not really have happened. Not here. No one was supposed to know how the ancient weapons were made. They were all destroyed when women came to power. Even mentioning the existence of these weapons had been done only in secret for two thousand years. Ahrik knew their history only because he commanded a *ketel*. Until he heard the boom and saw that dust-covered man wobble and fall, Ahrik had thought that this indiscriminate, destructive power was gone from their world, from Dom.

Ahrik suppressed a rising urgency, tinged with guilt. He might have been able to stop this. He realized now that if Shahl was seriously hurt, it would damage the family name, but if he was dead, it would be disastrous for Ahrik. Zharla was supposed to have a choice. She would never forgive Ahrik for not protecting his brother, the one she wanted to choose. Better to have Shahl alive, well, and chosen by Zharla than for her to simply settle for Ahrik. A dead brother would haunt their marriage.

They were supposed to hear about the attack, not live it.

Ahrik wracked his memory for what would have made Shahl come back in here. He forgot something. Ahrik worked his way toward the counter, examining faces as he went. Kneeling down, he wiped blood and dust from one slick face. Not Shahl. The stench of blood made bile rise in his throat. He fought it down. He had seen many men wounded in training before, and he was no stranger to gaping wounds, but the scene before him was larger and more destructive than anything he had thought possible.

When he did not find his brother after a few moments, a new sense of panic began to take hold. His training kicked in. He forced himself to breathe slowly, to think how he could find Shahl.

The cinnamon. In Shahl's pocket.

He smelled it now, despite the dust. The tang led him to a balding, middle-aged man wedged between the serving counter and the stone floor, slick with blood. His face and torso were a mess, and Shahl was pinned underneath him. Ahrik hoped the man's body had shielded Shahl from the blast.

Ahrik gripped the dead man and pulled. But he rushed it, and Ahrik's hands slipped free, slick and red. He got down on his knees to find better purchase, then sank his shoulder into the dead man's side and pushed with his legs. The body slid off his brother. To Ahrik's relief, Shahl breathed out and then coughed on a full breath of dusty air. He checked his brother for visible wounds. He found none, except for a bit of blood that trickled from both ears. His vitals seemed okay.

Shahl's eyelids blinked open. "Ah'ke?" he asked, dazed.

"She'le, can you move?"

Shahl nodded, and Ahrik pulled his brother's arm around his own shoulder, gripped Shahl around the waist, and lifted him to his feet. Ahrik turned to go back the way he came, but it was packed with people now. Healers fought to get in through the front entrance. Walking wounded stumbled and jostled to get out.

The leather market. The back way. If Shahl had any injuries, Ahrik hoped they were mild. He pulled Shahl through the opening in the counter and toward the kitchen. He was relieved when Shahl began to walk, mostly supporting his own weight. Other than an occasional grimace, Ahrik saw no obvious signs of pain.

A peace forces officer stood in the kitchen, an island in a sea of pandemonium. He herded people out the back exit. When the brothers arrived at the back alleyway, Ahrik paused to let Shahl catch his breath. He glanced up and down the street. Good, Zharla was gone. He didn't want her to sympathize with Shahl's injuries.

"Ah'ke." Shahl panted. "I need to sit."

Ahrik eased him down as gently as he could. "Are...are you okay, She'le?" Ahrik slumped down beside his brother. A healer came over, but Ahrik waved him away. "There's worse off in there."

Ahrik breathed a sigh of relief. The scent of leather refreshed his senses. Ahrik looked back at his brother, who winced as he tried to shift his weight. Ahrik felt a pang of regret at his harshness toward Shahl earlier. "Here, Shahl, let me..."

Shahl fended him off with one hand. "No, no, I'm okay. Just winded." He brought a hand up to his neckline and pulled out his necklace. He fingered the flame-shaped pendant, then breathed a sigh of relief. Shahl took a few deep breaths, then asked, "Ahrik, what was that?"

Ahrik rested his arms on his knees. He hung his head. This was bigger than his distaste for his brother. "During The War, they used explosive weapons, chemicals mixed together to create extreme kinetic force."

Shahl shuddered, as if cold, then narrowed his eyes in distrust. "Is that hearsay, or did you read that in a book?"

"Believe it or not, I read books. Just about useful things. Not like you."

Shahl scrunched up his face and sat up a little straighter. They stared in mutual challenge, silently rehashing an argument they'd had a dozen times in recent months. Even an explosion was not enough to cool Shahl's stubbornness.

Ahrik shook his head. "These kinetic weapons were supposed to be a thing of the past."

Shahl winced. "I . . . ouch . . . didn't think that kind of chemical reaction was possible."

"Oh, it's possible, but geothermal energy and subatomic propulsion make that kind of kinetic force unnecessary today." Ahrik's eyes glazed over. "It was once the foundation of human civilization."

"You surprise me, Ahrik." Shahl's smile mocked him.

Ahrik shot him a warning glance. "During The War, the most destructive weapons used atomic force, not a chemical reaction. Atomic weapons ravaged the planet. They destroyed the far side of the Emerald Moon."

"Uncontrolled fission?"

Ahrik shook his head.

Shahl let out an uncomfortable breath. "Fusion?"

Ahrik nodded.

A woman shrieked. "She'le!"

Zharla ran up, the family guard close on her heels. Her boots clicked to a stop on the grimy stone pavement, and her cloak flowed over the ground as she stooped next to Shahl. Worry strained her eyes. She looked back and forth between the two brothers, then at the trickle of ghoulish victims leaving the social hall. "Who did this?"

The silence that passed between the three of them spoke volumes. Ahrik knew the answer to her question, but he couldn't bear to face his own miscalculation. He would let them believe that it could have been the men's rights movement, or the antiwar party, or rebels from the Kereu. That it could have been some reactionary women's group, targeting traitors in the social hall.

Ahrik shrugged. "Whether we want it or not, war is upon us."

Zharla's shoulders slumped after she helped Shahl up. "Everything." She shuddered. "Everything is different now."

> An Esheli woman serves the Eshel, because it gives life. An Esheli man defends women's rule, because it gives order.
> We desire order because it is safety from The War, when all life ceased.

> Mantra of the Esheli Woman

2 | Auspicious Beginning

Few marriages have such auspicious beginnings.

Zharla Tamer-li, at the decision ceremony

Z HARLA disguised her exhaustion with a deep breath. The afternoon sun streamed into the parlor of the Tameri mansion, but
already she wanted the day to be over. She wanted to skip the part
where she destroyed all of Shahl's hopes and dreams. Zharla sat on
the deep violet, upholstered chair with gilt wooden armrests, gripping the wood to keep her hands from shaking, as if squeezing the
life from the leaping dolphins carved there, the symbol of the Tameri
clan. If there weren't so many old crones clinging to the old order
and holding society back, she'd have repudiated the clan long ago.

As soon as they were of no use to her, as soon as she had her seat
on the Council, she'd do exactly that.

Her suitors, Shahl and Ahrik, knelt on the short-pile rug before
her. The reek of the clan's incense wafting on the air almost overpow-
ered her, but Zharla smiled at Shahl. He wore a gentle fragrance, a
whisper of cinnamon to match the biscuit he had brought her, now
struggling in vain against the incense. With the price of cinnamon
from the Kereu so dear now, the plump biscuit was a queenly gift.

How she dreaded what she was about to tell him.

By custom, the young woman met alone with her prospective
husbands, since from the moment of decision onward, the marriage
could legally be consummated. The parlor, tucked away in a corner

of the Tameri estate, was arranged as normal, with the exception of the accoutrements for the ceremony on the side table and a bed in one corner. The thought of using that bed made Zharla's stomach churn. If she never touched a bed with Ahrik in it, it would be too soon.

Somehow, Ahrik brooded on his knees, and guilty pleasure needled Zharla. His training beads gleamed from their place in the rim of metal on his forehead. His rank sash wound around his waist, embroidered in gold and silver. He fingered the weapon at his side and focused his eyes on the ground in front of him. Zharla knew he hated how she supported Shahl's cause, and she read it all over him, feeling almost guilty at the thought.

Almost.

Zharla's eyes passed over Shahl once again, dressed in his scarlet silk tunic and trousers. She withdrew her handkerchief from the pouch at her waist and coughed back a sob. His face held so much promise. The choker chain around his neck held the gems for the *melmezi* classes he had taken. So few men were allowed to enter the *melmez* that he had every reason to beam with pride, but she knew he beamed now for another reason. He thought she was about to choose him. She forced herself to look away from his face, for if he met her gaze with his smile or his eager eyes, she would break. She tried not to think how this would transform him into a puddle of despair.

Zharla pressed her eyes shut to hold back tears and drew in a long breath, composing herself. She would give up all her wedding finery and all the pomp and all the riches and fame to have one moment alone with Shahl, to explain to him what had really happened, that this was not what she wanted. "Ahjoz will be watching," her mother had told her before the ceremony. Her mother had narrowed her demonic eyes. "If you break from the script, even if you still choose Ahrik, Shahl dies."

Zharla wondered if the attack at the social hall that morning was Ahrik targeting his brother, but she quickly suppressed the thought.

Impossible.

She released her grip on the arm rests and cleared her throat into her handkerchief. Twisting the handkerchief in her hands, she looked from one to another. "I'm glad you're both okay, after this morning."

It could have been much worse. Losing Shahl would have crushed her. He had so much to live for still, even without her, and his brand of innocent idealism only came around once in a generation. She couldn't help but take in Shahl's smile, and it nearly broke her, but she studied the handkerchief she twisted through her hands until the anguish keening within her breast had subsided.

Will he ever understand my sacrifice?

Zharla grew conscious of the necklace Shahl had given her earlier, before the attack at the social hall. The flame-shaped pendant now lay hidden under layers of chiffon, satin, and tulle. She looked for Shahl's matching necklace and saw it bounce outside his red tunic as he shifted his weight.

For days beforehand, Zharla had rehearsed the ceremony assiduously. She knew the two brothers had, too. Zharla recited the opening phrase: "*Hareshu li-Simhaleli ahlaka kalletni.*" ("The Lady of the Emerald Moon has graced me with your presence.") She motioned with her eyes to the side table, where matches, candles, and ewers sat, and where the musky stench of incense burned in metal censers.

The brothers rose and moved toward the table, reciting as they went: "*Tenen-li shi-ahleh sheret-li metnenini, fe-tenen-li shi-ahleh li-shehet mehreshini.*" ("Hers is the light that showed me the way, and hers is the light that lets me now see.") They lit five candles each, for ten total, faces solemn.

Ahrik's hands glided from one candle to the next. Shahl's shook. The carefree flames danced, an insult to Zharla's heartbreak. The candles represented the light of the Emerald Moon, which showed the Mothers the way out of the mountains and into the Eshel after The War, but a shadow clung to Zharla's heart that no light could chase away. She wanted to believe that Ahrik knew nothing of the script her mother had given her.

This shadow would cast a pall over their marriage, this collusion between Ahrik and her mother.

Zharla feigned a smile, and her eyes passed from one brother to the other, narrowing on one, softening for the other. *"Eshihetni fe-tenen raqbihu ehreshak,"* she said. ("Look to me now and I shall show you the light of Her will.") She wracked her brain for a way to tell Shahl, in a way only he would understand, that she was choosing Ahrik to preserve his life.

The brothers returned to their positions on the floor. *"Raqbihu hall etred, lek-raqbihu an-esh'het,"* they said. ("Her will only do I wish for, but Her will I do not fathom.")

In the final act of ceremony, Ahrik and Shahl leaned down to rest their foreheads on the floor. Zharla smiled to see Ahrik humbled like this. Beside him, Shahl's body quivered.

"You may look up," Zharla commanded them. She followed the script her mother had given her, meant to convince Ahrik and Shahl that none of this was planned. "Impressive, Ahrik. For a keteli, you have learned the Old Tongue well. As for you, Shahl, your command of the Old Tongue has always been unmatched." Envy flashed on Ahrik's face as Shahl looked up, that hopeful smile in his eyes. Only by focusing on her disdain for Ahrik could Zharla keep to the script, to make it look like this was what she wanted. If she dwelt on Shahl's goodness for even a moment, her façade would crumble.

Zharla poured all the enmity she could muster into her voice. "Look at me, Ahrik."

He met her gaze, his eyes full of scorn.

"What could you possibly want from me?" Zharla asked. "My mother told me I should choose you. Why?" Every part of her scoured soul begged to reveal her mother's threat.

Ahrik knelt, silent.

"At a loss for words, for once?" Zharla asked.

Ahrik looked down, his shoulders and neck burdened with false modesty. "I cannot change your mind about me."

Zharla squeezed the handkerchief. Her knuckles turned white with fury. Ahrik needled her. He must know about the script. She muttered in disgust and leveled a cold stare at him, but then sadness coursed through her once again. She could not postpone her hateful task any longer. Her mother had given her the words to say. "We make choices, sometimes hard choices," she muttered. She grit her teeth, then spat the next words out: "This is the hardest one that I have ever made."

She turned a mournful gaze on Shahl, and a bolt of fear flashed into his eyes. Zharla felt a tear form at the corner of her eye, but it came from deep in her heart. *"She'leni, She'leni,"* she said. ("My She'le, my She'le.") *"Haqrer shadhe'eke."* ("I have chosen your brother.")

Shahl disintegrated onto the floor, his forehead on the ground. His fingers interlaced with the hair on the back of his head.

"Please forgive me, She'le," she whispered.

His head stayed down for a long, painful moment. Then, raising his head with obvious effort, he nodded in mute acceptance. He stared into the middle distance, convulsed in silence. After yet another eternal moment he worked himself to a standing position and turned toward the door, still without looking at Zharla. A chasm tore open in the caverns of her heart.

Tears streamed down her face. In the moment she could have told him the truth, in a way only he'd understand, her mind had failed her. She had thought of nothing. She had failed Shahl. When he was almost to the door of the parlor, Zharla called, "Shahl." He half-turned, eyes fixed on the middle distance. "Broth—"

A sob choked off her words.

He nodded once, his visage forlorn, palmed open the door, and left.

After watching the door resolve behind him, Zharla glanced at where Shahl's forehead had touched the floor. Light glistened off the tear-moistened stone. But then she saw something else laying on the rug, just behind where Shahl's forehead had been, and she let out a low moan of despair. Shahl's necklace. She crumpled out of her seat and knelt next to the necklace, scooping it up while soft sobs wracked her body.

She fought back the convulsions and turned her head toward Ahrik. "Do you feel any sympathy at all for your brother?"

He said nothing, merely stared, as if she had uttered words he could not comprehend.

So uncaring. She bowed her head and cried for a long while, adding her own tears to Shahl's.

Her tears drained, Zharla sat up on the rug and fastened a fierce glare on Ahrik, their eyes on the same level now. "I shall have you, but you will not have me," she said. She would not lose Shahl only to lose to Ahrik. "If I never grow to love you, Ahrik Jeber-li, I shall not be surprised, but until that happens, you shall not know the gratification of my body. Our seed, if it ever grows, will be the product of love, not duty. Do you accept that?"

Quiet rage seeped into Ahrik's eyes. "You would ask a *shadhir* of the ketela to sever his military line?" A vein pulsed on his neck. "I'll be shamed." He stood up, and his hands fell to his side. He looked down on her. "How will my family serve the Eshel?"

His eyes bore a fire she had never seen before. It made her uncertain.

She gulped, then stood. She drew herself up until her eyes were nearly level with Ahrik's, gripping her hands behind her back so he wouldn't see them tremble. "I do not ask you to give up your bloodline, Ahrik, only to be patient until we both desire our blood to mingle. Do you accept that?"

"The rule of women needs the ketela. Do not ask me to choose between you and women's rule."

She laughed. "Oh, Ahrik, you are such a pawn t—"

Ahrik's weapon flashed from his side. Before she could scream, the blade was at her throat, just touching her still, breathless neck. Fear consumed her where uncertainty had once reigned. *Would he hurt me?* Her position in the Tameri family meant too much to Ahrik's posterity, but Ahrik was also impulsive and rash. Zharla tried to stay calm, to think through the situation. *What is his goal?* She took in a quick breath, and pain shot from her neck. She felt the icy prick of blood where her skin met the blade.

Ahrik's eyes bored into Zharla. "I never needed your love, and now I don't want it. It's your choice. I accept it. But know this: you will bear us a child. Maybe not soon, but you will."

From somewhere deep, a fire lit inside her. She spat in his face and felt the sting of blood beading out on her neck once again. She shoved him away and dabbed at her neck with her handkerchief. "You will not threaten me."

He found his balance, but his face was aghast with surprise. She stared, defiant. She moved into his space and shoved a finger into his chest. "You have no claim on my future child, not after you and my monster-of-a-mother took Shahl from me. My love for my child will be the only love I have." She gestured between them, to their relationship. "I'd rather die lonely and loveless than bring a child into this."

The corners of his mouth took an insolent turn upward, and he wiped the spittle from his face inside the hem of her dress. "My little brother is weak," he said. "I can control you by controlling hi—"

She slapped him. "That was a warning. I do not fear you."

Part of her regretted the violence. It would have saddened Shahl, but she felt more powerful than she ever had before. More in control than she thought possible.

The sneer on his mouth grew until it covered his whole face, but he gave no retort.

She checked her handkerchief and eyed him. She had the advantage. "Now, we will wait an appropriate period of time, so that those outside will think the marriage has been consummated. And when we emerge, both you and I will be as ebullient as they will expect us to be."

For nigh on an hour, Ahrik fumed and paced around the room, stopping on occasion to consider his wife in disbelief. As Zharla rose to muss the sheets on the bed, she observed, with delicious temerity, "At worst this was a draw, Ahrik. It was the best I had hoped for."

After the requisite time had passed, Zharla took his arm and led him to the door. She smirked at him before palming it open. "Few marriages have such auspicious beginnings."

She hoped that Ahrik did not notice how much her hand shook as she pressed her palm to the reader.

As soon as he was sure no civilian eyes could pry, Ahrik balled up his gossamer overshirt and plunged into the brush. The decision ceremony earlier that afternoon stung. He left Zharla on the street as soon as he could after the reception, after they pretended to head off to an evening together.

He should have worn his combat uniform instead of his dress uniform. He could have cloaked and slipped out of the reception with no one noticing. As it was, he had to go through each *hayli* checkpoint after getting off the last transporter station. At the last checkpoint before his base, he scoffed at the ill-disciplined carriage and lax protocol of the volunteer soldiers, the ones that Zharla and Shahl and every other clueless civilian thought he commanded. The *hayla* were practically civilians, not soldiers. He was glad to command keteli clones, not *hayla*.

If not for the ketela, women's rule would have ended long ago. The *hayla* couldn't win a war if they tried. And it didn't look like they tried.

Ahrik trudged toward the setting sun. His base lay on the landward side of Meran, in a secure military zone, and it could only be reached by military transporter or on foot. Today he made the trip on foot, to cool off from his new wife's insolence. Zharla insulted not only him but the honor of his ten thousand sons as well. For their sake, he could not forgive her demand at the decision ceremony.

Making the trip on foot also allowed him to test his sons.

He stuffed the gossamer overshirt into his sash at the base of his spine, where it was less likely to snag on a branch or the long grasses that grew everywhere on this side of Meran. The climate was too arid for the taller trees that grew farther north, but the plentiful afternoon sun encouraged the cedar shrubs and scrub grass that populated the valley next to his base.

Ahrik's anger leaked away as he neared his base. With his ketel, he was whole. He would never feel this completeness with his brother, and especially not with his new wife. His clones were his sons, but they were more like brothers than Shahl would ever be. Among his ketel, he felt no fear or inadequacy. The power of all produced perfection.

He came to the last rise before his base and crouched down, stilled his breathing, and listened. He suppressed what remained of his anger. It was time to lead his sons, not think of his wife.

He guessed there were two squads tracking him. He played this game whenever he came home on foot. He eluded the patrol squads, and they would track him without being detected. He lost today, of course, when he charged into the brush like a hedgehog, but he wanted to see if he could catch them being careless after he gave himself away so easily. He sensed nothing. He smiled. They were out there, watching him.

He ascended the ridge at a crouch and was not surprised to see Leren waiting for him at the top. Ahrik acknowledged him.

Leren nodded back, then knelt in the age-old fealty salute, one knee and two palms on the ground, with his head bowed. He commanded Ahrik's 3d Hand, one of his five units of two thousand. He was the strongest-willed and ablest of Ahrik's five hand commanders. Leren was often the first to speak at planning councils, and he trained his hand more vigorously than the other hand commanders.

Ahrik wondered if he should tell Leren and the other hand commanders what really happened at the decision ceremony. They'd bled and sweat and trained together for their whole lives, and Ahrik didn't want to keep any secret from them. They might secretly snicker at him for not losing his virginity, or they might respect him more for bringing them into his confidence. He couldn't decide which.

The scar on Leren's face made him easy to recognize. It ran from his chin to his ear, the result of a training accident the previous year. One of his subcommanders mistakenly used a sharpened qasfin instead of a dulled practice blade during a sparring session. The subcommander was sent to the ranks, but if the wound had been any more serious the punishment would have been death. Such was the justice of the ketel. One did not make such mistakes. The integrity of the whole depended on it.

Ahrik returned Leren's salute by bringing his right hand to his heart. "How long were your men shadowing me this time?"

Leren rose. "From the stream on the far side of the valley, Father, two hundred meters this side of the last *hayla* checkpoint. The wind shifted, and one of my sniffers caught your scent. After the lookers located the source, it was easy enough for the two squads to stay on your flanks."

"Where are they now?" There was a brief pause while Leren closed his eyes and communicated with the two squads via the tendril link, casting his thoughts directly into the minds of his squad leaders. Ahrik could not achieve such an intimate connection at such a low level of the ketel. He did have a strong connection with his command company and with his hand and subcommanders—the commanders of five hundred and one hundred—but beyond that, he relied on his subordinates for tactical control.

Ahrik absently felt for the lump on the base of his neck, where his own tendril communicator was implanted years ago. From the age of five, he and his sons worked to synchronize their thoughts to be able to communicate like this. It was only possible because they shared so many genes and so many experiences. He thought of the decision ceremony. If he didn't tell them what happened, would the tendril link still work? Ahrik closed his eyes and sighed. If he didn't have the tendril link to his sons, he had nothing.

Presently, twenty men melted out of the brush. Hands and faces covered, and in full battle gear, they knelt in the fealty salute and chanted in unison, "The Eshel is our mother and we live for Father."

"Well done, sons," Ahrik said, brimming with pride. Praising his ketel never got old. "Commander Leren, I suggest you reward these men."

Leren gave a curt nod, then paused to communicate with his subcommanders over the tendril link. Then, to his twenty men, "2d and 5th Squads from 3d Company will replace you."

The men walked along the ridge, in the direction of the lower base entrance, meant for ketelis, not officers. They shared subdued smiles.

Ahrik's personal aide, Ayen, approached from the direction of the main base entrance, his red command company collar bobbing at his brisk pace. His face bore a quizzical look. He gave the ready salute, hand over heart. "Father, heard you were here."

News traveled fast in the ketel.

"Ayen," said Ahrik. "Assemble my sons tonight. I have news. I would have cast it ahead over the tendril link, but I wanted to give it in person."

"Yes, Father." Ayen paused to send the order, then considered Leren and the two departing squads. "Father, permission to ask a personal question?"

Ahrik nodded, and Leren drew close, forming a tight triangle with Ahrik and Ayen. A flock of swallows swooped past, angling for insects in the waning light.

"Something troubling you, Father?" asked Ayen. "The attack in-mountain? The decision ceremony? You don't normally wear your dress uniform to scramble through the brush." Ahrik smiled with satisfaction. Ayen knew him well. He was the right man to be his aide.

Ahrik moved toward the main base entrance, which was marked by a waist-high stone pillar just beyond the crest of the ridge, the only sign of civilization in the area. Ahrik smiled as he read the engraving, the Oath of the Ketel, written in the Old Tongue:

*Shalagh fenenu. An-qerer qulna fe-an-efret feneku. Slagh-li
an-felesh bel-zhoreq ketel-li. Eshela-li ghidushe fe-nihye al
Qadushe. Shlegh anu feneshe.*

Ayen and Leren walked up to the base entrance as well. Ahrik
furrowed his brow, then opened and closed his fists. He wrestled
with whether to tell them. He ran his fingers over the engraving.
"Did you know I was there, at the attack?"

Both of Ahrik's subordinates gasped.

"I saw an ancient weapon used firsthand," said Ahrik. "They're
barbaric. How did Man ever come up with anything like that?" He
shook his head. "We have to find out who used them."

Ayen nodded. "The intel shop is already on it."

Leren looked at Ahrik askance. "That's not all, is it, Father?"

Ahrik pressed his lips together.

"The decision ceremony, Father?" asked Leren. He furrowed
his brow, and his scar caught the sallow light. "She chose you. We
thought you'd be happy."

Ahrik's hand hovered over the palm reader, which was on the
same pillar as the oath. *Shalagh fenenu.* ("We are one.") They'd find
out eventually. Better now, on his terms.

Ahrik sighed. "She said we wouldn't have children until..."

"Until?" asked Ayen.

"...until we love each other."

Ayen's eyes grew wide. "So, Mistress Tamer-li and you didn't..."

"We did not." Ahrik pressed his palm to the reader. The ground
to the right of the pillar dissolved, revealing the ramp down to Ahrik's base. He paused in the entryway. "The marriage is legal, even
if it's not consummated. Only you two and the other four hand
commanders will know about this. Check?"

"Check, Father," they said in unison.

Ahrik glimpsed at the setting sun. It touched the horizon. Its
fire burned an angry red.

"Ayen," he said as they entered, "bring me a combat uniform.
This one's a mess."

Shahl took in the clink of glasses and the soft murmur of the tea shop. Here, no one would know him and he would not know anyone else. It was the kind of place to escape, at least for a time, to let night fall fully so he could go through with his plan under cover of darkness. He checked the messenger bag at his feet. It held everything he'd need, including all the cash he could find at home while everyone else was away celebrating Ahrik's marriage victory.

He found a seat close enough to the door to make a quick exit, but in a corner, where he had space to himself. The tea shop was on the street where he and Zharla used to meet for their evening strolls, and she'd told him to meet her here when they were at the social hall this morning, before the accursed decision ceremony, before the attack.

Midnight drew near. He saw little chance she'd actually come, but he had to let her prove he meant nothing to her. *Why do I punish myself like this?*

He'd had his cry, but he was strong enough to put his past behind him. Now was the time for action, even if the rejection still cut him to his core, like a pin lodged in his chest, doing no real damage but pricking him with searing pain whenever he moved.

"Yes?" asked the waiter, startling Shahl. The man wore an over-worked expression, but he was built like a mountain.

"Mint tea," he said, recovering himself.

"Nothing stronger? We have—"

"No," Shahl said. He placed some cash on the table. This was the kind of place where you didn't pay with a biometric account. He wanted to become anonymous and make a new life, not live in the old one.

He sat and sipped his tea when it came, until a young man close to his age sauntered up and broke into his solitude.

"Care to play?" he asked. He held a game board and pieces under his arm.

Shahl sighed. He'd expected someone to come up to him eventually, in a place like this, with few social norms and even fewer questions asked. If he had wanted to be truly alone, he would have gone up the mountain. Few people went up there at night, which is why he and Zharla went up there sometimes. Used to go up there. Shahl shut his eyes and swept the memory from his mind with a painful sigh.

Shahl opened his eyes and looked at the young man, game board held out before him, like an offering. Shahl shifted the messenger bag under his table to make room. "Something tells me you're not going to accept no for an answer."

The young man set the board down. "You've been here for over an hour, and nobody else has come by. I figured I'd give it a shot."

Shahl shrugged a vague assent, and they began arranging the pieces.

"What's your name?" the young man asked.

"No names," Shahl said. Leave no trace.

The young man made the first move. The tea shop murmur and clink of glasses hovered over them, unheeding.

"Did you hear about the attack?" the young man asked Shahl, after a while.

A part of Shahl wanted to tell him about everything that happened to him that day, but the experience was still too raw. Shahl nodded and took one of the young man's pieces with a flourish. "I heard it was Kerewi rebels."

Shahl felt a twinge of guilt at the little lie, but it might be true, and after this afternoon he cared less for things like the truth.

The young man took one of Shahl's pieces. "The rebels, huh?" he said. "How is that rabble supposed to fly halfway around the planet to attack a social hall?"

"Rabble?" Shahl asked. He pushed his chair back from the game and folded his arms. "You don't think they're capable of something like this?"

"Oh sure, they might want to, but they can't. From what I hear, there's no support for the rebels, even over there in the Kereu."

"Where do you get your information? The government caller networks?"

The young man stood. "What are you? Some kind of rebel sympathizer?"

Shahl sprang to his feet, sending his chair clattering to the floor behind him. After everything that happened that day, he would not put up with this callow surliness.

"I am loyal." Shahl poked the young man's chest, hard. "Are you?"

The murmur of the tea shop grew silent.

The young man found his footing. "Is that the best you can do?"

The young man cocked his fist, but the waiter grabbed his arm with a meaty hand and held him back. "No."

Regret washed over Shahl. *When did violence come so easily for me?* He would have just let the young man hit him, with how little he cared. Shahl put up his hands to defuse the situation, then deflected his gaze. "I've had a rough day. I shouldn't have done that."

The young man peered a challenge at Shahl. He smoothed his tunic, then sat. "Okay, okay. Let's just play."

Shahl nodded and sat down himself. "Consider this: the rebels might actually have legitimate grievances. We destroyed their capital and killed thousands of Kerewa ten years ago, when we won the War of Unification."

The young man just nodded and made his next move.

They finished the game in silence. Shahl let him win, which was hard to do. The young man wasn't very good. As he packed up the game, the young man asked, without the boldness he showed before, "Why are you just sitting here?"

"We all have our reasons." Shahl's tone was a bit sharper than it would have been a day earlier.

"You're not a regular."

Shahl considered him, then checked the time on the wall. Well past midnight. "I'm going to give you the advice I wish I'd gotten two years ago. When it comes to love, don't trust anyone."

The young man furrowed his brow, searching for the logic in the advice.

Shahl didn't care. "When you think a woman loves you, don't believe it. Ever." *I should have lived by those words today.*

The young man tucked the game board under his arm. "What happened to you?"

Shahl grunted and hefted the messenger bag onto his shoulder. He shook his head and made his way to the exit.

"Hey, wait!" The young man followed Shahl outside. "What's your plan?"

"Besides never loving again? Leave Meran. Disappear." Shahl turned and slipped into the night.

> Every keteli soldier binds his wrist with metal as a reminder to keep the secret of the ketel safe. To reveal this secret is death to the Eshel, and risks a return to The War. Any keteli found in open society is punished with death. Any commander who reveals the secret of the ketel is punished with death, and his military bloodline is snuffed out.
>
> Secret Law of the Mothers, Article I, Clause 19

3 | Night of Consequence

SHERESH SHEHUR-LI: I see you got the two of them together. Well done.
MATRON TAMER-LI: You got what you wanted. Give me what I want.
SHERESH: Starting next week.
MATRON: Fine.

Voice recording found in the Tameri clan archives during the inquest into the rise of Ahrik, RY 2519

AHRIK drank in the power of the ketel. He watched a video feed in his office as his sons assembled in the cavernous main hall. By rank and file, they ordered themselves in the dim subterranean light. Ayen, his aide, went out to give the five-minute warning.

The enemy is nothing before the power of the ketel.

Ahrik turned off the video feed. He smiled with pride. Women's rule was a cause worth living and dying for. Ahrik thought of this before anything else. Zharla and Shahl and the rest of the people who thought like them were fools not to see this.

The message center on his desk compiler chimed. He ignored it. Nothing could take him from this reverie.

The door to his office dissolved, and Ayen slipped through. "Four more minutes to midnight, Father."

Ahrik nodded. Ahrik's duty to protect the Eshel was why he had to have a child by Zharla. If Ahrik performed well in battle, his son's ketel could be the first ketel of one hundred thousand to be cloned in generations. The heroism of Ahrik's father in leading his own ketel in the War of Unification sealed Ahrik's promotion to a ketel of ten thousand. He yearned to grant the same to his own son, a life of glorious service to women's rule.

Ayen moved to his desk, opposite Ahrik's, and cocked his head at the compiler display. "Father, th—"

Ahrik cut him off with a warning grunt. "Ayen, why do you serve in the ketel?"

Ayen adjusted the metal band on his right wrist and eased himself up, then moved to parade rest in front of Ahrik's desk. "Father? I don't follow."

"Why do you fight, Ayen? All you've ever known is preparation for war. You're not part of Esheli society, and the only world you know is right here, among my ten thousand. Why do you do it?"

If Ayen thought the question was a test, he didn't show it. He pressed forward with perfect military discipline. "This is all I know, Father. I live to serve the Eshel. I'd die to protect you, Father of the Ketel."

Ahrik rubbed his chin. He stood and smoothed his uniform. "I serve to honor my father's memory." Heleq Jeber-li had been an *aanin*, commanding a ketel of 1,000. When the Kerewa launched their unprovoked war on the Eshel, the Esheli confederation closed ranks to confront the threat. After three years of war, many Eshela lay dead but the coalition that the Kerewa had raised to exterminate the Esheli people had also begun to show signs of wear. In a courageous bid to end the war without further loss of life, Heleq's ketel led an airborne assault on the enemy capital, Kereu City. Since the Kerewa did not know that Esheli scientists had developed transporters capable of crossing the ocean so swiftly, the defenders of the city were taken by surprise.

Ahrik smiled at his aide. "If I die with his name on my lips, I will have done all I could for the Eshel."

Ahrik crossed over to his book shelves. He fingered the three-volume history of the War of Unification. "Ayen," Ahrik asked, "do you know what it means to die for the Eshel?"

Ayen scratched his head. "I have not yet felt the glory of death, Father."

Ahrik raised an eyebrow. "After my father's ketel attacked Kereu City in the War of Unification, the Kerewa lost the will to fight. The leaders of the Esheli confederation were merciful, though. They brought the Kerewa into political power. Thirty recorded generations after The War, the planet's only two habitable continents finally became unified. My father died to make that happen. He died with a purpose. His death brought peace to the Eshel."

"May we all die so well, Father," said Ayen. He glanced toward his desk, as if something waited for him there. "Father?"

Ahrik rose and stepped toward the door. "Speak, Ayen."

"Did you see the message, Father? Supervisor Sheresh is coming tomorrow morning."

Ahrik felt the color drain from his face. He leaned on the cold stone of his desk. The chill assaulted the palms of his hands. His supervisor never came to visit. Never. Something must be wrong.

Ahrik and Ayen locked eyes. They both knew what this meant.

Ahrik renewed his approach to the door. "Did he give. . . a reason for his visit?"

"No, Father." Ayen rushed to palm open the door for Ahrik. "Father, just one question, if I may." The door dissolved, and the murmur of ten thousand men met them from down the hall. "Why do we fight, Father?"

With all his energy, Ahrik focused on not showing his true feelings. The attack that morning spurred a swirl of thoughts, and his confrontation with Zharla at the decision ceremony did nothing to calm his mind. His military bloodline might end with him because of his insolent wife. The very notion of men's rights was an insult to Ahrik and his loyal sons, but the attack made Ahrik think that the trouble in the Kereu was more than just a flare-up. That the Chief Elders might not have it under control.

"That's easy, Ayen," Ahrik lied. "We fight to destroy the Kerewi rebels. To destroy them root and branch." Ahrik said a silent prayer to the Lady of the Emerald Moon, asking that Ayen not see his lack of conviction.

Zharla felt so...empty. *Have I done the right thing?* She drew a bath, to forget her pain and steel herself for the unhappy marriage that awaited her. She poured salts into the churning water. She could have escaped with Shahl, somehow cheated his death. Even if he couldn't cheat death, would a few hours with him have been better than what she robbed from him, the knowledge that she had chosen him? Then again, she could not live with his death on her conscience.

She sighed at the time piece on the wall. Almost midnight. She rued the task, but she needed to face Shahl as she said she would.

The scented steam filled her lungs with life, but her heart would not be put at ease. She slipped into the water and tried to focus on something else. She studied her stone surroundings. The walls of the washroom were carved to evoke the dim interior of Meran Mountain. They were a deep, moist green, with a trickle of water cascading down the back wall and into the large stone basin in which Zharla reclined. She reached up to a lever on the wall to raise the temperature of the water. Steam mixed with the scented salts.

She planned how to defeat her mother, overcome her domineering ways. Zharla and her mother agreed on one thing and one thing only: Zharla should be the next appointee to the Council of Elders. Positions on the Council did not come open frequently, but Zharla had clear advantages: young, passionate, and well-placed to get the business vote. Her mother was also right that having Ahrik by her side was politically expedient, even if it meant living in celibacy with a man she despised.

But men's rights were real, and if women's rule didn't reform itself then the system would break. There was no telling what would happen then. After the attack that morning, Zharla knew that the chances of a global cataclysm like The War were real. Zharla would never be as faithful an advocate of men's rights as Shahl, but she was always willing to give his thoughts a sympathetic ear. For the sake of peace, the men's rights movement needed an ally on the Council.

This was the only way. If she couldn't have Shahl, then she would endure his brother to accomplish what Shahl would have done in his brother's place. Only that, she decided, would make this celibate misery worth it.

She gripped the sides of the basin and leaned her head back with an exhausted breath. A sudden chill prowled into the room, like a panther on the hunt. Her eyes narrowed into alertness. The chill didn't come from a sudden, cold breeze. In Zharla's washroom such a breeze was impossible. Something was not as it should be, a sinister premonition in the recesses of her mind.

She sank a little lower into the water. *It's probably nothing.* She called out, "Hello?" More softly, she asked, "Renla, is that you?" How foolish. Renla had long ago retired for the evening, and her presence would never induce such a sensation. How embarrassing.

Of course nothing was wrong.

Driven by curiosity and by the need to show courage, Zharla got out of the bath, passed through the drying field, and gathered her thick robe around herself. *It's time to get out, anyway.* She slipped the necklace he'd given her over her head. She owed it to Shahl to go to the tea shop, in case he was there. He deserved that much, at least.

She padded toward her bedroom, then stopped to choose night-clothes from her dressing room.

She laid her clothes over the desk chair and peered around her room, checking to see if anything was out of place. Like the washroom, Zharla's chambers were fashioned of quarried stone, as were all the buildings of out-mountain Meran. The bedroom's two windows faced the sea, to let in the morning light and the salty sea breeze. It was never truly cold in Meran, even in winter, so the windows consisted of little more than a framed opening in an outer wall, with a *kall* field over the opening to detect intrusions and control atmosphere. The drapes were drawn, and the only source of illumination was the lights in her room. She trusted that light now to shut out an unsettling disquiet.

She crept around her room to make sure everything was in its place, examining the sparse yet exquisite furniture. She looked under her bed, framed with wrought metal, and glanced toward the window to check the position of the *sutur*, its wooden, trapezoidal frame sitting on the ground, its two sets of strings running perpendicular to one another. She moved back to the polished stone desk with carved stone legs and the wooden chair with the night clothes draped over it. She looked over to the small metal table by the bed. Nothing seemed amiss.

Nothing at all.

She reached for her night clothes, then her chambers went completely dark. Her heart stopped cold. Fear rippled down her spine. The darkness enveloping her did not cause her terror. She could think of any number of plausible explanations for the lights going out. Rather, in the split second before being plunged into darkness, in that moment between mere caution and spine-tingling terror, she had seen a figure standing across the room.

"Zharla." A voice in the darkness. Shahl's voice.

How could he be here? He knew how scandalous it would be for him to be in her private chambers, and he wouldn't even be able to get in without someone knowing. Surely he had a good reason to be here.

"She'le?" Her voice shook, but she should have sensed no warning in her mind from Shahl's presence.

"You will please forgive my turning out the lights," he said. "I'm not really supposed to be here." She was sure now that the voice belonged to Shahl.

"You cannot be here." She fumbled for her clothes. Adrenaline pumped through her veins. She wracked her memory for something close by that she could use as a weapon, just in case.

"I have not come to pay homage to trifling conventions, Zharla. I have come to tell you something." His feet shuffled toward her in the dark.

Zharla eased her body closer to the desk. There were styluses there that could serve as crude weapons. She tried to buy time. "What is your plan now?" she asked. "Are you going into the presbytery? You told me once you might do that, if you weren't chosen."

He chuckled and shuffled toward her again. "Oh, no. I must have you."

"What?" *Did I mishear?* Shahl had evil on his mind, and there wasn't enough light in the room to see where she had lain a stylus on the desk that morning, before she met Shahl at the social hall. Not like this. It shouldn't be like this. "Not now, my She'le. Maybe later, after time has passed, when Ahrik is away at war."

"I am the one you love, not Ahrik." Her fingertip brushed a stylus, but in that moment, in the thick darkness, strong hands grabbed her arms and neck from behind. *What?* In panic, she realized that at least two or three men, besides Shahl, were behind her.

A sharp pain lanced through her throat. Something liquid flowed into the muscles of her neck. She screamed, but no sound came out. Her vocal chords constricted. She flailed her arms and legs, but her arms were held fast, and more hands clutched her ankles and thighs. Her robe was torn off. She screamed again and again, but no sound came out. She lashed out with her arms, but her fists struck only air.

The men that held her slammed her onto the bed. Dazed, she stopped fighting for a bit, but kicked ferociously when they spread her legs apart. Her writhing and twisting had no effect. Her mind brimmed with alarm. Their grip was too tight. A shadow hovered close over her. "This is because I love you."

Then Zharla felt the violation. Pain flashed like lightning from her center. She fought back with a violence she had never known, even though it made the pain more excruciating. This vile shadow took from her the one thing that she alone should give.

"No!" she screamed in silence. She arched and twisted her back and gnashed with her teeth, but the men simply held her tighter, yanking her hair and extremities without mercy, digging into her thighs, her torso, her chest with wicked fingers. Pain flooded every part of her body. It lanced over her, exacerbated by confusion, despair, and denial, and left no piece of her being unscathed.

Her eyes finally adjusted to the darkness, and through a mist of anguish and silent sobs of pain, she began to make out the face of the man that did this to her. Her eyes saw Shahl, but she battled the belief that it could really be him. *How could he do this? All our years of friendship, all our secret meetings, did they mean nothing, after all?*

Then, in one dizzying instant, Shahl's face disappeared. The hands that held her left. The sharp pain retreated. But everything else remained. The oppressive pain remained, coursing through her. The confusion and bewilderment remained. Her silent shrieks, heard by no one, remained. The image of Shahl's face remained, seared on her mind.

Zharla wept, laying on the bed, fully exposed to the darkness. She tried to sit up but only managed to support herself on one elbow. Her head swam. This could not have happened in her own room, in the one place where she should feel safe. She had to go back to the washroom. She had to scrub herself clean. She had to free herself, in some puny way, from the violence she had suffered.

She tried to get out of bed, but her body did not respond. Zharla was in another world, as if this terrible thing had happened to some other her. She swung a leg off of the bed, but then the hard stone floor came up to meet her, much faster than it should have.

Ahrik strode to the podium. He looked over his ten thousand sons. They filled the cavernous hall. The sight took his breath away. He hailed them. They chanted. *Ah-rik! Ah-rik! Ah-rik!* It began softly but grew by degrees into a steady, stomping beat, all in perfect unison. The chanting rang off the stone walls of the cavern. Magnificent.

He raised his arms in salute. "My sons!" His voice was amplified, but he could barely hear himself for the pulse of his sons' chanting. He motioned for quiet, and his ketel reluctantly gave up the chant. Ahrik felt the beat even after he began to speak. He lived for moments like this, when nothing else mattered but the power of the ketel. It almost made him forget that he had no idea why Sheresh wanted to see him the next day.

"My sons," he repeated. "Ours is the honor to serve the Eshel!" Cheering. "We will serve her in any place, at any time, and against any enemy!" More cheering. Shahl was wrong about this war. Men didn't need more rights. The Kereu didn't need more concessions. The cheering bolstered his faith in their righteous cause.

He waited for the cheering to die down. "I know you want to fight for the Eshel. Tomorrow we deploy. I didn't relay our deployment orders. Until now." The quiet in the assembly hall brimmed with an exultance nearly as powerful as the chanting.

"My sons, the dream of combat is closer. Our orders"—he paused, and he could almost feel his sons lean closer—"are to enter space training." The cheering this time thundered off the walls of the cavern, and his sons took up the chant once again: *Ah-rik! Ah-rik! Ah-rik!*

Ahrik let their praise wash over him. Every doubt was gone. When the chanting died down, it was too soon. Thoughts of his supervisor's visit tomorrow were gone. He continued, "My sons, we are the first ketel of ten thousand to undergo space infantry training. We will sweep away the rebel refuse from space, just as the Army of the Eshel sweeps it from Dom!"

Ah-rik!

"Long live the Eshel!" His ketel would conquer.

Ah-rik!

"Long live women's rule!" His sons would live forever in glory.

Ah-rik!

"Long live peace!" He was invincible.

Ah-rik! Ah-rik! Ah-rik!

In the slight nip before dawn, Shahl shuffled onto the platform of the intercity transporter station, hefted his messenger bag onto his shoulder, and boarded the day's first transporter to Mekele Eshel, the planet's capital city. He did not look back.

The transporter ride to Mekele Eshel passed in eerie quiet. They sped away from dawn in Meran and toward the creeping predawn of Mekele. Shahl's old life receded and a new one loomed. The dawn would catch them soon enough, since Mekele was only two hours behind Meran, but Shahl tried not to think of the life he'd left behind. *Look forward*, he told himself.

Meran stood for the empty place in his heart. Zharla rejected him, but why she would make herself so unhappy, he could not say. Her choice carried the pain of a twisting knife. He could not let it go. Something made him go back to that pain, even though that was the thing he wanted to be farthest from.

Ahrik had made Shahl leave Meran just as much as Zharla. Ahrik was the city's favorite son, the celebrity who would carry on the family's proud military tradition. Shahl could not bear to live in such a shadow. They came from the same family, but Shahl couldn't understand his family's infatuation with past glory, nor the insistence on maintaining the illusion of social standing.

The transporter on which Shahl traveled began to pass through an electrical storm, which made the trip even more eerie. They traveled close to the speed of sound, toward the wee hours of the morning; the sky overhead was gorged with clouds. All around them, lightning danced. The transporter capsule extended ten meters, aft to stern, with translucent skin. A handful of other passengers huddled against the grim ride. Lightning illuminated them like ghouls. A young couple sat across from him, exchanging furtive whispers. He averted his eyes from that reminder of what could have been.

Being in Mekele would not remove the pain of loss. Shahl would have been a dedicated husband to Zharla. She could have been so happy, but she chose his loathsome brother instead. Shahl was sad for himself and the life that could have been, but he was heartbroken for Zharla, for what she'd given up. These emotions lodged in his heart and left him wanting to dwell as much as possible on something else, like the antiseptic details of boson drive transport.

Look forward.

The transporters were, besides walking, the principal means of getting from one place to another, be it within Esheli cities or between them. The transporters traveled through *kall* particle fields that made it possible to travel at speeds well over the speed of sound. They couldn't go that fast tonight because of the storm, but Shahl still marveled at the power of the transporter system.

Without two critical technologies, the particle compiler and the boson drive, the transporter system would be impossible. Shahl opened his eyes to fish his handheld compiler from his bag. He was about to thumb it on when he realized that doing so would probably bring him news of Meran and Zharla's choice of Ahrik. He put the compiler back in his bag and slumped down in despair.

He looked to the front of the transporter capsule. There, the driver guided the transporter with the help of his internal compiler. Using properties of the mineral *kall*, compilers controlled the movement of subatomic particles in a gas environment, usually pure nitrogen or xenon. Particle compilers were capable of trillions of calculations in a second, and they allowed drivers and supervisors with implanted compilers to manage switches and schedule changes at high speed.

The transporter system also relied on the boson drive. Based on the same principle of subatomic regulation that underlay the particle compiler, the boson drive systematically alternated the subatomic force binding boson particles together. Regulated properly, and depending on the elemental composition of the surrounding environment, this could create propulsion in any direction one desired. It could even mask the effects of acceleration and deceleration and, in space, negate weightlessness.

Rain stroked the transporter's skin, but when the sky lit up behind them, no thunderclap followed. The only thunder that reached them came from the front. When it did, though, the thunder claps came quick and intense. Not a few times, Shahl startled at a particularly close lightning strike or an especially powerful roll of thunder. The storm kept him on edge, even though he knew he would soon be starting a new life in Mekele.

Suddenly, his veins filled with ice. A colossal sound, like he'd felt in the social hall attack, consumed the transporter. His heart threatened to beat out of his chest. In that moment between sensing mortal danger and then understanding that the threat was benign, alertness washed over him.

The tension flowed out of him as he realized that they were decelerating, and the thunderclaps that had been following them finally caught up. He sat back and relished the symphony of power that the thunder played.

As the music faded, he once again became aware of his physical surroundings. They had passed through the storm, and the light of stars faded into the out-mountain lights of Mekele ahead. Other passengers stirred. Two men near the front moved to retrieve bags from the overhead shelf. A wizened old thing softly hummed a folk tune to herself in the back of the transporter. By her black, flowing robe, black head covering, and the absence of a good number of her teeth, not to mention the Merani tune she emitted, Shahl could tell she came from in-mountain Meran.

The young couple sitting across from Shahl continued their furtive conversation. Shahl tried to ignore the caresses they shared, but each caress they shared twisted, by degrees, the knife of Zharla's betrayal. The young couple, sharing the love that Shahl should have had, were probably from Mekele. They sat too close together the whole time. Their modern, tight-fitting clothing and their immodest displays of affection reeked of Mekele's freewheeling, carefree social mores. No self-respecting Merani would engage in such unseemly behavior.

But Mekele was a melting pot, one that Shahl hoped to melt into. Mekele was divided into four quarters, one for each major Esheli city, and Shahl planned to go to the central temple, which was in the Merani Quarter. There he could become someone new in the presbytery. He would build a new life, a life with meaning, where he could immerse himself in books and maybe help one or two people along the way.

As the dawn caught up with him in Mekele, Shahl thought that perhaps melting into a new city might take the sting out of the last twenty-four hours.

Look forward.

> *Shalagh fenenu. An-qerer qulna fe-an-efret feneku. Slagh-li an-felesh bel-zhoreq ketel-li. Eshela-li ghidushe fe-nihye al Qadushe. Shlegh anu feneshe.*
>
> Qerer Ketel-li

> We are one. There is no other bond and no enemy among us. Death is nothing before the power of the ketel. The Eshel is our mother and we live for Father. I am us.
>
> Oath of the Ketel

4 | Fight or Flight

Victim [name redacted] exhibits injuries consistent
with sexual assault. Physical description of assailant
matches Shahl Jeber-li. Genetic profile also a match. No
signs of forced entry into room.

From the peace forces report on the attack, 3 Teshrin
Ewel RY 2498

A STARTLED cry yanked Zharla to consciousness. Blades of morning light sliced through the drapes and pierced her eyes, wors-
ening the pain throbbing in her head. She lifted her head from the
cold, hard stone, eyes bleary, to see feet flying down the steps from
the door. Renla. She flung the bed cover over Zharla's naked body.
Zharla shivered and looked down at a small, dark red stain on the
bed cover. The sight of it spurred her mind to clarity, and she recon-
structed the events of the night before.

She was raped. Shahl raped her, but she still did not want to
believe he could have. *How did I misjudge Shahl for so long?* The physical
pain was one thing, dulling her senses, making every movement a
chore, shooting from her core to her fingers. The pain in her mind,
though, was worse. Much, much worse. Her entire world lay in
ruins, destroyed. Every hope now hung in the balance, contingent
on overcoming this one monstrous, violent act. She felt a terrible
loss of trust in everyone around her, had aged a lifetime.

She lay on the floor as Renla tried to comfort her, but Zharla
shook her off. She reached up to her neck, laced her fingers around

the necklace Shahl had given her, and yanked. Pain shot through the back of her neck, but it was nothing compared to what she felt inside. With an animal yell, she hurled the necklace against the wall of her room. The necklace pinged and landed who knows where. Then she collapsed into Renla's arms and convulsed with sobs.

Ahrik was halfway through his morning exercise routine when the bell to his personal quarters chimed. Swearing under his breath, he finished his thirty-second circuit of left jabs at the punching bag and reached for a towel. Sheresh was early. A visit before morning roll call was never good.

"Come," he called.

Ayen entered. His face was timid and apologetic. "Ah... I'm sorry, Father. He's here."

Ahrik snapped his towel in irritation. This visit would bring bad news.

"Where?" Ahrik asked.

"On his way to the waiting chamber, Father. Three minutes."

Ahrik pursed his lips. Sheresh had risen to his office during the long peace in the first decade after the War of Unification, when there was little real chance to prove himself. Now that there was a war on, Ahrik wondered why Sheresh didn't fade into irrelevance. Sheresh must have the ear of some Chief Elder, or share her bed every once in a while. Ahrik saluted him, like all superiors, but his stomach churned every time he did.

Ahrik doused off, dressed, and forced a smile to his face before entering the waiting chamber. Ayen had the room arranged for a visit, Ahrik noted with approval. Fresh fruit sat in a bowl on the tea table, along with a carafe of chilled water. Ayen had also brought extra chairs in, just in case.

Sheresh stood in the corner, perusing the bookshelf. Ahrik's books. Ahrik hid his irritation. He gave a salute and Sheresh returned it, brushing his hand to his heart. Sheresh was too arrogant to respect the uniform he wore. As Ahrik expected, Sheresh had arrived in full military dress. He meant to embarrass Ahrik, but Ahrik always had a complete dress uniform in his quarters, for this reason.

Ahrik smiled at this small victory. "News from the front, sir?"

He brought himself to his full height. He wanted to get the bad news over with quickly.

The supervisor sat down on Ahrik's couch and scoffed. "There's a more urgent matter first. Your orders have been changed."

Ahrik stiffened with anticipation.

The supervisor continued. "You will be sent cross-planet today, not to space training."

Ahrik clenched his fists, then relaxed them with a slow breath. He crossed over to pour himself some water from the carafe. He forced down his irritation and mustered a safe question. "Sir, what will our mission be cross-planet?"

"Rear support and garrison policing. You and your men don't have combat experience, so we can't throw you into the front, but your ketel would be a valuable reserve unit to have on hand." Sheresh picked a piece of fruit from Ahrik's tea table and tossed it up and down, smiling.

Ahrik's eyes flared, and he fought to keep his voice level. "No combat mission? We are ready, sir. Don't take away space training without giving us combat."

"This decision is not open to discussion, Shadhir Jeber-li, and I didn't come here to bandy about it with you. The Transport Section of the Supervisor Staff has made the necessary arrangements. You'll receive further instructions cross-planet." Supervisor Sheresh bit into the fruit. Juice leaked from the corners of his mouth.

Years of military discipline were all that stood between Ahrik and his anger boiling over. He was afraid to speak, not because he feared Sheresh, but because he feared saying something that might harm his sons later.

Sheresh dabbed at his mouth with a tissue. "There is one item of concern that seems to have surfaced. I was hoping to enlist your assistance." The supervisor formed the words around a mouthful of fruit, but Ahrik could tell he was choosing his words carefully, but not why. Ahrik fumed inside, but he was, above all, a soldier. There would be another time to fight such battles.

Sheresh swallowed. He paused. "You remember your counterpart, Alrem."

Ahrik gave a wary nod. Of course he remembered Alrem. They were about the same age, and they both commanded a ketel of ten thousand clones. Outside his own ketel, Alrem was one of his closest friends. Supervisor Sheresh would know that. He was probably hiding something.

"Alrem went missing for a month. He was found last week."

Putting on his most innocent expression, Ahrik asked, "Sir, how does a man with ten thousand soldiers sworn to protect him simply disappear?"

Sheresh shrugged. He was hiding something. Ahrik could see it in the slight quiver of his lower lip and the ever-so-slight twitch of his eye. Sheresh took another bite and munched on the fruit, content to let Ahrik's question mull, unanswered. "I would like you to find out what you can about his experience, why he went missing, and why he was found a thousand kilometers from his ketel."

Ahrik could tell his supervisor wanted the discussion to be over, but he wouldn't give up that easily. "Is there anything more you can tell me, sir? It seems odd—"

"That is all I know," Sheresh said, swallowing his fruit too soon. An uncomfortable silence filled the room.

The supervisor placed the remains of the fruit on the table in front of him. He stood, but did not move to leave. Ahrik narrowed his eyes. A warning hum flared in his mind. Sheresh had something else to say, but he didn't quite know how to say it. This was out of character.

"There's more, sir?" Ahrik asked.

"I regret to tell you that, yes, there is."

Ahrik shifted his weight, as if preparing for a blow. This must be the real reason Sheresh came in person. A messenger or tendril communication would have done to change travel plans and give him the news of Alrem. Ahrik backed up to his desk. He wondered if Zharla had changed her mind about the marriage. No, she couldn't do that.

"Last night"—Sheresh cleared his throat—"your wife was raped. She was found just this morning."

Ahrik's face darkened. He fumbled for a handhold on the desk behind him. For as little as he liked Zharla, a serious wrong had been done to her and her family's honor. This was a wrong against all the women of the Eshel. A challenge to women's rule itself.

"Who?" demanded Ahrik. His pulse rose through throat and temples.

"We have reason to believe that. . . This will not be easy to take, Ahrik. The truth of the matter is that. . . ah. . ."

"Sir?" Ahrik's senses were riveted.

". . . your brother is no longer in Meran."

Ahrik stood in stone silence. He clenched his fists, knuckles white.

Sheresh hesitated for a moment. He measured Ahrik. He went on. "Apparently, he took a transporter last night to Mekele, and—this is the most damning evidence so far—your wife claims it was Shahl who did it."

Ahrik trembled with rage. "I will kill him."

Sheresh cleared his throat. He avoided eye contact with Ahrik. "No one knows where he is."

Ahrik tried to focus on his next course of action. He was going cross-planet today with his ketel. He might be able to steal into the city on a transporter before they left, to see Zharla. It depended on the plans that the Transport Section had made. He would make the attempt to see Zharla, but he could not let it come at the cost of making his sons think he was abandoning them. If there was a chance for revenge...

"Sir, I must go to my wife."

"You will do no such thing," said Sheresh. He moved toward the door, then stopped and said over his shoulder, "She has her family, and you know your duty. Besides, you are the last person she wants to see now, Ahrik. You know it. I've heard the rumors, and you woke up here, not there. Stay with your men."

Sheresh left, and Ahrik slammed his fist over and over again into the couch. He screamed into one of the pillows, then collapsed onto it. He centered his breath and cast to Ayen over the tendril network, *Orders changed. Deploying cross-planet.*

Shahl stepped off the receiving platform at Mekele's main transporter station, tired, hungry, alone. He wandered in no particular direction and stared into the middle distance, the early-morning foot traffic bending around him. Traffic was light, lighter than it had been the few other times he'd come to Mekele. Dawn had just broken here. The other times he'd come, it had been a much more sensible hour. Since this was a one-way trip, the time of day didn't matter at all.

He sighed, trying to release a young lifetime of regret, but his vacant eyes gathered focus instead around a small, slender figure coming toward him. His head came up, and he recognized the girl that had sat across from him on the transporter. Where was her companion?

"Hey," she asked, "you okay?" Her face bore a delicate smile, one that feared nothing at all, but her voice cut him to the core.

What injustice is this, that a simple kindness quickens the sting of rejection? What hope do I have that life as a pir'e will smother this pain? Zharla's choice was never supposed to hurt like this.

When he didn't answer, the girl twisted her mouth as if considering a silly question. "You know you can get your luggage over there, right?"

Shahl frowned and stared at her. He lifted up his messenger bag, which contained all the possessions he had in the world. Soon, even that would be taken away. A *pir'e* owned nothing.

"Oh," she said. With a tilt of her head and a bob of her shoulders, she turned and lilted off.

Oh, to be so carefree. He called after her. "Excuse me."

She stopped and turned. Her face registered mild surprise, one eyebrow raised in half amusement. "Yes?"

"Do you know where I can get something to eat?" Shahl noted, with utter pain, that there was almost no life in his own voice.

"Try the Merani quarter. Its food stands are close," answered the young woman, pointing in the direction of an exit. Outside, clouds masked the faint glow of sunrise. "You'd better hurry, friend," she said. "That storm we passed is coming."

She turned again, and this time her exit was final. Shahl's sad gaze followed her for a moment, but then his feet, and his empty stomach, shuffled him toward the exit.

By the time Shahl found food he recognized, he was drenched. Out-mountain Mekele's four quarters had their own unique character. With its narrow alleyways, polished stone architecture, and densely-packed houses, Shahl imagined that the Merani Quarter could feel like home. If not for the pouring rain and early hour, he imagined that the pungent smell of saffron and thyme would meet his nostrils, the merchants' pitches competing for his ear. At that hour, however, Shahl saw only rows of closed shops, except for the occasional *mligh* stand offering Mekele's working classes something to fuel their bellies for a hard day's labor.

Shahl scarfed down a *mligh* sandwich, a wide, square flat bread rolled up around an assortment of roasted vegetables and meat. The spicy kick reminded him of home. One of the few good memories left to him.

The awning under which he stood offered something like shelter from the downpour, though not from the sickening feeling that he would soon have to go out in it. To extend his stay a little longer, he stood listening to news piped into the little food stand over the caller network. In the primitive years after The War, callers used in-mountain caverns to relay news to a city's inhabitants, but now, when so many lived out-mountain and newer technology was available, callers fed their voices into particle compilers that transformed and transported the artificial sound on kall tendrils.

In this quarter of Mekele, caller networks delivered more news from Meran. Shahl took in the caller's sing-song chant, the sound intoxicating. Construction of the new Merani port facilities would be completed next week. The peace forces had narrowed their investigation of the social hall attack to a rebel cell based in the Eshel. Melmez Meran had held matriculation ceremonies for its new students the day before. The selection of the municipal council would take place four months later, earlier than expected.

The caller chant continued. "A woman was raped last night, and peace forces are searching for a man named Shahl Jeber-li."

Shahl stopped cold, eyes wide with shock. The caller gave a clear and unsettling description of Shahl.

How could anyone think I did this? Shahl lowered his face and inched over to see if the *mligh* stand owner's receiver had a video feed as well. It did. Shahl's face turned a deathly shade of pale when he saw his own image on the display.

The owner chuckled. "Hey, that could be either of us."

They did look similar. *Thank goodness for the rain.*

The last bite of the sandwich trembled in Shahl's hand, then fell onto the slick pavement.

"Don't worry, I'll get it," the owner said. "You're probably the only customer I'll have for a half hour or so, with the storm."

Shahl realized he would have to pay. Fingers shaking, he almost put his thumb to the pay scanner, but he realized that his identity and whereabouts would be revealed. He smiled apologetically to the stand owner, then fumbled with the latch of his bag and shoved his hand in to retrieve some cash. He handed it to the man and assumed it was enough.

"Thanks," mumbled Shahl. He turned to walk away, then stumbled on a chink in the paving stones. He caught himself too late, earning a scraped hand and a banged knee. Shahl limped on, into the anonymity of the storm, toward the central temple in the Merani Quarter. Toward a new life.

"Hey, you okay?" the *mligh* stand owner asked. A pause. "Your change!" Another pause, while Shahl put some distance between them. Shahl hoped it would be enough. He kept his pace even and slow, like he hadn't a care in the world. Even now, the rain sheeted down, muffling the sound of the owner's voice. "You gave me way too much!"

Shahl didn't respond. He put his head down and let the rain run over him. He had to figure out what was going on.

I am not a rapist. I could never do such a thing.

Was this some ploy by Ahrik to get rid of him, to make sure he would never be close to Zharla again? He fled Meran in the middle of the night. Did someone construe his leaving Meran as an admission of guilt? Who could be the victim? He hadn't known any women except Zharla, and she would never lie like this. Should he turn himself in or sneak into the presbytery before they asked too many questions?

The rain drained through his hair and off his forehead. Through the downpour he saw a figure trudging up the slope toward him, equally drenched and pathetic. They nodded in greeting as they passed one another, and he saw that it was a female peace forces officer. His heart sank and his shoulders slumped down even more. He might have to decide whether to run or fight the charges earlier than he'd thought.

He picked up his pace, hoping the officer didn't notice. He peeked over his shoulder. Maybe the peace forces officer wouldn't stop at the *mligh* stand. Maybe the *mligh* stand owner hadn't recognized him. His mind flashed panic when he glanced back and saw two figures conferring under the awning of the *mligh* stand. He didn't need to hear the words to guess at the conversation.

A woman's voice called out, "Hey, you! Stop!"

Shahl wanted to stop, to turn himself in, but he had no chance in the courts. The courts offered no mercy for a rapist. Better to murder somebody than rape a woman. If he was already a suspect, then he was essentially convicted.

He ran, but not so fast that he would slip on the slick stone. He couldn't turn back now. The fact that he was running—for the second time, it would seem to them—only reinforced his guilt. If he could lose himself in the Merani Quarter's warrens and alleys and make his way to the central temple, then maybe he had a chance. Becoming a confessant in the presbytery was a new start. He could take on a new identity, start anew.

Shahl heard footsteps behind him. Heavy boots. And they were gaining.

An alley opened to the right. Shahl ducked around the corner. He slipped on a smooth patch of stone but caught himself on some steps. His eyes followed the steps up, but there was only a landing with a second-floor doorway and a stone wall. No exit. He scanned the alley. Also a dead end. He scrambled up the stairs.

There was nothing to do now. He couldn't run anymore. A sneaking dread crept through his spine as the implication sank in. When it came to rape, the peace forces shot first and asked questions later. The courts convicted on the slimmest of evidence.

Shahl was a dead man.

Shahl half-turned on the steps. The peace forces officer slipped on the same section of pavement. But she didn't just stumble, like Shahl. She careened to the pavement. Her head hit the wet stone with a gut-wrenching smack. Guilt washed over Shahl. The officer lay motionless on the ground, and his dread deepened. They would add assault of a peace forces officer to the rape charge. There were no witnesses. The storm had forced everyone inside, even those normally out at this early hour. Shahl had no way to prove he hadn't touched the officer. They would find a way to make Shahl pay.

He was a dead man.

Shahl crept back down the stairs. Maybe he could squeeze past the officer on the ground and run away. Maybe she hadn't called for others to come. The rain was coming down in torrents now, and thunder clapped nearby, startling him. Shahl didn't see blood around the officer, which was good. He had no desire to add murder to the rape charge he would face. He just needed to get away, to have time to prove his innocence.

The peace forces officer stirred, and Shahl froze. So much for creeping by. She let out a doleful moan, and Shahl took a step back. Runoff flowed down the cobbled street. Shahl scrambled halfway up the stairs again and turned, on all fours to avoid slipping on the steps and tumbling to the alley below. He looked over his shoulder and, to his horror, the peace forces officer reached for her weapon. A distiller pistol.

A distiller? I have to escape. Distillers did not maim or incapacitate. They killed. They shot pebble-sized fields of matter-scramblers that reduced anything they came in contact with to a slurry of basic elements.

His heart pounded.

Shahl scrambled, slipped, and crawled his way toward the landing. Then he heard the weapon discharge: *Thunk!*

An eternity passed as he waited for impact. *Whoosh!* A miss, but he heard the sickening sizzle of the distiller charge turning the rain above him into hydrogen and oxygen. Scrambling. *Thunk! Whap!* The next charge struck the wall just beyond his head.

His stomach churned as a chunk of wall became a slimy, gray ooze sliding down to the steps. The acrid smell of sulfur made him want to vomit.

"Don't shoot!" he screamed, the panic rising in his eyes. "Please! Don't shoot!" Another eternity passed. Shahl expected these moments to be his last. He turned to face his fate, but the weapon did not discharge again.

"Don't move." Her voice shook. She crouched at the bottom of the stairway, her weapon raised. Shahl froze in fear, sprawled, crablike, just below the top step. Every ounce of him wanted to flee, but he could not. The officer started to stand, distiller pistol still raised, then she reached for the wall to steady herself.

"I'm innocent," Shahl said, creeping up to the landing behind him. The officer wobbled as she started climbing the steps. Her weapon wavered.

"Why...run...then?" Her speech slurred. She kept her hand on the wall, as if her world spun. That had probably saved his life. No peace forces officer could have aim that bad.

Shahl could think of no response that wouldn't damn him more. The officer groaned and steadied her arm. "You raped...that girl. Ought...kill you...now."

Shahl's voice cracked. "I...I didn't do it."

The officer was only two meters away now, while Shahl had gotten to the landing. He crept backward, to get as far as possible from that distiller pistol and the officer who carried it. He did not doubt her willingness to make good on her threat. She had probably aimed for his head before. Fear pumped through his body.

"You...tried...kill me." She tottered.

Shahl felt the wall on his back. Dregs of hope drained from his heart. "No, no. That's not what I wanted."

"You...tripped...me."

"Now wait a—"

She trained her distiller on him. Shahl winced and cowered. She was almost on top of him now, standing on the second step from the top.

"That...girl." She gave an odd grunt. "Had...no chance...beg." She trained the distiller on his forehead, but the pistol swayed. Her legs buckled, but she steadied herself with the cavity that her distiller had just put in the wall. She squeezed her eyes shut, then tore them open. She grunted again.

"St...stop...mov...ing."

"Please, sit down on the steps. You're woozy." Shahl reached out a shaky hand.

The distiller fell from her hand. In the alley below, metal clanged onto stone. If she fainted again, he could make his escape, but he didn't want her to fall into the alley. *Can someone survive a fall like that?* He reached into the darkened doorway on his left, feeling for something he could anchor himself with if he had to grab for the officer with his right hand.

"Give...back." Another grunt, head lolled to the side. "My... 'stiller." She let go of the wall and grasped at the air in his direction, but then stopped and raised both hands to her head.

"Let me help you." Shahl reached. *Please don't fall. Please don't fall.*

Her eyes glazed over. She teetered on the edge. Shahl lurched forward, grabbing for something: a sleeve, a hand, a weapon strap, anything. Her limp fingers slipped through his wet hand. Panic screamed in his mind, followed by a sickening crack and thud as she hit something hard below. The rain pelted him. He shivered with cold, even though the summer was high.

He slid down the steps. Perhaps she was still alive. Perhaps her injuries were not fatal. Perhaps her limbs had absorbed the force of her fall and her vital organs were not beyond repair. If she died, the peace forces would kill him on sight. He hoped for a miracle, even though he wasn't sure now that he deserved any mercy at all. If he had not run away from home, this peace forces officer would not be lying in a drenched alley in the grimy Merani Quarter.

Shahl scrambled to the prone body of the peace forces officer and knelt on the black residue of urine, spit, and trash that even the street cleaners and the rainfall could not erase from the paving stones. The officer's eyes stared blankly, and her chest neither rose nor fell.

This is not happening.

Her body lay propped off the ground, her head lolled back at an awkward angle. Shahl's hands slumped onto the black mire and he felt underneath her. Stone blocks. No give.

He ran his fingers through his slick hair, then leaned his ear close to her mouth, in hopes of feeling the warmth of her breath. Nothing. He reached for her wrist to feel for a pulse. Still nothing.

He put his face in his hands. "What have I done?"

"Her neck snapped on the way down," said a deep and resonant voice behind him, a voice that at any other time would have been comforting, but now held only foreboding. "Her body stopped on those stone blocks, but nothing stopped her head."

Shahl eased himself around on his hip, ashen. A man stood in the doorway across the alley, eating what sounded like roasted nuts. A witness? How could there be a witness? What glimmer of twisted hope remained in Shahl evaporated. No one could now doubt what he had done.

The man smiled in the wan light. "They're much less forgiving when you put a woman officer away."

Shahl lost the strength in his torso and caught himself with his hands on the gooey stone, all options expended.

"Get up, you poor excuse for a man," growled the figure in the doorway. Then, a bit less menacing, "Come inside. They'll be out in force soon, and you won't get away so easily the next time."

Shahl felt a hand under his arm, which gave him just enough strength to drag himself into the doorway.

Lifting his head, he saw darkness inside the door frame, with the bulky, slightly less dark man giving Shahl just enough space to pass.

A smell stung Shahl's nostrils as he passed the threshold: dank, human sweat, mingled with a hint of human refuse and some sweet fragrance that had no chance to cover it all.

Into the blackness Shahl stepped, then a sack came down over his head. His alarm spiked. He flailed out. He ripped at the sack on his head. No use. Many hands held him, and thrash as he might he could not free himself. The blackness lurked close, and Shahl struggled to breathe.

"The less you struggle, the less painful this will be," the deep voice said.

Shahl realized now that what he had mistaken for a calming quality before was actually a cold disregard for human kindness.

Shahl shivered. "Wha—"

Something hard—a fist, perhaps—struck the side of his head, just above the ear. Another fist knocked the wind out of him, and blows to the backs of his legs brought him to his knees.

He struck out with his arms, but they grabbed them and pinned them in an awkward position. Pain shot into his shoulders. Shahl lost count of the blows, assailing him from too many directions.

The beating stopped, suddenly, and Shahl drifted through pain and grogginess, a living nightmare. He was on the cusp of blessed unconsciousness, without being able to make its sweet embrace. Pain hunted his fading awareness.

He felt himself dragged down, down. Footsteps fell on either side of him, and two sets of hands held him up. Their descent ended, and the path stayed level for a long while. In the darkness, pain, and mental fog, Shahl could not tell how far they dragged him.

He moved his head, and they dropped him to the ground. "On your feet."

Shahl took a kick to the gut. He doubled over in pain while the two men laughed. He struggled to his feet and stumbled along in the dark as they pulled him faster than Shahl's aching body could move.

They stopped, finally, and tossed Shahl to the ground. Someone yanked the sack off his head, and tore back the shade on a window, and there was light everywhere. Shahl could see nothing for the brightness.

Someone yanked at his collar and pulled him close enough to smell sweat. "Here's your choice. We can set you outside for the peace forces to find, where they'll slime you like the officer you killed should've slimed you before. Or, you can stay with us and become part of our family. We'll teach you to survive. But you can't have your old life back, Shahl Jeber-li."

Shahl shuddered. *How do they know my name?*

You'll never believe our luck. The twin brother of Ahrik Jeber-li just fell into our lap. Prepare to indoctrinate.

Message from Pir'e Analt to rebels on the Emerald Moon, intercepted by intelligence officers from the Ketel of Sheresh Shehur-li

5 | War Is Hell

We have tasted the first blood of combat. What glory it
is.

Ahrik Jeber-li, after the Battle at the Transit Station,
4 Teshrin Ewel RY 2498

RENLA. Renla." Zharla could not afford to let her voice rise above
the soft sleeping sounds of the servants' quarters. She didn't
want Renla to start out of sleep and wake those who slumbered near
her. She rocked Renla's shoulder back and forth, coaxing her friend
back to consciousness. She wished now that she had pushed her
mother harder to allow servants to have private quarters. The Tameri
estate had enough rooms for it, but her mother always countered
that such was not their station. Zharla grimaced. She needed her
friend's help in exacting *tenqam* from the rapist. From Shahl.

In the twenty-four hours since the rape, Zharla's life had been
hell. Daylight did nothing to suppress the foul memory and physical
pain of the attack. She'd met with the peace forces investigators twice
that day, recounting the agonizing details both times, suppressing
the gag reflex that threatened her as she did so. Her mother offered
little comfort, her face a mask of pity, but whether the pity was for
herself or her daughter, Zharla could not tell.

Zharla read fear in the edges of her mother's eyes when she told
Zharla that afternoon, "I should have done more to keep you away
from that Jeberi boy."

The verbal mementos of consolation given by those closest to

Zharla offered no comfort at all. She had no stomach to answer the message Ahrik sent before he deployed that evening. For that, she would have had to be past emotion altogether.

The fall of night, one night after the attack, closed in around her. A persistent disquiet threatened her sanity. Darkness loomed all over again, in a monstrous cloud, a cloud that the peace forces did nothing to dispel. As long as they did not catch Shahl, the threat would hover over her every breath. Sleep fled, replaced by thoughts of revenge. *Tenqam.*

When the urgency in Zharla's whisper and the squeeze of her hand brought Renla to, her friend cast her a look of bewilderment. Zharla almost never came to the servants' quarters, and she never came at night. Before Renla could speak, Zharla placed a finger on her friend's lips, then motioned for her to follow.

Once safely out in the hall, no mean feat, given the number of people they had to step over, Zharla whispered, "We are going."

"Where?" Renla yawned.

"In-mountain." Zharla kept her voice low, with nary a hint of indecision.

Renla shuddered, and her face grew as dark as the night around them. "Again? I spent my childhood trying to get out of that place."

"Trust me."

Renla frowned and pulled a long, black shawl and scarf from the hall closet. Many in Renla's family covered in public, but Zharla did not. They held hands as they snuck out of the main gate of the Tameri estate, communicating with hand movements rather than speech, using the simple code they'd developed in their years together. Pressure at certain points and in certain patterns meant different commands and letters. The gate guards slept as they crept past, and they made for the transporter station.

Renla squeezed Zharla's hand, in code. *Where in mountain?*

Zharla gave an inscrutable smile and signaled back. *Far enough.*

Renla spelled out, *Shtera Umqi?*

Farther, Zharla squeezed back.

Just out of earshot from the guard post, Renla stopped in the shadow of an alleyway, arms folded. Her voice rasped from underuse, "Zhe'le, what's going on?"

"I need to buy something."

Renla bit her lip and furrowed her brow. "You're claiming *ten-qam*."

Esheli law allowed any female victim of rape the right to maim her rapist, but not kill him, if she was sure who it was and as long as the peace forces had not yet apprehended him.

Zharla could say nothing more than what her eyes already said.

Renla's eyes pleaded. She grasped Zharla's hand. "He could have meant so much to you."

Zharla breathed out and yanked her hand back. "I'm done cowering. I will see his guilt in the moment of truth, as he begs me for salvation."

Zharla set off for the transporter station again, her pace furious. They no longer held hands.

Renla rushed to keep up, to wrap her scarf around her head and neck, against the cold and the dark, searching eyes that lurked in the in-mountain night. As they paid their fare for the transporter, Renla whispered, "You know where he is, don't you?"

Zharla turned to her friend and squeezed a black-clad shoulder. "You know where I can buy a weapon, don't you?"

Harsh light sprang into the cell where Shahl lay, shivering and exposed, his clothes somehow missing. He gagged on the reek of stale sweat and dried blood. Even shielding his eyes, he sensed a shadow come into the room. A dark and ominous hum confronted him, from the same voice that had pulled him out of the alley after he killed the peace forces officer. "Put this on."

Something made of cloth fell by his side. Shahl worked himself into a sitting position, and when his eyes finally adjusted, he saw a confessant's shift and puzzled through the meaning of it all. "Isn't there an induction ceremony?"

"Have you not learned to stop asking questions?" The dark shape gave a flick of his hand, and a menacing shuffle of feet and clank of metal sounded from a different direction.

Shahl tensed. The dark shape laughed. Shahl heard only malice. "We could teach you another lesson, if need be."

Shahl gasped and pushed himself back into the corner of the cell. "No. I... I'm sorry. I'll put it on." He fumbled with the material, but after the beatings, his hands did not respond like they should. He wanted to scream at the world, but he knew what that would bring. He looked up in apology. He imagined himself smiling, but had no idea what emerged on his face. "I... I was planning to enter the presbytery anyway."

The shadow smiled, too, but in a much different way. "Finally listening to reason, I see."

The shadow withdrew and the door resolved with a menacing hiss. The moment of illumination ended.

Shahl sighed in defeat. *How have I come to this?* He gave up trying to put on the confessant's shift and stared into the darkness, gaze vacant. In the darkness, an inkling of truth flashed back at him. Ahrik. Ahrik would benefit the most from the falsehood his life had become. Just as soon as it settled on his mind, though, Shahl dismissed the idea. His own brother? Never.

The transporter burst from the tunnel, and until it crawled to a stop at Shtera Umqi, Zharla's vision consisted of one big blaze. Her dilated pupils adjusted, and she made out the ground far below the station platform, shifting this way and that in currents of humanity, hypnotizing through the transporter's transparent skin.

Zharla tried to make herself as small as possible for the press of people getting off at Meran's busiest in-mountain station, teeming even at this wee hour. Out of nervous habit, she twisted her hands around her handkerchief.

As she stepped off, she noticed a man trying to enter the door to the women's section of the transporter, unsure if carelessness or lunacy drove him. A chorus of female hissing and clicking met his impertinence. Seeming confused at first, but then wounded by the jabbing, pinching, and shouted derision, the man made a rapid retreat. Men were seen more often now in government, law, higher education, and trade, but most Merani women were loath to relinquish the last vestiges of women's privilege.

Good. Anything to keep another Esheli woman from being a victim like her. Men's rights were a sham if Shahl, one of the movement's greatest advocates, could do what he did.

Zharla looked a question at Renla beside her.

Renla pointed with her head. "This way, I think. It's been a while."

Weapons dealing was banned in Meran, as in all other Esheli cities. The reality of life in-mountain, however, sometimes required a level of personal protection that the peace forces could not ensure in Meran's twisting caves and warrens.

Zharla and Renla walked away from the light and people of Shtera Umqi and farther into the bowels of the mountain. Just beyond the light ring that cast out from Shtera Umqi, where the main cavern of central Meran gave way to passageways burrowed into the rock, the rhythm of machinery, the clink of steel, and the calls of vendors met Zharla's ears before she saw the long, straight alleyway with shop after shop full of weapons of every sort.

Two men stood at the head of the alley, their dress nondescript. Distiller pistols hung at their sides. Judging by the hard looks they gave the two women, they probably had a number of other instruments of death hidden elsewhere on their persons, and it occurred to Zharla that they might suspect her of hiding a weapon in the handkerchief she held in her hand. Zharla slowed, hesitant to walk between them.

Renla clutched her elbow and pressed on. "Stay with me," she hissed.

The two men exchanged an assessing glance, and one of them motioned for them to continue. Their bearing seemed almost military, but they were not peace forces or ketelis, as far as Zharla could tell. Their dark edge was like nothing Zharla had ever experienced. She glanced over her shoulder after a few meters, just a peek to make sure they weren't following.

When they were out of earshot, Renla gave Zharla an admonishing nudge. "Don't stare. They're *ah'sbi*." She scanned their surroundings with nervous eyes. "This is a mistake, Zhe'le. Are you sure it was Shahl?"

Zharla's look burned fierce. "Does the sun rise over Meran Bay?"

Renla muttered under her breath and flexed her fists, but led on.

They passed shop after shop. Zharla couldn't believe what she saw. This was no black market, but an open market. There could not be anyone in central Meran that did not know about this. Even side streets were lined with weapons shops. Zharla knew that the reach of the peace forces did not run as deep in-mountain as it did out-mountain, but she had no idea that the disparity was this great. She shivered at the danger, and became aware of every eye that glanced their way and felt the stares of some, feasting on the novelty of a well-dressed out-mountainer venturing too deep into their city, at night.

Renla may have been right. Zharla hoped never to come here again.

After walking a few dozen yards into the weapons market, they came to a shop whose lighting made it slightly less uninviting than the others. "Re'le," said Zharla, "let's try this one."

The artificial light inside the shop gave a blue glow to the vendor's wares. Zharla recognized some of the weapons hanging on the wall from her studies at the melmez. There were qasfina, the short, crescent-shaped weapons of the ketela, like Ahrik carried with him, and distiller weapons of various shapes and sizes. She did not recognize most of the weapons.

She looked at the shopkeeper, expressionless. "I need to send a message that won't be forgotten."

The shopkeeper coughed, then continued drinking his tea, his back propped against the wall. Zharla judged him overfed and over-clever. He gave her an in-mountain sneer. "Womun like yuh come 'round my shop lookin' for ruvenge or protuction. Which iz it?"

Zharla cocked her head in a challenge. "For a weapons dealer, you have a healthy dose of curiosity."

A worried look flooded into Renla's eyes. She drew closer to Zharla and eased her feet wider apart, clenched her hands into fists.

The shopkeeper raised an appraising eyebrow, then cast his eyes down. "Furgive me. I wuz only makin' tulk. My shop has the bust weapons in Meran."

The way he added that last assertion made Zharla believe it less. She looked an impatient challenge at the shopkeeper.

He peered at Zharla, as if to judge whether he could trust her with some confidence. "I think I have what yuh need."

He turned around and, with his back to her, worked at something on the rock wall. One moment there was smooth rock, and the next there was an opening. The lights in his shop dimmed. He turned to face Zharla, and in his hands was a thin, simple-looking wooden box, about a hand span in width and two hand spans in length.

The shopkeeper lowered his voice. "Before I opun this box, yuh must agree t'tull"—at this point, he broke into a perfect out-moun-tain accent, executed at a whisper—"no one that I have sold you this weapon. My fellow shopkeepers do not know that I have something like this." He shivered. "If they did, they would report me to the two men you saw as you entered the market."

Zharla had a sinking suspicion that she would regret finding out, but she asked anyway, "How did you get here from out-mountain?"

He lowered his voice even more and drew almost too close for Zharla's comfort. Renla leaned onto the counter, acting as a sort of counterbalance.

"I risk death by showing this weapon to you, or speaking the out-mountain dialect. The *ah'sbe* kills those who break its code."

Zharla's face contorted with curiosity. She could not tell whether he was being honest or whether this was some ploy to squeeze more money out of her. "Why sell this weapon to me?"

"I know people," he continued in a whisper. "Many people come into my shop who have been wronged, but all of them have done their fair share of wronging others. Not you. You suffer from some grave injustice."

Zharla stepped back in surprise, and Renla's hand was there on the small of her back, supporting her. *Have I betrayed so much about myself?*

She forced down her surprise and regained her composure. She spoke, her voice barely audible, with a descant of pain. "Open the box. Your secret is safe."

The box opened easily on small metal hinges. An ordinary looking knife rested on cushioned, black felt, oriented diagonally. The steel blade gleamed, even in the blue light, and its matte black handle boasted polished rivets that suggested a tine running its length.

She stood up to her full height and glanced around at all the weapons on the walls that seemed safer, more powerful. She raised her hands in disbelief and narrowed her eyes in warning. "It's only a knife."

"It's more than a knife in the hand of one truly aggrieved." His eyes darted about and he switched back to the in-mountain dialect. "Religious assassuns and those seekin' revenge for the murder of a family membur use it down 'ere, but I think it appropriate f'yuh."

"How does it work?" She lifted it out, the cool metal unfamiliar to her touch.

He offered a smirk. "You're th'furst to handle it. It'll respond unly t'yuh."

She looked at him with incomprehension. As she looked down at it, the shopkeeper switched back to out-mountain dialect, but not before he lowered his voice and checked to make sure the coast was clear outside his shop. "This knife's true function can only be unlocked by imprinting it with a clear memory of a grave injustice. Close both hands around the hilt and think only of that injustice. Fill the weapon with the pain and anger that you felt then."

In seconds, Zharla trembled with fury. The rape had scored her memory, had made her want to kill her attacker or die trying, transported into the vale of pain whose sides slid in upon her.

She heard a voice, as if from a great distance, and realized once again where she was. The shopkeeper called to her. She stood in the weapons market deep in the belly of Meran. As she became aware of her surroundings once again, she realized that her eyes had been shut tightly. She opened them, and to her amazement, the blade in her hand glowed white. She should have felt the heat of the blade melt through the handle, but she felt nothing more than her sweaty palm, heated as much by wild thoughts of agonizing violation as by the blade.

"Strike the wull. Go un," the weapons dealer said, giddy. She found a spot free from merchandise and plunged the blade into the wall. The wall may as well have been butter. The power exhilarated her. If the knife could cut through solid rock like this, imagine what it could do to the body of the man she had to destroy. She could not fail now.

She felt the heat of the blade dissipate as she thought on this. A slow trickle of molten ooze began to squeeze from the wound she had inflicted on the stone. Power flowed through her. She bled the rock itself. She slipped the blade out of the wall and saw that the glow had diminished.

"How—" she began.

"Ah, the secruts of knife-makin'. They say thut some weapun makers mine so deep thut th'fires beneath th'mountun purify ther blades."

She hefted the knife with false assessment. Even if she lost control of the knife, no worse harm could come to her than what she would already have inflicted. She need only touch it to the body of her attacker while it was hot.

Shahl would be expecting nothing like the weapon she held.

Ahrik had found hell on earth. The stagnant air of the Kereu stood humid and hazy. It sucked the life from his pores. His ketel had disembarked from their transporters and occupied the open stretches of moist, blazing dirt at the transit station. There wasn't a cloud in the sky. Or, all the moisture in the clouds had settled into humidity on the ground. The sun beat down in a novel kind of heat.

His ketel assembled in a clearing about a kilometer-and-half in diameter, surrounded by walls of jungle ten meters high and as dense as any vegetation he'd ever seen. On the gentle rise at the center of the clearing stood an observation tower of semi-permanent construction, while a raised receiving platform made a ring about 600 meters in diameter around the tower, with eight docking points for transporters to unload and load cargo.

Beyond the docking platform, Ahrik saw a ring of towers like the central tower, about 200 meters inside the jungle wall. He counted twelve towers and rubbed his chin. Over 250 meters between towers. They'd need at least a full hand to defend this station against a determined attack. Ahrik assumed there were defensive works between the towers, with interlocking fields of view making kill zones between the jungle and the trench line. If there were any defenders in those trenches, and he hoped there were, they'd been baking in the blistering sun far longer than mere mortals should. They were soldiers, though, so they took what the army gave.

Today, the army gave its worst. It had managed to fly Ahrik's ten thousand sons across the ocean using the latest airborne transporter tech, only to arrive at a forsaken clearing in the Kerewi jungle without a convoy of ground-based transporters there to meet them. He and his ten thousand stood ready to be transported to their first real deployment, but here they sat, simmering in an outdoor oven.

Ahrik checked the time on his internal compiler, huffed, and beat a path to the base of the central tower. A Transport Section staffer poked a wary head out of the doorway and emerged to meet him. Ahrik stopped and folded his arms in front of his chest. He wasn't about to see his sons suffer because the army couldn't spare a few lousy transporters.

The staffer gulped and shuffled to a stop before Ahrik. He gave a crisp ready salute, as if it might make up for his utter failure to meet expectations.

Ahrik returned the salute and grunted with impatience. "I want quick answers, keteli. Who is your commanding officer?"

"Sir, my father is cross-planet, convalescing in the Eshel. He was wounded in a freak rebel attack last month near Peshron."

"Who is in command at this transit station?"

"I am, sir."

The answer felt a bit too eager for Ahrik's taste.

The staffer drew himself up to Ahrik's height. "I am in Melel's ketel of one thousand, and I report to my standard commander at the main base in Peshron." There was no hand in a ketel of one thousand, only two standards of about four hundred and fifty clones and a command company. The staffer shifted his weight from one foot to the other and sent an insolent, expectant look in Ahrik's direction.

The staffer emphasized the last syllable of "Peshron," so it threw Ahrik off for a moment. All Esheli words received emphasis on the first syllable. He recovered, and accessed his internal compiler to check the army's order of battle. The Ketel of Melel was a minor unit. Melel's bloodline hadn't been promoted in three generations. Expendable, then. And useless, apparently.

Ahrik drew close to the staffer. "You mean to tell me that there is no human in command of the Kereu's main logistics link to the Eshel?"

"Sir?"

"Who gives you orders? Can this Melel maintain his tendril link with you across the ocean?"

"No, but we have a detailed plan and—"

"A plan?" Ahrik let the incredulity sweep over this face. "A plan can't react to the unexpected. What is your name, keteli?"

"I have not earned a name, sir."

Ahrik poked a finger into the staffer's chest. "If you have not done something to make you worthy of a name, why should I trust you with my men's lives? It's a wonder we haven't lost this war already."

"Sir, this is the finest transport company in the Kereu." The staffer planted his feet and met Ahrik's glare. "We haven't missed a transit window."

Ahrik set his hands on his hips and smirked. "Until today?"

The staffer's eyes widened in defeat. He cast his gaze down. "Something must have gone wrong, sir, or your men would be on their way to their destinations by now."

Ahrik hummed in concern at the plural. As far as he knew, they only had one destination. He had not known that his ketel would be split up. Ahrik ignored this new question. This staffer couldn't answer it anyway, to be sure.

"What's your amazing plan, then, keteli?"

"Sir, I recommend you review the map display upstairs, where it's a bit cooler."

Ahrik clenched his fists but slowed his breathing to cast to his five hand commanders, *On me. In the tower. Tell your men not to get comfortable.* "Keteli," he told the staffer, "you have very little margin for error."

Thoughts of escape whispered away from Shahl's mind, moonbeams fighting against a thickening sky, their delicate green light just out of reach and consciousness. His torturers made sure of that with another beating, another sack over the head, another trip to a new place, dragged and pushed the whole way. Shahl had no idea where he was, and every part of him screamed in silent pain. Zharla's rejection remained a mere shadow of memory, this new torture sunk so deep. It could have been weeks, or it could have been hours. Time passed as a fading dew, like the suggestion of water when dying of thirst.

When they tore the sack from his head and tossed him into yet another black room, Shahl almost felt relief, but he knew worse lay in store. He tasted the evil in the air.

A cool breeze flowed over his scalp, and he reached a hand to his head. Shaved. He could not puzzle out in his muddled memory when that had happened.

His eyes finally adjusted to the darkness. The patterns carved into the walls told him he was in a temple. It didn't reek of urine and sweat like the last place, but the cold, hard stone floor through his thin confessant's shift made him shiver. He crawled over to a wall and ran his fingers over the carvings. He recognized them. The same carvings appeared on temples back home in Meran. If he was still in Mekele, then this was probably the central temple in the Merani Quarter. He sighed and thought on simpler times. Entering the presbytery wasn't supposed to be quite like this.

Movement slithered towards him from the blackest corner of the room. An ill-used throat wheezed. "You know where we are, friend?"

Shahl froze. He had thought he was alone. The voice didn't belong to one of his tormentors from the last, well, however long it had been. Tentative, he cleared the croak from his throat. "How do I know you're a friend?"

Shuffling neared. Shahl positioned his legs and arms as if they were a shield.

"I'm in here just like you, aren't I?"

Shahl noticed a hint of fear that he hadn't heard earlier. This man was just as scared as he was.

More wheezing. "This is some sort of halfway house. You recognize it, don't you?"

Shahl rubbed his temples and wrinkled his nose at the man's stench, a new blend of odors to adjust to. Shahl knew he should fill the expectant silence with something. "I...I think we're in the central temple, in the Merani Quarter of Mekele." He scooted away from the wheezing. "Tell me—friend—where's this halfway house supposed to get us?"

The man chuckled. "The *ah'sbe* can't just throw us onto the street when they need to move us. They need to give us new identities, make us disappear. Looks like this time we're confessants."

Footsteps fell outside the door, followed by a muffled discussion. The door dissolved with a hiss and a dark figure appeared. Shahl could tell by the way he moved and the tenor of his breathing that he was the same one who had ushered him into this hell, back in the rain-soaked alleyway. All the fatigue and pain and hunger and disorientation of his torment came flooding back. The dark figure nodded in his direction. "You. Jeberi Slime. Come with me."

Shahl began to wonder if it was possible, if Ahrik had some role in all this.

◻

Ahrik worked the metal bracelet on his right wrist. He counted backward from ten. Three of his hand commanders and a few Transport Section staffers stood with him in the control room of the transit station's central tower. Ahrik considered the consequences of throwing clones from someone else's ketel out of a window.

"You mean to tell me, keteli," he said to a staffer, "that you received a distress signal from the convoy that was supposed to transport my sons? I pray to the Lady of the Emerald Moon that you had a good reason for keeping this from me. I sent two hands in that direction." Beral's 1st Hand and Leren's 3d Hand were assigned to operate out of Peshron. There was no convoy to transport them, so Ahrik sent them on foot, since Peshron was less than ten kilometers away.

Ahrik should have asked more questions before executing his plan. He cursed under his breath and fingered the clasp of Biriq, with a pointed glare at the transport staffer. He cast to Beral and Leren over the tendril link: *Beral. Leren. Possible ambush ahead.*

The staffer shuffled backward. "N...no good reason, sir."

"And you failed to tell me that twenty transporters' worth of supplies are coming into this station at dusk." Ahrik flipped open the clasp.

The staffer nodded his head, eyes now wide with fear.

Ahrik drilled his gaze into the staffers around the room. "This is the perfect opportunity for the enemy to attack. Next you'll tell me that the shipments always come at the same time of day."

Another staffer cleared his throat. "Ah...actually, sir. The last transporter always arrives at nightfall."

Ahrik closed his eyes and huffed. He checked his internal compiler. The solar schedule gave them...an hour before the last transporter arrived. He had to act. Now.

"You," he said, pointing at the Transport Section staffers. "You may only speak in response to a direct question from me. I am now in command of this transit station." *Ayen,* he cast, *bring protection squad. Embed rest of command company with units. Fight's coming.*

Ahrik turned to his three remaining hand commanders, standing at parade rest across the room. "Halel, your 2d Hand will entrench under the circular transporter platform. Protect those supplies as they come in. Shan and Arnan, 4th and 5th Hands will entrench just behind the outer perimeter. Defend this station. Shan, figure out who is in command of perimeter defense. Get their number one in here. Staffers, your squads will unload and store those supplies as quickly as possible. Are my orders clear?"

The staffers nodded and turned back to their consoles to coordinate the unloading. The three hand commanders rushed out of the control room, and the ten members of his protection squad filed in. Ahrik peered out the window. The first supply transporter appeared on the horizon. From the darkening horizon over the ocean.

The transporters that brought his ketel began to lift into the kall stream to fly back to the Eshel. Like the supply transporters, the transit transporters they came on measured some fifty meters in length, much larger than the civilian transporters back home. In the fading light, his sons hollowed out trenches with their distillers, the discharge tubes spewing slurry over the ground.

Ahrik frowned. He and his sons had just walked into a trap. The trap was meant for another quarry, but it was still a trap. The enemy had months to plan and gather forces in the jungle and surely lusted after enough supplies for a hundred thousand men for a fortnight. Taking this transit station offline for even a few days would be a huge win for the rebels.

He cast orders to his hand commanders: *All units cloak. Total verbal silence.* Outside, six thousand men disappeared. The sensory fibers grown into their combat uniforms adjusted to the environment. The discharge from their distillers stopped, and almost no evidence remained of their presence. Even if the enemy was already watching, he wouldn't be able to tell where his men were now. Concealed and covered. They could spring a trap of their own. Ahrik smiled.

The eighth supply transporter docked, and the first began its departure after unloading its contents. For all their faults, the Transport Section staffers worked fast.

Silence pounded in Ahrik's mind. He sensed a creeping fear that he could not show, not to his sons, and not to the others over whom he exercised impromptu command. He had read and heard about the fear of battle, but he never thought that it would grip him like this. He scarfed down a ration bar. His stomach still felt hollow. He wondered what his new wife was doing now. Probably sleeping through dawn, what with the half-day time difference.

He wondered if they had caught his traitor of a brother yet, a day after the attack on Zharla. He frowned. An odd thought to have now, before battle.

He wiped his forehead. With all the movement in and out, the control room was now as sticky as the air outside. He shivered.

Darkness began to swallow the sky. The twelfth supply transporter docked. Shan, his 4th Hand commander, cast: *Father, two perimeter defense commanders on approach.*

Falcon, the seeker on Ahrik's protection squad, whispered, "Father, two figures approaching our position. Shall we neutralize?" Falcon peered up a question at Ahrik with his abnormally large eyes.

"No. Perimeter defense commanders."

Ahrik checked the supply transporters outside. They continued to flow in and out of the station. Footsteps on the stairs. The door to the control room dissolved, and two figures uncloaked and saluted. Ahrik's protection squad fingered their weapons.

"Hold," Ahrik ordered. Then, he took a good look at the two arrivals: "You're from the Ketel of Alrem. Where is he? Commander Sheresh said I should speak with him." Worry stabbed at Ahrik. Had his friend just been ambushed in the jungle?

"We lost contact, sir," said one of Alrem's men. Strain creased his face.

Ahrik glanced at his insignia. The senior of the two company commanders.

"I'm sure I'll see him soon," Ahrik said with false confidence. No need to reveal his suspicions of an ambush, here on the cusp of battle. It took all his willpower to suppress the fear he felt. He turned and examined the tabletop holomap. He smelled the humidity in the room and felt the tension rise by degrees. He nodded to Alrem's two company commanders. "You will remain here, so we can coordinate the defense."

"Yes, sir," they said in unison.

"How are your men deployed?" Ahrik asked. At the same time, he cast to the two hand commanders on their way to Peshron and the possible ambush site: *Beral and Leren, any contact?*

None, came the reply.

"One man every ten to fifteen meters, sir, depending on angles," said the senior company commander. "Two crew-served weapon teams in each tower. Total strength in two companies: two hundred and fifty."

Ahrik winced. They would need eight times that number to defend against what was coming for them. He hoped his sons were ready, now that they were here, on the cusp of battle. Alrem's men wouldn't last long if Ahrik's sons did not engage.

Ahrik's blood pumped faster, and he dared not speak, worried he would reveal his fear. He began to sense the unease of his men, leaked back over the tendril links from his hand commanders. He took a few deep breaths and told himself he was prepared. His sons had worked their whole lives to achieve success at this moment. They were about to taste the glory of combat, to become men and defenders of the Eshel.

The second-to-last transporter docked.

Beral: *Father, arrived at the ambush site, but—*

Sickened emotion flooded through the tendril link. Carnage smoldered. Air thick with death. Trees felled and burning across the supply route. The transporter convoy nothing but wreckage. *Father,* Beral cast, *bodies everywhere. Hundreds of men massacred, many in pieces, some with throats slit, others with ghastly, open wounds.* More emotion flooded over the tendril link. The moans of the dying made an eerie chorus. The smell of Beral's men vomiting.

Ahrik reeled. He stumbled to the windowsill that looked toward Peshron. Beral was letting his men's emotions spill over the tendril link. He cast back to Beral, *Get a hold of your men.* Ahrik couldn't afford to lose a fifth of his force before the fight began.

But Father, Beral cast back, *this is. . . was. . . the ketel of Alrem.*

Ahrik began to feel sick. He set his mind to overcome. He stood on the floor of the tower control room and dug his fingers into the table display. His eyes burned with determination. He considered telling Alrem's two company commanders about their ketel commander, but battle was almost upon them. Duty first.

The last docking point opened up. Ahrik set his jaw. The last transporter approached. Darkness deepened. Another shiver passed through him.

Contact.

The night lit up. The last transporter exploded into flame on its final approach. The eastern quarter of the outer perimeter burst with light. Ahrik felt his six thousand sons at the transit station cower in their holes.

Ahrik ground his teeth.

The command tower buckled from the repercussions of what seemed like a hundred blasts. Ahrik lurched back. A hand caught him. Ayen, his aide. Their eyes met, and for an instant Ahrik let his true fear wash over his face.

Ahrik looked out the window once more, transfixed. The last transporter disintegrated on its approach, flaming pieces tumbling to the ground as it hurtled toward the docking platform. The ball of flame struck the platform with a thunderous crash. Fire lashed out.

Flashes of light from the treeline accompanied dull booms, hammering the outer perimeter. Each explosion was weaker and less forceful than the one that Shahl had lived through at the social hall in Meran, but together these bursts made Ahrik search his soul for shards of hope.

In the fading light, the jungle moved. Hundreds upon hundreds of men emerged. Rank after rank, they streaked at a breakneck run to cover the 200 meters to the station's outer perimeter defenses. The enemy's line extended over at least 400 meters.

Explosions rippled along the defensive perimeter.

"Sweet Lady of the Emerald Moon, save us now," Ahrik muttered. He fought down his panic. "Staffer, report."

"Docking Point Two in flames, sir. No contact from the transporter pilot or the unloading squad. Other squads moving supplies to the interior of the station." Ahrik did not hold out much hope of preserving those supplies.

Ahrik cast to Beral and Leren, *Under attack. Return to transit station.* To the three hand commanders still at the station: *Courage, sons.* Ahrik felt his hand commanders trying to wrangle their men's paralyzing fear. How many men did the enemy have? Did they destroy the Ketel of Alrem? Would they destroy his ketel? Despair threatened him for an instant, but he remembered his training. He calmed his breathing. Ahrik would need all his resources to survive the night. He had advantages, like prepared defensive positions and, he hoped, surprise.

He looked a question to Alrem's company commanders. Their drawn faces shook his confidence, until he realized they were deep in concentration, directing their men by tendril link. One said, "We are taking heavy losses from this bombardment, sir."

Ahrik looked through the window. Tiny black forms darted by the tower, men from Alrem's ketel, moving from other sectors of the outer perimeter to reinforce at the point of attack. From his three hands inside the perimeter, he sensed only fear. His sons huddled in their trenches, frozen by the chaos that had just exploded upon them.

Then Alrem's men answered the rebels' onslaught. Flares shot up into the night. Tracers from their weapons arced in from the towers first, joined shortly thereafter by those in the trench line. The staccato *boom, boom* of the enemy bombardment persisted and the human wave still advanced, but now the *thu-thu-thunk, thu-thu-thunk* and tracers of Alrem's distillers answered.

Deep down, Ahrik knew their fate hung like a weighted thread.

The enemy approached to within 50 meters of the outer perimeter. Their drug-infused war cry split the night, and in desperation Ahrik looked to Alrem's two company commanders. To his amazement, they did not mirror his despair.

One smiled. "Come, you dogs, come."

Twenty-five meters.

Alrem's tracers paused as the rebels closed the distance to the perimeter. Then the perimeter opened up with three times as many tracers as before. Tracers tore into the wide enemy front. *Thu-thu-thunk, thu-thu-thunk.* At the same time, the crew-served weapons trained their sights on the tree line, just as the enemy bombardment ended to let the attackers hit the perimeter.

The rebel war cry turned to clamors of fright. Enemy bodies piled up in kill zones. Limbs writhed in the throes of death. A keening agony went up from the wounded, and the breakneck advance turned into flailing, sudden retreat, and then into slaughter as Alrem's crew served weapons closed from the treeline onto the tracers coming from the outer perimeter. Many rebels fell in the wicked vice, but probably half made it back to the jungle.

One of the company commanders sighed at the lull in the battle. Reading Ahrik's face, he said, "Sir, that was only the first wave. They forced us to reveal everything we've got, and they know it. Each new wave will shift the attack to a new area of the perimeter, spread us out, wear us down." He drew himself up. "Request permission to fight with my men, sir."

"Granted." Ahrik lowered his voice almost to a whisper. Still, his own sons trembled in their trenches, paralyzed by the chaos of the ancient weapons. So many years of training, to cower in fear at the first sign of battle.

The other company commander said, "Sir?"

Ahrik nodded, and the two company commanders gave him the death salute, hands crossed over their hearts. They knew that this night, of all nights, would be their last. Ahrik saw it in their eyes.

There had to be another way.

He flexed his wrist against the metal bracelet. If the enemy ignored the rules of war by using the ancient, forbidden weapons, then so could he. "Staffer, how long until the next transporter is unloaded?"

"Sir?" He looked confused. "Three minutes, sir."

"Bring the pilot of that transporter online."

The staffer swiped at his compiler display, and the pilot's voice crackled, "Sir?"

"Pilot, this is one."

"Yes, sir?" The pilot's voice shook.

"When the next rebel wave comes, you will fly your transporter at the treeline. Orient your transporter to hit the treeline broadside. I want you at maximum speed."

There was a pause. "If I refuse, sir?"

"You will obey a direct order, or my men will shoot you out of the sky." Ahrik hoped the pilot didn't call his bluff. At that moment, he wasn't sure he could get his men to do anything.

"Sir, nothing like this has ever been done before."

Ahrik stepped closer to the communication port, for emphasis. "That's why it will work."

"Sir, what about the boson drive? I'd have to shut it down manually before impact. I need to stay in the transporter to accomplish what you ask." A pause.

"You have two minutes before execution."

"I'm just a transporter pilot." The pilot gulped. "You're asking me to die for you, sir." The crackling connection did not hide the tremor in his voice.

Ahrik gulped down the bile that crawled up his throat. Asking someone to die for him was not supposed to be this hard. They made it sound so easy in training. "I'm asking you to save the lives of hundreds of good men. Thank you for your service to the Eshel. One out."

There. It was done. Ahrik couldn't tell if it was easier to ask one man to die than to ask all of Alrem's men to do the same. That pilot didn't deserve death any more than Alrem's men did. Ahrik pushed these questions from his mind. There would be a time to answer them. Later.

The enemy bombardment resumed, but this time it fell on Ahrik's sons between the perimeter and the platform. How the enemy got a bead on his sons' positions so quickly, Ahrik could not fathom. His sons crouched down even lower in their trenches, and Ahrik shook his head in frustration. If this transporter-as-weapon gamble didn't work, Ahrik and his sons would watch Alrem's men die, men whom they had known for years.

The second rebel wave emerged at the treeline on an even wider front than before, but still all of Ahrik's sons cowered inside the perimeter. Ahrik dared not order them out. They might run from the fight. Alrem's men adjusted their positions as best they could in the face of the second wave, but their tracers diminished in intensity.

Ahrik closed his eyes. "Staffer, get that transporter in the air."

The bombardment ceased with sudden disquiet, and the second rebel wave broke into a run. The transporter lunged overhead. It picked up speed. When the intent became clear, the screaming rebels slowed their charge and redirected their weapons, but it was too late. The ground shook with the impact. The careening transporter tore a gash out of the jungle. As if on cue, Alrem's men advanced from their trenches and poured distiller charges into the retreating enemy. They formed up at the treeline to pursue.

Only then did Ahrik's sons begin to emerge from their holes.

Calm returned to the control room, and Ahrik turned to Ayen in disgust. "We have tasted the first blood of combat." He slammed a fist onto the tabletop holomap, scrambling the image. "What glory it is."

> The operation at the transit station was a success. The new soldiers and the new training regimen took the enemy by surprise. If the Ketel of Ahrik had not been there, it would have been a complete victory.
>
> ---
>
> Rebel after-action report, found after the War of the Emerald Moon, RY 2501

6 | Hunter and Hunted

Zharla Tamer-li just left for Mekele. She will lead you to her rapist.

Message from Aanin Sheresh Shehur-li to the peace forces station, Merani Quarter, Mekele Eshel, night of 3 Teshrin Ewel RY 2498

THE transporter arrived in Mekele, and Zharla clutched her cloak about her, not because of the midsummer weather, which was warm and pleasant in the capital, but because anonymity was her closest ally. Zharla left Renla in Meran to throw off her family and any peace forces that might want to follow her. "Tell them I'm sick in bed all day," she told Renla.

Zharla's husband, the hero Ahrik, was half a world away, probably settling down to a quaint lunch with his military friends. She and Ahrik were both better off without him here.

Almost two days had passed since the rape, and she felt her opportunity at tenqam drawing shut. The knife she bought last night lay strapped to her thigh, underneath her cloak. The peace forces were probably close to finding Shahl, so she must not have long. She did not want to be recognized and then have it all come undone because the peace forces got to Shahl first. She pulled her hood down low over her face and wasted no time heading for the Merani Quarter, to the main Temple to the Lady of the Emerald Moon.

Once there, she ascended the stone steps to the temple and passed through the massive stone entryway. She had visited it once years ago, as a tourist, but she'd forgotten how imposing and grandiose the structure was. Stone pillars the size of trees lined the central nave, reaching through the open ceiling, to the sky above. Graven moon charts chased over the floor and walls, for teaching congregants the phases of worship. A spur of Mekele Mountain yawned over the altar, and Zharla found it difficult to tell where the mountain ended and the temple walls began.

She stepped into the shadow just inside the entrance and scanned the temple. If she guessed right about Shahl, then he'd entered the presbytery, and he'd be here as a confessant, since all confessants in Mekele were inducted here. Staying close to the temple pillars, she crept toward the altar. Already the afternoon light cast the east wall's shadow halfway across the temple floor. The thick walls stood three or four meters high, and the stone pillars she crept beside may even have been carved from the mountain itself.

She approached the altar from the shadow of the last pillar. The altar loomed before her, a solid stone block, exactly cubed, near the alcove cut into the mountain. On the steps leading up to the altar sat the confessants, religious aspirants to the ranks of the *pira*, dressed in white, their heads shaved. Their anxious eyes followed Zharla's every step, eager to prove their worth to those seeking spiritual enlightenment. Confessants won religious converts not by skilled argumentation or soulful entreaty, since that was the *pira's* domain, but by telling any who would listen of how they had turned from transgression. They hoped that by so doing the unrepentant would want to experience such a change themselves, and would seek out the doctrines of the *pira*.

She scanned the confessants' faces. Even though their shaved heads would make Shahl difficult to recognize, she did not see his eyes peering back at her. She would remember those eyes, the last thing she saw before the rape.

Up until two days ago, Zharla was certain that Shahl had done nothing worth confessing. Now she was intent on making him regret the violence he'd wrought. When she found him.

She eased toward the nearest confessant, her hand close to the knife at her thigh, hidden underneath her cloak, and spoke before the confessant had a chance to waylay her with his story of conversion. "Where is your *pir'e*?"

The confessant stood up, hands at his sides, and stared at the ground a few feet in front of him. His voice shook with innocence. "I can take you to him, if you will give me a moment of your time."

Zharla sensed his inner conviction. A novice, no doubt. She opened and closed her fingers at her side, inside her cloak, stroking the knife, drawing comfort. "No. Just point me in the right direction, please."

Crestfallen but obsequious, he pointed toward the rear of the temple. A man lumbered toward her out of the dark maw of the mountain behind the altar. The *pir'e* was large but not fat, and taller than most. His red ecclesiastical robes swished at his sides as he paced toward Zharla with an air of humility that she distrusted.

"Daughter," he began, with a rumble low in his chest. "I—"

"I am not your daughter," she hissed. "I only preserve the sanctity of this place to honor the poor whose money built it." Zharla frowned at him, but kept her voice down. "I am not party to your dogmas."

"Please, there is no need—"

She held up her hand and took a deep breath, to release the tension. "Let me begin again. Do you have a new confessant in your midst? He would have joined in the last day or so." She gave Shahl's description. His name, she knew, would be no use, since those entering the presbytery discarded their old lives.

A good reason for Shahl to enter the presbytery. To hide from his crime. Maybe he'd planned this all along, if she didn't choose him.

"Ah, you want the power of new faith," the *pir'e* said.

Zharla let him believe the untruth. The less that people asked her real intentions, the better.

He nodded towards the front of the temple, as if Shahl was there. "That confessant is on an errand. You are welcome to wait in the pews."

Zharla inclined her head with something like deference, then turned to wait by the east wall instead, where the shadows were deepest. The freedom that had eluded her since the rape two days before was within her grasp, and time passed like eternity. She shivered and fingered the hilt of the heat knife in its sheath and thought on how sweet tenqam would be.

"Jeberi Slime. Stand up." A figure, that same deep-throated nemesis, grabbed a handful of Shahl's shift and yanked him close. "Let me tell you how this will go. You are going to be the best confessant that the Eshel has ever seen, got it? You recognize no one. You tell the story we gave you."

Shahl guessed it was still light outside, although the dimness of the temple's back corridors, carved into Mekele Mountain, made it hard to tell. He smirked at his captor, and something came over him, an insolence towards Ahrik and his ilk that made Shahl want to throw off the yoke he bore. "Or what? You'll kill me?" He shrugged. "I might prefer that."

"No, fool," the man said, smacking Shahl with an open palm and pushing him through a doorway. The late afternoon sun cast forbidding shadows into the alcove behind the altar. In a swirl of red robes, the large, deep-throated man shook Shahl and manhandled his gaze towards the east wall, near the main entrance to the temple. "We'll kill *her*."

Shahl squinted into the light, but he saw where the man forced his gaze. His heart stood still in his chest, for at that moment a figure emerged from the shadows of the temple pillars and into the fading light. The figure's face was shrouded by a hood, but Shahl could tell from the way the figure moved, and from some deep sense of foreboding, that it was Zharla Tamer-li.

"Father," the keteli healer panted, "prez th'Lady I found yuh." The keteli's uniform was soaked with a mix of sweat and blood. Ahrik looked for unit markings. A field healer from Leren's 3d Hand. The blood probably wasn't his.

Ahrik ran a hand over his close-cropped hair. As the rush of battle wore off, the time lag between the Kereu and Meran began to catch up with him. His internal compiler told him it was dusk, two days after the decision ceremony, but the early morning sun told him something different.

He hadn't slept since the visit from Sheresh back in Meran, before they deployed, over twenty-four hours earlier. The keteli healer intercepted him as he and his aide, Ayen, trudged back to the central observation tower after another battlefield circulation. Ahrik hoped it was the last circulation he would have to do. Precious few of Alrem's men still lived. Vicious hand-to-hand combat had awaited them in the jungle last night. Only Ahrik's two hands returning on the Peshron road had forced a final enemy retreat.

Then Ahrik saw a stretcher, borne by two other healers. They trudged up behind the first healer, moving in a way that said they carried precious cargo. Ahrik filled his lungs with air to hold fatigue at bay once again. "This man is from Alrem's ketel," he said.

Ahrik prayed that he was still alive. The losses would be a heavy weight between Alrem and him when next they met.

If they met again.

The healer shook his head. "Ut's Alrem humself, Father."

Ahrik's mind sprang to alertness. He scanned the man's unit markets, but found no rank insignia to confirm the healer's claim. His legs turned weak.

He looked a question at the healer, who nodded. "No rank 'signia, Father, but one'f 'is sons cunfirm'd."

"Bring him into the tower. Ayen, see that no one disturbs us."

"Yes, Father."

Once inside, Ahrik asked the healer, "Is he stable?"

"Father, he's schedul'd fer exfil on th'next transpurter, 'n five," the healer said. Ahrik heard the fatigue in the keteli's voice and saw the bags under his eyes. Guilt stabbed at Ahrik. He had no reason to be tired himself, compared to what his sons had been through.

Ahrik's chest filled with pride as he watched the healers go. His sons still put Ahrik first, even on the brink of complete exhaustion. Ahrik crouched down beside the stretcher and considered his old friend. His eyes widened in surprise when Alrem smiled at him.

"Alrem?" Ahrik asked.

"I can see the pride in your eyes. I felt like you once."

"This was no great victory, Alrem. I... I'm sorry... I should have saved more of your men." Ahrik sighed. "We are looking for survivors now." His words rang hollow. His own ketel had suffered so little—none killed, none missing, only a few wounded.

An unnatural sound rattled somewhere deep in Alrem's chest. He wheezed. "I feel my sons' absence in my mind." Then Alrem laughed. His face twisted in pain. He grabbed his abdomen. "Ahrik, this war comes at great cost, but those who pay have little say in how it's fought."

"The price we pay to defend women's rule."

Alrem snorted, then winced in pain. "I thought like that before I lost my first squad to those berzerkers. They are not men, Ahrik. They take no prisoners, and they go into battle with unhinged bloodlust."

"The power of the ketel—"

"Power?" Alrem scoffed. "Where is my ketel now? I once had ten thousand sons, but now I lead, what, fifty? Maybe fewer? We are not winning this war, Ahrik."

Ahrik shook his head. "We control the cities and the intercity transporter network. The local population supports the Republic, don't they? The regional security brief—"

"Lies. I was ambushed on that transporter network, and if we control the cities, then rebels control the streets." Alrem grabbed Ahrik's uniform with a bloody hand and pulled him close. "Where is my ketel now?"

Ahrik trembled. He tried to pull away. "I'm supposed to ask you something, Alrem."

Alrem laughed again, then cringed in pain. "Did Supervisor Sheresh put you up to it?" He waved his hand. "Ignore that. Stay alive. Keep your men alive. The army doesn't care about you." Alrem squeezed his eyes shut. "There is no glory in death."

Ahrik fixed his eyes on the ground. "Where were you?"

Alrem grasped Ahrik's hand. He coughed, and winced. "Feel no guilt for my sons you could have saved, Ahrik. The Chief Elders brought them here, not you." He gave a dismissive grunt, to tell Ahrik what he thought of the Chief Elders. "When we're back in the Eshel, I'll tell you where I was. Everything will be clearer than you could ever imagine."

Ahrik hung his head, but nodded an agreement to meet back in Meran. When the field healers came to take Alrem away, Ahrik turned to lead his men into a war he didn't know how to fight.

Zharla wiped her clammy hands on her cloak and tried to lick away the cotton in her mouth. The evening air brought no breeze, but her core quivered anyway. She fought down the fear of what it would feel like to plunge the knife into Shahl's body. She leaned on a stone pillar and tried to smell something pleasant on the air. The deep well of hard stone left her cold inside. She set her teeth against the task before her. If she let Shahl, her attacker, know he'd broken her, then a moment of violence would turn into a lifetime of despair. Any hope of picking up the pieces of her shattered life rested in her being stronger than him.

Zharla knelt, as any good congregant would, with her hood pulled deep over her face, a fragile, once-proud woman seeking her escape from a twisted world. Every few seconds, when she thought she could get away with it, she interrupted her feigned piety to steal a glance in the direction where she had last seen Shahl. She waited for her opportunity. For dusk to darken toward night. For the congregants to disperse. For Shahl to be as vulnerable as she had been.

He was the rapist, and she the victim. The thought gave her the will to do the deed. Now she was the predator, and he the prey. Her heart pounded, and she unfastened the clasp on the sheath under her cloak.

She saw him clearly, despite the overcast night and feeble, green moon. He pled some case to a group of congregants: a man, a woman, and a girl. The hypocrisy churned her insides. She couldn't let him escape his crime by going into the presbytery. Something animal stirred within her, and her soul crouched, ready to spring, to claw and tear and destroy.

The three congregants walked away from Shahl, and he called for them to stay and hear his story. She caught a faint snippet and felt the heat rise within her breast: "I did not mean for it to happen to her."

Did not mean for it to happen to me? Zharla welcomed the rage that poured over her. Her thirst for tenqam solidified into icy determination. Rape is no accident. He and at least two other men attacked her. The attack seared her mind, and, for the first time, recalling it made her stronger, not weaker. She bunched her cloak in her hands, stuffed it in her mouth, and screamed in silent violence. She would conquer now, or die.

When she regained control of her breathing, she lifted rage-blurred eyes to find Shahl. She did not see him. She wouldn't get another chance like this. Panic rose. She scanned the darkness of the temple.

Footsteps fell behind her. She sucked in her breath and gripped the hilt of the knife under her cloak. She whirled.

"A story of woe for a humble congregant?" Shahl said, his eyes cast down.

She answered him nothing, just remained still, in half-whirl, the hood low on her head, statuesque, one hand on the pillar behind her and the other inside her cloak, easing out the heat knife. His shift swished eerily as the motion that carried him to a stop behind her petered out. He must have followed the other three congregants to the temple entrance, then happened on her on his way back to the altar. If he moved toward her, she would pounce. Already the heat of her knife seeped into her leg as she coaxed it from its sheath and hid it behind her back.

He moved, but away from her, toward the altar. She followed him with her eyes, and a tear of hate slid down her face.

"Perhaps another time," he said, his voice soft. He gave no indication of having recognized her.

She peered after him, not willing to lose him once again. Zharla readied herself to leap forward, to catch him unaware. *Conquer now.*

He stopped, and she froze just before springing into action. He kneeled, then sprawled on the ground, face first, his arms and legs spread wide. Zharla drew her head back in shock. She did not dwell on this new form of supplication to the Lady of the Emerald Moon, this meaningless cry for forgiveness. This was her chance. She took it.

She pointed her knife toward Shahl and crept forward. He lay not ten meters from her, chanting some muffled dirge. She looked around. The temple had emptied of both congregants and confessants. Zharla and Shahl, two interlopers, alone at last. She took a careful step forward and focused her mind on the injustice of the rape. Her knife glowed with new fervency. She crept another step forward, and her cloak rustled. *Maybe the religious chant makes him oblivious.*

The knife turned from red to white hot. Only two steps remained before she realized sweet revenge. She planted her foot next to his leg and moved the white knife toward his neck. Still he did not move. Still he chanted, but she knew not why. With his face turned away from her, she could not see if his eyes were open or closed.

She held the knife over his inert body. She hesitated. If she wounded him too deeply, she may never know why he did it. *Why should I falter now, on the cusp of deliverance?*

Zharla weighed which might be greater: pure, violent revenge or the power of knowing why.

She drove her knee into his back and pinned his shoulder with her hand. He did not fight back. She moved the knife slowly, to draw out his pain and suffering as long as possible.

The last two centimeters between her blade and Shahl's neck passed with a clarity that slowed each moment in time. His hair singed first, sending an acrid smell into her nostrils. His shift began to crinkle and shy back from the heat next, turning from white to a foreboding black as it retreated from her blade. In that instant before the blade touched the skin, just as it began to steam and bubble, Shahl's body stiffened. But still he did not struggle. His chanting stopped. He did not scream, but he sucked in his breath. His hair and robe began to catch fire, but he did not cry out in pain. He only whispered one word: "Zhe'le."

She drew back her blade, just enough to pause his pain. *Why does he not fight back?* The blade left a wicked burn. Her grip weakened. White hot, the knife fell and sank up to the hilt in the stone floor. The calm in Shahl's voice overcame her. She heard pain and misunderstanding, guilt. He used the familiar form of her name. She did not know how, after the pain she had inflicted.

She stumbled back, but tripped on her cloak. She landed hard on the stone and pushed her feet against the floor until her back stopped against a pillar. She scrambled around the pillar, ready to make a run for it. She stole a glance back at Shahl.

He lay still, on the ground, his face now turned toward her. His eyes did not burn with anger, but reached out to her in sadness. He did not spring up and lash out at her. He raised himself up on one hand, the other probing the wound on his neck. He looked at her for a long moment, uncomprehending.

"Why?" he asked.

She reached for the clasp at her neck. She could probably outrun Shahl with his shift on, if she shed her cloak.

He unfolded himself and took a wobbly step toward her, his face awash in pain.

"Stop, Shahl."

He froze and winced. "Wh...why are you afraid of me?"

"What sick game are you playing, you...you...?" She could not think of a fitting epithet. He wasn't supposed to respond with sadness and puzzlement, but with the detachment that accompanied his attack, the detachment she saw in his face, heard in his voice, that black, black night. Her lip curled in a snarl. "After what you did to me?"

Shahl backed away, unsteady, eyes wide with confusion. His breath heaved as he leaned back against the impassive stone wall. "I am no angel, Zharla, but I have done nothing to you but be rejected." His voice held more than just physical pain. "A woman died because I made a poor choice, and I will answer for that in time, but you, Zharla? What have I done to you?"

"I...I saw your face, Shahl. I heard your voice in the darkness." Every moment was etched in her memory. "You were in my room. You. Raped. Me."

"Oh, no. No." Horrified understanding swept over his face. He looked down at the knife in the floor and reached for the burn at the base of his neck. "You're the woman who was raped. You're claiming tenqam."

The strength left Shahl's gaze. He slid to the ground and curled up against the temple wall, then whimpered.

Zharla saw her chance. She undid her cloak and leaped forward. She yanked the knife from the floor and brandished it at him. "Speak, Shahl!"

"What? No. I...I..." He sputtered. "I wandered the streets that night. I had tea at a shop. I waited for you. You never came." He sniffed back tears. "How would I even get into your room?"

She searched his eyes, his voice, his every movement, for some sign of dissimulation or derangement. She searched her own memory for any detail she might have missed. She did not think Shahl capable of lying, nor did she suspect him of it now.

She had not thought him capable of rape, either.

Zharla replayed the attack in her mind, and she was certain of three things: she saw Shahl's face, she heard his voice, and she was violated. Either Shahl had suddenly become an imaginative and convincing liar, or he was innocent. She searched his expression, the slump of his shoulders, the pain in his eyes, for any sign of deceit, but found nothing. The possibility that he was innocent lurked like guilt.

She swayed her head in despair, then shook the blade in his direction. "I cannot deny what I saw and heard and felt two nights ago."

He made no feeble plea for mercy, no blubbering confession of guilt. His gaze slid to the floor of the temple, then stared at nothingness. The longer her thoughts went undisturbed, and the longer Shahl held his peace, the more she doubted his guilt.

"Is your neck bad?" she asked after a beat.

He did not answer. At that moment metal scraped against stone behind her.

"Don't move," ordered a gruff voice.

She spun. A figure trained a distiller pistol on Shahl in the pale moonlight. His eyes glared past Zharla and bore into Shahl.

Moonlight glanced off of metal insignia on his shoulders. Three other figures moved to flank Shahl. Softly, quietly, Zharla sheathed her knife. She looked to the altar, wondering what had become of the *pir'e* and the confessants, and wondering why they had abandoned Shahl.

The peace forces officer who'd spoken moved past her. She followed him with her eyes to where Shahl rose from the ground. He grimaced with the effort, but stood with poise. He made no motion to flee, but offered his wrists to the peace forces officer.

His posture bore sadness, but his eyes bore pride.

"Hold still, now," the officer said with a growl. "We're in a temple, which is the only reason we didn't turn your head into elemental slime."

One of the other officers moved to bind Shahl's wrists, a woman not much older than Zharla.

Shahl winced at the bindings. "How did you find me?"

The peace forces officer grabbed his wrists and twisted Shahl around, then slammed him into the east temple wall. The other officers chuckled. "The next time you open your mouth," she said, "I'll break your jaw."

"I'd like to know," Zharla said, wrapping her cloak around her shoulders, pulling her hood low.

The first officer's demeanor changed as he turned to face Zharla. "I beg your forgiveness, miss...uh...ma'am. I don't think I should say."

"Did you come here to think, or to detain this man?" Zharla asked.

Flustered, the officer said, "Ma'am, you look important, but—"

"I am a woman, and I am from a consequential family." She waited, lips parted in haughty expectation, her will undeterred.

The officer sighed and holstered his weapon. "They said to follow a woman of your description here. When I made a positive visual match to the target, I waited for reinforcements to arrive. It didn't seem like you needed any help, so I didn't move on him. Please, ma'am, you were all right, weren't you? Please don't report me if you felt like you were in danger. I...I didn't know you were... um...consequential."

She nodded with false thanks. "The Lady has preserved me well enough."

The officer's face flooded with relief. "With your leave, ma'am." She nodded almost imperceptibly.

The officer turned to Shahl. "You, scum, move."

As the peace force officers pushed Shahl past Zharla, she peered into his face. He did not meet her eye. His visage still held that same sadness, a sorrow born of pity for the rest of the world. He would not go on trial. The rest of the world would.

Zharla witnessed nothing that convinced her of his guilt.

They were almost out of earshot when Zharla called after them,

"Officer." The one in charge stopped and said something to the others. They carried on while he took a few steps back toward Zharla.

"Ma'am?"

"What's his crime?"

"Rape, ma'am. Of a woman."

"Anything else?"

"No, ma'am."

Zharla gathered her cloak around herself and stumbled back to the transporter station, to the long ride back to Meran.

The plan is set. The days of Ahrik Jeber-li are numbered.

Message from Pir'e Analt to rebels on the Emerald Moon, intercepted by intelligence officers from the Ketel of Sheresh Shehur-li

7 | Trial

Men's Rights Groups Clash with Peace Forces over Jeberi Case

Caller network headline on the day after the verdict, 12 Eyir RY 2498

"Two minutes, Father," Ayen said. He eased himself to his desk and swiped open his external compiler. As if he could hide from what troubled his commanding officer.

Ahrik sank into his desk chair and cradled his head in his hands. His thumbs and forefingers made arches between his cheeks and his temples. "What am I doing wrong, Ayen?"

"Father?" Ayen asked. His voice twisted with unease at what was coming.

"We're three months into a six-month deployment, and my own wife hasn't returned a single one of my messages." She gave no word of preparations for Shahl's trial, despite weeks of asking. It would start tomorrow. He had to rely on caller networks, and they gave precious little information about such cases.

Ahrik's hands slumped down onto the desk and he looked up. Ayen stared back at him, face blank.

Ahrik stood and moved to the small wardrobe. He shrugged on his combat blouse. "I shouldn't have burdened you with that. You'll never be married."

Ayen rushed to dissolve the door before Ahrik got there. "I live to serve you, Father."

Ahrik paused at the doorway. "I pray your faith in me is warranted, Ayen." Ahrik caught the worry that flashed on his aide's face, but it disappeared when Ahrik looked at him square.

Ahrik had less than two weeks before his mid-deployment leave. He doubted their chances of winning this war. He had even begun to doubt himself, which he hadn't thought possible three months earlier, before he came to the Kereu. And now he knew his wife was even colder than he thought possible. No support at all. Ahrik felt alone, his power a figment of others' imagination. Ten thousand men lived to serve him, but they could do nothing for him at all.

Ahrik breathed in and fixed the imaginary mask of command on his face as he strode toward the conference room. His command company stood when he entered, with Ayen in tow. He looked around the room, intent on the hard work and dedication his sons had shown so far on their deployment. "Last update brief before my mid-deployment leave," he said. "Who's up first?"

Ayen began the brief with an overview of the past three months. "Father, our mission has progressed apace since the victory at the transit station."

He droned on and on. Ahrik didn't believe a word. Their victory at the transit station was not as decisive as they thought. In the three months that passed since, they engaged the enemy over and over but retrieved no enemy weapons and interrogated no rebels. The rebel wounded took their own lives. Retreating rebels executed wounded compatriots outright to prevent them from falling captive. If anything, the increase in the ferocity of rebel attacks since the battle at the transit station revealed that the rebel attack had been a well-planned and coordinated operation with an orderly and controlled withdrawal, not a rout.

Ahrik looked around the room and wondered if his sons really thought they were winning this war, or if they were telling Ahrik what they thought he wanted to hear.

Logistics and personnel briefed next. "Father, morale is high and your sons are ready for the fight."

Not true. Kerewi rain was their constant companion. The rain forced them to clean their distiller weapons and sharpen and oil their edged weapons twice as frequently as they did in the Eshel. Patrolling was different, too, because the extra water they had to carry slowed them down when they were on foot. When they patrolled in climate controlled transporters, they became more vulnerable to ambush. Rations often came poorly sealed. Hot meals were a mere memory of the tastes that they grew up with in the Eshel. They gave up on guessing what they were eating.

His sons even came up with a raucous ditty to decry their lot, "*li-Dar be-Kereu*" ("At Home in the Kereu"). There were competitions to see who could invent the verse that was most suggestive of their deprivations—of any sort. By the three-month mark, there were over one hundred verses, with the favorites sung at obscene volumes.

Operations followed logistics and personnel. "Father, we are conducting over fifty patrols per day in the area of operations, and we have yet to lose an engagement."

Ahrik wanted to ask the briefers what the point was. The slog of combat would be bearable if he thought his supervisors knew what they were doing. Ahrik's ketel was strung out in garrison across three major Kerewi cities and the three dozen or so towns in between, a fifth of the Kereu's population. This was not the mission Ahrik had prepared his sons for. They were trained to assault and destroy prepared enemy defenses, not to garrison the rear.

Over such distances, the tendril network that emanated from the base of Ahrik's skull was useless. The army didn't supply them with enough electromagnetic communications systems to make a difference over such distances, so Ahrik's safest, most reliable communications came by deploying small units of his ketel to outposts spaced just inside tendril range, creating a spider web that could relay tendril messages back and forth. But messages took too much time to relay, and the dispersion endangered his sons. Every week saw him lose a few more, and every casualty ate away at his ketel's morale and cohesion.

Ahrik interrupted the operations briefing. "What is our casualty count?"

"Father, we have suffered ninety-eight dead and 284 wounded," the operations briefer said.

Ahrik drummed a rhythm on the table with his fingers, unsure why the supervisors didn't use hayla units for this mission instead. They were expendable, volunteers organized into standard units of five hundred, and their true nature was not kept secret from the Esheli population. Their training took only a few months, not the lifetime of training that a keteli received. If a hayel died, the government simply recruited a new volunteer. If a keteli died, it left a gap. Once a ketel was mostly or fully expended, the ketel commander passed into staff service or senior command over hayel forces. The hayla were not clones raised as warriors from birth and educated with their father-commanders. They had no tendril network, which took years of psychological imprinting to develop. Hayla units were supplied with more robust electromagnetic communications systems than the ketela, with greater range, and they knew how to use them.

The ketela were the Eshel's shock troops, but the hayla gave the caller networks something to write about. The ketela took territory. The hayla held it.

If a hayel proved himself in combat, he might have his posterity made into a ketel. His seed was dedicated to serving the Eshel, assuming he could be trusted with the secret of the ketel. The first generation after being chosen was a ketel of ten, and then, if still found worthy, the next generation was a ketel of one hundred, and so on. The ketela were chosen. The hayla merely volunteered.

But Ahrik couldn't bring up the hayla here without destroying his sons' confidence in the mission. They should figure it out on their own. "Why is my ketel assigned to control so much of the Kereu's population?" he asked. "Ten thousand shock troops to police one-fifth of the Kereu. Why?"

"Father," someone from intel said, "those are our orders."

Ahrik chuckled. "Stupid answer." The room went still. "That's the answer I expected three months ago, before we deployed to this mud hole." He glared around the room. "I want an answer to this by the time I get back from leave."

He rose and strode back to his office. He saw a message from Zharla, at long last, but his face grew as dark as a moonless night when he read it. He couldn't get home soon enough.

A storm of confusion scoured Zharla's heart. She had to decide whether to testify for or against Shahl at his trial tomorrow. For weeks, Zharla's sense of justice had eaten away at her anger over the rape. After weeks of avoiding Ahrik's messages, she finally responded, to tell him she planned to go to the head judge in Shahl's case for answers.

Maybe the judge knew something that could help her determine his guilt for certain. Zharla's misfortune was to be the only witness to the heinous crime someone perpetrated against her. If Shahl was not guilty, Zharla could not say who was. She twisted her handkerchief in her hands.

Zharla sat in an anteroom of Meran's judicial complex, one of the few government offices still located in-mountain. The judicial complex sat near the peak of Meran, at the edge of the mountain wall. Artificial light reflected off polished stone furnishings, but centuries earlier craftsmen had carved striated patterns into the mountain wall so thin that now natural light also rippled through from outside.

A bell chimed, and the attendant—a diminutive man of about twenty-five, kindly featured but otherwise unremarkable—ushered her into an adjoining room. The judge sat in a stone chair padded with crimson pillows, her back to a wall of illuminated striations. She sat erect, one leg crossed over a knee, hands clasped in her lap. Her face wore a pursed, slightly strained expression that looked to be as permanent as her surroundings.

"Madam Judge." Zharla inclined her head.

The judge leaned forward. "Heiress Tamer-li, why are you here? You made your declaration. The peace forces apprehended your assailant."

"Shahl may be innocent, Madam Judge."

She arched a sarcastic eyebrow. "Oh, then I'll have to tell the peace forces they don't know how to do their job." The judge cackled, then set her hands on the desk before her and grew as serious as death. "Do you want to see justice done, child?"

Zharla bristled at being called a child, but this woman might have answers. The truth. "Yes, Madam Judge."

"Then at the trial tomorrow, say what you saw and heard." She scooted back in her chair, a signal that the conversation was now over, at least according to her. "Good day."

Zharla's face grew hot, and she breathed out in fury. "My testimony is worth more than that. In the dark generations after The War, the Mothers said that a child of the Eshel should only be convicted by honest testimony."

"Yes?" The judge's tone grew wary. Her lips pursed even more than before.

"Everything about that night is a trick played on my memory. I don't want to believe that Shahl could have done this thing." Zharla paused to think through her next words. She shoved her twisted handkerchief into her sleeve. "The peace forces have left important questions unanswered, Madam Judge."

The judge leaned forward and rested her elbows on the desk. "You have piqued my interest, child, but the peace forces' case is strong. His fluids were found on you, he was seen in the area at the time of the attack, and your own declaration matches the man in custody. You even conversed with him that night. Your doubt cannot be based on mistaken identity, I fear, so why should you doubt now?"

Zharla looked down and took a deep breath. "Madam Judge, my attacker was not alone. At least two others held my arms and legs, but the Shahl I knew didn't have two friends, let alone know anyone who would help him with such an act. Who helped him?"

The judge narrowed her eyes and stroked her chin. "This doesn't undermine his guilt, but it is a question worth asking."

"Also, my attacker and his accomplices got into my room undetected, but my room lies at the end of the second floor of the main building. The only way to reach it from the outside is to scale sheer stone walls. Even at his finest, Shahl could not pull this off. His brother might, but not him. How did the attackers get in?"

"Another valid, yet tangential, question." The judge shifted in her seat.

Zharla eyed the judge's discomfort. *She knows something.*

Zharla clenched her fists under her cloak. "There is one final sliver of doubt, Madam Judge. I confronted Shahl on the night the peace forces apprehended him, seeking tenqam, and he knew nothing of the attack. Shahl has always been a terrible liar. How did he feign ignorance of the attack?"

"Perhaps, Heiress Tamer-li, you did not know this man like you thought. Men can be unpredictable, like faithful dogs that turn wild after a small taste of flesh." The judge looked at her askance. "You have not yet related, child, your alternate narrative for how this horrific crime occurred. What new story, what different cast of characters, also answers your questions?"

Zharla avoided the judge's gaze. "This is why I came, to see if you had some insight."

Zharla knew in that instant that coming to the head judge was a bad idea.

"Child, I am perfectly willing to entertain your questions, but I am the head judge in this case. I cannot make premature judgments on either evidence or testimony."

"The peace forces didn't listen to me, Madam Judge. They said I was headstrong, afflicted by the trauma of a sad experience..."

"That seems accurate."

"...and that they had their man."

The judge stood and folded her hands in front of her. The maternal wisdom in the action took Zharla aback. "In order for justice to be served, someone will have to be punished. This crime was committed against every Esheli woman, not just you. The roles of men and women are changing. Would you have me put the welfare of one insignificant man above the welfare of an entire nation? Of women's rule?"

Zharla stood in turn and looked the judge square in the eyes. Yet another moment of decision passed in the gaze. "Yes."

"You are naive."

"The Law of the Mothers establishes justice for all."

"Where did you learn such tripe? At the melmez?" The judge chuckled, almost introspectively.

Zharla stared at the older woman in disbelief. If justice lay in the hands of women such as this, then Shahl was correct to push for men's rights, after all.

The judge smirked. "Are we done?"

Zharla had heard enough. She took a step toward the judge, and the judge's eyes widened in surprise. Zharla placed her hands on her hips. "My questions must be answered. Even my rapist deserves the truth."

The judge raised an eyebrow. "I admire your pluck, Heiress Tamer-li, but how do we administer justice if we never find the answers to your questions? Shall I let a man go free when a woman has been raped, his fluids have been found on her, and witnesses have placed him at the scene, all because the victim doubts her memory? Justice doesn't work that way. When you say justice for all, I think of all the gray hairs I've gotten trying to defend justice for most." The judge wagged her finger. "Don't you lecture me about justice."

"The truth will come out in the end," Zharla said, folding her arms in defiance.

Without a word, the judge sat down and shrugged her shoulders. She cocked her head to one side, a signal that their conversation was truly over.

In the cavern outside the judicial complex, Zharla placed a hand on the stone wall and bent over. She wanted to be sick, but at least she knew how she would testify tomorrow. She promised herself that she would never harbor in her soul the gneissic cynicism that the judge had in hers.

The wake-up chime sounded throughout the prison, and Shahl eased his body into a seated position. Everything hurt. It hurt to breathe, to eat, and to relieve himself. Just thinking on what he had become was an exercise in mental pain. Life in prison was not the soul-sucking hell he thought it would be. It was much, much worse.

And Ahrik was the cause of it all.

Prison life knew only one law: violence. And today was the day he would live free. No more daily beatings from fellow inmates. No more surrender to the unproductive routine of prison life. No more harried, fitful existence, running from physical and mental pain.

Tomorrow he went on trial. Today he fought back against Ahrik and those who plotted his destruction.

He shuffled out of his cell, like he always did. No need to make them think today was any different. Make them think he was an easy target. In his mind, he shook out his limbs and recited in his mind how he'd fight. Get his legs under him. Strike opponents with the force of his hips instead of flailing at them with his extremities, just like Ahrik tried to teach him over the years. He might end up in the infirmary, but he would be free.

Three of them came at him in the washroom, from behind. He saw them in the steel mirror while he washed his face. *Am I so pathetic that they don't even try to disguise their approach?*

One of them pushed him in the small of the back while another tried to dunk his head into the basin, but he spun down and away. He smashed his heel down on the foot of the one who tried to dunk him and brought his elbow up into the chin of the third assailant, who was probably just waiting his turn. The waiting assailant's head whipped up with a teeth-chattering crack. He staggered back in surprise, while Dunker cried out in alarm and pain. Other inmates in the washroom shouted. Some scattered. Some formed a circle, to watch.

Shahl didn't wait for Pusher to come at him, just bull-rushed him into the granite counter with the wash basins. Steel and water crashed all around them, and Shahl heard Pusher's head smack against the stone wall with a satisfying crunch. Pusher's body went limp, then slumped to the ground with a slick thud.

Shahl knew one, maybe both, of the others would be right behind him, so he immediately turned and braced himself against the wall. He kicked out with both legs and caught one of them square in the chest. Was it Dunker or Waiter? Shahl heard the air rush out of the man's lungs, but it didn't matter, because the other one came at him from the side.

Shahl didn't stand a chance once they recovered from his initial assault, and he knew it, so he just curled up and took the beating. His tormentors laid it on thick, probably because he'd fought back this time. Shahl didn't care. With his trial tomorrow, his life would end anyway.

He peeked through swollen eyes at the swirling water and blood on the floor and between the blows saw one of them lying still. Shahl smiled through blood-soaked teeth. He wouldn't be the only one going to the infirmary today.

When they were done with him, he lay on the ground, his breath ragged gasps. One of his tormentors stood over him, and a question rang in Shahl's ears: "Why d'yuh think we do thus t'you?"

Shahl coughed up something wet. "Did my brother send you?"

"One day, yuh rich lil' slime, yuh'r goin' t'be one'f us."

"I'm not... like you." He winced at the pain in his ribs.

His tormentor spewed a dark chuckle, emphasizing it with a kick in Shahl's side. "Thut's where yuh'r wrong. Yuh'r jus' like us." He crouched down, so close that Shahl could smell his foul breath. "Jus'.

Like. Us."

Shahl fought back the urge to vomit. All he could get out was, "No." He was beaten physically, but he would not relinquish his will to these men and their ways.

He would not let Ahrik win. Not this time.

Even though his eyes were nearly swollen shut, Shahl still felt the other man's menacing smile. "Thut's it?" He chuckled again, and another wave of stench flooded Shahl's nostrils. "I 'ave a message f'yuh from th'buss."

"Boss?"

"Yeah, the buss." He paused. " 'E says 'e thinks yuh'll get through thus. When yuh do, there'll be a prize."

"What could you possibly have—"

A sharp jab in his ribs shut him up.

"When th'buss 'as a prize, 'e 'as a prize. Guess whut ut'll be."

Shahl relented. "Money? Love?"

"Bett'r."

"It's definitely not the truth." He winced in anticipation of another blow to his ribs, but his opponent did not get the joke at the boss's expense.

"E'en bett'r 'n thut," the foul breath said.

Shahl rolled over onto his back. The day's ordeal was over. "Okay, what. . . is. . . it?"

"Th'bes' prize'f all: ruvenge." Another kick, but he hardly felt it for the pain in the rest of his body, and for the new sense of possibility that Shahl realized in that moment, the notion that he could do more than simply take his beatings and fight back every once in a while.

These ill-bred scoundrels and ruffians might actually be of some use to him. Maybe he would play along, see where it all led.

In Shahl's new world of violence and cynicism, revenge was a more worthy goal than resistance. Men's rights meant so little, after all, when revenge was a possibility.

The head judge rapped her gavel, and Zharla reached over to clutch Renla's hand. Her mother, sitting on her left, reached her hand out as well, but Zharla pulled back and scooted closer to Renla.

People packed the courtroom, to witness the fall of a son from one of Meran's most prominent families. Caller network representatives, men's rights activists, and even some of Shahl's extended family, their faces chagrined and curdled, filled the stone pews, and all eyes stayed riveted on the judge. Zharla wondered if Ahrik would have attended were he not at war. Probably not.

Zharla looked over at Shahl, sitting in a kall field enclosure on the far side of the room. He kept his eyes cast forward, intent, his face blank. Bruising puffed his face, and he moved slowly, with difficulty, as if his prison garb hid some deeper wound. If his hair had begun to grow back, they'd shaved it again. He did not look her way before the judge's gavel sent a spear of authority reverberating throughout the cold, stone courtroom.

As the trial proceeded, Shahl tore at her heart by degrees. With witness after witness, his aspect remained impassive. Not once during the trial did he even glance her way, much less hold eye contact. Zharla's eyes were dry now, after weeks of leaking out her anger and confusion, but a void loomed over her heart to see what they had done to him, or what he had done to himself.

Those in the courtroom murmured in anticipation after each witness, the case against Shahl growing deeper every time. They knew Shahl Jeber-li was on trial for rape, but not who the victim was, since female victims of sexual assault were kept secret. If anyone saw Zharla there, they'd assume it was because she was Shahl's sister-in-law.

After a brief recess, during which Zharla did not dare relinquish her seat, the head judge rapped her gavel once more. "Silence," she called out. The other two judges sat on either side of her, hands folded on their desks. One of the assistant judges handed the head judge a stiff square of cardstock.

Zharla held onto a slim hope. The head judge had raised Zharla's questions, and the peace forces had answered only with the physical evidence. Zharla took a deep breath and leaned over to Renla. "Wish me luck, Re'le. I think she's going to call me back to her private chambers to testify."

Renla squeezed her hand. "Zhe'le, I—"

The head judge's gavel cut her off. "Hearken," the head judge said, "to the verdict of this court."

Zharla gasped. "No."

"After careful consideration of the evidence, we have reached a unanimous verdict." The head judge's voice rang off the soulless stone walls. "In the charge of rape of a woman, this court finds Shahl Jeber-li—"

Zharla yanked her hand away from Renla and flew to her feet. "Wait!"

The head judge looked up, her face a mix of anger and surprise.

"Zharla," her mother whispered beside her.

The judge assumed a maternal air. "Heiress Tamer-li, I know this must have been a terrible experience, seeing your brother-in-law on trial, but, please, won't you be seated?"

"You haven't heard my testimony, Madam Judge." She hastened to add, "I have known him for many years. This man was almost my husband."

Murmurs of shock rippled throughout the courtroom, and her mother tugged on her cloak. "Zharla, please."

Zharla looked down to her mother. Their eyes met. For the first time in a long while, Zharla saw genuine concern in her mother's face. Zharla knew she should not interpret it as concern for her well being.

Her mother's eyes pleaded. "Whatever you say, whatever you do, it will not help Shahl."

Zharla narrowed her eyes and pulled away. "Mother, what do you know—"

"Silence!" the head judge called, rapping her gavel once more. She sat up straighter in her chair and the room grew deathly still.

On her raised bench, the head judge towered over the courtroom. She pointed her gavel at Zharla, a thick oaken haft thrust through a polished granite head. The thing trembled in the head judge's outstretched hand. Her voice came at a whisper, laced with fury. "I will not take counsel in my courtroom."

Zharla stood her ground. She set her jaw.

Renla reached for Zharla's hand. "Zhe'le, please."

The head judge slammed the gavel down, and the sound ripped like a shockwave over the room. "Heiress Tamer-li, you will sit, or you will be removed."

"Justice. For. All." Zharla said it at a whisper, but her voice carried like the clap of the gavel. Time stood still.

The head judge's jaw dropped, but she regained her composure and her eyes lit with renewed fury. "Bailiff."

A huge woman strode toward Zharla from the direction of the bench. There could not have been an ounce of fat on her. The bailiff was almost to the rail separating the attendees from the rest of the courtroom, but in an act of surrender, Zharla brought her hands up. "That won't be necessary, Madam Judge. Come, Renla." She looked down on her mother, but did not bother to offer a goodbye.

Waves of elation and despair flooded over Zharla as she weaved her way out of the courtroom with Renla. She had bested the head judge and probably caused a furor for the men clamoring for rights. She didn't need to hear the verdict to know what it would be. Zharla exited the courtroom, weighed down by emotion.

When she and Renla left the judicial complex, a crowd of activists shuffled forward, eager and expectant. "What's the verdict, Mistress Tamer-li?"

She waved them off. "I can't." Zharla staggered to the cavern wall and propped against it. She clutched her stomach. "Re'le."

"Back off!" Renla shouted. "Zhe'le, let's move away from the crowd."

Zharla took a few steps, but then stopped and doubled over. She retched on the carved paving stones, and Renla rushed over to hold back her flowing hair.

Zharla reached up and pulled Renla close. Bile dripped off her lower lip. "Re'le, lead me home." She coughed. "I...I think I'm late."

Zharla could have sworn they did a pregnancy test after the rape.

Zharla met Renla's eyes, and a horrified realization washed over Renla's face.

> MATRON TAMER-LI: Do you know what this will cost me?
> SHERESH SHEHUR-LI: Enlighten me.
> MATRON: I may lose the one I love most.
> SHERESH: You're capable of love?
> MATRON: Burn, you sunchild.
>
> ---
>
> Voice recording discovered in the Tameri clan archives during the inquest into the rise of Ahrik, RY 2519

8 | Innocence Lost

3d Hand, 1st Standard, is dissolved.

Order of Ahrik, after the attack at the unnamed village,
19 Eyir RY 2498

AHRIK sat, expressionless, and shooed away a fly in the command hut of 3d Hand, 4th Standard, the 3–4 Death Cheaters. Nothing could keep the stifling late summer heat from penetrating the roof and walls of this forsaken outpost, somewhere in the jungle of the Kereu. The ketel had suffered its hundredth casualty that day, a seeker in the 3–4. Ahrik had to be there for his sons.

Ahrik could do little to shoo away the weight of these casualties on this mind. Shahl's trial a week ago mattered nothing. Zharla's conniving interventions with the judge mattered nothing. Ahrik's mid-deployment leave in two days mattered nothing. Even the war mattered nothing.

"Father," said Ayen, "3d Hand commander on approach."

Ahrik nodded. "Empty the command hut."

The small staff filed out at a grunt from Ayen.

Leren slid into the command hut and saluted, even though saluting indoors wasn't necessary. "Father, you beat me here."

"I wish I could be happy about that, Leren." Ahrik motioned for him to sit.

"I'll be happy when this war ends, Father."

Ahrik wondered how many more would die before that end. He

nodded, then narrowed his eyes at Leren. "How's morale?"

Leren's shoulders slumped, and Ahrik's heart sank. Any answer to that question that wasn't immediate and positive was cause for concern. "We fight on, Father."

"The truth, Leren."

Leren sighed and shook his head. "The enemy has hit us hard in the last month, but especially the last week. They're everywhere, Father. They ambush patrols, attack outposts just at the change of guard, and they snipe at us all night. We're still learning the terrain, and our numbers are too few to pursue in force when they hit us and run. When they stand and fight, we win, but more rebels always appear to fight another day."

"So this seeker, the ketel's hundredth casualty, he's—"

"A sign of things to come, Father."

Ahrik stood and walked around the room, running his hands over compiler displays, dormant now for the remembrance ceremony. The hum of the air cooler pervaded the place, working furiously to keep the humidity at bay. Ahrik turned to Leren. "How do you motivate your men to fight?"

Leren stood and faced Ahrik. His lips curled in a snarl, and the scar on his cheek burned white. "One word, Father: hate."

"This enemy deserves no less."

"My thought exactly, Father. Their weapons make a civilized conscience burn. They make jagged, bacteria-infested wounds. Not like the clean wounds from distillers. Our weapons cauterize flesh, but their weapons make a man bleed. Do you know how many men I've lost that way? Father, it's a slow, agonizing death."

Ahrik just nodded. He knew how many sons he'd lost. He felt the vacancies in his mind. He would let Leren talk through his pain. He had no one else to go to.

"Father." Leren slammed a fist into his opposite palm. "When we capture those weapons? It does no good, because your supervisor's men come to confiscate them. Sheresh, Father!"

"Yes, I know," said Ahrik. "We know little about how their weapons work, and the enemy keeps attacking."

Leren cocked his head and rubbed the scar on his cheek. "Father, the enemy does not take prisoners. It may be time for...harsher measures..."

Ahrik should have seen it coming. Maybe Shahl was right. He always said that violence and hate only led to more violence and hate. Ahrik was about to say something like that to Leren, but a staff messenger burst into the hut.

"Father! Sir!" He heaved a breath. "An urgent message from the 3–1 Hell Scouts."

The 3–1 was a different standard from the 3–4 Death Cheaters, but still in Leren's hand. Ahrik furrowed his brow. "The message came by electromag, not tendril?"

The messenger nodded. He took another deep breath. "The 3–1 commander is dead. Assassinated, Father." Ahrik's face darkened. That was why they hadn't gotten a tendril message. Many ketelis would give their lives before letting such an important link in the tendril network die.

"How?"

"An explosion weapon, Father. A forbidden weapon. Inside the base."

"You mean, they lobbed it in, like they always try to do, and they got lucky?" Ahrik cast to Ayen, *Get my shuttle and protection squad ready.*

"No, Father, one of the locals hid it under her clothes. She set it off when she got close."

Ahrik reached for a wall, and the warmth of it made his head swim. His eyes glazed into the middle distance. Many rebels died trying to kill his sons, and most killed themselves before getting captured, but this? Commanders were not even supposed to display rank insignia, so no attacker should have gotten so close.

Ahrik flashed a questioning look at Leren, but Leren sighed and looked away, his eyes icy and unforgiving. Leren had already given his counsel. Ahrik closed his eyes and tried to find anyone in the 3–1 command group on the tendril network. Nothing. *Ayen,* he cast.

Hail 3–1. Order: Question all locals.

Ahrik looked from the messenger to Leren. He cast, *Leren, if I go there, what will I find?*

Leren returned a hard stare. *We are warriors, Father. We honor the Oath of the Ketel. We do not hide our weapons.*

"Keteli," Ahrik said to the messenger. "Leave us."

They will attack again, Father, Leren cast. *It does not end here.*

Ahrik ground his teeth and took a baleful step towards his subordinate. *What does this mean?*

Leren's gaze bore an utter lack of human caring, and his eyes spoke a silence that Ahrik could not penetrate. Ahrik had to go to the 3–1, to find the truth, but no part of him wanted to.

The mesmerizing cacophony of the morning callers drew Zharla from her slumber. Her stomach pined for nourishment, but she had no desire to eat. Her breakfast probably lay cold already, forgotten in the kitchen. A greater worry lurked in her belly, though. Only two days remained before Ahrik would return on leave. He would stay less than a week, enough to see Shahl's sentence carried out, but the thought of him nearby twisted her insides through tines of merciless torment.

Four more days. Shahl had only four more days to live.

Zharla lifted her head off the pillow and felt something amiss. Some hidden well of energy pricked her senses into awareness. A data capsule rested near the head of her bed, a square of paper affixed. She slipped the paper off, wariness in her movement. She did not recognize the handwriting, but she drew in a sharp breath when she read it. "Justice for all."

A new tremor of violation seeped into her gut. In all likelihood, Zharla reasoned, a personal courier had brought it from the head judge to Renla, with instructions to place it on her bed. The capsule probably wouldn't carry any of the head judge's biometric signatures, since judges lived under a stone-clad rule: all communication with witnesses took place in the courtroom or in judges' chambers, where surveillance and recording were possible.

Zharla suppressed the question of how the judge had put the capsule there, to focus on why. Zharla considered the possibilities as she shuffled to her desk. She peered out the window, to Meran Mountain beyond, then frowned at the data capsule. It might be new evidence in Shahl's case, but it also might be a warning against giving too much to the men's rights movement. Zharla trembled with anticipation as she slipped the data capsule into her desk compiler.

It turned out to be nothing. The smooth surface of the compiler sprang to life with a visual recording. There was no audio, just a video recording of two very young boys. She took a closer look, and they appeared to be Ahrik and Shahl when they were much younger, maybe three or four years old. The recording went on for about twenty seconds, and by the end of it, she was sure. Ahrik and Shahl were sitting on the floor, playing with some toys, and then the video ended. Unremarkable. Any significance escaped her.

She watched the recording again. She double-checked the contents of the capsule using her desk compiler. The recording was the only data stored on it. She ejected the data capsule, gathered a shawl around her shoulders against the creeping morning nip, and made her way downstairs. Renla stood eating her breakfast in the kitchen.

"Re'le, where's my mother?" She hoped her voice conveyed impatience.

Renla's quizzical look indicated that it had. "Your moth... She just went to her quarters." Then, as Zharla went in that direction, Renla called after her, "Your breakfast?"

"I'll only be a minute." Zharla wanted to see her mother's reaction first, see what she might have to do with this.

Zharla chimed the bell to her mother's chambers, and a faint voice called out, "Come in."

Zharla dissolved the door to find a darkened room. Her eyes adjusted, and she made out her mother, reclined on the wicker lounge chair next to the bed.

"Dear, what's this about?" Her mother gave a faint cough. "You brought a breeze in. Bring me a blanket from the alcove behind you. Yes, there."

Zharla attended to her mother's immediate requests, a task she had learned it was better to endure than chafe at. Then she broached the purpose for her visit.

"A data capsule? You disturbed my rest for a data capsule?"

Zharla knew that her mother had been neither sleeping nor anywhere close to it. It was just another ruse to win sympathy or induce guilt, or both. "It's important, Mother."

Her mother struggled to her feet, reaching out to get a hand up from Zharla. "Do you know why I demand so much of you, sweet Zharla?"

Zharla sighed and shook her head, tired that every conversation with her mother was a lesson in untruth.

Her mother smiled. "You are my only hope."

"Hope?" Zharla reached toward the wall-mounted compiler, the data capsule in hand.

"You're the only one I trust to preserve everything we've worked for."

At an almost imperceptible nod from her mother, Zharla slipped the data capsule into the compiler. Her mother moved too close.

As Zharla brought up the video on the compiler, she said, "Just because we work for something doesn't make it right, Mother."

She patted Zharla's shoulder. "And yet I still trust you to win the nomination to the Council, even after your performance last week at the trial of that Jeberi boy."

Zharla broke eye contact and tried to hide a shudder, then engaged the video. Nothing happened. Zharla checked the data on the capsule, then withdrew and reinserted it. The compiler was working, but she didn't see the video. Zharla ran a hand through her hair.

Her mother chuckled. "You could at least have brought me a recording with a clearer picture."

Zharla looked up. "Ah, it's working. Wait. . ." The recording had blurred. Stymied, she stopped the recording halfway through, then ejected and reinserted the capsule. It was even more blurry. She let it run.

"Is this what you wanted me to see, dear?" Then, without waiting for a response, her mother went on, "I see two boys playing on the floor, and one has a runny nose."

"A runny nose?"

"Yes, see. He just wiped his nose again. Now, about your nomination to the Council. What do you think about being in the final three?"

Zharla ignored the question. She saw what her mother saw in the video, then the recording ended. Her urgency heightened now, Zharla ejected the capsule, strode over to her mother's desk compiler, and inserted the capsule there. The recording was even blurrier. She stopped and restarted the power supply. Still blurrier. The video was unrecognizable now.

"Who was that recording of, Zharla?" asked her mother. "What about the Council?" Her brow furrowed with mock concern. "Are you okay, dear?"

"It's nothing, Mother." Zharla walked out of the room.

Shahl groaned at the morning klaxon, the sound as black in his mind as the last breaths of a wasted life. He reasoned that his sentence was just, but the crime they charged him with was an injustice against the truth. He was no rapist. Every day that dawned drew him closer to his inexorable fate, an obscene monument to the lengths that Ahrik would go to defeat his own brother.

Shahl rolled off his cot and, stomach to the grimy floor, reached underneath the rusted frame to move a pebble from one pile to the other. Every morning, one more pebble. Ninety-seven days since his arrest at the temple in Mekele. Ninety-seven days he would not get back, days he could have used to tell the truth, had he been given the chance.

He looked over to the smaller pile, from whence he moved the pebble. Four days remained to him in this life.

Exile to the Emerald Moon was a death sentence. No one came back. No one was really meant to. If the inertial stabilizers in the capsule didn't fail, one might actually survive atmospheric exit from Dom, and if the oxygen held out one might even make it all the way to the moon, but then the heat shield had to withstand entry to the moon's thin atmosphere, not to mention impact, when the inertial stabilizers would again matter.

Shahl had seen the pictures and videos of shattered capsules on the moon, of capsules adrift in orbit. He took another look at the small pile of pebbles under his bed, hidden where his jailers wouldn't see them, wouldn't destroy his one last grasp at humanity, to count the time until his doom.

I hope Ahrik is happy. Shahl wanted to spit in disgust, but couldn't gin up the moisture. His face softened. *I hope Zharla is happy. She is the only innocent in all this.*

Shahl pressed his hands onto the blackened floor and lifted himself to a seated position, with his back to the creaking metal frame of the cot. He sighed and waited for the second klaxon, for the door to his cell to dissolve, so he could begin one more pitiful day in the sad tale of woe his life had become.

The second klaxon sounded and the door to his cell hissed to dissolution. The murmured voices of his fellow prisoners passed as he shuffled to the doorway. One man paused to glance his way, a tooth missing in his conniving but respectful smile, one of the thugs Shahl fought in the washroom the day before the trial. Shahl nodded back a begrudged recognition, stymied, distrustful of the man's unwanted attention.

Shahl avoided eye contact with anyone else on his way to the washroom. He didn't want trouble today. Or tomorrow, or the next day. Let him die alone.

Shahl froze a few steps inside the entrance to the washroom and scanned his surroundings with skeptical care. A forbidding silence reverberated off the stone walls. Shahl wondered if he was late, or if he had misinterpreted the klaxons, or if he'd missed breakfast.

The thug with the missing tooth sauntered out of the shower alcove. Shahl flexed his hands and wrists and eased into a fighting stance. If he was going to die anyway, he may as well go down fighting.

Two more men appeared, one through the door Shahl had entered and the other covering the other exit. Shahl growled and moved to put the sinks at his back.

Shahl nodded towards the shattered sink from their earlier encounter in the washroom. "I can do some damage. You know that."

The men at the exits shrugged with a confusing level of disinterest and looked at the gap-toothed thug coming from the shower, who smiled in as conniving a way as he did before. He assessed Shahl with narrowed eyes. "Thus izn't whut yuh think."

"I'm going to die anyway. Let's not prolong it."

"Yuh won't die."

"What? Now ahs'bi thugs believe in an afterlife?"

The thug snarled and shrugged. "Whut w'said b'fore wuz true. Yuh wunt ruvenge, ur not?"

The question gave Shahl pause. He relaxed slightly. He hadn't thought the prospect of revenge serious until that moment.

It intrigued him.

Shahl grunted and folded his arms over his chest. "Why should I believe you?"

He chuckled. "W'could kull yuh now."

Shahl sized them up. "What do I have to do?"

The thug took a step forward and reached into a pocket.

Shahl jerked into a fighting stance.

The thug put a conciliatory hand up in the air and slowly, very slowly, drew something from his pocket with the other hand. "Jus' take thus on th'murning of th'exile, check?"

Shahl reached out to take the small pouch that the thug held out, but the thug snatched it back before Shahl could grasp it.

Shahl forced down his frustration. "You need me for something, or else we wouldn't be talking right now. We'd be fighting."

"Th'Buss said nut t'give it t'yuh till after yur two friends vizit."

"Friends? Oh. . ."

"Yuh jus' need t'say yuh 'ate 'im."

"Hate whom?"

The thug emitted an evil laugh. "Yur bruther."

"I don't hate him."

The thug just looked at him and sneered. "Yuh will." He nodded to his comrades. "Yuh will."

His comrades moved in on Shahl from two sides, then gave him what he expected they would all along. As he lay bleeding on the washroom floor, he began to think that hate might not be too strong a sentiment for what Ahrik did or didn't do to put him here.

Ahrik's shuttle settled into the muggy dust at the 3–1 Hell Scouts outpost. Bosonic wash rippled the soil and fluttered the trees. Ayen and Ahrik's protection squad fanned out, weapons at the ready. Ahrik strode off the shuttle, but slowed at the gruesome scene. The reek of death hung on the air. Ayen's face turned grim, and the protection squad surveyed the carnage.

Confused silence seeped back from the protection squad over the tendril link. After everything Ahrik and his sons had seen, violence could still shock them. The mangled body of the 3–1 commander lay nearby, with the bodies of a few of his own protection squad scattered about.

And no one tended the bodies.

Ahrik struggled to lower his heart rate enough to cast to Leren: *How can you let your men desecrate their dead like this?*

No response.

Ahrik took a step toward the commander's corpse, then froze. Not five meters from the slain commander lay a woman's head. The ragged neck showed that a tremendous force had yanked it from its body, and now it lay cocked on the ground, a pool of blood congealed around it. The face was off-kilter, like a floppy mask hanging on the skull. In an instant, he thought of that moment at the social hall in Meran, when he searched the bloody, dusty aftermath for his brother. Ahrik had seen a lone head in the midst of the destruction, the face just as off-kilter.

A harried, wild-eyed keteli from the Hell Scouts stumbled towards him from the village center.

"Keteli," Ahrik said. "Report."

"F... Father, aft'r our command'r wuz kulled, we 'mmediately begun roundin' up vullagers, l... like yuh urdered." The keteli nodded toward the village center. "Thus way."

Ahrik followed. He considered the keteli's haggard appearance and frayed uniform. This ill discipline began before today. Something was amiss in the 3-1 Hell Scouts. Ahrik scanned their surroundings for signs of trouble, then turned back to the keteli. "I want to oversee interrogations."

"Ch... check, Father."

Ahrik furrowed his brow. The keteli should not be so nervous.

The village consisted of a few dozen low-slung wooden buildings and a smattering of small homes. The hour grew late. The mosquitoes buzzed in force, along with a murderous assortment of other bugs. The tension between the ketelis and the straggling villagers hung over the air like a pall.

Ahrik made a rough estimate of the number of villagers milling about. He checked his internal compiler for statistics on this village. There should be at least three times as many villagers.

Ahrik picked up emotive shreds from the tendril network, even though the 3-1 commander was dead. The ketelis from the 3-1 fidgeted, but whether spoiling for a fight or fearing the vengeance of war, Ahrik dared not discern.

Ahrik, Ayen, and the wild-eyed keteli walked toward the interrogation building near the village center. The keteli motioned for them to wait, then peeled a villager away from a larger group, a man with a pitiful limp and threadbare satchel to match. When they were on the second of three wooden steps leading into the building, about 50 meters from where Ahrik walked, the whole front of the building disappeared in a flash of light and heat, and the ground buckled.

The blast knocked Ahrik to the ground. His head struck something hard and his vision closed in around him.

He was not unconscious long, less than a minute, but when he came to, he could not feel his tendril link to his sons. In fact, he couldn't even bring up Leren, the 3d Hand commander. Given how close Leren was in the chain of command, he should have been able to do that instantly.

Ahrik looked around him. His ears rang. The building where the blast originated was blown over, and he saw no sign of the wild-eyed keteli. Wood scraps lay scattered everywhere. Ahrik fished a splinter out of the meat of his hand. He sat, collected his scrambled thoughts, and steadied his breathing. He couldn't see any villagers, only a few of his sons, and they wore expressions even more grim and nervous than before.

"How many killed?" he asked a keteli who came to his aid.

"J...just one, Father, but it was Winner. Everyone loved him." The wild-eyed keteli.

Ahrik wondered what Winner did to earn such a name. And what happened to harry his mind in the moments before death.

Ahrik reached for his head and nodded his thanks to the keteli helping him. "Where is everyone?" he asked. "Who is in command of the 3–1?"

"Finding the killers," said the keteli. "I am in command now, Father."

Ahrik probed a tender spot on this temple and winced. *Ayen, on me*, he cast. He looked a question at the new 3–1 commander and his uncomfortably low-level rank insignia. "Where are the villagers?"

"Some died in the blast, Father. Some died in the. . ." The keteli trailed off into an uncomfortable silence.

Ahrik's eyes narrowed.

". . . in the aftermath," the keteli said.

Ahrik stood and staggered over to the epicenter of the blast. He saw villagers' bodies and parts cast in all directions, and he saw wounds from the tiny bits of metal that the rebels put into their explosives. But then he saw many, many bodies, scattered all over the village, cut down from behind as they ran. After the blast. Some still writhed in the final throes of death. Wounds deep and cauterized. Distiller weapons.

His bearings returned, and Ahrik heard the *thu-thu-thunk* of distiller weapons in the distance. His connection to the tendril network restored itself, and a sickening realization dawned. He half-ran, half-staggered back to the nervous commander. Grabbing him by the shoulders, Ahrik shook him and screamed, "Bring your men back! Stop them!"

"I tried, Father." The new commander shrugged, his will spent. "I can't."

Desperate, Ahrik ran toward the sound of the distillers, Ayen and his protection squad close on his heels. The *thu-thu-thunk* of the distillers continued, but tapered off as he neared the source.

By the time he saw the bodies, lined up neatly in the jungle on the ground a few paces off the roadway, the distillers had stopped. A surreal silence loomed over Ahrik's mind. He walked along the road. His legs grew heavier and heavier with each new group of bodies that he saw. When he came to the edge of the town, he heard sobs. Not from women and children, but from men. From his sons.

They had planned this. Such methodical death. "Ayen," said Ahrik, reaching to support himself on his aide's shoulder. "How could my sons do this?"

"Father, I—"

"No!" Ahrik squeezed his hair with a hand, then sank to his knees and slammed the ground with his fist. "I did this. My hatred. My lack of control. I spread my sons all over the Kereu so they couldn't communicate and support one another. I did this." His empty stare took in the middle distance. Shame overcame him.

"Father, I'll start the men on cleanup."

"Wait, Ayen." Ahrik breathed out in despair. "Order: 3d Hand, 1st Standard, is dissolved. Reapportion the Hell Scouts to the rest of the ketel."

War is hell.

LEREN: Now what? This is a mess.

MAN (UNIDENTIFIED): No, no. This could end up being a benefit.

LEREN: Benefit? How could you—?

MAN: Oh, come off it! Don't feign sympathy here! Your men did this. Your men put those people through hell, then snuffed out their puny, little lives.

LEREN: How can we see that as a good thing?

MAN: Who said anything about "we"? You're a clone. Do what you're told, and everything will work out.

Voice recording found in the archives of the Army of the Eshel two years after the War for the White Planet, RY 2521; it is not known why this was not discovered earlier, during the inquest into the rise of Ahrik

9 | Life and Death

Shahl Jeber-li Executed: Justice Is Served

Headline, caller network, 26 Eyir RY 2498

ZHARLA pulled her cloak closer. She dreaded the moments to come. "Renla," she said, "the chill autumn wind heralds more than colder weather."

"You don't have to tell him." Renla rewrapped the scarf around her neck and looked up and down the transporter platform, as if an answer to Zharla's quandary might lie among the hundreds of people milling about.

Zharla knew that her friend also faced a dilemma. She considered her friend with a wary gaze. "Do you have to enlist? I have enough family members fighting in this war."

Renla bit her lip, but said nothing. A bondswoman couldn't enlist without her mistress' permission.

Zharla lowered her voice to a whisper and leaned in to her friend. "Did any of this have to happen, Re'le?" The platform was packed with people, and Zharla worried what ears might hear. "I want to love my child like my mother never loved me. I feel no obligation to tell Ahrik I'm pregnant with the rapist's child, just like I have no desire to let you leave my side."

Renla forced a smile and shrugged her shoulders in a question. "Doesn't the Eshel deserve everything we have to give?"

Zharla grunted. "My child certainly does." This was her child.

Ahrik did not deserve to know. She smiled through pursed lips and cast a wistful glance towards the patch of sky that would bear Ahrik's transporter hence, as if pining for what could have been. "You can go home, Re'le. I should do this alone."

"Remember, Zhe'le, your secret is safe with me, whether you choose to tell him or not." Renla squeezed Zharla's hand, then disappeared into the crowd with a spring, but her young face bore the wound of not getting her way.

Someday she would fight, Zharla could tell. Zharla needed her nearby now, though, especially with a baby on the way.

Zharla pulled her bulky cloak higher on her neck and sniffed at the breeze. Meran's intercity transporter platform sat on the leeward side of Meran, and the morning sun had not yet crested the mountain, so most of the people standing on the platform were rubbing hands and stomping feet to ward off the northerly breeze. At least the cooler air made her wear clothes that hid her swelling belly.

A smallish figure with a crafty eye emerged from the crowd and stood next to Zharla. He wore a military uniform. She tried to avoid eye contact, but she recognized him as a superior of Ahrik's. She'd met him at the wedding ceremony, back when life held promise. What was his name? Balash?

"A brisk morning," said the officer.

"Yes," answered Zharla. Now she remembered: Sheresh. And he was one of the other two candidates for the council. She couldn't tell if the odd smell of deceit he emitted was real or only in her mind.

She felt his eyes on her, and knew in an instant she should not trust him. He struck her as one part officer and two parts politician. She didn't want to stand next to him, or even be on the platform at all. She would have preferred to wait for Ahrik at home, but most of Meran's social luminaries were there to meet him, and some gossip hound would notice his wife's absence. That would doubtless hurt her chances of making it onto the Council. So, Zharla held her nose and did her duty, standing on the overly chilly Meran transporter platform, next to an officer of whom she was not overly fond.

"This will be a great day for your Ahrik," Sheresh said.

She gave him a flat stare. "Ahrik is his own man, not mine."

Sheresh rocked on his heels and smiled with almost giddy anticipation, on odd gesture for a man twenty years past his prime. He looked at her as if her words did not register. "A great day, yes, a great day."

"Oh?" Zharla responded, more out of resignation than curiosity. If Sheresh was determined to prosecute a conversation, despite her best efforts to ignore him, this was as good a subject as any.

Sheresh's eyes held a secret that he could just barely keep from telling. "Yes. Your Ahrik"—the words were like fingernails raked over ice—"will have a great honor bestowed upon him this day."

Zharla smiled at the irony: news of his wife's pregnancy by a rapist was hardly an honor Ahrik would welcome.

"What honor is that, Supervisor Sheresh?" Had she just fallen into this man's rhetorical trap? Curse her curiosity.

His smile was smug. "You will see."

Annoyed with herself for being so inquisitive, she waited in silence for Ahrik to arrive. She shifted her weight back and forth. Her legs began to cramp. Her nausea had never quite left. She was not sure how much longer she could keep up the social façade of standing for unnaturally long periods.

She saw the black speck of a transporter on the eastern horizon, and the military choir burst into song. Zharla suppressed her rising nausea. Supervisor Sheresh looked at her, and she wondered how his grin could have possibly gotten bigger.

The transporter's deceleration brought a strong bosonic hum with it, and the closing strains of *"Ahati Meran she-Bene"* surrendered to the military rhythm of *"Eshelna Eshel-li"*. The chorus roused to its apex as the transporter came to a stop just a few paces in front of Zharla.

She maneuvered herself toward the door, an unwilling actor in other people's plays. Best to get this out of the way.

The transporter door dissolved. She expected to see a smile on

Ahrik's face, or at least something like relief at being home, but she saw nothing. His uniform was immaculate, his bearing ineffable and military, but his eyes showed no emotion at all.

Absolutely vacant.

Ahrik stepped onto the platform. "Zharla," he declared, his body rigid.

"Husband," she replied. She closed the final distance and let him embrace her, careful to keep her hands on his ribs so that he could not get their bodies close. She wanted no part of him to press against her.

The choir swelled at just the right time, as they consummated their embrace with a chaste peck on the cheek. Zharla cringed in her gut. When they broke their false embrace, the crowd cheered. *They actually believe we like each other. Amazing.*

The cheers subsided, and the supervisor climbed onto a stool and motioned for the crowd's attention. His smug grin returned. When he spoke, his voice carried a tedious rhythm. Despite his long-winded speech, the gullible people on the platform cheered and murmured their approval at all the right places.

How could this man possibly beat her onto the Council?

"People of Meran," called the supervisor, after what seemed a slurry of vacuous words. Cheering. "We welcome home today one of your brightest stars, one of your noble sons, one of the Eshel's finest warriors."

He lathered more praise on Ahrik, after which the crowd cheered its raucous approval.

He went on. "Ahrik is on leave from a glorious deployment."

Ahrik tensed. Zharla eyed him, unsure what to make of that.

The supervisor droned on about Ahrik's accomplishments, saying something about his ketel being "first to the fight," whatever that meant. Ahrik and his men saved a massive shipment of supplies from falling into rebel hands and destroyed a rebel force many times their size, with no casualties. Ahrik's was the invincible ketel, graced by the Lady of the Emerald Moon. Ahrik brought peace to the Kereu and security to its cities and towns. Ahrik led his men into the ranks of Esheli warriors of legend.

Despite the praise, Zharla felt the tension rise in Ahrik. His face wore a wide smile, and he waved to the crowd as their cheers washed over him. He looked the paragon of military myth, yet Zharla felt a disquiet in him that she partly feared, partly respected, with no idea what was really going on.

At that moment, the supervisor paused for dramatic effect. This was the big announcement. "And that," the supervisor shouted, triumphant, "is why the Chief Elders of the Eshel bestow on Ahrik's firstborn son the rank of *elef meyan*. May he also serve the Eshel in glory!"

The crowd erupted, and the cheers thundered through the platform. Zharla felt it in her feet. Ahrik's firstborn son would command a ketel of one hundred thousand.

This changed everything.

The crowd chanted his name, encouraged by Sheresh's undulating arms. In all the time since The War, thousands of years ago, no soldier from Meran had ever received this honor. The only ketel of one hundred thousand in recent memory had been from Hof Chelek, over forty years previous. This would be the first ketel of one hundred thousand for the new Republic.

Her son. The one she carried in her womb, if it was a boy. The rapist's son. As the crowd chanted his name, she craned her mouth next to his ear and whispered, "I'm pregnant."

He stiffened, the action ever so slight, ever so fleeting, but stiffen he did.

And he pretended to ignore her.

She studied him out of the corner of her eye. He waved, smiled, drank in the moment. Then he caught her looking and his face melted into seriousness. Fear crept into her face, and she did the first thing that came into her mind, something that would cement their new social standing. She threw her arms up, cheered at the top of her lungs, and hugged him close. She cringed once again as her body mashed against his.

Ahrik seethed. He gripped Zharla's hand in his. His ire grew
with every pleasant exchange and fake smile as they worked their
way off the platform. He stewed on the transporter ride home, even
though he maintained a disciplined public face and engaged Zharla
in meaningless conversation.

Now that his bloodline was to be promoted, all it would take
for the child she bore to be the father of one hundred thousand
keteli warriors was for her to publicly reveal that she was pregnant
and let people believe that he was the father. To his horror, she
made no effort to hide the bulge in her belly on the way home. He
hoped that she had already told somebody, anybody, that she never
consummated their marriage.

Ahrik made a beeline for the Tameri estate from the transporter
station. He pulled his wife straight to her wing of the main building,
letting onlookers believe by their fawning that they intended to do
what couples do that haven't seen each other in months. As soon as
the door to Zharla's chamber sealed, however, Ahrik leveled a fierce
stare at his wife.

"Why are you still pregnant, Zharla?"

She didn't answer immediately, just sauntered to her stone desk
under the east window.

He leaped towards her. "Why?!"

"Keep your voice down, Ahrik. People will talk." Zharla's smile
revealed a mischievousness he had never known she possessed. She
cast him a quizzical look. "Why shouldn't I wait for you to make this
decision?"

"There. Is. Nothing. To. Decide. My brother raped you!" He took
another step closer to her, fire in his eyes. His chest heaved with
anger.

She shrugged and turned away. "The life inside me did not decide how to come into the world." She fingered a stylus on her desk, her gaze impenetrable. "Perhaps it...she...should at least have a chance to decide how she leaves it. Besides, I just found out." She considered the *sutur* sitting under the southern window with studied nonchalance. "I'm as surprised as you."

Ahrik's aspect became quiet, but his voice filled with venom. "They didn't run a test after the attack?"

Zharla pushed up an eyebrow. "They didn't tell me the results."

He narrowed his eyes and slid closer, taking each creeping step with menace. "There's more to it than that, isn't there? You want my brother's impure blood to continue the line that should be mine." He stuck a finger into his chest, then pointed at her. "You're happy about it."

His eyes burned with fury. His fists clenched, as of their own accord.

Zharla remained silent. She drew herself up and finally looked his way. Ahrik read fear in her eyes, and realized his worst dread. "You haven't told anyone, have you?" he asked. "No one knows I am still a virgin, that we never consummated..." His legs weakened. "You want Sha...my brother...to carry on my legacy."

Disbelief flooded over him.

He broke.

Ahrik charged Zharla, animal hate in him. "Why? Why? Why?" he screamed, arms flailing. He smashed the compiler display on the desk with his fist. "Why?!" he yelled one final time.

All the while, Zharla stood frozen with one hand gripping the stylus and one hand clenched protectively against her belly, aghast. Only Ahrik's heaving breath reverberated against the cold, stone walls.

Again, Zharla drew herself up. She peered into Ahrik's face. "I want to see Shahl before he dies. Use your new promo—"

Stunned, Ahrik's face distorted in anger. "No!" he bellowed. He pulled his hand back to strike. He could break her jaw with one blow.

He did not strike. Zharla did something he did not expect. She did not cower or tremble. She did not run or dart out of the way. She simply closed her eyes and drew in a quick breath, her body still straight and tall, ready to receive the blow.

This was how those women, men, and children looked before his sons murdered them. Women and men resigned to their fate, but not surrendered to their fear. He encouraged this kind of hate in his sons. At that moment, his hand poised to strike, his ire powerful enough to kill, he remembered the eerie silence of a town whose people would never wake or breath or laugh or cry. He heard the whimpering of his men and saw the ghostly bodies of dozens and dozens of women, men, and children.

Until that moment, a part of him had thought that he was better than his sons for what they did, but he saw now what a lie that was. He was no better than them. He knew exactly what evil he was capable of.

He had come to the brink. He shuddered at his sins, at the blood that, he realized then, stained his own hands.

Zharla nodded to the prison escort and filled her lungs with the rancid prison air. "I'm ready to see him."

Ahrik fidgeted on the stone bench, then hissed, "If he tries anything, I'll kill him."

She waited for the escort to leave. The room, a stone cube three meters on a side, took on a worried air. "This prison is dreary and cold enough without your malice, Ahrik." She looked askance at him. "What happened to you in the Kereu? You've been on edge ever since you came home."

A cloud passed over his face. "You won't tell him about the pregnancy, right?"

She shrugged. "Why should he know?"

"You said you wouldn't tell him." Ahrik's voice held a note of warning, and a darkness of which she had not thought even him capable.

She answered his challenge with an irritated stare, then softened and patted his hand. "Don't worry, he won't try anything." She couldn't let him see how unsettled she was to see Shahl again. She choked back the dryness in her throat and changed the subject. "I claimed tenqam."

Ahrik folded his hands and stared at them for a beat. "How bad was it?"

She stroked her chin, to give the impression of having wrestled with this for some time. "I don't think he's guilty."

Ahrik's glower returned. "He raped you, Zharla."

She fished out her handkerchief and twisted it through her fingers. "I have questions."

"Were you raped?"

"Yes."

"Was it Shahl's face?"

"Yes, definitely."

"His voice?"

She nodded, face severe, pained.

"Where is your doubt?"

She returned his incredulous stare with narrowed eyes, her retort ready, but the door to the chamber dissolved and two guards walked in with Shahl.

Zharla sucked in her breath at the sight of him. His shackles clattered over the rough-hewn stone, and he moved with obvious pain. He looked thinner than Zharla remembered, his face sullen and puffy in the wrong places. He slumped onto the stone bench across the table and waited, looking slowly back and forth between Zharla and Ahrik.

Zharla cleared back the timber in her voice. "Guards, please leave us."

"I'm sorry, Mistress Tamer-li. Our orders are clear." The guard who spoke exchanged a look with his compatriot. "We must stay."

She turned her head, but did not make eye contact. "You need to leave."

Ahrik furrowed his brow and leaned into her field of vision. "Uh, why should they leave?"

Shahl turned his attention to Ahrik. Shahl's eyes flashed with deadened hate, an emotion that Zharla did not think him, in turn, capable of.

She saw that something swirled within Shahl, something deep and resolute. And frightening. Zharla pitied him coming to this.

Zharla turned to the guard and gave him a look of defiance that only a Tameri woman could give. "I want to be alone with my husband and brother-in-law."

The guard frowned with uncertainty at Zharla's withering tone.

Ahrik looked up his eyebrows at the guards and shrugged. "You won't win this one."

The second guard seemed to find some spine. "Mistress Tamer-li, we...ah...can't afford to have the prisoner do anything to you."

"He'll protect me," Zharla said, nodding towards Ahrik. "His son is to be the next *elef meyan*. Besides, he's armed."

The guards exchanged nervous glances.

Ahrik sighed. He removed his crescent shaped qasfin from its cloaked sheath on his thigh and set it on the table, his hand on the hilt.

Shahl curled his lip at Ahrik's blade, like a wild animal pinned in a cruel trap. That same hate flashed across his face once again, and Zharla's heart reached out to him.

The guards relaxed slightly. The first one handed a small electromagnetic transmitter to Zharla. "We'll make the door opaque, but we'll leave the sound link open in case there's trouble. Press this button, and we'll come back in. You have five minutes."

"Cut the sound link, please," Zharla said.

The first guard threw up his hands. "Mistress Tamer-li—"

Without warning, Zharla lurched forward and pressed one hand over Ahrik's, pinning his blade in place, and pressed the palm of her other hand against the point. "Do you want to explain to your superiors why I received a wound?"

The second guard gasped.

Ahrik crept his off hand towards Zharla's and hovered, ready.

Shahl grunted in admiration.

Zharla fixed the guards with a glare. "I've got your transmitter and my husband, don't I? I am safe."

Ahrik looked at her with a mix of admiration, wariness, and fear. Shahl slumped back and studied Zharla and Ahrik, as if he knew something they didn't.

The guards nodded and turned with resignation, murmuring to one another as they left the meeting room and resolved the door. When their voices cut off, Zharla knew that the room was sound-proof.

Ahrik eased his weapon from Zharla's grasp and sheathed it.

As soon as they were alone, Zharla turned to Shahl. "I'm pregnant with your child."

Shahl cocked his head back in stunned silence. Ahrik's boots scraped over the rough stone floor as he stood, the anger pulsing in his neck. "What happened to keeping it a secret?"

"Sit down, oaf. He'll carry our secret to a space-bound grave tomorrow."

Shahl whistled low and offered a slow shake of his head. "You're only half right, Heiress Tamer-li. You are not carrying my child."

A stab of pain lurched at Zharla's chest. Shahl had used her formal title, not even her name.

Ahrik sat, reluctantly, and fixed his gaze on Shahl. "C'mon, little brother. Do you honestly believe—"

Zharla put her hand up to stop Ahrik mid-sentence. "Go on, Shahl," she whispered. "How can I be sure?"

"I don't know what you saw or heard or felt, or anything," Shahl said, "but I did not commit this crime. I was not in your room that night. I have no way of proving it, but I was at the tea shop, waiting for you."

Ahrik looked from Zharla to Shahl, dumbfounded.

Shahl continued, "I was never tried for the death of the peace forces officer in Mekele, the morning after you were...attacked."

Zharla fought back tears.

Shahl gave a hopeless shrug. "She died as I fled. The callers said they were looking for someone with my description. The rain made the stone slick. I didn't want to hurt anyone, but she ended up dead and I ended up here." He shrugged in utter defeat. "My sentence is just. It's just for the wrong crime."

"She'le." Zharla reached for him.

He pulled away. "Don't touch me." His mouth twisted and he turned his glare on his brother, as if suppressing some deep reservoir of emotion. "You know something, Ahrik, something you're not telling us. Is it about that peace forces officer? I told the investigator about it, but she ignored me. What are you hiding, Ahrik? I...I hate you...for..." He trailed off in frustration and looked at Zharla for a beat, then at the stone tabletop. "Am I guilty of someone's death? Yes. Are you pregnant with my child? Absolutely not."

Ahrik gripped the metal bracelet he always wore, his knuckles white with pressure and his eyes distant, as if reciting words into the middle distance. His look was cut from the very stone that surrounded them, as if Shahl had hit close to the mark. Zharla puzzled through the ramifications.

Shahl slumped down in his chair, listless, defeated, done speaking.

Ahrik cradled his head in his hands and heaved a breath.

They sat there for a long moment before Zharla, drying her eyes with her handkerchief, whispered, "I'm done."

She pressed the button on the transmitter.

Ahrik stood on the exile platform and waited for the sentence to be carried out. The rising sun lipped the horizon, layering the ocean with ocher smears. Only a handful of people stood in the chippy fall air, there on the northern outskirts of Meran. Zharla stood next to him, with Renla, both dressed in obsidian black.

Ahrik wondered what his parents would think if they were here. He twisted his face in consternation. He didn't know what to think himself.

Only the tinge of the salt breeze and the muted rush of lapping waves accompanied the solemn preparation for death. Shahl's capsule would be launched up into the morning sky, toward the Emerald Moon. If he lived, it would be the will of the Lady of the Emerald Moon. But he would probably die. No one had ever returned from a sentence of exile to the Emerald Moon.

They brought him over to the capsule. He appeared even more pathetic than the day before. Ahrik's mind drifted back to when he and Shahl would dig for crabs in the sandy beach and chase after gulls, on mornings not unlike this one. They would race up and down Meran Mountain before dawn, on mornings not unlike this one. Guilt clawed at Ahrik now that he didn't let his brother win just once.

The guards laid Shahl down in the capsule that would shoot him out to space. Shahl, docile, just slipped in, like some other power had already taken hold of him. No argument or resistance. Dignified. The capsule was set to break open as soon as the oxygen ran out, so Shahl's likely fate was to be instantly frozen, if he wasn't battered against the debris floating in the moon belt first, or smashed against the regolith on the moon itself. Ahrik thought back to their encounter yesterday and stole a glance at Zharla, with her swollen eyes and handkerchief twisted nearly into a rope.

If Shahl was guilty, it was like no guilt Ahrik had ever seen.

They strapped Shahl's body and head into the capsule's restraining harnesses. It felt wrong that this could happen to his brother.

Next to Ahrik, Zharla choked back a sob and sat on a bench. She covered her face. Her shoulders shook. She would never love Ahrik. He reached down to place a hand of comfort on her shoulder. She swatted it away. She would never give herself to him. His military bloodline was ended.

He deserved it.

The guards sealed the capsule with chilling nonchalance. They turned on the oxygen tank and boson drive, and started the countdown timer to Shahl's release into space. With a *whoosh* and a *thunk* of disturbing finality, the capsule shot out of the shaft and quickly disappeared into the sky. Ahrik followed it until the shining silver speck merged into the rising sun. Shahl's fate was no less capricious than any of the ketelis who now lay in the steaming ground of the Kereu, or of the innocents who died in that terrible moment before he went on leave. Ahrik could not say that Shahl was guilty simply because chance had dictated death for him. In war, chance chose who lived and who died, with no right to appeal.

Shahl was no less a victim of circumstance than Ahrik's sons who were chosen for death in the chaos of battle. Tomorrow, Ahrik would return to his sons back in the Kereu, to fight for three more months. Three more months of meaningless violence. Shahl was no more guilty than Ahrik. His sons murdered innocents. Ahrik's guilt might even be greater. The thin crowd wandered away from the platform. He sat down on the bench and nudged Zharla. "The Lady chose me to live. The Lady chose Shahl to die."

She looked at him with swollen red eyes. In her hands, she twirled two necklaces with flame pendants, one that Shahl gave her, and one that he left at the decision ceremony. "He's gone. What should I care of the Lady?"

Ahrik saw his chance at redemption, however slim that chance was. He looked away from Zharla's forlorn gaze. "You were right to keep the baby."

Intercepted capsule. Subject was barely alive, but stable now. Awaiting further instructions.

Message from Emerald Moon rebels to Pir'e Analt,
26 Eyir RY 2498

10 | A Son Is Born

What kind of justice did Shahl Jeber-li receive? He spoke out for men's rights, and they executed him.

From Pir'e Analt's sermon, central Mekele temple, the week after the exile, 2 Kenen Ewel RY 2498

T HE late autumn wind whipped up Zharla's sense of déjà vu while she stood on the intercity transporter platform. She shielded her eyes from the setting sun and peered into the distance, searching for the speck that would become the transporter to bring Ahrik home from his deployment. Six months at war, apart from a few days of leave, and he was coming home to a much different Meran than he'd left.

Soldiers stood on the platform now, weapons slung on packs, traipsing up and down in twos and threes, as if the rebels might try attacking here in Meran again. They hadn't, not since the attack at the social hall, but the city had become tense in other ways. Men's rights rallies were more frequent, and even though Zharla didn't support the rallies directly, the pira were starting to take up the call in their weekly sermons.

The city was restless, but whether spoiling for a fight or anxious to avoid one, Zharla could not tell.

Her mother stood by her side, sour and immovable against the fell wind. "Dear, what are you thinking?"

Zharla rubbed her hands against the unseasonable nip. The thirty or so other people on the platform sheltered just as helplessly.

She and her mother were the only ones there for Ahrik, since he sent ahead to say that he wanted no official welcome. No choir, no pronouncements, no uniforms, no fanfare.

"You didn't have to come, Mother."

Her mother smiled, as if Zharla's statement was the beginning of a quaint disquisition. "I'm here for you, dear. You bear the future."

Zharla pressed her lips together in annoyance. As soon as she had announced her pregnancy two months ago, after the execution, her mother and everyone else aside from Renla and Ahrik began to fawn over her with sickening platitudes, dripping with triteness. They all believed that Ahrik was father to her child, the next *elefmeyan*, the hope to end all war.

"Yes." She patted her swelling belly with a contrived maternal air. "He will be something."

Her mother rested a hand on Zharla's elbow.

Zharla suppressed a shiver and avoided eye contact.

"You know, dear, you could improve his chances of success dramatically by being on the Council of Elders."

Zharla turned a frosty glare on her mother. "And you think renouncing the men's rights movement outright would put me there?"

Her mother breathed with forced nonchalance. "Ahrik's own supervisor, Sheresh, is now the top contender for the place you should occupy. His connection to the military is important now."

Zharla peered into the distance, as if Ahrik's arrival could save her from her mother's infernal attentions. "Armies don't win wars. They fight them."

"You have a military connection..."

Zharla scoffed. "Go home."

"...and you have the merchant vote..."

Zharla slid towards her mother, so they were within breathing distance.

"...so a renunciation of the men's rights movement would almost certainly let you beat out Sheresh."

Zharla narrowed her eyes at her mother. She forced down the ire in her chest, aware that people might be watching. "So this is your plan for my life?" she muttered, just loud enough for her mother to hear. "You've already killed Shahl. What else can you take from me?"

Her mother cocked her head in mild surprise. "I'm trying to ensure your success."

Zharla shook her head. "What blessed concern." She pressed her eyes shut. "Mother, we can't win this war without reforming the place of men in society. Shahl knew that. I know that. Accept reality."

Her mother gave a little laugh, as if that settled the question. "Ahrik is the best thing to happen to us since—"

" 'Us'? Mother, when it comes to Ahrik there is no 'us'."

Her mother hummed, refusing to concede the point. "You will come around. You'll see."

Zharla's eyes narrowed in distrust. "Mother, what are you planning?"

Her mother brightened. "Ah, here he comes."

Sure enough, a speck appeared on the horizon, framed by the setting sun. The beauty of the image stood in stark contrast to the worry and pain in Zharla's heart. The streaming reds and oranges of the fall sunset caught Zharla's breath in her throat, while the sickening realization of Ahrik's return churned the acid in her stomach.

She sighed. "Here comes our man Ahrik Jeber-li, august Shadhir of the Eshel, hero of the Kereu, golden son of Meran."

"You're too young to be cynical."

Zharla stood taller at the patent offense of her mother's words. No one who had lived what Zharla had lived could be accused of naivete or cynicism. "Tell me, mother. What would Ahrik the Great have to do to fall from grace, in your eyes?"

"That is not a valid question."

"And once you believe something, can you unbelieve it?" Zharla's eyes swept the horizon. Ahrik's transporter had grown from a speck to a smudge.

"How ridiculous."

"My point exactly, mother." Zharla stomped her feet once again, this time not entirely to ward off the weather. She huffed with frustration and slid away from her mother's now silent form.

Zharla had just begun to distinguish features on the transporter, even individual forms through its clear walls, when her mother cleared her throat with haughty expectation. "What are you planning to name him?"

Zharla searched the air for some semblance of peace. Finding none, she leaned towards her mother with as much patience as she could muster, then placed her hands on her belly. Her thoughts detoured unexpectedly to the life growing within her. She had a chance to break the cycle of mistrust between mother and child. She smiled. "Nayr."

Her mother stood in silence, staring into nothingness, almost brooding.

"Mother? What do you think?"

The transporter began to decelerate. Zharla felt the hum of bosonic wash in her chest. She tasted the tinge of ozone on the air.

Her mother glanced at the transporter, then at Zharla. "Aren't you going to ask Ahrik's opinion?"

Emotion washed over her, like the transporter's bosonic field, when she thought who the father really was, that secret she'd shared with only three others, and which she determined now to carry to her grave, like Shahl had. She pursed her lips. "I'm the woman here, Mother, not him."

Her mother raised one searching eyebrow. "It's an inauspicious name. Sounds too much like fire."

The transporter decelerated to a stop at the platform.

"Mother, this boy will spark a peace unlike any that Dom or the moon has ever seen."

Her mother didn't respond. The doors of the transporter dissolved open, and she directed her steely gaze to the search for her prized son-in-law.

A breeze whooshed down the platform. The hum of the boson

drive faded. Zharla scanned the faces exiting the transporter but saw none she recognized.

"Did he say which section of the transporter he'd be in?" asked her mother. She swept her attention over the exiting passengers, her eyes revealing a growing confusion.

"He's only written me one line in the last two months, and that was to tell me he didn't want a big to-do for his return." Zharla began walking down the platform, examining the faces of those who passed.

"Is this the right transporter?" her mother asked.

"It's the one he told me he'd return on." Zharla scrunched her mouth, perplexed. There weren't that many people disembarking.

"I don't see him, dear."

Zharla's brow furrowed. "Nor I, Mother. Nor I."

Shahl crept towards consciousness, but limned on the verge of slipping back into blackness. His body wouldn't move. His brain slogged against some general anesthetic. He became aware of taking a breath, something he did not remember doing in a very, very long time. Something cold touched his lips. Something warm and refreshing slid down his throat. Soothing voices flowed around him. He thought he felt a smile on his face. He hadn't smiled for a very long time, either.

Maybe he was dead, and his ordeal was over. He imagined the smile broadening on his face, then once again slipped into black.

Ahrik cloaked during the transporter's approach, then slipped away from the platform unnoticed. He smirked to see Zharla and her mother wander away from the platform. He saw no reason to return to his wife. She was about to give birth to another man's son, a son that the world thought was his own.

He didn't fault the life that grew within her, but he did fault her obvious contempt for him. She made it plain in the way she looked at him, in the way she spoke to him, and in the way she ignored him when she could. Her disdain accentuated his sense of inadequacy. If not for his sons, for his duty to defend women's rule, Ahrik would rather have faded away into nothingness.

Ahrik did not want it to be this way. He didn't want to build this wall between himself and his wife, but the intimate specter of death and destruction had accompanied him for six months. Heavier thoughts than confronting his wife weighed him down. Their petty rivalry paled in comparison to the pain he and his sons lived for half a year.

Still cloaked, he crept over fences and through brush toward his base. With his cloak engaged, he skirted all the hayla checkpoints. The hayla were an affront to his dead sons, the lie that society deluded itself with: while his secret clones suffered and bled and died in anonymity, the hayla took all the credit for their success.

How little success his ketel managed in six long months.

Once he hit the open ground north of Meran, he paused and took in the sunset. That sun set on his dead sons, over there in the Kereu. And many innocents. He groaned, deep in his heart. For three months, no one in the ketel talked about the massacre that now hung like a cloud over the 3d Hand.

There was nothing to say about something that everyone knew.

War was a nasty, hateful, unforgiving business. He threw his sons into battle and proclaimed the rightness of their cause, but Ahrik doubted the Eshel's moral superiority. He wanted to protect innocent Kerewa, he really did, but he could not tell which ones meant them harm. Even though he told his sons that they fought for the peace of the Eshel, no song of glory would bring back the ones whose bodies lay in the fetid earth of the Kereu.

Ahrik trudged up the final ridge. His gaze remained fixed on the small stone pillar and the oath it bore. He was certain of one casualty in this war: the truth. The only truth that Ahrik saw now was of those men who fought and died around him. Of lives flung into abyss and chaos. Nothing else mattered anymore, perhaps not even that fanciful oath.

He paused at the entrance to his base and nodded to the two guards crouched in the knee-high grass. He and his sons didn't salute in the open anymore. The enemy used this in the Kereu to identify commanders.

He ran his fingers over the Oath of the Ketel carved into the stone post at the crest of the hill. *Slagh-li an-felesh bel-zhoreq ketel-li.* (Death is nothing before the power of the ketel.) How its meaning had changed in so short a time.

His conniving, pregnant wife could wait, as could the soft, detestable Supervisor Sheresh and the fake parties he would throw to show off Ahrik, his star military commander. Too many good men lay incapacitated with wounds in Ahrik's secret underground base, in the healing complex, for Ahrik to put on such airs.

Ahrik passed through the gate and thought about the oblivious Merani citizens he'd passed at the transporter station. The irony of his ketel's sacrifice became clear. The very people he told his sons they were fighting for had no inkling of the sacrifice his sons made. His sons fought in anonymity. They died with only their comrades to mourn them. They lay in unmarked graves where they fell, with nothing but their comrades' hearts and his ketel's death register to mark their passing.

Ahrik trudged through the stone corridors of his base. The dead were the lucky ones. They didn't have to live with a suppressed conscience or a broken body, and they didn't have the burden of mourning those for whom fate had chosen death. That Ahrik could have been so lucky to come back dead.

He felt the untruth of this thought when he slipped into the dim light of his base healing complex. Row upon row of his wounded sons lay on dozens of cots in the massive cavern, in various states of consciousness and agony.

The Chief Elders, the Army of the Eshel, and the Esheli people might count these men's lives as naught. He did not.

He once thought that the life of a keteli, given in anonymity, was worth the peace of the Eshel and the safety of women's rule. The hayla who died received burial ceremonies and public interment and monuments and songs for their brave deeds. So did keteli commanders like him. But the clones, expendable, received nothing but the thankless opportunity to fight again. If they lived. Lying in row after row of healing beds, three hundred and forty-three of them, Ahrik saw that their courage was worth every individual praise that the hayla received.

A weak artificial light glanced off the rock walls of the cavern. He walked down an aisle and reached out to his sons over the tendril network. Most of them, when they sensed him near, sat up in their beds and raised their right hands over their chests in salute. Others lay still, unconscious, chests rising and falling. Some were missing right hands or arms, so they raised their lefts. Ahrik lost count of the types of injuries. Some had bandaged heads or torsos. Some had limbs in traction over their beds. Some had no bandages at all but lay moaning in pain. All had eyes sunken by the pain of loss and the trauma of battle.

He stopped in front of a keteli with vacant eyes. The keteli had no apparent injuries. Ahrik wondered about his story. Whether he'd earned a name.

"What happened, keteli?" Ahrik asked.

The keteli convulsed. "I...I...I dun't know. I...I can't hun... hundle it."

Ahrik shuddered at how close to the breaking point he felt himself, like this keteli. Ahrik looked at the keteli for a beat. "Your comrades are with you. I am with you."

A healer slid over from a nearby station. He hovered at the end of the bed.

The keteli clenched his knees up to his chin. A spasm of convulsions ripped through him.

Ahrik knelt beside him. "Which hand are you with?"

The keteli held up three trembling fingers.

Ahrik rested a hand on the keteli's arm, and the keteli's shaking subsided. "Will you let me in?" Ahrik whispered, reaching out over the tendril link.

The wounded keteli's eyes grew wide with fear, and he convulsed. Worried looks glossed over the faces of the men around him. One or two cast awkward glances in Ahrik's direction. The healer rushed to the opposite side of the bed and gave Ahrik a questioning look. The keteli screamed, eyes still wide, and the healer restrained him.

Ahrik dared not look at the faces of the men around him, for fear of what he might see there. Pity? Despair? Contempt? Ahrik could not deal with the flood of emotions that threatened to engulf him.

He'd never felt so alone. His base housed just under nine thousand of what he thought were his closest friends, but there he stood, in the middle of the healing complex, unable to provide comfort or give praise or even understand what was going on. He'd grown up with these men, spent grueling hours with them in combat training, and connected with them in endless meditation sessions to develop the tendril network. With his hand commanders and subcommanders alone, he'd spent countless hours simply talking.

Yet in that moment, when the healer restrained the keteli, Ahrik's only companion was himself. Forced solitude. Helplessness assaulted him, and he wondered if his sons saw it, too.

If Ahrik could not help them, he could not influence them. If he could not influence them, he could not command. Their devotion defined him. Their detachment made him irrelevant. Ahrik wondered how Alrem dealt with the loss of his ketel.

He should visit his old friend.

Without a word or a glance at any more of his sons, Ahrik stalked the rest of the way to his chambers. He resolved the door behind him, sat on his bed, and stared into space. Where did he go wrong? How many life and death decisions did he make in six months? His ketel, his sons. War made them strangers. For the first time in his life, he wanted to feel tears on his face.

Ahrik suppressed his nervousness with a scowl and set himself on a chair in the midwife's consultation room. His gaze of contrived perturbation swung between Zharla and Renla, her bondswoman.

Zharla gave him a look of flaccid appeasement. "I know you don't want to be here, Ahrik, but this baby is coming in one week. We should at least give the impression of getting along."

Ahrik let the sarcasm rise in his voice, masking the fear fluttering his stomach. "Perhaps you would prefer that I pretend to be my brother."

Zharla wagged a condescending finger at him, an almost comical gesture given the healing shift she wore. "You need me."

Renla bit her lip and wrapped a finger through a stray, red curl. She kept her peace, but her eyes missed nothing. Ahrik saw how suspicion brewed behind her eyes.

It set his teeth on edge. He focused his inner resolve on keeping the secret of the ketel, but now that secret threatened to break open here, in the midwife's examination room. Renla might be able to see his nervousness. If Zharla suspected anything amiss, Ahrik did not know if he would have the mental wherewithal to keep the secret.

Ahrik shrugged at Zharla, too tired to argue the reality of their political truce yet again. He had no way to get answers to his growing questions about this war without Zharla's political connections, and the story of her illegitimate son would destroy support for her candidacy among the conservative military faction.

Ahrik nodded and shifted in his seat. He needed to play along with the fiction of their truce, at least for a little while longer. They were about to take cells for the creation of the ketel of one hundred thousand. Zharla and Renla knew nothing about that. They had not taken the blood Oath of the Ketel that decreed death to any who revealed the ketela's true nature, that the Eshel's shock troops were genetically engineered. If this secret got out, it would destroy society.

Ahrik considered what difference it would make for his sons if Zharla and Renla knew about the ketela. It probably wouldn't give any more meaning to his sons' bitter sacrifice.

Zharla smiled with finely tuned nonchalance, which gave her a sickening resemblance to her cold and calculating mother. "You haven't been yourself since you got back three months ago."

Ahrik shivered at the chill her look sent down his spine, but he spread his arms wide. "I'm here now. Let's get this over with."

Zharla sat on the examining table and Renla took the chair between the table and Ahrik, Zharla's street clothes and cloak folded nearby. Zharla cleared her throat and smoothed her shift when the technician dissolved the door. Renla reached out and squeezed Zharla's hand, then cast a wary glance in Ahrik's direction, assessing him with a wariness that Ahrik hadn't witnessed before.

Ahrik searched her eyes in turn for any suspicion over cloning or the ketela. This moment, here in the midwife's office, was critical to keeping the secret safe. Ahrik adjusted the metal bracelet at his wrist and muttered a prayer. The secret must stay safe.

He couldn't find a comfortable spot on the chair.

Renla's gaze swept over Ahrik even more than before.

Despite his prayer, a pang of guilt struck Ahrik when the technician prepped Zharla's belly and brought out a huge needle.

"What is that for?" Zharla asked the technician, who was about to plunge the needle in.

Ahrik studied the technician's response. The technician paused. Ahrik tensed. Renla's eyes settled on him once again.

When the technician opened her mouth, she spoke no trace of a lie. "This sample is to conduct one final test for chromosomal abnormalities, Mistress Tamer-li, to be ready when the baby is born. It is standard practice for all officers whose sons are chosen for rank advancement. Any chromosomal abnormalities would probably nullify the advancement and require us to wait for another son."

The technician went about her work. Zharla relaxed, but Renla's stare remained riveted on Ahrik. He met her gaze. Her eyes narrowed to suspicious slits.

In that moment of guilt, a part of him wanted to tell Zharla what was really going on. He did not know how long he could live this lie. In reality, so little of consequence divided Zharla from him. The government and the army lied to everyone. To Zharla about the clones, and to Ahrik about the war. The two hundred thousand clones in the Army of the Eshel fought and died in anonymity. Few would suffer if everyone knew that a few men like himself led a double life, on the one hand acting as heroic icons for the Republic's masses and on the other leading tens of thousands of clones in war. Were it not for his blood oath and the consequences that went with breaching it, he would tell her outright. But he was not ready to break that oath. Not yet.

The Oath of the Ketel, for all its faults, defined him.

Under Renla's penetrating gaze, a twisted thought came to Ahrik, the technician's hand poised to plunge the needle into Zharla's womb. Chromosomal abnormalities would save Ahrik the shame of lying to his wife. But Zharla wanted a perfectly healthy son that would break Ahrik's military bloodline forever.

The technician looked a question at Zharla.

Zharla looked at Ahrik with eyes of victory and nodded at the technician in approval. "Go ahead."

Ahrik studied her face. Did she suspect something, too? No, her look ranged between pity and haughtiness. She knew the child was healthy. She thought she had won a victory.

The war weighed on his mind, and Ahrik didn't care as much about his military line as he used to. One hundred thousand more clones would just mean more men for the government to chew up in its wars.

Renla's perceptive, fiery eyes took in Ahrik's every facial movement, it seemed. She suspected something.

The technician left. Ahrik suppressed a sigh of relief. "Fine," he said, shifting his head in Zharla's general direction. "I'll be more involved, for appearances' sake."

The secret of the ketel was safe, and Zharla looked at him like she'd won a victory, but Ahrik knew they had both lost.

Zharla thanked the courier and resolved the front door, then examined the paper envelope. *Well, this is interesting.*

The square envelope bore the official seal of the Army of the Eshel. She eased the seal open as she paced to the parlor to deliver it. She sucked in her breath as she read:

Shadhir Ahrik Jeber-li:

Report with ketel in two weeks at sunset. Preparation for space training.

Aanin Sheresh Shehur-li

She leaned against the door jamb to the parlor and rested the paper on her swollen belly, unsure how she felt about this new development. *At least he's going away again.*

Ahrik looked up from reading some obscure book on war, his eyes tired, but whether from fatigue or the stress of their tenuous marriage, she couldn't tell.

"This came for you by courier," Zharla said, waving the message in his direction.

"It came opened?" A peeved look crossed his face.

Zharla suppressed a twinge of guilt. "It looked...important."

Ahrik read it, grunted, crumpled up the message, and tossed it into the bin. "This is not the first time I've received such a mess—"

Renla cleared her throat and slid through the doorway to the parlor.

"What is it?" Zharla asked.

She nodded towards the handheld receiver on the wall. "Mistress Zharla, it's Aanin Sheresh, for your husband."

Zharla smiled. In her family's home, her husband was merely that: her husband.

Ahrik grumbled and stalked to the receiver, palmed it on, and put it to his ear. "Yes, sir... Fine, sir, thank you... Yes, I received it... Great news, sir... Yes, I agree that it is, sir... We're ready, sir... Fine... Very well... I'll ask her, sir... Thank you again, sir... Lady's blessings to you, too, sir."

Zharla gave Ahrik an expectant look.

He closed the connection and sighed. "He wants to congratulate me, or us, on the space training by dining with us tomorrow. He wants us to choose the place."

"We'll have to break bread with him?"

"I like it as little as you do."

Zharla chuckled and tossed the envelope into the bin as well. "This is the first time in our married life that we have agreed on something."

He looked at her, blinked, and gave a detached grunt. "I won't let it get to my head."

They walked home after the dinner with Sheresh. A chilly breeze blew off the coast, and Ahrik gathered his cloak around his neck. As they passed through the subdued out-mountain markets of Meran, the caller networks announced news of the war.

"Sounds like the war is going well," said Zharla. An attempt to fill the void in their marriage with something other than silence.

Ahrik gave her a skeptical glance. "War means that something is not going well."

Zharla looked confused. "They're announcing the things you did."

Ahrik shook his head in sorrowful disbelief. "What do you make of these war reports, Zharla?"

"I'm sure there's some truth and some falsehood." She turned toward him in discomfort. Her belly bulged in front of her. "Which is which?"

Ahrik considered his words with care. "Did we bring security and prosperity to parts of the Kereu? Yes. Do the Kerewa love me? No. The butcher's bill of this war, of any war, cuts deep."

"A stunning admission from one who brings us victory."

Ahrik coughed. "I'm not certain we would know victory if it walked up and struck us in the face."

"For the second time in as many days, we agree on something, Ahrik Jeber-li."

Ahrik ignored the humor. "This is serious. If they can convince enough of us that we've won, then we've won." He shivered and looked over the lights glowering around the bay. "I wonder why we're in the Kereu at all."

"So, why fight?"

Ahrik stopped walking. He stared at her and grasped her arm, purposefully but not violently. "Hear this now. My duty is in my blood. If I fail to do my duty, I let down the generations of men and women who came before me and made me who I am. If I fail to do my duty, I let down my comrades, who expect me to uphold the trust of my office. If I fail to do my duty, then my so... I mean... my men will die and I will have let them down."

Zharla gazed at him.

Ahrik shifted his stance, horrified that he had almost let slip the secret of the ketel. "When I went off to war, I thought I was going to defend you and all those people like you who have no idea what peace costs, and to stake my claim to history and the glory of the Eshel. But the first time I held a dying man in my arms, that myth drained out of me with his lifeblood. I fight to avenge my dead, Zharla, and to keep the living from having to be avenged. Nothing more, nothing less."

Zharla shook her head. "So... simple."

Ahrik opened his mouth to respond, but two men blocked their way out of the quiet side street they had entered. Another slipped in behind them. The dark pall of their eyes said they had violence on their minds.

Adrenaline coursed through Ahrik's veins. Instinct took over. He checked for weapons and saw only short blades in right hands. Their left hands were empty. If they had distiller weapons, then they would have to reach for them. His only ally was speed.

He whipped Biriq from its cloaked sheath and pushed Zharla toward the wall of a building, as far as possible from the assailants. With feline speed, he leapt forward and severed the last two fingers on the right hand of one of the men in front of them, and then reversed the motion to catch the other with the point of Biriq on his knife hand. The point pushed through, and he felt the man's fingers against his elbow. The satisfying clang of two metal objects falling to the cobblestones followed soon after.

He moved toward Zharla next. As Ahrik expected he would, the third assailant lunged at his wife when Ahrik parried the first two. The third man's reaction was too slow. Ahrik's blade caught his right forearm in a slashing motion, leaving an ugly gash from wrist to elbow. As a third metal object clanged to the ground, Ahrik gripped the third man's neck at the pressure points, just under the jaw, and slammed his head against the wall. Ahrik squeezed, then drew his face close. The other two ran off.

"Follow them." Ahrik shoved the man in the direction of his fellow assailants, but he crumpled to the ground instead.

The adrenaline cleared. Ahrik's breath heaved. His mind became lucid once more after the burst of violence, like a dream that put him right back in the Kerewi jungle. His thumping heart slowed, and he glanced over to make sure Zharla was okay.

Her face wore a mask of fear, and she leaned against the wall, her head ducked down in wariness and fear. He reached toward her, but she cowered.

"Don't touch me," she said, pushing herself farther away from him. "Are you a man or an animal?"

He drew in a centering breath. "The streets of Meran used to be safe at night."

"Yes, I—"

She clutched her belly and tensed with pain. Her eyes shot open and she gripped his shoulder like a vice.

The next contraction came less than five minutes later, and they went straight to the midwife.

The genetic traits in this batch are extraordinary. All of the main traits—stamina, strength, high metabolism, sensory perception—are manifested on a consistent basis throughout the batch, instead of the typical, sporadic distribution. The secondary traits are also distributed throughout the batch, although many clone sections exhibit multiple secondary traits, instead of the norm, which is to have only one secondary trait per section. In short, the new one hundred thousand will be super soldiers.

From the genetic cultivist's report on the Ketel of Elef
Meyan Nayr Tamer-li, 5 Mezit RY 2499

11 | Into Space

First to the fight

Motto of the Ketel of Ahrik

A MALE voice rasped in Shahl's ear, jerked him from a chemical slumber. "How would you like to be known?" The man sniffed and moved, a large person hefting his weight. "'Shahl' will not do."

"I'm not sure"—Shahl coughed—"that I want to be known at all."

Shahl's surroundings danced into a blur recognizable as almost real, as light plays through a rough-cut prism and gradually resolves into reality. He lay helpless in a healing bed. Where? On Dom? On the Emerald Moon?

His breath came in ragged bursts, along with his memory, but the nightmare of his mental and physical pain continued, unabated. The serenity from earlier waking moments proved the calm before the storm.

Pain sizzled through his body. His senses sharpened still more. He recognized pain in its most benign form now. That rasping voice held pain deep, deep down, but whether the man behind the voice caused the pain or endured it, Shahl could not tell.

Thick fog clouded Shahl's head, and his voice croaked with underuse. "Where am I?"

The voice rasped, "The faster you accept your new life, the better off you'll be."

Shahl blinked open his eyes and looked in the direction of the voice. The rest of his body would not respond. He judged his inter-locutor a captor, not a liberator, and he dared not risk the hope that liberation awaited, at hand. Shahl narrowed his eyes. "Let me go."

The round man with the raspy voice winced and graced him only with eyes of forlornness and pity.

A woman's voice cut in from the opposite side of the bed. "When we cracked his pod, he was blue from lack of oxygen. We could call him 'Blue'."

Shahl struggled to catch a glimpse of the woman, but the round man's negating groan drew his attention back.

The man frowned. "This is how he'll be known from now on."

The woman hummed. "'Biriq'?"

"The name of Ahrik's blade? Too ironic."

"What about something from the Old Tongue? 'Met', the word for 'death'?"

Shahl strained to move his eyes in the direction of the woman's voice, but his body still wouldn't respond. She must be behind his head.

"Too close to the tired ideas we're trying to overthrow," said the man.

The woman's voice brightened. "How about 'Anda'?"

"'Belonging'? He belongs to the rebellion now?" The man laugh-ed, but it came out as a wheeze. "It's perfect."

Shahl tried to arch his back and push against whatever held him down, but he could not move. Through gritted teeth he said, "Let. Me. Die."

The woman patted his shoulder. "There now, Anda. Everyone here knows one truth: only fate decides our death."

"Let. Me. Go."

"You'll die if we do, and we need you to live," the round man rasped. "Help us. We can help you."

Shahl groaned and tried to turn away from the voice. His will to resist withered with an expiring groan.

In his old life, the man once known as Shahl would have rejected his new name, but in his new life, he did not have the energy to fight such things. He did as he was told.

The man took a step back from the bed. "What's your name, son?"

"Anda," he croaked. "I am Anda."

Ahrik sat in his cramped cabin at the stratospheric training station. He tapped aimlessly at the blank compiler display on the small metal desk crammed into one corner. One month into their two-month space training rotation, and he'd finally decided to write a note to Zharla. He just had no idea what to say. The baby was probably taking over Zharla's life, but he didn't care to ask about a child that we wanted nothing to do with.

He could tell her about their orders to interdict rebel resupply from the Emerald Moon, or about the unnamed keteli that got sucked out of an airlock. When they retrieved his body, the space freeze was so deep that they had to use a stasis field to keep him from splintering as he warmed up. No way was Ahrik going to let his body be transferred back to the Eshel with that ghastly look on his face, the limbs flashed at odd angles.

Zharla wouldn't care about that.

Ayen walked in. They long ago did away with waiting for Ahrik to call him in. His aide's interruptions were too frequent.

"Father," said Ayen, "two meteors hit an interdiction patrol craft. The kall fields held, so there was no loss in pressure, but one keteli was killed by a meteor that entered at his right shoulder and exited his groin. The patrol leader was blinded permanently when the other meteor struck a pressurized oxygen tank and exploded."

Ahrik stood. He frowned. "Why didn't the electromag watchers warn the interdiction patrol about the meteors? Did their sensors fail?"

Ayen shifted on his feet and studied the ground. "No, Father." He stole a glance at Ahrik. "Two watchers fell asleep on duty."

Ahrik swore. He fixed his gaze on Ayen. "Are they running the gauntlet?"

Ahrik wondered if he trained them too hard. Maybe, if they had more time to rest...Ahrik pushed the thought from his mind. The training wasn't too hard. The real thing was always worse. If anything, the Kereu taught him that.

Ayen nodded. "Father, Hand Commander Halel gave the watchers the option of running the gauntlet as a squad or only sending out the two watchers who fell asleep."

"They chose to run it as a squad, didn't they?"

Ayen nodded again.

Ahrik smiled at the leadership this showed. The two fatigued watchers would almost certainly die if they ran the gauntlet alone. Unlike gauntlets gravside, which involved long sticks or the flats of keteli blades, gauntlets in space had to use distiller weapons. Those being punished were pushed out of an airlock ten kilometers from the space station, given fifteen minutes each worth of oxygen and enough fuel for a minute's worth of propulsion, and told to get back to the station alive. One company from a different hand was chosen at random to constitute the gauntlet, which meant that about two hundred distiller weapons stood between the culprits and safety. The distillers were set to stun, but with ten men instead of two running the gauntlet, more bodies could absorb the distillers' stun charges, with extra fuel to course-correct, if needed.

"Let's go to the command module. I want to see how they fare."

From the wall-size display in the command module, Ahrik saw the squad begin its journey back to the station. They'd have to pass through two rows of shuttles with bay doors open, so the company with distillers could shoot at them as they passed.

The squad clustered together and linked arms and legs. This protected as many propulsion units as possible from the stun charges. Their route back to the station was ragged, since distillers and mistimed propulsion sometimes pushed them off course. They were almost to the station airlock when one keteli from the squad veered off and slammed into the station's hull. The squad formed a human chain to retrieve the keteli, but his body looked limp as they pulled it into the airlock.

Ayen sighed. "They were almost there."

Halel, Ahrik cast over the tendril link. *Are you at airlock? Report.*

Father, cast Halel, *squad leader caught stun charge to propulsion unit. Broke femur clean through. Knocked out cold. Snapped air line on impact. Hypoxia. Cognitive functions severely degraded. Will be sent gravside in induced coma.*

"Such is the discipline of the ketel, Ayen. A few suffer now so more live later." Ahrik wasn't about to write that in his note to Zharla, either. He didn't believe it. These clones were just as human as him and Alrem and Zharla and Renla. Someday society would have to count the true cost of this war.

Anda willed himself through a last set of arm curls. The weight was a pittance compared to what soldiers like Ahrik lifted, but Anda was never meant for this life. They had dragged him out of the healer's bed much more quickly than they should have, and now he had to exercise to the point of collapse twice a day. He had to build muscle mass and bone density in the Emerald Moon's fraction-grav, they said, even though they lived in a hab with artigrav. He set down the hand weights and took off at a run around the track.

His new tormentor was Esh'a, the woman who'd named him, and he couldn't get a good read on her. She wasn't like the other tormentors, violent and crass, and she tendered Anda praise on occasion, at least after her fashion. She kept her hair pulled back into one long, black braid, and her glare was as fierce today as always.

"C'mon, Anda," she yelled. "How are you supposed to survive gravside without exercise?"

Anda didn't care for his new name, but he cared even less about his old life. After two laps, he stopped in front of Esh'a and panted, hands on knees. Sweat dripped onto the metal grating at his feet, and he wrung his nose at the smell he emitted. "Why...should I... ever go...gravside...again?"

Esh'a cocked her head, and a wisp of black hair slipped onto her forehead. "They didn't tell you? You're going down on a mission."

He stood up and tried to control his breathing, hands on hips. "What mission? I thought I proved Dom's impotence by staying alive up here."

She shrugged. "If they say you go, you go."

"If I refuse?"

She pulled up her sleeve, revealing a nasty scar on her forearm, in the shape of a circle with a line through it. "They have ways of encouraging you to go along."

Anda shuddered. "What is it?"

"It's our symbol. We're two worlds, not one, the Eshel and the Kereu."

Anda turned away and took a step toward the track, but Esh'a grabbed his arm.

"I used to think like you," she said, "like I had a choice."

Anda shook his head. "What's this all about, the rebellion?"

She motioned for him to sit. "You deserve a break." Esh'a rubbed her temples. "The Republic is based on an unjust settlement. The central government in the Eshel has exploited the people of the Kereu for ten years. A few of us made it on the Emerald Moon, and the Eshel left us alone for a long time, but when the big Esheli mining conglomerates took an interest in our minerals, they started pushing us around up here, too."

Anda stroked his chin. "That explains the sudden spike in fighting a couple of years ago."

She nodded. "There were always pockets of resistance in the Kereu, but things ramped up when Moon got involved."

"Are the Tamera involved?"

Esh'a pursed her lips. "Heavily. Matron Tamer-li supplies half of the rebel's weapons and has a significant presence out by Station

Prime, where Moon's largest mines are."

Anda froze, mid-thought. "There can't be enough people here on the moon to supply fighters to the rebels, and most Kerewa live in the cities, under Esheli government control. Where do the rebels get all their fighters? I've heard estimates of a half-million combatants on each side."

Esh'a stood up with an abruptness that startled Anda, her lips pursed. "Okay, Anda, break's over. Two more laps, and faster this time. Go!"

Ahrik didn't want to go gravside before his ketel's final training exercise, but Sheresh requested a personal audience. Ahrik didn't even bring a change of clothes. He saw no reason to sleep in a bed while his sons had to bunk in stasis fields up in the stratospheric space station.

He ground his teeth and forced himself to focus on the ground coming towards him at an improbable speed. He wanted to see if he could overcome the vertigo. Space elevators didn't decelerate until they were almost at the ground, but most passengers didn't feel it because of the internal stabilizers.

But this elevator was different. Ahrik had to take a civilian elevator because the military one wasn't scheduled to come down for another day. It wouldn't have gotten him to the audience with Sheresh in time. He looked around the elevator cabin in disgust. Carefree traders and politicians lounged on the overly luxurious deceleration couches, dressed in their finery and snacking on dainty treats. A waiter came by to offer Ahrik mligh bites with almost no caloric value, they were so small. Ahrik turned away the waiter with a glare. Such dainties meant nothing with a war on.

The other passengers grumbled when Ahrik asked the elevator pilot to leave the hull transluced as they descended, but they would not dare challenge his military uniform, with its shadhir rank sash.

As they approached the surface of Dom, the rest of the passengers lay in their couches and closed their eyes. Ahrik focused on breathing, and telling himself that he would not smash to the ground. His stomach churned while they came to a stop, but he didn't vomit. He smiled in satisfaction, knowing that this skill might come in handy someday.

Ahrik stepped onto the platform at the elevator station. His legs wobbled, but he muscled through it. A short transporter ride into Meran took him almost directly to Sheresh's office. He saw the Tameri estate through the transporter's kall tube. He assumed his wife and her son were home, but he saw no reason to see them. What was the point, even if he had more time? Their marriage was almost a year old, and he'd only been home for three months of it. He still hadn't sent her that message. Hadn't even written it.

The ketel would go straight from two months of space training to another six-month deployment somewhere. His sons wouldn't go home first. Neither should he.

Ahrik shook out his legs as he walked from the transporter station to the headquarters of the Army of the Eshel. The artigrav in space was close to the real thing, but there was something about having cold, hard earth under foot.

Ahrik strode over the stone-paved streets of out-mountain Meran. They relocated the headquarters here a few years after the War of Unification, when real estate in-mountain turned into a premium because of the peace boom.

A breeze blew in off the ocean. The fragrance of algae and salt hung on the air. New port infrastructure gleamed by the docks. The imposing architecture of the headquarters building ahead of him proclaimed the army's importance, but the blocky design revealed a stunning lack of imagination.

When Ahrik was finally ushered into Sheresh's office, Ahrik's legs now firm under him, the supervisor didn't bother to stand. He peered up from his desk compiler and drummed his fingers next to the display. "Ah, Ahrik. So nice of you to come down."

Ahrik swallowed a retort. This meeting was unnecessary. A message would have done well enough. "Thank you for taking the time to meet me, sir."

Sheresh didn't offer Ahrik a seat. "Have you been to see Mistress Tamer-li yet?"

Ahrik hesitated, unsure of the answer that Sheresh sought. "My duty comes first, sir."

Sheresh stood and walked around to Ahrik's side of the desk. He gave Ahrik's shoulder a jocular slap. "That's why I like you, Ahrik. Dedicated to the cause."

Ahrik flinched and stole a glance out the window, hoping his supervisor didn't see. "I try, sir."

"You're the best we have, my boy."

A new, more sinister churn formed in Ahrik's stomach. He smiled and nodded once, eager to be done with this encounter. "Sir, I came for orders."

"All business, as usual." Sheresh licked his lips and skirted the desk once more, planting himself in front of his compiler display. "Let's see. Your orders: 'Space interdiction. Patrol over the Kerewi hemisphere'."

"Glad we're training for this mission, sir." Ahrik had expected the orders to be interdiction, but he could never be sure. The army had a way of giving him missions his ketel hadn't trained for.

Sheresh held up a hand. "There's more."

Ahrik tensed.

Sheresh looked down at his compiler display and carried on, as if nothing were amiss. "You must not enter the space over the Eshel. You are not to use lethal force unless and until the enemy discharges distillers at you. You are not to pursue craft from space into the atmosphere. Civilian vessels have far weaker reentry shields than military ones, and if they take evasive maneuvers, they could burn up."

Ahrik fought to keep his mouth from gaping open. "Sir, I..."

Ahrik couldn't finish. These conditions were preposterous. If

Ahrik's sons managed to detect the fast, cloaked smuggling vessels while the smugglers were still in space, and managed to somehow stop and board them, then they could conduct space interdiction operations over the Kerewi hemisphere.

But not over the Eshel. Or with distillers. Or by pursuit from space. Or by doing most of the things they'd just spent two months training to do.

"Question, Shadhir Jeber li?"

Ahrik fought to compose himself. "Those are our written orders, sir?"

"Yes." Sheresh handed him the square orders card.

A quick glance told Ahrik that the orders said nothing of the conditions that Sheresh just placed on their interdiction mission. Nothing about staying away from the Eshel or not using distillers or not pursuing from space. The churn in Ahrik's stomach turned into nausea.

He breathed and focused on forcing it down.

"Very well, sir. We'll do our best." He saluted and went back to his sons, without stopping to see Zharla and her son.

"Do you understand your mission, Anda?" The fierce tone of the question made Anda's hand move to his left arm instinctively, to feel the new scar under his sleeve. He was standing in front of the man with the rasping voice. After all these weeks, he didn't know the man's name.

Anda nodded.

"Well?" The man shoved him to the ground.

Anda gulped and scooted away from the short, stocky man. Anda's hip throbbed where it struck the ground. His back hit a wall. He could go no farther. "Go to the. . . gravside rendezvous point and. . . and wait for instructions."

"Simple. You are ah'sbi now. You belong to our family. Esh'a?" he rasped, then turned and walked out.

Anda lurched to his feet and tried to stand at attention. He gave Esh'a an awkward salute. He wondered if all soldiers lost the will to resist like this.

Esh'a slapped down his hand. "Don't salute me." She motioned toward the waiting ship. "You ready? I'm taking you down."

"What's the point of all this?"

"The cause?"

"The violence."

Esh'a shrugged. "I follow orders."

She stroked his shoulder. Her touch sent a thrill through him, but her fingers also brushed the scar on the back of his neck, bringing back the awful memory of the night he spent as a confessant in the central temple at Mekele.

Anda flushed. He tried to conceal his shock at being touched in such a way, after so many weeks or months—he had no idea how long it had been—of a life ruled by brutishness and blood. This could be some new kind of torture, psychological. He eased himself away with a smile in Esh'a's general direction and boarded the ship. "I guess we all follow orders, right?"

His life felt so wrong.

Esh'a shrugged. "Just promise me one thing, Anda. Watch your back. Only trust yourself. Okay?" Her hand grazed his forearm, the lightest of caresses, as they began to strap in.

"Sure," Anda said. For the first two hours of the flight, until Dom filled the view pane of the ship, sweat beaded on his brow and he clutched his knees to keep them from shaking.

Ahrik walked into his command module on day ninety-nine of a 180-day deployment, expecting that this day would be as mind-numbing and uneventful as the other ninety-eight. Same thing, day after day: nothing. No smuggling, no gun runners, no interdiction over the Kereu. Ahrik began to wonder where the rebels got all their fighters and weapons.

He slumped into his chair and drummed his fingers on the metal desk at the exact center of his open, circular staff planning area, in a small stratospheric station somewhere above the Kereu. He scrolled through his messages. They told him nothing he didn't already know.

His lead intelligence officer approached. "Father, you should see this."

Ahrik sat up. He stopped drumming.

"What is it, Brain?" After the Peshron campaign, Ahrik made more of an effort to learn the names of those who had them. Brain had a largish head, bred for cognition, and a keen intellect. A very good intelligence officer.

Brain nodded to his handheld display. "Normal commercial activity over the Kereu usually consists of transit between the suborbital elevator stations and occasional exploratory trips to the Emerald Moon."

Ahrik leaned over the display. "Nothing out of the ordinary over the Kereu." Then Ahrik caught the image over the Eshel and furrowed his brow. "How'd you get that data?"

Brain gulped and shifted his eyes in nervous arcs. "Father, we um…"

"Yes?" Ahrik's stomach fluttered with concern. If Sheresh saw this data, he would conclude that Ahrik had disobeyed his instructions to stay away from the Eshel. Ahrik began to think of disciplinary options that would justify this error. Summary reassignment? Another gauntlet? "I ordered you to ignore the Eshel."

"Yes, Father, but we were worried about smuggling into the Eshel from over the oceans, then we happened on this." Brain enlarged a section of the dynamic model projected over his handheld. "The new sensors have only been online for a day, but my team already observed two vessels break from Army-approved flight patterns into the Eshel."

"Go on." Ahrik narrowed his eyes. He wondered what he would

find if he pointed the sensors directly at the Eshel.

"Father, one vessel merged into the Meran-bound flight stream from the atmosphere over the lesser ocean, to the east of the Eshel, but our sensors could not tell where it originated."

"Curious." Ahrik leaned forward, increasingly aware that he had a decision to make. Fate and future weighed on this decision, and Ahrik had nothing to guide him but his intuition.

"Father, the second vessel followed a trajectory from the Emerald Moon toward the western Eshel. We originally thought this was a returning exploratory mission, but it did not stop at one of the orbital stations, or even one of the suborbital elevator stations. Every other exploratory mission to the moon has stopped at one of those stations."

Ahrik cocked his head, now thoroughly intrigued. "Where did it go?"

Brain shrugged. "It disappeared, Father, but we now know that someone is smuggling something from the moon to the Eshel."

Ahrik stroked his chin. "And probably to the Kereu, as well." The weight of the decision confronting Ahrik grew by degrees, like the pressure change of a planetary descent. Brain's revelation made the implication plain: Sheresh's instructions stood head-to-head against the truth about this war. Sooner or later, one of them, the truth or the instructions, would have to give way.

"No, Father. It disappeared from our sensors." His voice gave the hint of an anxious warble.

"Cloaked? At entry velocity?"

Brain nodded.

Ahrik gave a low whistle. "That's advanced tech."

Ahrik made his decision at that moment. He pushed down the squeaming eels of uncertainty that writhed against his sense of duty and an obedience learned over generations of discipline. He saw no way back from this struggle between orders and truth, only a way forward.

His gut churned, but he gave Brain a confident smile and clapped him on the shoulder. "Excellent work, Brain. Continue to track and record any abnormalities."

"And what of the Eshel, Father?"

"Be discreet."

Ahrik knew of only two ketela tasked with interdiction over the Eshel, each of one thousand. Compared to his eight thousand five hundred or so over the Kereu, Ahrik did not see how two thousand men could control that much flight activity over that much space. Ahrik calculated. Those two ketela only had enough men for about fifty squad-level patrols at any given time, and that was at maximum operating tempo. Fifty squads to patrol two-fifths of the entire globe's volume of space.

"Brain, if I wanted to smuggle something from space into the Eshel, could it be done?"

"With ease, Father. Neither of the two ketela over the Eshel has a sophisticated sensor network, and there are huge dead zones. The smugglers probably know about them. That vessel coming from the Emerald Moon yesterday may have been following a series of dead zones."

"Can you be sure?"

"No, Father, but..."

"...but it's worth looking into. Brain, work with operations and planning to figure out what's going on with these abnormal flight patterns, but I don't want anyone else to know what we're doing. Come to me directly when you've found something." Ahrik smiled. "First."

"To the fight," Brain answered.

Ahrik broke from slumber with a sudden wariness.

"Father, we found something." Ayen rocked Ahrik's shoulder. Only four hours had passed since he fell asleep, but that was more rest than he was used to. He forced the cobwebs from his mind and rose up on an elbow.

"Thank you, Ayen." Ahrik sat on the edge of his bunk, then considered his aide. "You do your job well, but your waist looks like it's never seen this war. In the next rotation, we'll see about a line assignment for you."

"Thank you, Father." Ayen shuffled his feet in discomfort. Ahrik wanted his men to be uncomfortable. That pushed them to be hard, to be alert, to be good soldiers.

Ahrik stood and reached for his uniform. "What did we find?"

"We got one, Father."

Ahrik grinned with steely eyes. The ketel was due to end its six-month interdiction deployment in two weeks. Ahrik wondered how old that would make Zharla's boy. Eight months? So much time away from Meran that Ahrik almost missed it. If he could just avoid his wife and her son.

Ahrik brought his mind back to the present. They had tracked dozens of abnormal flights since Brain's revelation three months earlier. But they had not captured a single smuggling vessel. Until now. He shook the fatigue from his body and beamed.

Ayen smiled back. "A weapons expert will meet us there."

When they arrived at the main hangar, a nondescript merchant vessel brooded before them, silent and steaming. It measured twenty meters from stem to stern, long for a space-going vessel, and wider than most Ahrik had seen. Where Ahrik expected to find identifying markings he saw only scraped and filed metal. Irritated, Ahrik noted distiller damage on the engine housings.

"Squad leader," he asked, "why is there distiller damage here?"

"Ut's not frum our weapuns, Father," said the leader of the interdiction squad. "W'found thus vessul driftin' an' pulled 'lungside."

"Father," the weapons expert added, "that damage may not be from distillers at all. See the scoring? It's too ragged. Something less energy intensive did that."

Ahrik nodded. He saw it now. "What was it carrying?"

"The cargo hold was empty, Father, but I have my weapons team searching the vessel top to bottom."

Ahrik frowned. "Where is the pilot?"

At a bark from the squad leader, two ketelis dragged a man from the other side of the vessel. He was large for a pilot. A stream of dried blood made its way from a field dressing on the man's temple, and another dressing on his arm was soaked red. Ahrik gave the squad leader a questioning glance.

"He, uh, r'sisted whun w'boarded, Father. He sunt one'f m'men to th'healers with a brokun urm." For that, Ahrik gave the man an icy glare, but wanted to do more.

"Let him go," commanded Ahrik. The man crumpled to the floor. Ahrik narrowed his eyes. He couldn't tell if this man was connected to the war in some way, or if he was innocent, like those people in the village. Ahrik shook off his second-guessing and steeled his composure. No reason to let his sons know how he really felt.

"Revive him." Immediately, healers attended to him. They moved the captive pilot to a sitting position while other ketelis fastened his hands behind his back. Ahrik reached down and grabbed the man's chin. As he lifted the pilot's head, the man's eyes passed from grogginess to consciousness to some form of comprehension.

"You recognize me and my rank insignia," said Ahrik, a sense of keen assessment in his eye. "What was your destination, pilot?" Ahrik squeezed, his anger rising with every moment of silence that passed. "What was your cargo?"

The pilot's eyes bulged with fear, then something clicked in his jaw. Ahrik released his grip, suddenly unsure of himself. Ahrik had not squeezed him hard enough to break anything. The pilot's eyes shifted from fear to insolence, then he clenched his teeth, hard. Something in his mouth made a sickening crack.

"Poisun caps'l!" shouted the squad leader.

One keteli hammered the man's chin with his fist. Blood splattered across the floor. The other keteli pounded the man's back. The man coughed as he toppled over, then went into convulsions. A healer rushed over and stabbed something into his neck. The man stopped his convulsions, but looked up at Ahrik, eyes victorious.

It happened so fast it took Ahrik by surprise. "Revive him!" he shouted.

A bloody smile spread on the pilot's face. His eyes rolled. The healers tried to revive him, but in vain. Ahrik swore. What could he have learned if he'd kept the pilot alive? What opportunity had he just lost? The man convulsed once again, then lay still.

As two ketelis hefted the body away, Ahrik saw the weapons expert pause. He received a tendril message. "Father," he said, "they found something inside. It might be contraband."

They approached the vessel's main hatch, and a keteli came out to explain that one of the men found a rivet missing. They pulled up the panel and found a series of black metal objects, unlike anything they had ever seen.

Ahrik boarded the vessel, then stopped short. The weapons expert gasped. Tense, Ahrik ordered, "Everyone out." He spun toward the weapons expert: "Except you." To the squad leader: "Secure the hangar. No one enters or leaves until my intel lead says so." To his intel lead, he cast: *Brain, come to main hangar. Bring debriefing team.* Ahrik didn't want to risk word of this getting out by aural communications.

"Well," Ahrik asked the weapons expert when they were alone, "what do you think?"

"Sweet Moon, Father. They're just like the ones we found during the Kereu campaign, only brand spanking new. There could be hundreds stashed in the hull space."

Ahrik's head swam. He reached for a bulkhead. These were ancient weapons, but they looked new. And they came from off-planet. This whole time, Ahrik thought that secret Kerewi factories produced the rebels' weapons. But if they came from off-planet, then this war was much, much bigger than he had imagined. "Pick three men to help you dissect this vessel," Ahrik said. "Word of this must not get out."

The weapons expert grinned with satisfaction.

Ahrik paused on his way to the hatch. "What's your name?"

"Haven't got one yet, Father."

"That could change soon. This could be the most important task you ever perform for me. First."

The weapons expert's face lit up. "To the fight, Father."

Ahrik stepped toward the exit hatch but again stopped short. To the right of the hatch, partially hidden by the vessel's frame, hung a small identification plate, half-pulled from its moorings. Confused, Ahrik rubbed it with his thumb to be sure he read it right. It was unmistakable. The smugglers must have missed it when they stripped the vessel of its markings. He stole a glance over his shoulder to be sure the weapons expert hadn't seen, then ripped it off, wincing as the metal dug into the skin of his fingers.

Ahrik stuffed the small strip of metal into his tunic, then pulled it out again, just to be sure he hadn't misread. It bore a ten-digit identification number, with the Tameri clan's leaping dolphins underneath.

> SHERESH SHEHUR-LI: Can I count on you?
> LEREN: All I have to do is ignore him? He'll do the rest?
> SHERESH: He'll do the rest.
> LEREN: What of the officers' conspiracy?
> SHERESH: I have that under control. [pause] Now, are you ready for the day of your liberation?
> LEREN: More than ever.

> Undated voice recording found in the archives of the Ketel of Ahrik

12 | Revelation

It is often argued, of Ahrik and Zharla, that Ahrik was
the strong one, that he had a plan. My research
suggests otherwise. Not only do we know too little
about Zharla, but there are indications that neither one
had a clear idea how things would work out, much less
that they would rise to rule the planet.

Professor Ezhen Alem-li, Melmez Meran, during the
reign of Nayr, RY 2528

ZHARLA flew down the stairs to the kitchen, where Renla and two
other servants cleaned up the aftermath of dinner. "Renla," she
said, her tone direct, "please come."

Renla turned, recognition in her fiery chocolate eyes. She shook
water from her dripping hands and ran them through a drying field.
"A stroll?"

Zharla nodded and motioned toward the door. They broke into
the crisp autumn evening, holding hands like they had on countless walks before, when they developed a code to transmit simple
messages by squeezing different parts of the hand.

Wrong, Renla sent in code, followed by the question signifier.

Zharla smiled and said, "Nayr is only nine months old, but he
has the strength of a two year old and the attitude of a twelve year
old. I need some air."

Other servants watch, squeezed Renla. Another question.

Zharla chuckled. "That's not the problem. Mother is fed up with

Nayr breaking precious family heirlooms. She practically ordered me to move out just now."

Renla bit her lip and tucked a wayward curl into her cap with her off hand. *Sorry, Zharla.*

Zharla laughed and waved off the apology. "Ahrik comes back from deployment in a week. I have half a mind to move out just to keep him and my mother apart. Sometimes I think she loves him more than me."

Loves?

"Well, likes anyway. I'm not sure my mother loves anyone these days. She turned irascible and moody after Nayr was born. Something's going on, but I can't tell what."

After?

"Well played, Renla. Mother has always been a bit like that, I suppose." She locked eyes with Renla. "But Mother looks at Nayr with eyes of fear." Zharla shook her head. "And Mother fears no one."

They crunched down the gravel walkway. A bird landed on the grass and hopped over to the flower bed to peck for food.

Zharla and Ahrik had been married almost eighteen months, but they had only lived together for three of them. Not that she minded, but she worried that Nayr lacked a father figure.

They arrived at the gate, and the old guard Ahjoz approached, his hand up in apology. "I'm sorry, Mistress Zharla. No exit today. There is a rally coming up from the port."

"Ahjoz, we're just going for a stroll."

"Your mother gave clear instructions. I'm sorry."

Zharla frowned. Ahjoz kept her in as much as he kept strangers out. But she loved the old man and his humble charm, despite his loyalty to her mother.

She led Renla back the way they had come, but when they reached the long, evening shadows where the garden trees came closest to the corner of the house, she pulled Renla behind a bush. She eased her head out to see if Ahjoz had seen. He sauntered back to his place in the gatehouse, oblivious.

A devious smile crossed Zharla's face. With a satisfied look at Renla, then signaled, *Way out.*

Renla gave her a confused look.

Back gate, signaled Zharla. *A-H-J-O-Z not know.*

Generations ago, Tameri women had made themselves an escape route from their estate, just in case things ever took a turn for the worse. Its secret location and how to access it had passed from mother to daughter. Where the wall of the complex met a spur of Meran, separated from the housing area by the orchard, the wall bent to follow the contour of the mountain. Here, if one knew where to look, was a simple scanner that scanned for only one thing: gender. The opaque kall field door looked exactly like the mountain wall in which it was set. If one was a woman, the door dissolved. If one was a man, it remained opaque and very uncomfortable to pass through.

Zharla led a dumbfounded Renla to the place. Shadowed between the wall and the trees, Renla whispered, "I've lived here all my life and never known about this?"

"Re'le, this is only for moments of utmost need."

"What drives your need now, Zhe'le?" Her voice steeled with anticipation.

Zharla placed her hand on the scanner and the tunnel opened. Faint lights blinked on inside. She squeezed to Renla, *Justice.*

Renal furrowed her brow at the tunnel. *Matron know?*

They entered, and the door resolved.

Zharla shook her head. "She doesn't know about this tunnel. My grandmother brought me here before she died. Told me never to tell my mother. I didn't know why back then, but I do now."

They walked the short distance to the opposite end of the tunnel, and a similar door to the first opened onto an obscure alley.

"So this is how you took all those walks with Shahl without your mother noticing," Renla said.

Zharla smiled, reminiscing on her erstwhile innocence, trying to shut out the torment that replaced it. She took a deep breath while the tunnel door reformed behind them, then exhaled.

The world outside the compound looked as normal as ever, but the grumbling chants and drum beats from the rally suffused the scene with a shifting, disturbed air.

Zharla looked an appraising question at Renla. "Have you ever seen a men's rally?"

"I was blessed with less defiance than you," said Renla.

Mischief crossed Zharla's lips. "Not much less."

Fair, Renla squeezed.

Zharla and Renla moved toward the distant, unnatural rumble of the rally, holding to the shadows in the simmering dusk, to avoid both recognition and the peace forces. When the way became too narrow, Renla followed closely, her lips pursed, gait uncertain. When the distant rumble of the rally became audible as chanting, a peace forces patrol passed by at a trot. The two women crouched in the shadows, bodies tense until the patrol passed. The rumbling crescendoed as they drew nearer the rally, and the chant became clear: "Justice for all! Women's rule must fall!"

The two women crept as close as they dared, crouching 50 meters away and peering around the corner of an alleyway. The only other spectators were a handful of underemployed, ill-clad young men across the street, carrying on in the jocular, scatological way that such individuals do when life presents more challenges than opportunities. A line of blue-clad peace forces screened the marching protesters as they moved fitfully up the cross street, moving from the port to the mountain. They were a motley group, despite the apparent coherence of their chant and the rhythm of their scattered drums.

There were not only men, which surprised Zharla, but women also. Their dress suggested a representative cross section of Meran's socioeconomic spectrum. Filthy dock workers and smart-looking professionals marched with men and women of ill-repute and errand boys, caps still on their heads. Street urchins and the homeless had found their way into the ranks, pushing carts or dragging behind them what pitiful possessions they called their own. Some rally-goers just shuffled along, neither marching nor chanting, demeanor distinguished by disinterest more than fervor for a cause, real or imagined.

Zharla turned to Renla, keeping her voice just loud enough to be heard. "Shall we join them?"

A worried challenge crossed Renla's eyes. "You know I will not leave you."

Zharla grabbed Renla's hand and started toward the procession.

"Hold it," said a deep voice behind them. A man lumbered out from behind some crates piled in the street. Despite the poor light, Zharla could see he was dressed in red presbytery robes. His broad shoulders looked like they did not know want, and his eyes searched and darted like someone whose conscience bore a weight.

Zharla blinked back tears at the memory this man conjured, from the night she sought tenqam from Shahl. "You're the pir'e from the central temple in Mekele. What are you doing so far from home?"

"I came for the rally." His voice carried like a deep and threatening grumble, as if he could speak with greater power, but chose not to. "What's your excuse?"

Zharla saw fear in his eyes. He knew something.

The pir'e moved between the two of them and the rallying mass passing up the street, then looked over his shoulder, as if they had stumbled on something they shouldn't. His carriage took on an unexpected tenor of nervousness. "Go home."

Zharla stood her ground, but Renla grabbed her hand. *Let's go.*

"No, he's hiding something." She narrowed her eyes at the red-robed pir'e. "You knew Shahl was inno—"

A deafening sound consumed her world. The force of the blast slammed Zharla into a building, cut off her words. Then, ringing silence. And blackness.

When Zharla came to, panic stirred on the night air. A frantic, faraway voice called to her from somewhere close, "Mistress Tamer-li? Mistress Tamer-li?" A large hand shook her shoulder, with surprising tenderness.

Her eyes flickered.

"Are you okay?" he asked.

She tasted blood. Her head throbbed. Her leg felt wrong somehow. She lay on the hard ground. The image that came into focus was of a stranger. No, not of a stranger. Of the pir'e.

Where is Renla? Her arm tensed, and she struggled to lift her head to inspect it. A stream of blood had made a path from her shoulder to her wrist, spreading out fitfully at her knuckles. Her fist clenched something. Through the dissipating mental fog, reason began to return, cutting through the tinny ring in her ears.

"Where is Renla?" she mumbled to the pir'e from Mekele.

"Your friend?" The pir'e's eyes darted left and right. "I'm sorry. There was...there was nothing I could do." Blood stood caked on one temple and under his ears. "It wasn't supposed to be like this," he muttered. "Are you okay, Mistress Tamer-li? I...I need to go."

The pir'e passed into the dusky gloom like a deep shadow, and Zharla looked down at her clenched fist. She didn't remember holding anything before. She coaxed her fist open, and with her good arm, reached in to pull out a scrap of paper.

She puzzled through the letters, then wild confusion gave way to a sickened understanding. Panicked, she looked around and called, "Renla, where are you?"

Ahrik chewed on his thoughts. He stood while Supervisor Sheresh sat. Sheresh kept his office cold, the papers on his desk arranged in neat rows, as if to intimidate whoever entered. The window behind him let in what remained of the evening's fading light over Meran Bay. The drumbeats of a rally thrummed the air.

Sheresh looked up from his work. "So glad that you could come down, my boy, and with only one week left in your deployment."

Ahrik wasn't thrilled that he had to make yet another trip down the elevator for a face-to-face with his supervisor, but Ahrik requested this meeting. He wanted some answers, even though he wasn't sure he'd like what he heard. He straightened. "Glad to be here, sir."

"How's it going up there?"

"Fine, sir." Ahrik shifted his weight. The polished stone squeaked under his combat boots. "Sir, I'd like to discuss my report on the vessel we interdicted."

"I read it," said Sheresh. His voice came out in an unnatural deadpan, noncommittal, as one would expect a candidate for the Council of Elders to use. Sheresh gave Ahrik an absent look, as if the report were a mere afterthought. "I saw nothing to discuss."

Ahrik cocked his head in dismay. "Sir, the rebels have resupply routes off-planet. They have new, explosive weapons like those used in The War."

"I know our history, Ahrik." Sheresh raised an eyebrow, then went back to the papers on his desk. "Anything else?"

Ahrik gulped. "I meant no disrespect, sir. It's just that we may be facing an enemy we're not prepared for."

Sheresh eased himself up out of his chair, knuckles resting on the edge of his polished stone desk. "You doubt the power of the ketel? I can arrange an investigation, Ahrik."

Ahrik pursed his lips and gathered his thoughts before proceeding. "No, sir, that won't be necessary. I only meant that more men might die than need to, or the people of the Eshel might suffer needless sacrifice because we didn't prepare for these new weapons."

Sheresh smirked. He sauntered around the desk and stood in front of Ahrik and gave a pursed smile. "A fine sentiment, caring for the welfare of others. But it is not your job to cultivate such high-minded altruism." As he said this, he brushed his hand over the commendations on Ahrik's chest, then straightened the sash at Ahrik's side.

"No, no," said Sheresh. "You were born to win wars. The men of your ketel were bred to win wars. They may die, and you may die, but neither you nor they will measure the cost. That is the Chief Elders' job. That is their burden to bear, not yours."

Sheresh gave an imperious smile. "I thank you for your concern. Duly noted. But you will do your duty, and mind your manners. This is the last time that I will hear even a hint of protest from you. Is that clear?"

"Yes, sir." Ahrik's body remained rigid, at attention.

"Now, if you have any actual evidence that the rebels are using the ancient weapons—oh, laughable fantasy—then present that and I will consider it. Do you have any evidence?"

"Your people requisitioned it, sir. Again."

"That is problematic, isn't it, Ahrik? You see, I have many people. If you can give a more accurate description of these people, then please send a formal request over, and we'll take a look."

Ahrik exchanged an impassive stare with his supervisor. "Very well, sir."

"Dismissed."

"Thank you, sir." Ahrik saluted.

Ahrik descended the steps of the headquarters building and slid into the dusk. He heard and felt a blast from the direction of the road leading from the port to in-mountain Meran. Briefly, he wondered whether he should go check in on Zharla before going back up the elevator to his sons. He decided against it.

The attacks were becoming more frequent.

He never sent the request.

"Mistress Zharla! Mistress Zharla!" A servant rushed into the parlor where Zharla lay, resting her knee. The servant thrust a piece of stiff message paper toward Zharla, then caught herself and showed the appropriate deference. Zharla eased herself up on the couch, wincing at the pain in her knee, twisted cruelly in the blast the week before. She shook out her sore wrist before taking the square paper from the servant. One week since Renla went missing, and Zharla more expected a death notice than a ransom demand. Expectation turned to disbelief when she read the astronomical sum:

Three million *keina*, one for each of the Kerewa that the army has murdered.

Zharla slumped back onto the couch. At least it wasn't a death notice. But she could never gather that sum from her personal accounts. She would have to go to the clan business board. Or to her mother.

"Is it bad, Mistress Zharla?"

"Could it have been good?" Zharla sighed. "When is the next board meeting?"

The servant shrugged. "Your mother is meeting a military officer in the boardroom now."

Zharla sat up. Unease assaulted her shaking legs as she stood. "Who?"

The servant signaled her ignorance.

Zharla limped to the business wing of the estate, brushing off the servant when she rushed to support her. Zharla paused at the door to the boardroom and turned to the servant. "Go check on Nayr."

An uncomfortable silence met her when she entered the boardroom. Her mother, face fuming red, stood glaring at Sheresh. Ahrik's supervisor, in turn, whipped his head toward the door when she entered, but the prominent vein in his neck and the attitude of his stance told Zharla that she had just walked in on an argument.

Confusion tore at Zharla's balance and weakened her knees. She shoved down the question why her mother was meeting with one of Zharla's principal opponents for the Council seat. She slid so that the two antagonists could not see her grip the jamb of the door behind her back, for support.

Then she saw the look in her mother's eye, and a sickening clarity settled over Zharla's mind. They were talking about her and, by the depth of their silence, scheming some evil scheme. Zharla stared down at the shorter military officer. The very sight of him stoked her ire. She eased her gaze toward her mother. "I heard you had...a visitor."

Her mother inclined her head in cursory assent, with her usual contrived, plaintive grace. "Is everything alright, dear?"

Sheresh cleared his throat. "I heard about—"

Zharla froze him with a glare and breathed a moment to calm her temper. When her natural composure returned, she addressed her mother once again, "A word, Mother?"

Sheresh shuffled past Zharla, waddled almost, with a look at her mother that said their discussion was far from over.

Zharla resolved the door behind him and set her hands to her hips. "What was that about, Mother?"

"Just some pressing business, dear," said her mother. "How can I help you?"

"Is he angling for your support with the selection?" Zharla bore her gaze down on her mother and caught the way she broke eye contact, ever so briefly—*hiding something!*

"This wasn't about...that."

Zharla knew when she would get no more out of her mother, so she smiled and cast down her eyes with deference. "No matter. I trust you, Mother." She peered up and restored the confidence to her voice. "I've come to request Renla's ransom."

"How much do they want?" her mother asked. Her mother shifted her hips, discomfort obvious. Strange.

"Three million *keina*."

"Done," said her mother, too quickly. She gave a wan smile, then stepped to Zharla with the tired simulacrum of a hug. Zharla waited a painful beat to make the affectation appear real, then disengaged, holding her mother at arm's length.

"Thank you," Zharla said to the middle distance between them, to avoid making the eye contact that she could not bear to hold, not with such a woman. Zharla fought to smile through the suspicion hanging over her mind, an ominous cloud lurking overhead.

She turned and stretched out her palm to dissolve the door. *That was easy. Too easy.*

Tomorrow wouldn't be too soon to leave this house.

Ahrik checked his internal compiler to make sure he had the right address. Zharla's new house stood on a cobbled street in a posh district halfway between the port and the mountain. The midday sun shone full onto the front door. Ahrik looked up and down the street. The house in front of him had no number, but the numbers on either side told him this was the place.

A grim-faced guard with a drawn distiller stood watch outside, pacing. Her incisive glare would be enough to scare away all but the most committed visitor. Ahrik tried to remember the name of the grizzled head guard with the white whiskers, in case this guard challenged him. Ehloz? Ahjoz? When the guard turned toward him on her circuit of pacing, Ahrik spied the leaping dolphin sigil of the Tamera on the guard's breast. This must be Zharla's house.

Ahrik wondered if an unnumbered house on a quiet street was a step up or a step down for Zharla. He wasn't sure he was ready to step back into her life. Ahrik struck out across the cobbled street and nodded to the guard. Would the door scanner even let him in?

The guard nodded to him in recognition and he stalked up from the cobblestones to the front door, skipping the middle step. When he placed his hand on the scanner, the door opened. The readout even gave his name. He gave a sigh that settled somewhere between relief and trepidation. He chuckled to think that they might even be expecting him.

"Well, I'm here," he said when the door resolved behind him. If they expected him, they did not show they cared. "Zharla? Renla?"

His wife limped around a corner, paused to give a curt hello, and continued on her way. Ahrik reared his head in mock affront and considered why he left his sons to come here. "I've won the war, and I'm here to stay." He gave a sarcastic shrug and sauntered after Zharla into what he presumed was the study. "Zhe'le?"

"Don't call me that."

"What? No pleasing welcome for your victorious warrior come home?" Ahrik frowned. "Why are you limping?"

"I hurt my knee about a week ago. Don't worry about it." She considered him through suspicious eyes. "Something is seriously wrong around here, and I've been trying to get to the bottom of it for the last week."

"You've realized that our relationship is dysfunctional?"

"No." She sighed. "No, not that. Sit down." She called to Renla, in the far corner of the house, it seemed, "Do you have Nayr?" A faint, affirmative reply left her to turn her attention to Ahrik. She stared at him a moment, inscrutable. "We're still interviewing applicants for the servants' positions, and until they're hired, we're a bit shorthanded with Nayr. That boy is quite a handful, you know."

He grunted. "You do realize why I'm not inclined to help, right?"

"Really, Ahrik?" Zharla rubbed her temples. "I'm sorry. Please, just listen. This has been very difficult to sort through."

A different side to Zharla opened up, one Ahrik had never seen. She was unsure. Uncomfortable. Just like he felt. He leaned a shoulder against the wall but kept his surly attitude in ready reserve. "I'll listen."

Zharla nodded toward the sky. "In the weeks before you came home, things began to fall apart here on the ground. Renla was kidnapped, ransomed, and released."

He gave something between a shake of the head and a shrug of the shoulders.

She pursed her lips, but continued. "This sort of thing is becoming more frequent. We have an armed guard outside the house..."

"I noticed."

"...and neither Renla nor I go out without an armed escort. The men's rights demonstrations are more frequent and better attended, and there have been attacks at rallies. I was at one when it was attacked by an explosive weapon." She moved toward her desk.

"Wait. A week ago, you say?"

She nodded.

"A rally near the road from the port to Meran Mountain?"

She nodded again, suddenly wary. "What is it?"

Creeping guilt slunk into his consciousness as he put two and two together. He should have gone by to check on her, after all. "Are... are you okay?"

She frowned in mild surprise. "So concerned? I had a concussion, and twisted my knee, but I'll get over it." She sighed, as if struggling with the words, then leaned against the edge of her desk.

He waited. He felt the tension in her voice.

Genuine worry crossed her face. She shuffled through some papers on her desk. Of a sudden, she looked up at Ahrik with resolution, as if she found the words she sought. "There's a connection between the Tameri holdings and the war."

He grew serious and very, very attentive. He felt in his pocket for the metal scrap with the Tameri dolphin sigil, the one he'd ripped from the smuggling vessel, but thought better of bringing it out. Not yet.

Zharla looked out the window. "I began to grow suspicious after it was so easy to get the three million *keina* ransom from my mother."

Ahrik whistled at the sum.

Zharla moved to sit at her desk chair. "I poked around, very carefully. I found some things that didn't add up."

Ahrik didn't say anything, just sat down on a footstool and inclined his head to listen.

Zharla pulled a paper from the pile on her desk. "I found shipping manifests, mostly, but also expense reports for meetings that I didn't know happened in places that I didn't know the company did business."

"Company officials have gone to the Kereu?"

"No, nothing that obvious, but the timing and location of the meetings is odd, not in line with inventory or selling cycles, and in places where competitors are strong, where it doesn't make business sense to break into."

He gave a more thoughtful grunt. "And the manifests?"

"Nondescript at times, but what's most disturbing is that the fuel allocations for trips don't always match the distances or cargoes. Either some of the cargo is much heavier than what we normally transport—unlikely, since we deal in minerals—or the transporters are going much, much farther than is represented in the manifests."

He swore.

"Ahrik! Not in my home."

"Sorry. Habit." He fumbled in his pocket for the scrap of metal. "What's the connection to the war?"

"I happened on something in a warehouse last week." She shifted in her seat while he waited, expectant. "It doesn't look civilian."

Ahrik raised an eyebrow.

She reached down and plunged her hand into a desk drawer, giving a furtive glance toward the window and door. She opened her palm to reveal a cylindrical metal object, pointed at one end but flat on the other, one portion of the object of a brassy color and the other a more flinty gray.

Ahrik gasped. "Sweet Lady of the Emerald Moon."

"Oh, good, you know what it is."

Ahrik rubbed his face in his hands. "This is not good. It's very, very bad." Things were worse than he imagined. He weighed how much he could trust her.

"What is it?" she asked, pulling forward in her chair.

He pulled the small strip of metal from his pocket. He tossed it onto the desk, where it clattered over the polished stone surface.

Zharla stole a glance at it and then looked at Ahrik with disbelieving eyes. "Where did you get this?"

"I found it."

"If this is going to work, we need to be open and up-front with each other."

"Not. Yet." Ahrik already asked himself if he'd shown her too much. He risked the secret of the ketel by going further.

An uncomfortable beat passed between them. Zharla sighed. "It definitely came from one of our transporters. Can you tell me what was on it?"

He looked at her, an "Are you seriously pushing the issue?" look in his eyes. "Can you memorize the number and check it against your shipping manifests?"

She shrugged. "I recognize the number. That ship went in for repairs a while back and hasn't come out for some reason. Put that with the metal cylinder I gave you." She stood and peered out the window, eyes moist. "I wish that none of this had happened."

"You don't know how much I agree."

She came around her desk and sat on the edge once again, her face less than a meter from his. "Ahrik, my life is a vast, dramatic play over which I have little control. From choosing you over Shahl and the rape"—she shuddered—"to the attack at the rally and now this. I was supposed to be one of the most powerful women in the Eshel, but look at me now. I'm a pawn in my own game."

Ahrik nodded. "I see."

"No, you don't. You are in complete control of your life. Ten thousand soldiers at your beck and call, who will give you exactly what you want, when you want it."

He scoffed. "I wish it were that easy."

"By all appearances, it is. Everyone in the world lives under the illusion that I actually am one of the most powerful women in the Eshel, and you got to marry me. You're the war hero. You're the rising star. Your life comes on a platter. Mine comes with a chain."

Ahrik stood. "Your life and mine both, Zharla." He rubbed his chin, lost in thought for a moment. "If you're okay to walk down to the bay, there's someone you should meet."

Zharla couldn't meet the gaze of the men passing them in the military healing center. So many of them were...unwhole. Their uniforms were pressed and their gaits crisp, but a feeling of unease accompanied them down the corridors. She could only guess at the reasons these men needed healing.

And Zharla was not used to guessing.

She had heard an urgency in Ahrik's voice back at the house, a yearning that welled in her own soul, so she agreed to come. She endured the physical discomfort of the walk, and now the psychological discomfort of the healing center. Maybe, before all was said and done, they would both have to do many things they were uncomfortable with.

For a better future, for Nayr, for the Eshel, she hoped it would all be worth it.

She strode closer to Ahrik as they wended through a maze of sanitized corridors and nondescript recuperation rooms. She leaned forward, without touching him, and whispered, "I've walked by this healing center hundred times, tucked into Meran Mountain." She suppressed a shiver. "I never knew it held so much pain, that the cost of war might be so high."

Ahrik paused and considered her, a degree of begrudging respect in his aspect, as if he almost wanted to be pleased. "There are many things about war and those who fight them that would surprise you, Mistress Tamer-li." He nodded down the corridor. "Come, I want you to meet Alrem."

They entered a huge sitting room. Meran Bay sparkled like a crystal bowl through floor-to-ceiling windows. Ahrik rushed over and embraced a man she assumed was Alrem. The tenderness with which Ahrik hugged his friend touched a chord in her breast, and she choked back the pain of missing Shahl. She looked away, to think on something else.

Alrem advanced toward her with the bearing that she now recognized all military men must possess. He bore no bandages, nor did he move with a limp, or any other sign of physical malady. Curious.

He bowed his head and smiled a disarming smile at Zharla, and they touched the backs of their fingers in the unfamiliar greeting. "Mistress Tamer-li." He raised an appraising eyebrow at Ahrik. "It's about time I met your wife."

Behind Alrem's winning smile, Zharla sensed a deep sadness, a dignified but not pitiful longing. Ahrik had told her on the way over that Alrem had lost most of his soldiers in the war, but he seemed as even-keeled and well-adjusted a social creature as she'd ever met. If Ahrik hadn't told her, she wouldn't know the pain he felt.

She inclined her head in return. "Pleasure to meet you, Alrem."

They all moved to a corner of the room and sat on cushioned stone chairs, then Alrem and Ahrik carried on in the most normal way in the world, as if he and Ahrik had never been set apart from society to be the most potent force the world had ever seen. Ahrik had never acted this way around her, jovial, engaging, pleasant. In his world, he was perfectly normal. In hers, he was an enigma.

"Ahrik?" she asked, interjecting into the two men's conversation. "The facilities?"

Alrem pointed with one hand. "Around the corner. To the right."

"Thank you, Alrem."

He nodded and smiled. Like a soldier, but not like a soldier at all.

When she returned, before she rounded the corner, she slowed at an uncharacteristic burst of laughter from her husband. "Well," Ahrik said. "What do you think?"

Zharla stopped. Guilt pricked her conscience for eavesdropping.

"She's great. A little distant and hard to figure, but you're lucky she chose you, Ahrik." Alrem's unvarnished honesty made Zharla smile.

"No, I mean—"

"For the Ahit?" Alrem chuckled. "Yes, we need someone on the outside."

What are they talking about? She stood behind the corner, squirming with discomfort, and heard only silence while, she assumed, some nonverbal cue passed between them.

"We should tell her about the White Planet," said Ahrik.

White planet? Another pause.

She heard a sigh, a negative sound in response to Ahrik. "When is your next deployment?" asked Alrem.

"Two months. We're scheduled for a one-month bridging stint in space."

"Let's wait till you get back, then approach her," said Alrem.

Who are these men? Zharla asked herself, rounding the corner.

Alrem beamed, then stood and inclined his head with consummate grace. "Mistress Tamer-li, welcome back."

> Return the Tameri servant. Take the extra cost out of my share of the ransom.
>
> ---
>
> Handwritten note from Pir'e Analt to Renla's kidnappers, discovered during the inquest into the rise of Ahrik, RY 2519

13 | Battle of Nejru Gulch

I couldn't have known they would use atomics.
[Swears], nobody knew they would use atomics.

Aanin Sheresh Shehur-li, recorded testimony during
the inquest into the rise of Ahrik, RY 2519

ANDA shifted on his cot. He winced at the stab of pain in his back
and sighed, then stared at the blank walls and ceiling. The
time since his last beating blended into everpresent pain. The scabs
healed over. The tenderness and bruising remained.

Someone would pay for all this, for turning his life into a living hell.

At least better air circulated here than in his cell on the moon.
The food was better here, but he didn't know if that was the pain
playing tricks on his ability to taste. They spoke to him differently
here, when they spoke to him at all. More like a faithful pet and less
like a future meal. Esh'a even spoke to him with less pity, although
she had always treated him better than his other tormentors.

He rubbed the sleep from his eyes and groaned over what the
day held in store. The rusty metal springs of the cot groaned when
he rolled off. He shuffled to the wash basin in the pale dawn light
that filtered through the high window, illuminating slate gray walls.
He wondered what day it was.

He examined his reflection in the polished metal mirror. He
looked ten years older than he remembered, but they had a good
reason for keeping him alive. He just needed to figure out what that
was so he could finish the job and get on with his life.

Anda splashed water on his face from the metal basin and sucked in his breath. The bruises on his face were especially tender. Every day of pain and torment made it easier and easier to blame Ahrik for putting him here, or at least for letting him be put here. He had hid something from his own brother for their entire lives, and Ahrik was powerful enough that he could have stopped what happened to Anda.

But he couldn't do anything about Ahrik now. He shrugged and gestured a query at his reflection. "Will they tell you your mission today?"

The door to his room dissolved and he whirled. Eyes wary, he wrinkled his nose as fresh air rushed in. He must smell bad.

Esh'a stood in the doorway, dressed in the gray garb that matched the inscrutable flint of her eyes. Her hair was pulled back in her long, black braid. A hulking mass of a human flanked her, one of the ah'sbi thugs who beat him without mercy.

His mouth went dry at the sight of him, and his eyes darted to Esh'a, looking for any signal for what would happen next. The uncertainty almost made him want to pray to the Lady of the Emerald Moon. Almost.

"Anda," said Esh'a. "Come." She rarely spoke to him in this commanding tone unless others were present.

Something was up.

They set off down the hall. Biting back the pain, Anda stumbled along to stay beside Esh'a and as far from Hulk as possible. Hulk grumbled at him to pick up the pace.

Anda ventured a question, half-expecting to get shoved into the wall for speaking. "Where are we, Esh'a?"

Hulk growled at him, but Esh'a cut off Hulk with a look. "The Eshel."

With an uneasy glance at Hulk, and a little extra effort to widen the distance between them, Anda asked, "*When* are we?"

Esh'a smiled. "Today is the last day of recorded year 2499. Your son will be one year old in three months."

Hulk guffawed. Anda knew better than to deny the rape. His bruises were too tender to forget what would happen.

Maybe today was the day he would start to get revenge. Anda knew that striking out in revenge wouldn't really change his lot, but it would give him the satisfaction of sharing his pain with someone else. Ahrik's callousness put Anda here, made pain his companion, so he was as good a target for revenge as any.

They brought Anda to a room filled with dusty communications equipment. Hulk melted into some dark corner, and someone else materialized, the one who'd been with Anda in the Mekele temple before the confrontation with Zharla, the one who'd called Anda "friend."

An ethereal beeping chirped from one of the communication terminals. Esh'a motioned with her eyes for Friend to sit down at the controls.

"Why is *he* here?" asked Friend, sliding his hands into the control slots.

Anda scratched his head and asked himself the same question.

"Boss wants him here," said Esh'a. Her braid swished when she turned to face Friend.

Ahrik wants me here. When Anda was still Shahl, Ahrik treated him with persistent disdain. He crushed Shahl's spirit at every opportunity. Shahl fled to Mekele, where the ah'sbe trapped him and made him into Anda, a pawn in someone else's game, a slave of the day to day.

Anda needed revenge. Revenge for what they did to him, but especially revenge for what they did to Zharla. No woman deserved that, much less Zharla, a woman of such supreme dignity and grace. Death would be too lenient a recompense for the hell and torment they had made Zharla suffer. His tormentors wanted Anda to feel sorry for himself, to focus on his own tragedy, but the true victim was Zharla.

The communications equipment near Friend buzzed on. The large, wall-mounted compiler display bloomed to life. It showed a map of a space station out in the Nejru Gulch, the gravitational inflection point near the Emerald Moon.

Esh'a turned to Anda with her inscrutable smile. "For the first phase of your mission, you will witness the downfall of the vaunted, invincible Ketel of Ahrik."

Anda returned the smile with a guilty twinge of pleasure.

Ahrik froze. He dropped his razor in the basin and reached for the towel. The alarm rang in his gut even before it penetrated his brain over the tendril network. He wiped the shaving foam from his face and threw the towel on the ground. Brain, his intelligence chief, cast to him from the command module of the space station, *Father, under attack. One team member coming to you with situation report.*

Ahrik had one leg shoved into his combat suit when Ayen poked his head into the cabin. "Father—"

"Suit up, Ayen. Brain's man is coming." Ahrik slipped his arms into his suit and pressed the organic adherence seams with a soft *slurp*. This was supposed to be a bridging deployment, a one-month stint to fill the gap until the next ketel arrived for its regular, six-month tour. Ahrik volunteered since he didn't have anyone back home to spend the new year with, and because the Nejru Gulch was too important to be left unguarded, an ideal place to monitor mineral and trade flows from the Emerald Moon to Dom.

But the rebels hadn't operated here since the war began. This was supposed to be easy, so he deployed half his ketel and left the rest at home to meet the new year in comfort. No reason to displace eight thousand men when he only needed four.

Now he wished he'd brought them all.

Ahrik slapped Biriq onto his thigh and grabbed his distiller pack. He leaped from his cabin. In the anteroom, Ayen adjusted his own suit and reached for his distiller and qasfin. Ahrik pulled the straps of his distiller pack on then set his pack to charge. Ahrik and Ayen looked each other up and down in a precombat check. Distiller. Qasfin. Sealant. Medpack. Utility knife. Combat helmet. Backup life support system. "First," said Ayen.

"To the fight," answered Ahrik. Never did the phrase have such a rueful meaning. Many men would die today. Ahrik cursed himself for not bringing the full ketel.

In the corridor, a keteli from his intelligence team hurried toward him with a handheld. He had no name tape. He hadn't earned a name. A holograph swirled to life in the kall field to represent the Emerald Moon and the debris field in its orbital plane, along with the Nejru Gulch. As the keteli neared, the ketel's three positions came into focus: the space station, the substation, and the moon base.

Ahrik strode toward the command module, the keteli and Ayen on his heels. His combat helmet clanked against the back of his thigh. "Report, keteli."

"Father, forty seconds ago we observed a massive electromag disturbance in the moon's orbital plane." The keteli hurried to keep up with Ahrik. "Reconnaissance from interceptors out in the debris field shows over one hundred squad-level transporters approaching this station at attack velocity." At this, the holograph transformed to show individual rebel ships, broken into three successive waves.

Ahrik calculated. That was almost three thousand berzerkers descending on his tiny little station. He stroked his chin. *Brain*, he cast, *sound the general alarm*.

"Escorts?" Ahrik asked.

"None, Father."

"Command ship?"

"Negative, Father."

The alarm blared. Ahrik narrowed his eyes, weighing variables. This was a frontal assault. Mass versus distiller power. He frowned at the intel keteli. "How'd we miss this?"

"Father," the keteli said, "the rebels slingshot around Dom, using the debris field as a blind."

Ahrik nodded. *Brain*, he cast, *something doesn't add up. Keep your sensors open for a follow-on force.*

Yes, Father.

They entered the command module, and his command squad stood at their terminals.

"As you were." The command module was a sphere, and his command squad's thirty terminals were arranged in concentric semicircles on one side of the bowl, facing huge compiler displays mounted on the opposite wall. The other two squads in his command company were split between the other command modules in the space station, controlling operations at the substation and the moon base, respectively. Members of the protection company manned the station defenses and guarded the command modules, so all told there were about fifty men in Ahrik's module, and only about two hundred and fifty in the whole station, with one hand each deployed at the substation and the moon base.

Ahrik turned to the intel keteli before standing at his command podium. "Good holograph. I'll call you Graph."

Graph nodded his thanks, then returned to his intel terminal, locking the handheld into its dock.

Ahrik found his two hand commanders over the tendril link. *Beral and Halel, prepare for battle.* Ahrik's 1st Hand, commanded by Beral, was stationed on the moon base, and his 2d Hand, commanded by Halel, was stationed in the substation halfway between Ahrik's station and the moon. In addition to his command and protection companies at the Nejru Gulch space station, Ahrik had only two flights of ten interceptors each. He'd soon find out if they could fight. Two hundred and fifty men against three thousand rebel berzerkers. Bad odds.

Ayen, he cast to his aide, *deploy reserve interceptors, and redeploy Flight Two from recon to engage the enemy.* Flight Two was reconnoitering over a thousand kilometers of space, so they might not even engage the first wave before it reached the space station. One reserve flight against thirty-odd armed transporters in the first wave. It was not a good day to be an interceptor pilot.

Ahrik found the two flight leaders over the tendril link. The extra cognition necessary to reach so far down the chain taxed Ahrik. *Flight leaders*, he cast, *one here.*

Yes, Father.

You have your orders. We're counting on you. Stay out of our five kilometer kill zone. We don't want friendly casualties. Ahrik sucked in his breath. *First.*

To the fight.

Ahrik rubbed his forehead. He didn't even know their names. First to die.

Death. An unexpected sense of guilt swept over Ahrik. He had not been gone from the Eshel two weeks. He'd been married less than two years, and he could count the conversations he'd had with his wife on one hand. If he got out of this, he would change that.

He nodded to Brain. "Report."

"Father, one hundred and eighteen squad-size vessels on approach, in three waves. First wave will arrive in eleven minutes."

"Father," said a keteli from operations, "all teams are at battle stations. Flight One reserve has launched."

Ahrik considered the station defenses. This was a Zharek-class station, with eight spherical modules, three for command and five for living quarters, connected by passageways. "Engineer, engage the mag-fields to channel the enemy away from the command modules."

"Check, Father," said an engineer.

"Give me visual," Ahrik ordered. A moment later, the compiler displays sprang to life on the opposite side of the command module, illuminated with the position of the space station and the substation, as well as friendly and enemy craft. "Where are they going to hit us, Brain?"

"Father, if that first wave keeps its speed up, it might overshoot us and go straight for the substation or the moon base."

"Keep tracking it. No signs of a follow-on force?"

"None, Father."

"Father," a voice called, "the three waves are six, twelve, and fifteen minutes out, at current speeds. Flight One is nearly in range."

"The enemy will have to decelerate to engage our station, Father," said Graph.

Ahrik nodded his agreement and drew in a calming breath, then gathered his mind to cast out to his sons over the tendril network. *Sons, this is the time that we have prepared for all our lives. The enemy thinks he has surprised us, but he will feel our sting.*

A silent cheer rose over the intimate connection of the ketel. Ahrik could almost see the confidence descend over his module, the moment of calm before the ocean wave shatters itself against jagged rocks of fury.

Beads of red light began to blossom among the enemy as the reserve interceptors engaged the first wave. Ahrik pursed his lips with satisfaction. Two beads of blue light blossomed as two interceptors were lost.

"Twenty seconds until first wave is in range of station defenses, Father."

"Keep the interceptors out of our kill zone," ordered Ahrik. "I don't want to lose any more interceptors than I have to."

"Father, one hundred and two enemy transporters left. Twenty-one in the first wave."

"Communicate that to Halel and Beral. Our interceptors are doing their job." Two more beads of blue light flashed on the display. Only sixteen interceptors left.

"Father, the first wave has... accelerated," said Brain. "They're going to bypass us." The space station's point defenses opened up. The muffled *thu-thu-thunk* and *tha-wunk* of distiller weapons echoed their grim work of death throughout the station. The *zip* and *zing* of the attackers' answering projectiles punctuated the air. Kall fields sucked and slurped to restore atmospheric integrity after the hull punctures. Here and there Ahrik heard cries of pain, and felt them over the tendril link, but his sons manned their stations and gave as good as they got.

Ahrik swung his gaze to the main compiler display. The first wave of attackers passed by, through the silent and unforgiving vacuum of space. Half the enemy craft in the first wave were either gone or drifting, the vector of some taking them to a certain yet agonizing death in the nether reaches of space.

"Report," said Ahrik.

"Fifteen interceptors left in two flights, Father," said Graph. "Fifteen of forty-two vessels in first enemy wave got past. Second wave is decelerating, and all interceptors have engaged."

"Father," said Brain, "the second and third waves are not decelerating fast enough to engage us, and the trajectory of the first wave will take it past the substation."

"To the moon base?" asked Ahrik.

Brain shrugged. "The moon base's defenses will vaporize the rest of the first wave."

A bolt of fear crossed Ahrik's face. He did not know what the enemy had in mind. This might be the uncertainty of combat, or it might turn out much worse than Ahrik expected.

"Father," called someone, "the moon base reports a ground attack on widening flanks, similar to what we saw at the transit station in the Kereu."

This was a double envelopment, not a frontal assault. The enemy target was the moon base. Premonitions of anxiety crept through the seams of adrenaline in Ahrik's consciousness. He was suddenly unsure of his own confidence. He tried to lick some moisture into his mouth. "Tell me when the ground assault is contained."

"Father, our flight leaders report nine out of twenty interceptors lost. Interceptors disengaging from second wave now. Halel's substation has deployed four flights to engage the first wave as they pass."

Halel, Ahrik cast, *your interceptors need to prevent that first wave from getting to the moon base.*

Check, Father, cast Halel from the substation.

The space station's point defense systems opened up on the second wave, with even more vigor than on the first, an eerie juxtaposition to Ahrik's internal disquiet.

"Father," said Graph, gulping.

He must feel it too.

"Father," Graph repeated. "Two transporters from the first wave have accelerated. The substation interceptors won't catch them before they get to the moon base."

"Show me," said Ahrik. "Warn Beral about them, and order Halel to focus his interceptors on the enemy transporters that they can reach." On the command module's display, two tiny points of red light broke away from the first wave, at what Ahrik estimated was only five hundred kilometers from his station. The three dozen or so blue interceptors from the substation engaged the remainder of the first wave.

"Father, we're down to five interceptors defending our station. Forty-two enemy transporters remain in the last two waves."

Ahrik glanced at his station on the display. "Order interceptors to focus on the third wave." He closed his eyes and pursed his lips. His pilots weren't going to make it.

Down past the substation, two red lights blazed toward the surface of the moon at a fearsome speed.

"Father," said Brain. "Those two interceptors from the first wave have used the last of their fuel. They can't decelerate."

Blue interceptors swarmed over and through the red transporters that remained behind from the first wave. A deep disquiet insinuated itself into Ahrik's core, then a brilliant flash of white erupted from one of the red points at the center of the melee, consuming everything that had been there just a nanosecond before. On the display the blast looked small, but Ahrik knew it was massive.

The battle was lost. They had just witnessed weapons not used for an age.

"Dear, sweet Lady," muttered Ahrik, staring in disbelief. "Atomics." Shaking himself from his stupor of astonishment, he gathered his wits about him and screamed, "Mag fields! Get the mag fields up!"

Ahrik threw himself to the floor, and the whole station rocked back and forth, bobbing through the shockwave. Ahrik wanted to be sick, not for the motion, but for the good men that he knew were about to die in a fight turned sour. More than a thousand berzerkers were bearing down on their little space station, and Ahrik guessed that the substation had sustained heavy damage. If the rebels used atomics on the moon base, too, then Ahrik would lose two hands in one day.

It was a bad day to be in the Ketel of Ahrik.

A bad day for a new year.

Ahrik jerked himself up. His sons counted on him to lead. He planted his feet on the still-swaying floor. "Report," he ordered. If this was his day to die, so be it, but he would die fighting.

"Father," answered Brain, "the shockwave decelerated the second and third waves. They will engage our station, after all."

Ahrik sensed the fear in Brain's voice. This would be his first close combat.

"Father," said Graph, "the blast knocked out our peripheral sensors. We're blind to anything beyond our station."

Ahrik tried casting a message to Beral and Halel over the tendril link. Nothing. The blast knocked out the tendril link, too. It would take a while to reestablish. He couldn't even sense the ketelis who were in the command station with him.

Happy new year.

"Sons," he said, "we're going to have to do this the old-fashioned way."

The clank of enemy craft latching onto the hull echoed throughout the station. Ahrik hoped the magnetic channeling had worked and the enemy would only breach at the passageways. Much better to pile up berzerkers at the entryways of the spherical modules than have them drop right on top of them.

Ahrik primed his distiller and muttered, "Come you demons of war, come be the first to die."

Anda leaned toward the compiler display. His anticipation built. "The empty circles on the map are ours, and the filled ones are Ahrik's?"

"That's right," replied Esh'a.

Anda cocked his head to one side. "Where is Ahrik?"

Esh'a pointed at the display. "See the moon base and the substation in low lunar orbit? A high level source tells us he's in one of those two places. Besides, most of his forces are there." She nodded with sagacity. "He's big on personal protection."

Anda rubbed his chin and scrunched up his mouth, unconvinced. He knew to expect the unexpected from his brother.

Friend leaned back and put a foot on the desk in front of him, unconcerned with protocol or decorum. "What about that smaller station, the one in higher orbit?"

"Not likely he's there," said Esh'a, "but we're making a diversionary attack there, just in case." She squirmed with excitement. "Keep an eye on the moon base and the low orbit station, because—"

A powerful blast burst onto the map near the low orbit station, engulfing the ships in the vicinity.

Anda sat up in his chair. Some of the empty circles slowed and converged on the smaller station, in higher orbit. Other circles continued to converge on the moon base and the station in low orbit. Deep unease settled at the pit of his stomach. He suppressed it. Ahrik deserved this.

Friend spoke the question that Anda dared not ask. "What was that?"

"Our secret weapon," Esh'a said. A smile broke out on her face. "We're going to win this war."

Friend chuckled. "Asking who won a war is like asking who won an earthquake."

Esh'a slapped his foot off the desk and glared. "Shall I teach you a lesson?"

Friend sank lower in his chair and focused his eyes on the communications terminal.

Esh'a turned to Anda. "You'll see, Anda, the Butcher will be dead soon, if he's not alrea—"

Another blast erupted at the moon base.

Anda leaned forward more. Something felt wrong about this new weapon. But Ahrik had it coming. "The Butcher?" He chuckled and shrugged at the display. "How does this relate to my mission?"

"Later," Esh'a said, too much haste in her voice, just like the time she cut off the conversation when Anda asked about the number of fighters the Emerald Moon could produce. She was trying to avoid something. Esh'a yawned. "If this works, you may not even need to infiltrate his ketel at all. The Boss will decide."

"Who's the Boss?"

Esh'a raised an appraising eyebrow. "You can meet him when you're ready."

Something about Esh'a's response told Anda that he might already know the Boss, but by a different name. Anda grunted at this newfound suspicion. If true, it would help explain all the training and the beating. Anda's capture and exile and torture and training and molding into a soldier was planned from the beginning. Maybe Ahrik didn't plan it this way exactly, but if Ahrik had trusted these thugs to dispose of Anda, and then they turned on him like this, then Anda saw the justice in all of it.

Anda would play soldier, if that's what it took to exact revenge on Ahrik.

"Graph," Ahrik said. The *clang-clang* of enemy transporters and the *thu-thu-thunk* of the station's distillers rang throughout the command module. "Throw me the electromag, and someone get the station address system online." The electromag was a backup comm system for when the tendril link failed. Usually, only the uncloned hayel forces used them, but now Ahrik had to reach years back in his memory to the obscure course on tactical electromag comms. "Right," he had said at the time, "like the tendril link will ever fail."

"Father," said an engineer, "the atomic blast fried the station address system, too."

Ahrik squeezed the electromag and it buzzed to life. At least the army got hardened backup comms right. "Sting," he said, hailing his protection company commander in another command module, "this is one."

A pregnant silence followed, filled with the sound of berzerkers banging and cutting through the hull. All the sound came from the passageways, none from the hull of the command module itself, so the channeling had worked. The odds weren't all against them.

The electromag crackled. "One, Sting here."

Ahrik sighed with relief, then checked Biriq on his thigh. "Secure the docking bay in your module, and tell your two in the last module to do the same in his. We'll need a way to leave this steel death trap if it can't be held."

"We'll hold, Father."

How many men would have to die to make that true? "Station a team there anyway, and keep the docking bay intact." Ahrik looked at Ayen, who took three members of the command squad with him to defend their own docking bay. "And be ready to go vacuum if they get inside blade range, Sting. First."

"To the fight."

Ahrik flexed his left hand inside the distiller grip and stole a questioning glance at the engineer, who nodded in return. Good, they had control over life support and grav.

Ahrik sealed his helmet and face guard onto his combat suit, then waited while his internal compiler synched with his suit and weapon systems. The rest of his sons in the command module finished suiting up. All systems were a go.

Ahrik turned on his suit's general electromag channel. "Trust your training. Let's send this sludge back where it came from." The suit link used a low-power electromag signal, so only the men in his module could hear him.

He hoped they didn't hear the fear in his voice. No help was coming. This was war the old way, a bloodthirsty contest of wills.

Ahrik took his position near the command podium. He glanced down at the self-destruct control, which would train the station's own distillers on itself if he scanned his retina into it. Better to disintegrate the station than let the berzerkers get it intact. He flipped the switch to arm it, just in case. He peered into the faces of his men, who were waiting for berzerkers to pour into the command module from the hallways at either end.

Ahrik waved at the engineer. "Cut grav and life support on my mark." He scanned the module and clicked on his local electromag. "Engage your suit's local systems if we lose life support, and prepare for a quiet fight." He considered this a moment, then added, "Set distillers on the lowest lethal power. I'd like to save as much of this station as we can."

The muffled screams and sickening thump of men in visceral hand-to-hand combat reverberated from somewhere else in the station. Ahrik tried to sense the fight through the tendril link. Still nothing. He sneered. "Come, rebel slime."

Graph took cover behind a compiler display. He nodded at Ahrik. Ready.

The anticipation of combat pumped through Ahrik's veins. He might never get to feel like this again. He might never feel *anything* again. He wanted to remember what life was like, to feel the solid comfort of the Eshel under his feet once again.

To do right by Zharla.

Loud thuds echoed from the two hallways leading into the command module. Two more rebel transporters had attached to the station.

Sparks sprayed from the hallways. The dull clank of hull pieces hitting the deck echoed from both directions, but where Ahrik expected the enemy to come pouring out, he saw only smoke. The enemy did not charge or leap through the smoke. They staggered, as if they had not yet made the transition back to grav. As if they hadn't recovered from a night of drug-crazed partying. They were dressed in nothing but life-support masks and loin cloths, with small air tanks strapped to their backs. Their eyes darted with bloodshot fury, and their slate gray weapons blazed with wild death.

Ahrik clicked on his electromag. "Cut main lights. Engage."

The main lights went off and the dim emergency lights flickered on. The *thu-thu-thunk* of distillers erupted, cutting through the enemy like scythes. The rebels were also slathered with phosphorescent paint, making them easy targets. Ahrik thanked the Lady for a bit of luck on a day filled with death.

The enemy's weapons spouted fire in return. The *ping-ping-ping* of their metal projectiles ricocheted off the bulkheads and rang out through the command module.

"Engineer," yelled Ahrik into the electromag, "switch the polarity of the hull's interior mag field."

The ricocheting died off as the hull absorbed the enemy projectiles, but he still saw a number of his men hit at odd angles, blood seeping from wounds, the result of low-velocity ricochets.

His sons, crouched as they were behind their hasty barricades of chairs, tables, and compiler gear, got the better of the utterly exposed enemy. The enemy mostly crumpled as they reached the choke points from the passageways. Ahrik didn't want to disengage the gravity and give the enemy cover behind floating comrades. But then Ahrik noticed that the enemy wounded kept coming, dragging or pushing themselves across the floor on whatever able extremities remained to them. Some of his men drew their qasfina and finished off the ones who got closest. Possessed of some hellish drive, the only thing that stopped the berzerkers was a blade through a temple or the carotid artery. The floor of the command module became slick with the mingled blood of his sons and the enemy, cenobites of unholy terror.

Ahrik knew then that this was a fight to the death. One berzerker came close to Ahrik's sector, and the other two ketelis there had not yet noticed him, so Ahrik flipped Biriq and drove the killing point down into the man's temple, smashing his mask. As the berzerker stared up in his death throes, Ahrik saw an enemy with an unnatural grip on life, an inhuman desire to kill or be killed.

Ahrik surveyed the room. Phosphorescent bodies surrounded them on three sides, and still they poured in from the hallways. A keteli on Ahrik's right paused to adjust his distiller pack, and he caught an enemy projectile in the face. His facemask turned red. His body went limp. Ahrik had only fifty in the command module to begin with, and now at least fifteen of his sons lay on the deck, motionless.

Then the tendril link came back online, jolting Ahrik's mind into awareness of the battle. In the two other command modules, the fray was perilous. Sting's module had fallen. Ahrik's sons in that module ebbed out of his mind. In the last module, the situation was almost as dire. The station swarmed with berzerker phosphorescence.

Kill or die. Ahrik chose kill.

Engineer, he cast, *cut grav...*

He hesitated, but he needed an advantage.

...and cut the life support system. The tendril link was still weak, but Ahrik felt the impression of assent.

Sons, prepare your wounded comrades, so they don't freeze. Another mental murmur of assent.

Ahrik hooked his boots under the lip of the command podium. A great whoosh rushed through the station, and the fight raged on in utter silence. As soon as the air rushed into its holding tanks, the temperature dropped. The enemy still staggered into the command module, and his men still poured distiller charges into them. Fire still leaped from the enemy's weapons, from those enemies still physically able to use their weapons. Occasionally one of his sons would get hit, and Ahrik sensed a few of his wounded sons freezing, their vacuum insulated suits punctured, ineffective against the cold. *Sons, seal your comrades' suits,* he cast.

The berzerkers slowed. The complete silence contrasted with the pell-mell from moments before.

Ahrik's stomach fluttered when gravity left the room. The bodies of dead and wounded berzerkers floated from the ground, trailing rivulets of blood. His own casualties, strapped down with adhesive tape, stayed where they were. Those still able to use their distillers joined in one final, collective burst as tactical squads communicated over their own tendril links. Then the distillers stopped, keteli blades came out, and those able to do so pushed off from their positions to finish off the enemy.

The fight took on a surreal quality. In the sickening phosphorescence, blades flashed through freezing bodies, sent into sudden shock by the plummeting temperature. Congealed, then frozen, dots of blood floated up the room, like some grim, hallucinogenic snowfall.

Red pellets pinged off Ahrik's mask. The rebel weapons stilled in his mind. *Engineer*, he cast, *reengage grav.*

His sons sprang to the deck. Most brought out their distillers and began the torturous process of clearing the station, compartment by compartment. The rest inspected enemy casualties. Healers began working on Ahrik's sons, after which they moved to the very few enemy who were worth claiming as prisoners, clinging to what life remained in them from loss of blood or exposure.

Ahrik got the all-clear from his tactical team leaders—all enemy killed, wounded, or subdued. *Reengage life support,* he cast. He wondered how many of his sons he just froze to death.

He removed his combat helmet and mask and gulped in the thin air. Face grim, he surveyed the wreckage and death around him. He saw the compiler display Graph had concealed behind. A shattered handheld lay next to it. Ahrik fell to his knees next to the crumpled form on the ground. No name tape. The face mask was stained red, with one perfect, round hole in the center. Ahrik slumped against the hull of the module. He had such awesome power at his beck and call, but he couldn't keep his sons alive.

Ahrik grimaced and looked around for his intel chief. "Brain, report." Ahrik's voice bore the timber of failure. He had to know the status of the moon base, too, and of Halel and Beral. He pushed himself up to a standing position against the hull and hitched his combat helmet and distiller onto the latches at his hips.

Brain stood with a somber stance. "Our station is secure, Father. Two interceptors returning to Docking Bay Three for repairs."

So few pilots returned. Ahrik nodded to Ayen as he returned from the docking bay, then peered at Brain. "What about the substation and moon base?"

Brain's face fell. "We're still blind, Father."

Ahrik slammed a fist against the hull. He had to know. "Ayen. Brain. On me. To the substation."

Ahrik strode to the docking bay. Outside his shuttle, a guard saluted him, hand over heart. He still wore his combat suit, smeared with blood, eyes weary.

Ahrik paused before entering the shuttle. "Any of that yours, keteli?"

"No, Father." He smiled, perhaps only for Ahrik's benefit. "One'f m'squad mates died tuday. One-five-tuh-three. Filch. Best furager in th'hand, Father."

Ahrik tried to put conviction in his voice. "Filch will live on in the glory of the Eshel."

The keteli's eyes moistened. "Check, Father."

Ahrik palmed open the shuttle door. The movement felt empty, and cold regret clutched at his heart.

Ahrik frowned at the instrument display in front of Bat, his pilot. They approached the substation. A warning played in Ahrik's mind. "Transluce the hull."

The substation came into view, barely more than a pinprick of light. Something wasn't right.

Father, Halel cast to him. The tendril link wavered. *Turn... back. Radiation... extreme.*

"Bat," Ahrik ordered the pilot, "hold our approach."

Bat sighed with relief. He had pronounced ears that could sense sound and radiological pulses that others could not.

"Five thousand meters out, Father. Approach halted."

Ayen and Brain looked at Ahrik. Their faces registered concern.

"Radiation levels too high," Ahrik answered. *Halel,* he cast, *status report.*

All secure... Medical center overloaded... Lost all but five pilots... My hand... half-strength... survivors... radiation sickness. No contact... 1st Hand... moon.

"Father?" asked Bat. "I track two craft leaving the moon's atmosphere. Electromag signatures are similar to ones we tracked gravside for six months, during the last deployment."

Ahrik needed answers. He only had seven interceptor pilots left, and probably fewer interceptors. "Are we still cloaked, Bat?"

"Yes, Father."

"Follow, but be discreet." *Halel, use the medical facilities at Command Station. Continue hailing Beral on the moon.*

Check... Father.

The hull opaqued once more. Ahrik slipped his helmet onto his head and sealed his facemask.

Ayen leaned in. "Father, with all due respect, let's mark the location and have a team come back and monitor for the next rebel ships that leave on this trajectory."

Brain put on his helmet and gave Ayen an are-you-really-contradicting-Father look.

Ayen's shoulders slumped as he reached for his own gear. "It's just... your person is too valuable to the ketel..."

As Ayen trailed off, Ahrik considered him. He was only trying to do his duty. Ahrik's eyes fell. "Too many men died for me today."

Ahrik examined the schematic on his compiler display. They gained on the two rebel craft. Their trajectory took them into the oppressive nowhere of space. The stars shone less densely in this direction. The rebel craft slowed almost to a stop.

Bat rubbed his chin. "What are they looking for?"

"What is out here?" Ahrik asked. "Go visual, Bat." The hull of their craft shimmered to translucence, and Ahrik saw the two craft, not two kilometers away, yawing back and forth.

"Father," said Bat. He shrugged at the compiler display. "We've left the orbital plane of the earth and moon, only three degrees off the z-axis. Father, if there's a 'down' in space, we've found it. There's nothing here."

Ahrik furrowed his brow. He had to decide how far to follow. Ahrik doubted the rebels would set up another ambush after the attack they just launched, but he couldn't be sure.

"They're moving, Father," said Bat. He sucked in his breath. "Ohwouldyoulookatthat."

Away from moon and planet, and further "down" from where they and the rebel craft floated, a ripple shuddered in space. Stars drifted, as if the universe had reached out and dabbed its finger into the pool of space-time and then sat back to enjoy the mind-bending show.

The rebel crafts' engines burst on and then glowed blue as they accelerated toward the ripple.

"Father?"

"Release a buoy, then follow." Ahrik was risking his life, but that paled in comparison to the thousand men he lost today. He had to get to the bottom of this war, for their sakes. A sinking fear in his gut told him that the answer had just slipped through the space rippling in front of them.

Ahrik's shuttle plunged in. When they came out, so quickly that Ahrik could not tell exactly what it was they had come out of, they were in a different. . . somewhere. The sun—*a* sun—was off to port and forward, in the opposite position from where they'd just left it, and a planet lay dead ahead, instead of astern. Ahrik's stomach tightened at the vertigo. The sun burned a more brilliant yellow than the orange of their own sun, and the deep blue planet was swathed in white clouds. So much life. "Bat, any signs of an ambush?"

"Just those two craft, Father. They're proceeding like we're not even here."

The rebel craft shot toward the planet.

"Sweet Lady," said Brain. "What is this place?"

Ahrik recovered his breath, then remembered his talks with Alrem. It was true, after all. He gave a grim nod in the direction they faced. "That, my sons, is the White Planet."

> Why did they kill so many? Why did they use atomics? It did not need to be this way. They may kill me because I wrote this. I don't care.
>
> Leren, 3d Hand Commander, Ketel of Ahrik, journal entry, 1 Kenen Sheni (New Year) RY 2500

14 | Bitter Homecoming

Your husband, Shadhir Ahrik Jeber-li, has returned
from deployment. He is now in the Military Healing
Center in Meran.

Message from the Army of the Eshel to Zharla Tamer-li,
4 Kenen Sheni RY 2500

ZHARLA meandered toward the healing center. She attempted in
vain to wrangle Nayr's boundless energy into focus. Earlier that
day, on this most inauspicious of anniversaries, she had entered the
parlor to find Renla a nervous wreck. "I can't handle him anymore,"
her friend had pleaded.

So, Zharla dressed Nayr and coaxed him toward the bay. Her
precocious little boy skipped and ran and explored like a child two
years his senior, with a mischievous curiosity to match. She urged
Nayr along the cobbled streets of out-mountain Meran even as he left
no errant stone or lesser life form unexamined. At the park facing
the army headquarters, he held up a scorpion and asked if he could
eat it, before Zharla slapped it from his hand and scooped him into
her arms, at her wits' end.

She paused to take a breath after they crossed the park to the
healing center. She squeezed Nayr just a bit closer. *I never thought my
own husband would be in here.*

Ahrik was supposed to be gone for another a month, but he was
home two weeks early. And wounded, by implication of the message
she received that morning. How? His message before shipping out

was short: "Hello, all's well. Sent off to defend something near the Emerald Moon."

She had even sent a message back: "Stay safe." And she had meant it.

How does my life take such turns?

In the weeks before he left, her perception of Ahrik had shifted from disdain to tolerance, even something like progress and communication, and now this. If he died, she dared not think what effect it would have on her life. She used to think such a thing would be of no import, but now she doubted if she could build a future for the Eshel without Ahrik as an ally.

She had no answer for the questions swirling in her mind. Just more questions. Nayr defied her expectations, Ahrik remained an enigma, and society crumbled around them, it seemed. Even the rape still haunted her consciousness, leaving a trail of questions of its own.

She hefted Nayr to her hip and puffed up the stairs. Surely even her worst enemies could not have imagined such twists for her life.

A neatly dressed minder led her through the labyrinthine corridors of the healing center. Nayr skipped half the way and sang nursery rhymes the other half. When at last they arrived at Ahrik's room, she glanced at the minder. "I can find my way back, thanks."

She stepped just inside the room with Nayr and resolved the door behind them. "Ahrik?"

His head lolled upward and he narrowed his eyes.

She pushed confusion aside and approached. "It must be worse than I imagined." She scanned his body. "I don't see a mark on you."

Something like recognition slipped into his eyes. "Ah, my wife. Good."

He closed his eyes as if he were going to sleep.

"That's it? No explanation? No expressions of everlasting love? Not even a 'Happy New Year'?"

He strained himself into a sitting position. She reached out to help, but he shook her off with a toss of his head. "If you must know, you're one of the few people on this forsaken rock that I trust now, at least outside my ketel. Forgive me... I don't make any sense." He squeezed his knuckles into his scalp. "I'm... not quite myself."

"So mysterious." She straightened the cushions on his cot and cast him a quizzical look. "Why are you here?"

"I... My brain is scrambled. I"—he stared at Nayr, then nodded in the boy's direction—"who's that?"

"Ahrik, this is our... my... forget it."

Ahrik slumped farther into the cot. "I think... I've got something to tell you." He scratched his head. "Can't piece it together right now." He struggled back into a prone position and rubbed his temples, then looked over at Zharla, expectant. "You and the boy can go now."

Zharla crossed her arms. "Do you know what day it is?"

He stared into the middle distance. "I don't know what year it is."

"It's our betrothal anniversary. Eighteen years."

He gave her a blank stare. "I'm sorry you have to celebrate it like this."

She turned with a frustrated grunt and stalked out, Nayr in tow. "Celebrate" wasn't the word she'd use.

Ahrik remembered sitting, at some point long ago. In a closer present, three other individuals were in the room with him. His surroundings clouded around him. How long had he been here? Where was he before? In space? Oh yes, a battle. But there was something after that. Something... odd.

His wife. She needed to know something. He fought to think what it was, but failed.

One of the blurry individuals in the room approached. None of the details resolved themselves. A sharp pain lanced up his arm, and the person slunk away. Ahrik's heart nearly beat out of his chest, and his mind whipped to awareness. All of it came into crystal relief: the room, the three people in it, the Battle of Nejru Gulch, the White Planet.

The White Planet. He had to tell Zharla. He had even more questions now, about what he saw there. She could help. Like Alrem said, the Ahit needed someone like her on the outside.

Sheresh sat on a stool in the corner of the room. The room was well lit, but Sheresh leaned forward and cowered a bit, as if someone might catch him in some indiscretion. The other two individuals in the room were ketelis, a healer and a recorder, by the markings on their uniforms. They were from Sheresh's original ketel, if the physical resemblance could be believed, although the two ketelis looked fitter and less presumptuous than their father.

Sheresh grunted in the ketelis' direction. "Has it been long enough? Welcome back, Ahrik. I trust you rested well."

"Yes, sir." How long had he been out? Where was his ketel? Ahrik centered his breathing to connect over the tendril link but got nothing. What was wrong with the tendril link?

The keteli recorder stared at Ahrik with a frightening intensity. He hung on Ahrik's every word and action, storing data in the internal compiler at the base of his neck. He too controlled his breathing, for maximum data processing. Ahrik would have to be careful what he revealed through nonverbal cues.

Sheresh slapped his knee and let out an exasperated breath, like someone burdened with a task far beneath his station. "I want to help you make sense of what happened," he said. "We had to induce forgetfulness for a day, until everything was set up for this session. Your wife may have wondered what was going on." Sheresh nodded with false confidence. "You'll explain it to her."

Yes, Ahrik had a lot to explain to her, but as little as possible to tell his supervisor. "Thank you, sir." Ahrik thought a moment before asking his next question, a question to cover the nervousness that surrounded the lies that were coming. "Have my sons been debriefed?"

"Brain and Bat, as you call them, and your aide Ayen?" Sheresh smirked. "Yes, they have." He stood and took a step to the side, like a cat circling a challenger. "Tell us what happened after the battle ended. We have data and recordings for everything up to then." Sheresh bared a smile. "But not after."

Ahrik's mouth went dry. Did something happen to his sons after he left his command station over the Nejru Gulch? "Sir, if there is blame for what happened, I bear it, not my sons."

Sheresh clicked his tongue with indifference and dragged his stool closer. The scrape of metal on stone grated against Ahrik's nerves.

Sheresh narrowed his eyes, as if deciding whether he could trust Ahrik's next words. "Go on."

Ahrik didn't like where this was going. "Sir, we encountered two enemy craft, traveling on a perpendicular trajectory from the lunar–planetary orbital plane at high speed. We gave pursuit while cloaked, then arrived at some sort of portal or gate in the fabric of space. The enemy craft passed through, and so did we."

"You abandoned your ketel?" Sheresh scraped his stool closer.

"Sir, the implications of a dimensional gate, or whatever it was, under rebel control were huge. What we found may win us the war."

Scrape. Sheresh raised his eyebrows, with a mix of curiosity and amusement. "Oh?"

Not the reaction Ahrik had hoped for. Could Sheresh actually strike him with that stool? Ahrik scrambled through his mind to find the right details. His mind couldn't parse fast enough to maintain the appearance of normality. "Sir, we came to what we called the White Planet. We pursued the enemy craft to a continental land mass with a size and climate similar to the Kereu. We maintained our cloak the whole time, and if the rebel craft detected our suppressed electromagnetic signature, they did not react. Sir, the atmospheric entry was rough on my shuttle, so when we landed we had to make spot repairs."

"How long were you on the ground?"

"Twenty-two hours and thirteen minutes, sir."

Sheresh stretched his shoulders. He padded danger close, as if testing his prey. "What did you do during that time?"

"I left Bat to conduct repairs, sir, and took Ayen and Brain to conduct reconnaissance on rebel activities. We had to know what they were doing there, on the White Planet." Ahrik paused. He gulped, wondering if Sheresh could smell his lie. "The rebels picked up weapons and supplies, interacted with the inhabitants of the planet, then left."

Not an outright lie, but the only truth Ahrik wanted Sheresh to know. Something deep and dangerous lit within Sheresh. Some wicked deception lay behind his supervisor's eyes, an evil absent a few months ago, during the interdiction deployment. No longer the craftiness of an ambitious military officer, but the deceptiveness of someone who's compromised his values to get where he is.

Ahrik hoped that Zharla would understand this turn. She might even know what happened to Sheresh to make him like this.

"Is that all that happened on the... ah... White Planet?" Sheresh yawned and scraped the stool still closer. He stopped about three meters away.

Ahrik did not want him so close. He eyed Sheresh's every move, fought to control his breathing and facial expressions. "Sir, we encountered about thirty men on the last day, armed with the kinetic explosive weapons that the rebels use. We withdrew, since our focus was intelligence collection. We didn't engage them with distillers, since we didn't know what the effect of introducing new technology would be. We didn't know how many more of them there were, or what sort of control they exerted on—"

Sheresh kicked the stool and sent it skittering over the chiseled stone floor. He fixed Ahrik with a glare. "Tell me about the locals."

Ahrik cleared his throat and sighed to hide his unease at his supervisor's ire. His supervisor's deceit lurked and haunted, prowling like a wraith. Still, Ahrik had passed his own lie, about what they'd really done on the White Planet.

But Ahrik needed Zharla. Sheresh's behavior showed that everything Ahrik had believed since his first youthful breath was a lie. War bore no glory, only pain and death. Those who instilled that delusion in him since his youth, like Sheresh, had succumbed to it themselves. Why else did Sheresh send Ahrik to fail on his first campaign in the Kereu? Why else would Sheresh prevent Ahrik from interdicting over the Eshel, where he found rebel weapons in a Tameri vessel? Why else would the quietest place in the war, the Nejru Gulch, suddenly flare up when his ketel arrived for a simple gap deployment?

And now this latest piece of evidence: Sheresh sedated and interrogated Ahrik when he found the White Planet, the key to winning the war. Sheresh didn't want to end the war. He wanted it to go on and on and on.

Something was rotten, far above Ahrik's or even Sheresh's level. Ahrik used to think that war was simple, that political leaders gave the military an objective, and the military achieved it. No more. War was an inherently political affair, and the messiest, basest interests in the Eshel competed for the brittle and honorless ephemera of power.

Merchants. Military supervisors. The Elders. The officers who trained him for all those years to be a part of society but separate from it. Even the rebels. Ahrik could name no one with clean hands in this war, including himself.

Only Zharla knew this world well enough to cut through his confusion.

Ahrik met Sheresh's irked stare with a summer's calmness, devoid of guilt. Ahrik's own lie was nothing compared to the monstrous lies that Sheresh spewed.

Sheresh began to pace. Ahrik saw Sheresh clearly now. What Ahrik mistook for confidence for so many years was actually a false pride, a dishonor and disrespect that Sheresh bore for the many lives that Ahrik's sons had sacrificed with real intent, to defend the Eshel.

He reached for Biriq. His sheath was empty. No matter. Ahrik drew power from the rightness of his cause. Even if everyone around him, including his own supervisor, fought for themselves, he could fight for something that mattered. He would fight for the Eshel.

And he hoped Zharla would, too

"Sir," said Ahrik, following his supervisor with wary eyes, "we saw only a tiny sample of the White Planet's population. They were humanoid, their skin a bit richer in hue than ours, and a little taller on average, since their gravity is about ninety percent of ours. The social organization seemed primitive, but on our gradual exit from the atmosphere, we noticed a number of cities with very dense energy usage. We did not land in one of those areas, and it's unclear how these areas relate to one another. Is there one unified sociopolitical structure, like Dom, or is it more fractured?"

Sheresh paused his pacing for a moment, perhaps considering his next question. He scratched his cheek and eyed Ahrik, weighing his trustworthiness. "The enemy deployed atomics against you at the Nejru Gulch. How will you respond?"

The sudden change in topic caught Ahrik by surprise, but his reply was automatic. "Sir, there is nothing more powerful than the ket—"

Sheresh emitted a sinister laugh. "No, Ahrik. We will deploy new weapons."

Ahrik frowned. An empty growl rumbled in his throat. A sinister air paced, along with his supervisor. "New weapons, sir?"

Sheresh's smile darkened. "My men briefed your weapon specialists." He drew in a haughty breath and resumed pacing. "We have harnessed the power of nature, Ahrik. The enemy may have atomics, and they may have those uncivilized explosive weapons, but we can now unleash earthquakes and storms and volcanoes and tidal waves." He glared into Ahrik's eyes, for obvious effect. "They are called atmospherics and tectonics, and they will turn the tide of this war."

Ahrik's sinking heart flooded his disquiet at this new deception. Destruction wouldn't work. He tried it in the Kereu, and the enemy tried it with atomics at the Nejru Gulch, but neither he nor they were defeated. No, the key to this war lay in discriminating between those who wielded violence against the Eshel and those who did not. No weapon, he now realized, could do that.

If the Army of the Eshel deployed these weapons against Kerewi population centers, there would be nothing left to govern. It would cause a return to The War, just with more destructive weapons. Ahrik tried to puzzle out whether they would even work on the moon. "Sir, we cannot deploy these weapons in the Kereu. They would not work. Do you propose we attack the Emerald Moon? That's where the rebel bases are. That's where the portal is. The moon is the key to reaching the White Planet."

Sheresh stopped his pacing and withered Ahrik with an imperious stare. He strode up and leaned down so his face was only a few centimeters from Ahrik's, then whispered, venom in his voice, "This war is not to be won on the Emerald Moon, boy. This war will be won in the Kereu." A sneer crossed the supervisor's face. "Go. Tend to your affairs."

Ahrik's core trembled, but with military poise he scooted his chair back, rose, saluted, and departed. As soon as he was out of sight of the healing center, he cloaked himself and broke into a full sprint. For home.

Zharla had Nayr walk to in-mountain Meran, so it took at least twice as long as if she'd simply carried him. He did not run out of energy. Nayr was different, so perceptive and full of life, that perhaps he could escape the vortex of violence and pride that seemed to envelope Ahrik. Even if Ahrik wanted to be good, she was not sure he could. Maybe she could still influence Nayr. She could make him better than his parents.

"Hole me, Mama," Nayr said, in his persistent but endearing way, when they arrived at the government offices. Zharla slowed her pace, but doubted she was really walking too fast for a toddler who could run faster than most three year olds.

She stopped and crouched down beside Nayr, then stroked his wavy wisps of hair. The great doors to the government complex yawned behind them, pillars of dun granite carved from the mountain in an alcove just above Shtera Umqi. The somber cast and impatient smell of people going about their government business flowed through the air, unheeding, diffident. Zharla kissed her son's forehead. "Nayr, you're one. You walk." She rose. "Here, hold my hand."

To his credit, Nayr did not protest or throw a tantrum. He gripped Zharla's hand like a vice and peered at her with uncertain eyes. "Whea goin', Mama?"

He sensed her inner turmoil. An intense curiosity drove Zharla here, to the judicial complex, but a warning siren rang, far off in her consciousness. With the passage of almost two years since the rape, she saw a chance, finally, to solve the mystery of Shahl's trial. But the weakness swirling in her bowels reminded her that she was not sure the truth would bring comfort. She smiled at Nayr, like any mother would when trying to set an innocent mind at ease. "We're going on a walk, sweetie. You need to use some energy."

They passed through the great pillars, by the soldiers and peace forces officers scanning for weapons and, supposedly, for ill intent. People streamed in and out on their government business. As they weaved their way towards the judicial offices, Nayr performed the age-old duty of any young child: "Mama, thea yet?"

Nayr's feet dragged from the walk, long even for him, yet he asked the question in a way that showed he was prepared to ask it over and over again. An indomitable will, this boy had.

Zharla sighed. "Yes, we're here. You've been so patient, so be a good helper and let's rest a little, okay? Are you hungry?"

Zharla rifled through her bag for the snacks that Renla put there that morning, but Zharla's shaking hands would not cooperate. Her mother was a traitor in a war she did not understand. Her husband had only just started to emerge from an enigmatic shell, and then he was wounded. Her son showed physical and mental qualities that no one-year-old should. It was like she came here to confront the judge to escape it all. She suspected she was simply running in circles.

Zharla gave a wry smile. "Here, Nayr," she said, handing him his snack. "Try not to spill those."

Zharla did not have an appointment, since she did not know whom she could trust on this end, and since the judge herself might be part of her mother's traitorous conspiracy. When she and Nayr entered the office of the judge, the assistant looked confused. "May I help you?"

"I'd like to see the judge, please," Zharla said, with forced politeness.

"And you are...?" Then the assistant froze. Recognition passed over his face. "You."

"Is the judge here?" asked Zharla.

"She'll be back shortly, Heiress Tamer-li. Will you wait?"

She nodded, then turned to her son. "Nayr, sit down, please."

Done with his snack, he handed Zharla the wrapper. "Moah?"

She wasn't in the mood to argue, and the decorum of the judge's office militated against it, so she brought out another snack and handed it to him. She looked in her bag. Only two snacks left, which would buy her about ten minutes of silence with the judge.

Lush fabric rustled behind her, followed by the smell of expensive perfume. Zharla turned.

The judge strode up, stopped, and considered Zharla and her son with a surly air. "Is this the brat?"

Zharla stoked the fire in her eyes and gave another wan smile, this one of a different sort. "Madam Judge, this is my son, Nayr Tamer-li, and the military heir to Shadhir Ahrik Jeber-li."

"Yes, the one who will command one hundred thousand. Very impressive." She shrugged with annoyance. "You might as well enter." She moved toward her chambers, then whirled. "On second thought, walk with me."

"Nayr," whispered Zharla, beckoning him to follow. Nayr gave her the I'm-about-to-whine look, but Zharla scrambled to pick him up before he could make good on it. She grunted with the effort. The boy felt like he was made of stone.

They followed the judge into a poorly lit corridor, then stopped at a semi-secluded spot, marked by a subtle turn in the passage and an alcove with a stone bench. The judge sat. "Okay. Out with it," she said. "I can't guess what reasons you have for coming here, but I can assure you, they aren't good."

Zharla shifted Nayr to the other arm, and he nestled his head into her shoulder, squeezing his strong, chubby arms around her neck a little tighter. Zharla smiled inside, but then realized that all the questions she had articulated so clearly in her mind before she came were a mere jumble now that she sat with the judge in the subtle turn of the passage. "Why is my life such a mess?" just didn't seem to cut it, given the circumstances, but that was what she found herself asking the judge nonetheless.

"Oh, dear me," said the judge. Her demeanor softened. "It's been as bad for you as it's been for me, has it?" She averted her gaze, almost ashamed, if such an emotion could be ascribed to such a haughty individual. "If I'm the one you're coming to with that question, then there are few people indeed that you can trust."

Zharla, eyes moist, nodded almost imperceptibly. If she opened her mouth, a sob would escape, and her emotions would overcome her better sense.

The judge's shoulders slumped and she searched Zharla's face, many questions in her own eyes. "You are no longer that child who came to plead for the life of a star-crossed luster."

Zharla set Nayr down on the floor and gave him the last of the snacks, then folded her hands on her knee and pursed her lips. *You do not know him.*

The judge shrugged apologetically and buried her head in her hands. The situation called for Zharla to make physical contact with the judge, some gesture of human understanding, but Zharla refused. This woman had convicted an innocent man. Her Shahl. Zharla waited, still.

After what seemed an eternity, and a sigh that lasted almost as long, the judge lifted a tear-stained face and stared at the middle distance. "I did a bad thing with that boy whose life you pleaded for, Heiress Tamer-li, and now I want to make it right." Her shoulders convulsed with a choked-back sob. "Or at least try."

Heat kindled within Zharla. She fought the temptation to lash out. If Nayr weren't here...

The judge worked her eyes through the space toward Zharla's face, "I should have given more credence to your questions. I should have..."

A pair of individuals walked by. They looked like lawyers, and they avoided eye contact. After the echo of their steps died to nothing, Zharla turned and, to her surprise, found the judge looking at her through red-rimmed eyes.

"I'm dying," the judge confessed, looking into the middle distance. "Poison." She hunched over and lowered her voice. "I think it's related to your case."

Stunned, Zharla stared. She turned her attention to Nayr, suddenly grateful that he was oblivious. At least it comforted her to think he was oblivious. He was so precocious that she couldn't be sure.

"Wh...what am I supposed to do, Madam Judge?" For once, Zharla's concern was genuine.

"You are a good woman, Heiress Tamer-li, but you must hate me. Don't try to save what's beyond salvation."

"No woman is beyond salvation," quoted Zharla. "So said the Mothers of the Eshel."

The judge laughed, an undignified and reckless guffaw, as if the truth of her perfidy had just occurred to her, and liberated her. Her head shook back and forth in a rueful arc. "I hope you never lose that innocence, or naivete, or whatever it is."

Zharla gaped. She did not realize that she had any innocence or naivete, or whatever, left to lose. The rape, the war, her mother's treason had squeezed every drop of youthful credulity from within her breast. She waited to see what the judge would do next.

The judge coughed, a disturbing rack of a cough, and squinted at Zharla with bloodshot eyes.

"Take this for what it's worth, young woman."

Zharla reached for her shoulder, tentative.

The judge growled and shrugged Zharla off with another self-loathing, obscene guffaw. The judge shivered. "I might betray that boy all over again for lucre, if I thought I could get away with it." She shook her head. "There's only one thing I would do differently, Heiress Tamer-li."

"Wh... what's that?" A morbid curiosity drew Zharla inexorably toward the judge's next words.

The judge stood up, a bit unsteady, and took a half-step toward her office. She considered Zharla with troubled, regretful eyes. "I would trust no one."

Zharla refused to believe that any woman could descend to such a state, but part of her also wanted to despair as this woman had. Zharla read the judge's face, pitied her sorry statement, especially ironic for a woman as powerful as the judge.

The judge's voice broke into Zharla's stilted reverie. "Have a good life, Heiress Tamer-li. Look after that boy."

Zharla answered her only with silence.

Nayr asked for more snacks, but Zharla had nothing left to give.

Ahrik rounded the corner and slowed to a trot. He scanned for shadows and movement as a matter of reflex. He saw Zharla's house and wondered when he started considering it home. Probably after the drug-induced haze of the healing center but before seeing his supervisor's treachery laid bare. Zharla was the only person he could trust outside the army, and he could trust precious few within it.

Ahrik hugged the shadows and kept out of people's way on the street. No point in giving someone the shock of their life by colliding with someone they couldn't see. The languid late afternoon foot traffic didn't worry him too much on this score, but he wasn't willing to take any chances.

He drew in a cleansing breath in the shadows opposite Zharla's new house. How much could he trust her with the questions swirling in his mind? She betrayed Shahl two years ago, at the decision ceremony, so he needed to be sure she didn't give Ahrik the same treatment if he too bared his soul.

Ahrik grimaced. He certainly couldn't trust her with the secret of the ketel, the secret of the clones, but he still needed her. Only she could unravel how the Tameri clan was wrapped up in this war, and how they were connected to the military hierarchy, and why they would smuggle off-planet weapons for the rebels.

And he needed her for a deeper and darker purpose. If Sheresh and his co-conspirators tried to control Nayr, which was likely because he would one day command one hundred thousand ketelis, then Ahrik would certainly need Zharla to protect Nayr. And if it ever came to civil war, controlling the Tameri wealth would....

He refused to finish the thought.

Ahrik crept to the shadow's edge across the street from Zharla's house and allowed himself a brief smile. He was beginning to hope that their marriage could be more than a business transaction. Ahrik was not the man he used to be. Maybe she was different now, too. Maybe they could move past simply tolerating each other.

Ahrik's compiler alerted him that a node in his tendril network was nearby. Confused, he focused his mind on the tendril link. One of his sons was just a few meters from his position. A clone in an urban area was a serious breach of identity protection. The clone's cloak might fail. He could be recognized.

Father, I'm across the street from Mistress Tamer-li's house, behind the large trash receptacle.

Leren, Ahrik's 3d Hand commander.

Nervousness sloshed through his thoughts.

Checking to be sure no passersby took note, Ahrik backtracked toward Leren's location and crouched in the deep shadows of the alley. He looked toward the place he sensed Leren's face to be and cast, *Why are you here?*

Leren's answer revealed his discomfort. *Father, had to report on ketel's status, but didn't know whom to trust. Ayen had the coordinates of this place, and the group voted that I come.*

The group? Is this how decisions are made in my ketel? Why didn't Ayen take command?

A sad pause. *Father, request permission to use voice.*

Even at such a short distance, casting over the tendril link would tax anyone in an anxious state, like Leren. Under normal conditions, conveying detailed information in person was more efficient by voice than by tendril link.

Leren had bad news, then. Very bad news.

Ahrik sighed and did a quick check to make sure no one in the street had approached the alley. He whispered, "Granted, but stay cloaked."

"Father," said Leren, also at a timid whisper, "Ayen is a nervous wreck. The enemy detonated a third atomic after you...left us for the White Planet. They hit the subcommand station. 1st Hand Commander Beral and all his subcommanders down to the company level passed onto the death register, killed in an atomic blast on the moon. 2d Hand Commander Halel and many of his subcommanders are also dead, and most of his men suffer from severe radiation sickness. My men of the 3d Hand have had little to do since that incident in the Kerewi campaign, and morale in 4th and 5th Hands is at an all-time low." Silence reigned for a beat. "Father, we need you back."

Had one of his hand commanders not been crouched before him, Ahrik would have crumpled to the floor, crushed by the weight of these losses. A third atomic. Two hand commanders dead, and the other three useless. Ahrik's heart ached for the hundreds of men who died in anonymity in those atomic blasts, and for those who had suffered so much since from radiation sickness.

He reached out to steady himself on the cold, unforgiving stone of the building in whose shadow he hid. He filled the silence by focusing on his breathing, chasing these burdens from his mind. He needed to be strong. For his sons. For those who still lived.

He filled his voice with a conviction he did not feel. "Leren, announce sunrise assembly tomorrow." He pursed his lips. "We will overcome."

"Check, Father."

"Leren."

"Father?"

"First."

"To the fight," Leren replied, a new tinge of loss in his voice, too.

Ahrik heard Leren pad off, then turned his attention to Zharla's door, forcing himself not to dwell on the disarray in his ketel. He could go back to his men now, but so many questions remained unanswered, questions Zharla might be able to answer. Ahrik had so much to tell her that might connect the dots. The White Planet. The slaves captured here on Dom and taken there.

He had finally pieced together what was driving this war, and he trembled at the choices he might have to make. He needed Zharla's decisiveness now more than ever. He couldn't go to his ketel like this. He had no strength to give them, only questions.

He needed answers.

He did a final scan before crossing the cobbled street. A subtle smile eased onto his face when he saw Zharla stroll around the corner, lost in thought, with Nayr in tow, locked to her hand. Ahrik panned his gaze the other way and saw Alrem on approach as well.

Just the two people he needed to see.

Zharla palmed open the door and shooed Nayr into the house, then noticed Alrem. Passersby saw Alrem's uniform and made way as he approached the door and gave Zharla a greeting of friends.

Ahrik couldn't hear what they said. He uncloaked and slid from the shadows, then weaved through the people passing on the street.

"...idea when he'll be back?" Alrem asked.

"Here I am," Ahrik said, sidling up to the steps. Surprise registered on Zharla's face, satisfaction on Alrem's. He and Alrem embraced. Ahrik nodded a greeting to Zharla. A face poked itself between the doorframe and Zharla's cloak, and Ahrik smiled at Nayr. Ahrik might as well try to connect with him on some level, if he was ever going to win his wife's trust.

"Hello there," Ahrik said. The face disappeared behind Zharla.

"Say hello, Nayr," said Zharla. The boy gave something like a wave and mumbled something like a greeting. Zharla grimaced. "Come inside. I'm sure there's a reason you're both here."

Ahrik worked his way to a seat in the parlor and tried to get comfortable. Renla came in with tea, dried fruit, and nuts, then sat in a corner and bored her stare into Ahrik. Occasionally, she sized up Alrem as well, in a way that did nothing to put Ahrik at ease.

Zharla, absent for a moment while Nayr settled down in the next room, entered and took her place on the couch. The leaping dolphins carved into the arms and the embroidered upholstery told Ahrik that it was the same couch she had occupied at the decision ceremony, a lifetime ago, when she crushed Shahl's heart and made Ahrik feel he had won something.

Ahrik studied Zharla's manner for some clue that he could trust her with his life. The weary chill of what could have been, of what should have been, drifted over his consciousness. He wished now that the fateful day of decision had gone differently. Shahl should be alive, and maybe Ahrik should be in his brother's place.

Ahrik avoided Renla's glare with quiet determination. He tried to absolve himself of the looming silence by rubbing his temples. This war called for a new decision. "Zharla," he said, "we are losing this war." He turned to Alrem. "We need to tell her about the ketela."

Zharla looked confused. Alrem sprang to his feet. His glass of tea fell to the floor and shattered. Renla leaned forward in her chair, a study in punctilious concentration, her body tense, every muscle prepared to uncoil.

Alrem drew his face up in a twist of rage and incomprehension. "No."

Zharla grunted, as if taking in some spectacle of sport. "Which is the problem, Alrem, the war or the ketela?"

Ahrik knew what Alrem meant, and he knew the precise distance to his own weapon, Biriq. He measured a bead on Alrem. "Sit down, brother. You'll change your mind when you hear what I have to say." He turned to Zharla. "The ketela are—"

Alrem leapt over the tea table and threw himself at Ahrik. "No!"

On instinct, Ahrik slid to his feet and shifted his weight. He dodged Alrem's wild swing, then cradled him towards the chair Ahrik had just vacated. At the same time, Ahrik jabbed his fist into Alrem's stomach. Not enough to hurt him permanently. Just enough to knock the wind out of him. To immobilize him.

Alrem tangled into the chair and gasped for breath. He did not spring back to continue the fight.

Ahrik gave his friend a pointed look, then returned his attention to Zharla. "The ketela are too weak to protect women's rule." Ahrik narrowed his eyes at her. "Now's not the time to tell you why."

Renla poised herself to lunge, half out of her chair, eyes wide, prepared to meet any danger that might come Zharla's way.

Zharla looked at Ahrik askance. Nayr appeared at his mother's side, not afraid, but menacing, challenging Ahrik. Zharla sniffed in dissatisfaction. "Someone better start explaining something, Ahrik. No one brings violence to my home without a very good reason."

Ahrik helped Alrem up and into a new chair. He gripped his friend's shoulder. Alrem had only been doing what he thought was right, to protect the secret he'd been trained a lifetime to protect. Ahrik gave his friend an "Are you all right?" glance, and Alrem nodded in response. Ahrik whispered, so only Alrem could hear, "I'm sorry, I should have warned you first."

Ahrik righted his chair and set himself down, then leaned forward to rest his elbows on his knees, with a mix of conspiracy and fear. "There's no easy way to say this. Esheli trading families—to include yours, Zharla—are turning kall into cash and drugs for the rebels, who have themselves found a reliable source of weapons off-planet, in return for captured keteli soldiers, sold as slaves."

"Off-planet?" Zharla asked. "You mean..."

Ahrik nodded, "A different planet from our own."

Zharla let out a breath and glared in skepticism.

"We have to reimagine our thinking about this war," said Ahrik. "I've seen this other planet, the White Planet, where Alrem was taken as a prisoner. Alrem, I suspect that your captors were going to sell you as a slave until they realized that you were a ketel commander and not a mere keteli. Had you disappeared, it could have endangered their slave–kall–drug–weapons trade, because the Esheli leadership would have been forced to find out what happened to you. They brought you back to the Kereu, so you could be rescued.

"I spent two days on the White Planet, observing this vile trade and seeing my hope for winning this war disintegrate. The rebels gave the locals drugs and slaves, and the locals gave the rebels raw, unfinished kall and weapons of the kind my ketel has found a number of times in rebel possession."

"They trade our kall for captured keteli soldiers?" Zharla asked.

Ahrik stood and turned to the window. "Our soldiers must be effective in the wars on the White Planet."

Zharla hummed with distrust. "How could you tell they were captured ketelis? Surely the rebels didn't leave them in their uniforms."

"I...recognized some of them." A very uncomfortable silence settled on the room. Saying much more would endanger the secret of the ketel, that human cloning was practiced on a wide scale. Zharla couldn't know about the clones. No one could. He avoided eye contact with Alrem.

Ahrik gave a pained sigh. "There's more. We analyzed a nugget of the White Planet kall. It was more pure than what we find here, and there appears to be more of it, and closer to the surface, on the White Planet than here."

"Once the rebels ship the kall back here, how do they refine it?" asked Alrem.

Ahrik looked at Zharla and sighed. "Some months ago, we found evidence of a link between Esheli merchants and the rebels, but that was in the transfer of weapons, not kall. Then I remembered your shipping manifests, Zharla. Shipping kall from the White Planet would explain unusually high fuel costs."

Zharla chuckled. "This is preposterous, Ahrik. How could I have heard none of this?"

Ahrik merely shrugged. "My supervisor, Sheresh, kept me drugged for a day after returning from the White Planet. He's hiding something. In two years of war, we have not found a single unregistered kall processing plant in the Kereu. Those refineries must be here, in the Eshel." Ahrik turned to Alrem. "The military cannot investigate this. We need Zharla."

Alrem stood and moved next to Ahrik, his back to Zharla, then whispered, "She needs to take the oath."

Ahrik nodded. No one outside the ketela had ever taken the oath, which swore members to protect the secrecy of the Ahit, on pain of death. How could she take the oath without even knowing the secret of the ketel? Could she be trusted? "She won't like taking an oath she doesn't understand."

Ahrik glanced over Alrem's shoulder. Zharla glowered back at him.

Zharla glided to her feet and cleared her throat. "Renla, take Nayr. Leave us." Her voice carried menace, overlaid with fear. She padded to where Ahrik and Alrem stood near the window. When she rested her hand on the small of Ahrik's back, she noted, with relish, that he tensed at her touch.

"Pray tell, dear gentlemen, why do you stand here whispering secrets?"

Alrem shot Ahrik a look of fear. Ahrik cleared his throat and turned so that Zharla's hand no longer rested on his back. "Zharla," he said. "We...ah...need to tell you something."

"What is the Ahit, Ahrik Jeber-li?"

Ahrik's eyes widened with surprise, and he was, for once, dumb.

"I overheard you at the healing center. Alrem, please resolve the doors behind Renla. There's a switch by the palm scanner that will soundproof the room." Zharla never really thought she'd have to use that.

Ahrik followed Alrem with his eyes, as if to delay the inevitable. He evaded her gaze, but hummed with discontent. "The Ahit swears to uphold and protect women's rule."

Alrem flipped the switch and sat in a corner, eyeing the two of them with a wary aspect.

"What else?" asked Zharla. She shook a finger at both of them. "I'll not have treason in my home."

"Don't you dare," Ahrik warned. "Not after everything we've given the Eshel." He clenched and unclenched his fists, turned, and made as if to slam his fist on a table, but then checked himself.

He took a deep breath and turned back to her. "Shall we sit idly by while society falls apart, Zharla? If we lose this war, it will change life on this planet forever. Maybe end it."

Zharla scoffed and threw up her hands. "What could I do to stop that?" She twisted her mouth and shook her head. "It should never have come to this, Ahrik, and you know it. What's your plan, overthrow women's rule to save it? And you want me to swear to keep this treason a secret?"

"You're no lover of women's rule."

"I could still join the Council."

"This was a bad idea," Ahrik said to Alrem.

He took two ferocious strides to the door, but Alrem put a hand up to stop him. "She knows too much, Ahrik. She must take the oath."

Zharla sensed the violence on Alrem's mind. He rose and took a baleful step toward her. She sucked in her breath. Her heat knife was in her study, locked away and completely out of reach. Ahrik might actually let this happen.

She looked down for something to throw.

A metallic ring sang in her ears. She looked up, but froze. Without even turning around, Ahrik had drawn his blade and placed it at Alrem's throat. Alrem stood as still as stone, but a fury like raging water filled his glare.

"She lives," said Ahrik. "No matter what. She lives."

For a long moment, Zharla looked back and forth between them, considering her options.

Neither Ahrik nor Alrem moved a muscle, as if waiting for her decision. Ahrik was prepared to harm his friend to keep her safe, a realization that made Zharla's world swim.

She sat down on a chair by the window and folded her hands in her lap. She did not know if she could betray women's rule, nor if she could trust Ahrik with her life. Squeezing her eyes shut to hold back the tears, she whispered, "I'll take the oath."

Both men breathed a sigh of relief, and she wondered if they had planned the whole thing. Zharla examined Ahrik, but she saw honesty on his face, a face weighed down by worry and pain, not deceit.

Ahrik sheathed his blade and placed a hand on Alrem's shoulder. "My friend, this must be done."

Alrem nodded and sighed in assent.

Ahrik looked to Zharla and smiled his thanks.

"I'll only help you," Zharla whispered, "if the choice is between women's rule and chaos. But Ahrik..."

"Yes?"

"...the Lady help us if we aren't wise enough to tell the difference."

> By my blood, by my soul, by the Lady of the Emerald Moon, my life is forfeit if I betray the Ahit.
>
> Oath of the Ahit

15 | Trust No One

SHERESH SHEHUR-LI: Keep that daughter of yours under control.

MATRON TAMER-LI: You worry about what's yours. I'll worry about what's mine.

SHERESH: Don't double-cross me. I'll come for you. I'll hunt you down.

MATRON: Threats? Come now. I am long past threats.

Voice recording from the Tameri clan archives, 4 Kenen Sheni RY 2500

Aʜʀɪᴋ paced. From his desk, around the punching bag, to Ayen's desk. Then back, around the punching bag, to his desk. He'd sent his aide out to supervise the training exercise. Ahrik needed to be alone.

Zharla's mission was simple: make contact with a pir'e in Mekele, at the central temple, and act like a potential buyer for black market weapons. Ahrik's intelligence pointed to one Pir'e Analt. He didn't sell the weapons themselves, but he knew who did. Zharla had left early that morning, and she should have been back by now. He could send his ready squad after her... but no, that would just tell her that he thought she depended on him.

Ahrik paced. She depended on no one. Besides, going after her now might blow the Ahit wide open. Not just Ahrik, Alrem, and Zharla's cell, but the whole organization. How many Ahit members were there? No one knew. Ahrik only knew a handful, but even that knowledge was dangerous. If he was caught, the powers that be would find the others. Ahrik knew what methods they'd use. Nothing would stop them.

He slammed a right hook into the punching bag on his next pass. If he sent his ready squad, and if anyone saw that they were clones, then the questions would lead right back to him. His clones could not go public. Not yet. It would destroy too much. No, better to suppress his personal worry for Zharla. Just wait for word. Another punch into the bag. A left jab this time.

Ahrik waited. This war had destroyed his faith in deity, or he would pray. Instead, he just paced.

Anda sat in yet another darkened room. Before him sat yet another man shrouded in shadow. Anda had gotten used to mysterious conversations. The mystery and the beatings were a necessary evil, he'd found, a means to a vengeful end.

His interlocutor had obvious concerns about his identity, but Anda assumed this was Boss. Anda thought he recognized his voice. It was just as deep and resonant as the day Anda ran from the peace forces officer in the driving rain, then watched her fall to her death. This shadowy figure stood in the door that dreary morning and offered Anda sanctuary, after a fashion.

Anda squinted into the murk. He couldn't be sure this was him.

Boss shifted in his chair. It groaned under his weight. "Anda, my friend, thank you for meeting with me"—as if Anda really had a choice—"but why do you doubt our cause?"

Anda didn't begrudge this man his question. Let him have his theatrics. He was just doing what thugs and criminals do. Ahrik was the real villain. Anda just needed to play his part. To get the revenge he wanted.

Yet for some reason the rebels kept Anda here instead of sending him out to do what he came here to do, what they trained him for all these months.

The dark shadow of Boss shifted in a way that Anda now saw was supposed to be menacing. Anda did not fear him. In the weeks or days or hours since the rebels used atomics at the space station—however long it had been, Anda couldn't tell—Anda realized that the rebels needed him more than he needed them. They wanted him to blend into the Ketel of Ahrik, to infiltrate close to Ahrik. The rebels' bid to kill Ahrik at the space station failed, and now they needed Anda to finish the job.

Anda smiled and tossed his hands up with a melodramatic air. Time to get answers. "I am so glad we're friends, but I'm not sure this is 'our' cause. I have no doubt that you feel justified in this cause, but my role remains unclear."

"You doubt me," rumbled Boss in his soothing baritone. "Do we need to remind you why you should not doubt me?"

Anda played along. He squirmed. Painful memories burned in his mind, but he knew they couldn't do that to him now. Anda could almost taste his freedom. "No, no," he blurted, "we're past that, right? I'm a new man. Let's not go back to the old ways."

"Yes, that's what I thought. Now, about our cause."

Anda broke in, his voice timid and uncertain. He saw no reason to break the charade now. "I...I don't even know your name. How could I possibly do what you ask? How could I kill my own brother?"

"He would kill you, if given the chance."

"A long time has passed."

"The Butcher of Kafron must die." Boss rose from his chair, and shadows played games with the dim light in the room. He loomed over Anda, and the dim light showed swatches of swishing red. A pir'e. This was the same man who captured him all those months ago.

Anda rubbed his chin. They called his brother the Butcher, but he'd never heard of Kafron. Sounded Kerewi. Anda furrowed his brow, but shrugged off doubt. "If you trust me with this mission," he said, "then I need to trust you."

"You need to trust me?" Boss rumbled with laughter. "How do I gain your trust, Anda?"

"Where are we now?"

"Mekele. Central temple. Merani quarter."

Anda shuddered with the suppressed pain of that memory, of the heat knife, of Zharla, of his arrest and exile.

"Yes," said Boss. "You remember." He drew a step closer and squeezed Anda's shoulder. His face almost came into the light.

Anda patted Boss' hand and gritted his teeth. "Tell me why I should kill my brother."

Anda heard nothing. Instead, he felt Boss grin with unfettered malice. "I thought you'd never ask. Watch this recording. You will trust me. The Butcher of Kafron must die."

If Anda didn't know this vile creature for what he was, he would say Boss' voice had become sweet.

Boss plumped his own chair. "Come. Sit here."

Anda creaked into the chair. He watched in confusion as a video recording began to play on the compiler display. The sound on the recording was muffled, but he made out dozens of men loitering in a jungle town. All the men looked something like his brother. Some sobbed, some stared at the ground, and others moved bodies to some sort of collection site. So many bodies. Men, women, and children. None in uniform.

The color drained from Anda's face. He was grateful the room was far too dim to discern much color at all.

"Where is this?" Anda whispered.

"In the Kereu. Keep watching."

One of the soldiers picked himself off the ground. He broke away from a group of soldiers, anger slathered across his face. Ahrik. Anda didn't know how he knew, but he knew. Even with all the look-alikes, Anda recognized his brother's face.

Ahrik spoke with one of the look-alikes, this one a bit heavier-set than the rest. An aide, perhaps. Ahrik's stern face said he was directing the look-alike to do something.

Anda knew what happened. The sickening truth clutched and slid over his mind. He asked anyway. "What happened?"

Boss said nothing in response, as if he saw no need to speak.

The picture on the display panned, and Anda's breath caught in his throat. There, on the display, was a look-alike, not of Ahrik, but of Anda, or of the man once known as Shahl. If he hadn't been looking closely, Anda might not have seen how this soldier differed from the rest, since he and his brother looked so similar.

Anda slumped down in his chair. He stared at the middle distance. Realization percolated into the depths of his worried heart. Zharla needed to see this recording. She needed to see just how deep Ahrik's deception ran. "So, clones fight the Eshel's war in the Kereu, and at least one of these clones looks like me..."

Boss grunted.

"...and that is how you expect me to infiltrate the Ketel of Ahrik and exact revenge on the Butcher of Kafron."

"Yes, Anda."

Anda couldn't see it, but he was sure a dark smile crossed the other man's face.

"We must exact justice for this great crime," said Anda, trying to make the declaration sound believable. He just wanted to leave this place, the Mekele central temple. To do the job, to prove to Zharla what really happened. Someone else in the Eshel must know of these clones. He could expose Ahrik for the butcher that he was. He could prove the truth of Zharla's rape.

Anda saw it all clearly. Ahrik knew. All along, he'd known, deep in the blackest recesses of his heart.

Boss breathed out in satisfaction. "I see that you trust me now."

"Yes," Anda lied.

A door hissed open, and someone else entered. Whispers. Boss hummed in thought and turned to Anda. "I have to meet someone."

Anda swiveled in the chair and nodded at Boss. "I...I need to watch this...again."

"Certainly." Boss grunted with a contented air and moved for the door. As soon as the door resolved, Anda whipped his fingers into the compiler interface. He could prove his innocence. He could rid the world of the scourge of Ahrik and make things right with Zharla. He fumbled around on the murky desk for a data capsule. After too long, his fingers found what they sought. He slipped the capsule into the compiler and copied the data.

He dared not trust a hope. He could have his old life back.

The door dissolved with a serpentine hiss. "All done?" asked Boss, with even more menace than usual.

"Y. . . yes, I think so." Anda went back to being obsequious.

Zharla sat on a sun-warmed stone pew in the central temple in Mekele. She considered the lazy, late morning breeze and the unexpected twists and turns of her life, and it occurred to her that, until she'd joined Ahrik's little conspiracy, she hadn't felt like she belonged anywhere. Since her wedding day, when Shahl was taken from her, she had not felt a part of anything bigger than herself. She had Renla, and Nayr was easy to love, but hating her husband wasn't a fulfilling pastime. Much better to do something with her disappointing life, even if it was with men she didn't understand for a cause she mistrusted.

She'd asked Renla to wait outside the temple for her. Zharla was on a mission for the Ahit and, after all, she'd promised not to reveal its secrets. For what that was worth. As she sat on the cold pew, she tapped out a complex rhythm in her palm. Ahrik had taught this to her as a way to identify Ahit members she didn't know. Every Ahit member knew it.

Or so Ahrik said. At least it was a way to avoid thinking about her life, withering away in a winter of solitude and disappointment.

Across the temple, she heard the full-bodied declaration of a pir'e's wooden staff rapping against the solid floor. The rhythm was very, very fast, but it was the Ahit sign. She wouldn't have recognized it as a rhythm at all if she weren't listening for it. The pir'e stepped into the light and out from the altar's alcove. He was nondescript, except that his face wore a brashness than one does not expect of an ascetic.

She narrowed her eyes. She knew him, from the night she confronted Shahl, and then later when the men's rally was attacked. She studied him from under her hood as he approached.

He stopped a few paces away, then cocked his head. Surprise registered on his face. "Mistress Tamer-li?"

Zharla smiled at catching the pompous pir'e by surprise. No need to reveal, yet, that she knew the Ahit sign. Ambiguity gave her power. "So you're Pir'e Analt."

He leaned against his staff and gave an assessing hum. "Ahrik told you my name. Why are you in my temple?"

Your temple? "It's only two hours on the transporter," Zharla said, peeved at his insouciance.

"Your presence puzzles me, my dear." He presented her with a smile that did nothing to lessen the insolent pitch of his shoulders.

Zharla's hackles stood on the back of her neck. "I am not your 'dear,' Pir'e Analt. Who were you expecting?"

Analt gave a helpless shrug. "I am just a simple pir'e."

Zharla tapped out the Ahit sign so only he could hear. The temple stood empty around them, but Zharla wasn't taking any chances. "Your false asceticism may fool the teeming masses. It doesn't fool me."

He considered her through eyes clouded with challenge. "Why are you here?"

"Protection."

Analt nodded his head, deep in thought, then looked at her with genuine admiration. "If the Tameri clan needs protection, then the Eshel is in a sad state." He rubbed his chin. "That husband of yours can't get you weapons?"

Zharla stood and moved toward Analt with what she hoped was an imposing step. "Can you help me or not?"

He sighed. "With all the unrest in the Eshel, I am worried about evil forces corrupting the people. How do I know these weapons won't be used for ill?"

Zharla tried not to laugh. "What are you really worried about?"

"What if the peace forces can't control the smuggling?"

"The peace forces are in on it." Zharla frowned a challenge back at him.

He measured her for a long moment. "I didn't think you had this in you," he said, "yet here you are, putting your life and the lives of untold others in the balance." He settled onto a stone pew. "I've gotten wind of a supplier who thinks a member of the Tameri clan wants to buy weapons."

Mother. "How would the supplier have gotten that idea?"

"I am just a simple pir'e." The words sounded even less convincing the second time.

He reached into a pocket and pulled out a scrap of paper. "This is the address of the cafe and the meeting time later today. It's back in Meran. You'll have to hurry."

Zharla snatched the scrap of paper and turned to leave, but Analt cleared his throat. "Mistress Tamer-li, trust no one."

She turned to face him, her eyes like hard stone. "Why should I trust you?"

"I helped get your servant back for you, and I could do the same if they ever took your son."

Zharla's mind turned to flame. She slid forward, invading his space, but not touching him. "Threaten my son at your peril."

He stared, unfazed. "We want to get to the bottom of this war, too."

" 'We'?"

"The pira network. Surely you don't think that the Ahit are the only ones concerned about where the Eshel is going. I move in both worlds, Mistress Tamer-li, helping where I can. Be careful. You've just stepped into the dark side of a dark world."

Zharla exited the temple with a scowl and met Renla. She put the pir'e's threatening airs behind her. Zharla's world could never be darker than it was on her wedding night.

■

Ahrik woke and bolted upright, sweaty and alert. When did he fall asleep? He clutched the seams of the couch cushions and looked around his office. Horrifying images invaded his mind, images of men, women, and children lying on the wet ground of the Kereu, and he realized why he'd woken with a start. He checked his internal compiler. Late afternoon. Zharla still wasn't back. He looked down to the floor and saw the book he'd been reading. A bland history of the War of Unification. That's why he'd fallen asleep. And he'd picked it up in the first place to avoid thinking about why Zharla wasn't back yet.

Ayen, he cast over the tendril link. *Alert ready squad. Sensitive mission.*

■

Zharla chose a seat near the back of the cafe and ordered a *hender*, a tamarind-flavored sweet water. Renla arrived a few minutes later and sat at a street-side table, out of the way and unobtrusive, but within sight of Zharla, so she could run away and alert others, if needed. By the look of displeasure on Renla's face, not to mention the rant she'd launched into on the walk to the cafe, Zharla knew she was displeased beyond measure about what her mistress and friend had chosen to do.

Renla was a source of constancy, but Zharla needed more than that now. Renla was a dear friend, her loyalty unassailable, but she was a servant. Renla's family was sworn to the Tameri clan by oath, so if the Tameri clan's fortunes changed and they could no longer afford servants, Renla and her family would be forced to search elsewhere for support. In these dark times, Zharla hoped for the kind of loyalty that was free of obligation, the loyalty that she could only win from someone like Ahrik.

And maybe, just maybe, something more lurked there. Zharla dared not trust that hope, if that's what it was.

The appointed time for her meeting passed, and with each minute her feet shifted a little more and her cup drained a little farther. Her heart beat with anticipation, and she was about to get up and leave the stress of it all behind when a well-dressed man approached her table.

"May I?" he asked. His hair was short, his bearing practiced and disciplined. Zharla sized him up. A military man, and not one used to asking permission to sit. As she expected, he sat, without her invitation.

"Who are you?" she asked.

"You're new at this, aren't you? Just get the deal done."

"What deal?"

"Don't fool with me, Tameri," he said. "I didn't need your name to tell me you were the buyer. You look high-brow, you're obviously waiting for someone, and your friend watching over there gave it away."

Zharla suppressed a wince and stole a glance at Renla. The man's arrival had taken Renla by surprise, as well. Setting a brave façade, Zharla asked, "What'll it be, then?"

The man raised an eyebrow at her. He shook his head and muttered something about sending a child to do a man's job. "I had been authorized to offer ten thousand units, but now only one thousand are on the table. You can't handle a larger order."

Zharla sneered. "Why are you breaking your military oath?" The pause that followed told Zharla that the man did not intend to answer. She pressed. "I can tell I'm right by your reaction, your bearing, your look, your hair, your speech. At some point you swore your life to women's rule and the people of the Eshel. What happened?"

Incredulity passed over the man's face. "Should I walk?"

"Okay, okay. I'll take the thousand units."

"Are you sure you want to go through with this?" He shook his head. "Leave the cash at the port dead drop. Two million keina."

"Got it." By his tone, Zharla could tell his price was exorbitant, but she played along. Then, out of the corner of her eye, she saw Renla stare, not at her but at someone else in the cafe. Zharla glanced in that direction and saw a man sitting alone, with nothing but an external compiler in front of him. In the moment her eyes scanned in that direction, she didn't recognize him, but it was clear he'd just sat down.

Zharla smiled at the man across from her. "You have someone else with you, too, don't you? What are you up to?"

"That doesn't matter, Tameri."

Life in the cafe careened on, heedless of them, but Zharla tapped out the secret Ahit signal with her toe. The man froze as realization washed over him, and Zharla saw him reach inside his coat with indelible clarity. She reached inside her cloak. She saw the glint of his distiller pistol as he pulled his hand out, and her fingers found the leathery hilt of her heat knife, but then she fumbled the hold.

Panicked, she also caught sight of Renla standing up and running, not away, as she was supposed to have done, and not toward Zharla as she might have been expected to, but toward the other stranger in the cafe. She saw the stranger stand, turn, and trip as he started to run, and Zharla saw Shahl's face.

The shock passed in a flash, because the wrong end of the first man's distiller moved toward her chest as the heat knife fell from her grasp and clattered to the floor. She heard a shout of "Peace forces!" and heard the gentle *thunk* of a distiller. She expected to feel a hole gape open in her chest, but instead felt the thrill of being whole, of seeing the man's hand and wrist evaporate into a fine, iron-sulfuric mist, and his distiller clang to the floor.

A masked, black-clad figure stood over her as she leaned over and tried to slow her breathing. Customers rushed for the exits. Then Renla was there with a hand on her back. The moment of sheer panic passed, and the adrenaline shrank to a mere deluge in her veins.

"Zhe'le, they got them," said Renla.

Zharla had no idea who "they" and "them" were, but she was happy to be alive.

Two days had passed since the incident at the cafe, and Ahrik could no longer put off revealing his deepest secret to his wife. He had to take her to his base. She would witness the chaos she had just uncovered in the Ketel of Ahrik, and what it all meant for her dark past.

His greatest worry was that she wouldn't believe him when he told her that all this had surprised him as much as her.

He ordered his men to clear out so Zharla wouldn't see any of them before he was ready. He and Zharla entered his office, where Ayen had rearranged the furniture. Two chairs sat close to one another, with two other chairs, farther apart, facing them. Ahrik motioned for Zharla to sit in one of the first two chairs, and he took the seat next to her.

"Your base is deserted," said Zharla. "This raises more questions than it answers."

"You need to... I need you to see this. There's no way to tell you what's going on. I just have to show you." Ahrik stared into the middle distance.

His life was forfeit, from this moment forward. Generations of faithful duty, crushed like fallen leaves.

Zharla leaned over and, with two gentle fingers, turned his face toward her. "You've swathed yourself in mystery for the last two days, and you may recall that I almost had my chest ripped open in the cafe. Forgive me if I'm short on patience."

He sighed. "I'm sorry, Zharla. I have no idea how to deal with this. What we found at that cafe two days ago has forced me to reevaluate everything I thought I knew, and I know it will be the same for you."

"Spare me the heroics, soldier. We both know you're not so gallant as all that." Zharla closed her eyes. "I'm sorry, Ahrik. I shouldn't have said that."

Ahrik bit his lip, humble. "What you are about to see will undermine what you know about Esheli society, about me, about Shahl, and about the rape. I'm sorry, but there's no good way to talk you through that."

Zharla's face grew cold when Ahrik mentioned the rape. "You had better be right, Ahrik Jeber-li. By the Lady and the Moon, I don't take kindly to empty promises."

From her seat, Zharla scanned Ahrik's office. Nondescript. Utterly utilitarian. Exactly what you'd expect from a military commander. She eyed her husband. *What tortures Ahrik so?*

The door to his office dissolved, and the man from the cafe entered, flanked by two black-clad, masked men, dressed just like the ones who'd saved her life. They must have been from Ahrik's unit. She leaned over to him. "Where are the female soldiers?"

He simply flicked stormy, sorrowful eyes toward her and turned his attention to the distasteful task to his front.

The two guards sat the man down in one of the empty chairs in front of Zharla and Ahrik. The stump below the man's right elbow was bandaged, and he was blindfolded. The two guards chained him to the chair. Zharla winced at the violence with which they did so.

Ahrik peppered the man with questions, interspersed with unnatural pauses while Ahrik simply stared into the middle distance, as if having a conversation with someone in his head. The man looked like he might have been tortured. She tried to push the thought from her mind, but he was so forthcoming with his answers that it was hard to.

The bandaged man had commanded a ketel of ten but had turned to the rebels after being passed over for promotion because he had no children. He was a low-level arms dealer who took captured rebel arms from an anonymous contact and sold them to the rebels, who were stockpiling weapons in and around Esheli cities.

The door dissolved again and two guards brought the man's accomplice from the cafe in, half-naked and in a disastrous state.

Zharla sucked in her breath. "Shahl."

Ahrik's arm shot out to keep her in her chair, his look fierce. "It's not what you think."

She considered this new prisoner. He didn't quite look like Shahl. Something was off about him. Then she noticed the two guards. They weren't dressed in black, but in uniform. They had no masks. The room swam.

They looked like Ahrik.

"Ahrik," she whispered after reorienting herself. She fixed her gaze on the two guards. "Who are these. . . men? Why are you holding these men as prisoners instead of the peace forces?"

"Just give me a moment, Zharla, and I will explain." He returned his attention to the prisoners and asked the one who looked like Shahl, "Do you have a defense, keteli?"

"No, Father," he rasped.

Father?

The man hung his head, his carriage feeble, "I have betrayed my blood oath to you, Father."

Zharla's mouth tasted like sand.

Ahrik sighed, got up, and approached the broken man. "Then your sentence will be just." He brought his blade out and gently placed the inner point at the man's throat.

Zharla's alarm spiked. "Ahrik, what are you doing?"

He ignored her. "By my authority as father of this ketel, I sentence you to die."

"No, Ahrik," Zharla said, her voice barely above a whisper. With all her soul, she wanted to look away, but she could not. Some sick, animal desire within her clawed its way to the surface of her consciousness, forced her eyes open, forced her to see and hear the inevitable.

Ahrik still ignored her. "May your blood serve the land and people of the Eshel."

The condemned brought his head a little higher, welcoming the sentence.

"Stop, Ahrik!" Panic laced her voice. Zharla could not let it happen. She had stood aside while new and shocking questions flooded her mind, but she would not stay her hand while Ahrik acted like a law unto himself. She forced down question after question, like why the men look so similar to Ahrik and Shahl, but not quite the same.

Her heart stopped. One of these look-alikes was her rapist. She knew it as surely as the Emerald Moon would rise that night.

Ahrik did not move, as if waiting to see what Zharla would do.

A well of courage swelled within her, forcing down the panic she felt. She stood, strode over to Ahrik, and gently, very gently, rested a hand on his arm, the one holding the blade to the condemned man's neck. "No more blood. You don't want to do this."

Ahrik let a breath exhale, but did not move his arm or his blade. Without looking at her, he whispered, "If I promise not to kill this man now, will you agree to have this discussion in a few moments, when we are alone?"

He seemed to plead with her, but wrestle with himself inside.

Zharla nodded. She pitied him whatever choice he had to make at that moment.

"Good," said Ahrik, nodding toward the bandaged prisoner. "I don't think this man has told us everything he knows."

The blindfolded, chained man trembled. Zharla stared, unsure if he shook with fear or rage.

She and Ahrik returned to their seats, and Ahrik sheathed his blade.

The chained man spat on the floor. "How dare you violate the keteli code," he said. His voice dripped with insolence. "How. Dare. You."

Zharla gaped. "Ahrik, this man has no grounds to speak of loyalty and trust." She got up and walked over to the man. She wanted to grab him by the scruff and shake him as hard as he could, but she bent down, her head close to his.

"Zharla, step back," said Ahrik.

Too late. The man flipped his feet and jerked his body, and his head came toward hers at a horrific speed. He made contact, and she staggered back. She brought one hand to her nose, and it came away bloody, but the other hand reached for her heat knife. Rage surged within her. She saw exactly where she would plunge it, directly in the center of the chest, where the chains framed a perfect square target. She brought the knife back to her hip and her opposite hand forward, ready to lunge like she'd learned.

Just before she lunged, the man convulsed, then went limp.

Ahrik's hand rested on her arm. "No, Zhe'le." His voice was almost afraid. "Do not trust what you feel now."

For just a moment, it did not register that he had used her familiar name, but when he did, she understood why.

"No more blood," she said. In an instant, another man was by her side, another Ahrik look-alike, but not one of the guards. She cast a look back at Ahrik, asking if all ten thousand were like this.

The man helped her sit back down and gently wiped the blood from her face and hand, then tilted her head forward, giving her clean gauze for her nose. He showed her how to squeeze the bridge of her nose with her thumb and forefinger, with a look that said, "Like this."

A healer. She nodded and pinched her nose. "I... I'm okay."

The healer peered into her face with genuine concern, but Zharla cringed at the revolting vertigo of how much he resembled Ahrik.

One of these Shahl look-alikes raped her. She thirsted for the moment to confront Ahrik. He was the only one who would understand. Not even Renla would know what to make of it all.

Ahrik looked at her, waiting for her to be ready.

She had too many questions to be ready. She breathed out in

frustration. "Why did the chained man go limp?"

Ahrik's smile faded and he looked away. "We do what we must to protect those we...those around us." He returned his gaze to her. "I'm sure you have many questions, and I promise to answer them, but let me finish this interrogation."

She nodded in agreement. "All these years, I knew you even less than I thought."

After a pause while Ahrik once again stared into the middle distance, the chained man jerked awake. Ahrik turned his glare on the man. "What do you have to say for yourself?"

The man's voice quivered with fear instead of rage. "S...someone else was supposed to m...meet me at the cafe, I th...think I got the wrong T...T...Tameri. S...supposed to be older."

Mother had probably gone to the cafe, then left when she saw Zharla there. Zharla groaned at the possibility that her mother suspected that Zharla was on to her.

Zharla lifted her fingers from the bridge of her nose. The blood must have stopped by now.

Ahrik grimaced at the bandaged prisoner. "We'll hand you over to the peace forces."

Zharla smiled in triumph. Ahrik was a different man with his ketel. Away from the ketel he would not dispense death like medicine, but with the ketel he seemed inclined to. She yearned to see Ahrik change so that he became more like the even-keeled Ahrik, the one away from the ketel.

Ahrik consulted the middle distance again, and silence prevailed for a beat. Zharla felt a dribble of blood settle above her upper lip, and she wiped it away and pinched the bridge of her nose again. The keteli prisoner, the one who looked like Shahl, still stood at attention, although the effort of doing so clearly taxed him. The two guards, Ahrik look-alikes, flanked him, eyes straight ahead, somehow taking everything in.

Ahrik considered the two prisoners for a moment, then transferred his gaze to the guards. "Leave us," he ordered, rage simmering through his voice. He nodded toward the two prisoners. "Confine them."

When they left, Ahrik cradled his face in his hands for a long moment, while Zharla tried to make sense of what she'd just witnessed. Ahrik looked up at her like a man beaten, unsure of himself. "I'm not sure you realize this, Zharla, but my world has fallen apart."

"Your world?" she asked, incredulous. "I never really knew the world I was in to begin with. What now, Ahrik?"

"We go home." His eyes darkened as his ire grew.

"I want answers, Ahrik."

"Not here, Zharla. Not here." He clasped her hand and pulled her up from her chair.

> The plan to breed the super-soldiers for the Ketel of Nayr was a success, but the methods used with Zharla Tamer-li exposed the whole scheme before its time.
>
> Report on OPERATION GENESIS, found in the archives of the Army of the Eshel during the War for the White Planet, RY 2520

16 | The Stage Is Set

CHIEF ELDER, TERRITORIAL SECURITY: There is no rebel presence in the Eshel.

[Ten Minutes Later]

CALLER: There are rumors that rebel forces have established a beachhead at Hof Chelek. Is this true?
ELDER: [shocked] How could you possibly know such a thing?
CALLER: Are rebels in the Eshel?
ELDER: Th... they will be thrust into the sea by dawn.

Newscaller conference, 10 Kenen Sheni 2500

AHRIK trudged back to Meran through the underbrush, Zharla at his side. The day waned crimson, to match his inching rage, blinding him to his physical surroundings. He fought to control the vertigo that had turned to anguish, then to ire. How could one of his sons lie to him? Blood from his veins. A son bred and raised up in the Oath of the Ketel, to defend him, Ahrik, against all enemies. He shivered at how deep the betrayal might go.

Rarely did men betray alone.

He did not know how he could find and destroy those responsible for this treachery without destroying the ketel itself. If he let on that he knew of a plot against him, then fear would keep the confederates from exposing themselves, but if he accused any of his sons unjustly, then he would lose the trust of thousands. He couldn't just execute a keteli as an example, as he was about to earlier, because that would undermine the trust he sought from his wife.

"Slow down," Zharla said, "I'm running to keep up."

He stopped and glowered at her. He regretted bringing her to his base. She had prevented him from enforcing the keteli code that was the basis of trust between him and his men. He knew the code was brutal, but she had no place casting away something that had served the Eshel well for generations. He spared the other man, the one with the bandaged arm, because killing him felt wrong, especially with Zharla right there. The keteli was the real problem. Ahrik didn't know how to find the traitors in his own ketel, and he didn't know how to restore the loyalty and trust of the rest.

But Zharla deserved the truth, after all everything she'd lived.

His visage softened. "Sorry, my mind is elsewhere."

She tugged his sleeve. "Elsewhere? Where else could it be, Ahrik? We need to start answering the questions swirling around us."

He looked away. He had no cause to blame her, really. The answers to these questions held the truth about her rape, as well as questions about himself, his ketel, and the war. He ground his teeth. But he would violate his oath if he told her the truth she deserved to hear. He would break his oath more clearly than he already had.

He scouted the ground for a place to have the unwelcome conversation with his wife. "This is as good a place as any. Sit down and face me."

She pursed her lips, on the verge of protest, but to her credit she did as he asked. Ahrik gave a grateful smile. This scioness of a family fortune made sitting in the scrub brush look dignified, severe in her poise and beauty.

He pushed her beauty from his mind. "I know this is unnatural, but I have to go to extreme lengths to be sure that no one overhears this conversation."

"Even your ketel, who, it turns out, all look like you? They can't know?"

He ran a hand through his close-cropped hair. "One question

at a time. I thought I could trust my men, but it is clear now that someone in my ketel has betrayed me. If anyone finds out we've had this conversation, then I am dead, and you are, too, so I can no longer trust my men."

"Are you frightened, Ahrik?"

"Frightened? No, not frightened." He sighed. "Tired." He shook his head, and even that small effort exhausted him. "Everything is...harder now."

She fiddled with the hem of her skirt, shook her head, and looked at him with a mix of worry and pity. She adjusted her tunic, and two flame pendant necklaces slipped down her wrist, wrapped and intertwined like a bracelet. Zharla caught him staring and said, "It's complicated. You and Shahl are both a part of my life."

Ahrik nodded, recognizing that he may never change that. He took in the sunset for a beat. "Do you remember Zharek Jeber-li?"

"He wrote the *History of The War*."

"Yes, and twenty-one generations my ancestor. He also helped redevelop cloning technology in the aftermath of The War, which led to a great number of improvements in agriculture, livestock development, and medicine. You also know that human cloning is banned."

Anger flashed in her eyes. "I thought so until today."

"Zharek helped perfect human cloning, and he advocated for the development of the ketela, the elite units of the Army of the Eshel."

"Ahrik, to 'perfect human cloning' is not a 'great contribution'."

"My ten thousand? They're not volunteers, or hayla, like the public believe. They were cultured from cells taken from my mother when I was in the womb and then artificially gestated. They were given genetic traits to make them better soldiers: hearing, sight, strength, endurance, intelligence. That is why they look almost like me, but not quite."

"They don't all look like *you*, Ahrik," Zharla said, a menacing tone in her voice.

"I learned that only two days ago, Zharla, when I got the report from the cafe. I can only assume that some of Shahl's cells were taken at the same time they took cells from me, while we were both in utero. These clones of Shahl are the betrayal I spoke of. Knowing that there were clones of Shahl in my ketel, one of my sons should have come forward after the... attack."

Zharla stared at the ground and shuddered, as if to suppress the memory.

Ahrik reached out a hand but stopped short of touching her. "I've kept things from you, Zharla. Important things. I'm trying to set things right now." His eyes clouded. "Please be patient."

Her face eased a bit.

"From the age of five," he said, "my ten thousand and I ate, trained, and learned together. We meditated together for hours on end, in order to establish a tendril link between our internal compilers."

"Tendril link?"

He nodded. "This tech isn't available on the civilian market. Like scribes or recorders, we have internal compilers"—he pointed to the base of his skull—"but ours send signals to the compilers around them. It takes hours and hours of group meditation to calibrate the compilers to everyone's unique brain activity, but once this is done, we can talk to each other through our thoughts, as long as we're focused enough and not more than, say, a few kilometers apart."

"If I had a compiler installed, you and I could learn to send our thoughts to one another?"

Ahrik frowned and scratched at the dirt with a finger. "No, it only works between members of a ketel, whose neural pathways are already very similar. The tendril links also need to develop from an early age. It's too late in life for you."

"You expect me to believe that you never knew one of your soldiers was a clone of Shahl?" Accusation ran through every syllable.

He shrugged and realized that his anger had transformed once again, this time to resignation. "I can't make you believe me, Zharla. I don't even know how many of his clones there are."

She pressed her eyes closed. Tears leaked out, but she sniffed them aside. "There's at least one more. That man you have is not the one who raped me."

"Had I known there were any, when it happened, I would have told you right away. I cannot prove it to you in any other way than by laying bare my secrets to you now." Ahrik caught his breath at this, the most honest moment in his young life.

In the silence, crickets chirped their welcome to the impending night.

"I believe you, Ahrik," whispered Zharla. She gave her attention to Meran Mountain, illuminated in the purpling light of sunset over Ahrik's shoulder, off towards Mekele. She stopped and stared at him, in the throes of some monstrous revelation. "Nayr has one hundred thousand clones. Where are they?"

He acknowledged this new information with a nod. "At a base about three kilometers north of here. This whole area is a closed military zone."

"Should I be worried that someone in the army thinks they need one hundred thousand genetically-enhanced soldiers?"

Ahrik tore at a blade of grass. "If someone can hide clones of Shahl from me for all these years, right here in my own ketel, despite all the time I've trained and slept and eaten and learned and fought with them, and if they, whoever they are, can hide the identity of your true attacker, then they would stop at nothing to achieve their goal. I'll wager they are willing to end this war by bathing Dom and the moon in blood." He shuddered. "That would serve no one."

Ahrik resolved, then and there, to give every breath that remained to him to keep that perilous future from becoming true.

Zharla's gaze misted. "Such an end would destroy Nayr, would turn him into someone he's not."

Ahrik frowned with introspection. "War does that."

"Oh." She stared at him for a moment, understanding on her face.

"I didn't choose my soldier's life." He took a deep breath. "I accept it."

"In three years, when Nayr is five, he'll go away to his ketel, to learn with them?" Zharla asked.

"It will only be during the day, at least for the first few years, but, yes, his education starts at the age of five. His compiler will be implanted and he'll begin socialization with his clones. He will always be apart from them, but a part of them, too. He will not be able to perform his duty without them, nor they without him. This is why I'm telling you this now, Zharla. You...we...must teach him that he is not the man that they want him to become. We need to teach him not to be—"

"Like you?"

Ahrik's face registered the sting in her soft-eyed rebuke. He deserved it. "Like me. No, like I used to be. At least, I want to be different now."

Zharla smiled. "You are a good man, Ahrik."

Emotion coursed through him. It was the first time she'd ever complimented him, at least without sarcasm or guile. Guilt fought this emotion, though. He shook his head with sudden vigor. "I've done bad things, Zharla. Evil things."

She considered him in the light of the setting sun. "Thank you for not killing those men back there. I didn't know you very well when you left for that first deployment to the Kereu two years ago, but it did something to you. For the worse in some ways, but also for the better."

Ahrik ventured a smile. "The first time you see death is always a shock, but it wears off."

A tear, glistening in the setting sun, traveled down her cheek. "No, Ahrik. No." She wiped it away and sucked in a deep breath, nostrils flaring, her eyes closed in fervent study of some far-off, poignant thought. "Today was important for you, not for me."

He shut his eyes and let the import of the moment wash over him.

Zharla rose from the ground, as effortless a movement as any soldier ever made. Then her hand was there, extended to him. "Let's go home."

From that instant on, until the day he died, he could always close his eyes and recall with clearest memory the moment he first put his hand in hers.

The officer club hummed with over-jubilance. Too many of their number would never come home, and too many, it seemed, forgot it. Through harried, tired eyes, Ahrik looked for those he knew, chatted in passing with some, nodded in greeting to others. He caught Alrem's attention from across the room. Ahrik had Nayr with him, so it was hard to maneuver toward his friend, especially when he had to carry the boy.

Nayr was almost two, and Ahrik was tired. The boy was able to walk, so Ahrik set Nayr down, promising himself not to pick him up again.

It felt odd, being with the little boy everyone thought was his son. For the first time, the two of them were in public together, without Zharla. She said it was to keep up appearances, but Ahrik now recognized the importance of the bond they would share, even if he was not the boy's father.

Ahrik stopped at a relatively somber group of officers. He recognized a couple of other Ahit members. Arnab was slight of build, with sharp eyes and an even sharper wit, rarely used of late. Kimen bore a deep red scar that traveled from his ear and down his neck, then disappeared in the collar of his uniform. His grim frown matched his dark complexion. Ahrik saw an open seat and sat, then Nayr clambered onto his knee.

"How goes the war, brothers?" Ahrik asked, nodding towards their game of *chartak*.

Arnab gave a discouraging shake of the head and a quick glance at Kimen, then Ahrik noticed that Kimen's mood took on an even more brooding aspect. Ahrik grunted. They weren't sure if he was talking about the game or the actual war. Kimen looked at Ahrik with almost dead eyes. "If you must know—"

Arnab sat up. "We're winning." He pointed to the game of *chartak* and continued as if Ahrik's question had been about that all along. "Kimen and I have defeated their two most powerful armies and are about to occupy their capital."

"I don't think so," said an officer across the table. "We've got a lot of fight left."

"We shall see how long that fight lasts," Kimen said. A devious smile cut through his tone, as if he still meant the war that they all sensed was about to break open in some new, horrific way, in real life.

The men returned to their game, and Ahrik whispered to Arnab, "Can we talk?"

Arnab nodded and made for the exit.

Ahrik turned to the boy and tried to appear patriarchal. "Nayr, stay with Aanin Kimen. I'm going to talk to Shadhir Arnab."

Nayr just said, "No."

Ahrik placed Nayr in the seat next to Kimen. "You sit here."

"No."

The finality and determination with which Nayr said it took Ahrik aback. The boy thought he would win this contest of wills.

Ahrik would not be defeated so easily. "You stay. I go."

"I come wid you." He latched onto Ahrik's leg with surprising strength, and his eyes flashed something between desperation and panic.

At the threat of tears, Ahrik relented. He furrowed his brow, not sure what he was supposed to have done differently. He took hold of Nayr's hand and declared with contrived firmness, "Fine, but you walk. I'm not holding you."

" 'Kay."

By the time Ahrik found Arnab outside, Nayr was in his arms once again. He had to figure out how to deal with this. Nayr nestled his head into Ahrik's neck, trying to escape the cool ocean breeze as the early winter day conceded light for dusk. The breeze carried the moist scent of algae and the threat of fog. It would be a murky night.

"What news, Ahrik?" asked Arnab.

"What's wrong with Kimen?"

Arnab cocked his head in frustration. "You dragged me out into the cold to ask that? Kimen is his old, gloomy self. He complained earlier about a supposed rebel attack at Hof Chelek. Nothing is confirmed yet, so I cut it off."

"Wait. Hof Chelek? Whose ketel is there now?"

"Daf'e and Razh'e are both stationed there." Arnab reached out a calming hand. "Ahrik, it can't be true. I'm sure we'd have heard if—"

Ahrik shrank back. "Call it a feeling. What did Kimen base his belief on?"

Arnab shrugged. "He hasn't heard from Daf'e in a while." Arnab cleared his throat. "It's nothing. How many times have comms failed in this accursed war?"

Ahrik fixed him with a stony glare. "Dark forces are afoot, Arnab. You were an attaché to the Council of Chief Elders two years ago. Do you still know people in the caller networks?"

"Yes, but...whoa." Arnab held up his hands. "Stepping into politics isn't right."

Ahrik drew close and waited while a pair of officers tumbled out of the club, bragging about battlefield exploits. He scanned the street outside the club, then whispered, "Every Ahit member knows that there comes a time when we have to bend the rules."

"Why is now the time?"

"I...just trust me." Ahrik searched Arnab's face for any sign that he might not follow through. "There's little harm if I'm wrong. Just have one of your caller friends ask the question. If the Chief Elder handles the question, fine. Nothing to worry about. If she fumbles it, we'll know a great deal."

"I don't like it, but I'll do it," said Arnab. He nodded his farewell and tromped into the streets of Meran, creeping with fog.

Nayr tugged at Ahrik's collar. "How goes woah?"
Ahrik looked at Nayr. "I don't think we're winning."

Zharla sat at her desk, stylus frozen above the compiler display, and fixed her attention on the caller broadcast.

Ahrik walked into the parlor after returning home from the officer club, Nayr asleep on his shoulder. Ahrik nodded towards the broadcast. "What's going on?"

Zharla started and laid down her stylus, keeping one eye on the broadcast. "Oh, how was your jaunt?"

"Fine," Ahrik said, fixing her with a question. "You never watch the caller networks with that kind of intensity."

"It's bad."

Ahrik laid Nayr down on the couch, his head resting on the vivid purple pillows, his small body framed by the Tameri clan's leaping dolphins.

"I assume you haven't seen this yet, Ahrik." Zharla accessed the compiler next to the display and played back a portion of a newscaller conference with the Chief Elder over the Territorial Security portfolio. Zharla shook her head in disbelief. "This happened just a few minutes ago."

"There is no rebel presence in the Eshel," the Chief Elder said. Then Zharla skipped to the damning exchange between the Chief Elder and the caller network representative. Ahrik grinned with full exuberance.

Zharla looked up at him in horror. "You had something to do with this? Were you going to talk to me about this first?"

"I just planted a seed." He placed a hand on her shoulder, and she didn't shudder or pull away. "She did the rest herself. We have some clarity now, a real chance to turn this war around." He gave her a quizzical look. "I thought you'd be pleased."

Zharla snorted. "It will get much worse before it gets better,

Ahrik. Workers and unemployed men have already gathered at the port for demonstrations, and the kall markets ended the day down ten percent. In less than an hour."

"I hadn't thought of that." Ahrik cast his gaze to the ground. "Oh?"

Just then, a message chattered into the army receiver on Ahrik's side of the parlor. Ahrik snatched up the printed card as soon as it came out.

"Well?" asked Zharla, slightly peeved.

"We muster at dawn. All available ketela called to the colors."

"Sweet Lady," Zharla said, resting her head in her hands. "Help us now."

> Ayen, mobilize the ketel. Prepare for a fight measured in years, not days.
>
> ---
>
> Decrypted electromag message from Ahrik Jeber-li to his aide on the night of the Army-wide muster

17 | The Education of Nayr

> I, Sheresh Shehur-li, declare an oath to defend the
> people and land of the Eshel, and to uphold the rule of
> women against all enemies, and I do so without
> reservation or dissimulation, of my own free will, by
> the Lady of the Emerald Moon.
>
> ―――――――――――――――――――――――――――――
> Oath of office of the first man to be appointed a Chief
> Elder, 17 Kenen Sheni RY 2500

ZHARLA chopped a banana and slid the pieces into a bowl, then set to work slicing some grapes in half. As soon as word of the rebel invasion got out, the servants they'd hired, both young men just graduated from the melmez, asked to be released from service. Zharla didn't mind the extra work anymore. It kept her mind off the war and this sudden turn for the worse.

She finished slicing the grapes and shoveled them into the bowl after the bananas, then handed it to Renla. "Re'le, the soldier that Ahrik sent to protect us—Leren?—he wears an unsettled look."

"Why?" Renla took the bowl of fruit, then waved in front of Nayr, beginning the adventure of mealtime.

Zharla tied a bib around Nayr's neck and gave a noncommittal shrug. "Something's wrong with the situation."

"Gape! Nana!" Nayr flapped his chubby little arms and bounced in his high chair.

Renla handed Nayr a spoon. "Zhe'le, he's not a Shahl look-alike, so he can't be—"

"My attacker? No." Zharla rubbed her chin. "He's one of Ahrik's top soldiers. He commands two thousand, I think. Ahrik tried to explain it to me, but it was a lot to take in." Zharla shook her head. "I'm sure Ahrik would have an inkling if one of his top commanders was involved in my attack." Zharla rinsed her hands and ran them through the drying field. She turned and shrugged. "I'm trying to stay positive." She slumped into a chair at the table.

"It's not all bad."

Nayr tossed a banana on the floor near Zharla's foot.

"No, I suppose not," said Zharla, picking up the wayward morsel. "I could be hungry, cold, and living in-mountain." She chuckled. "I could be a man."

Renla gave a nervous laugh herself. Nayr had gotten most of the food into his mouth. A few grapes made it to the floor, but he munched away happily. His bib was a mess of mashed up banana. Renla handed Zharla a new bib and flashed an unconvincing smile.

Zharla furrowed her brow. "What's bothering you, Re'le?"

Renla turned to look out the window and tucked a curl under her cap. "Do you ever think that your life could have been different?"

Zharla glanced a question at her friend and blew a strand of hair from her face. "Are you questioning oath servitude, Re'le? It binds me as much as you."

Renla looked at Zharla, a mix of fear and nervousness on her face. "Do you really want to discuss this now?"

She and Renla stared at each other. A shared experience bound their families together, but it had always been more than that between them two.

Zharla leaned forward with an air of suspense. "Will you enlist if I release you from your oath?"

Renla bit her finger and shook her head with worry. "My family wants me to marry so I can keep my position, so my child can grow up bonded to Nayr." Determination flashed on Renla's face. "But I want to fight. Someone has to show the rebels what's what."

Zharla sighed and searched Renla face for any shred of doubt.

She found none. If only Renla knew what such a choice would mean.

"Mama. Done!" yelled Nayr, showing off his empty bowl.

Zharla stood and worked him out of his chair. "You could die."

Renla grunted. "Better than being... trapped." Renla allowed a question to sneak into her eyes. "Like you."

Zharla cleaned up Nayr and sent him on his way, then folded her arms, weighing the situation. "You think I'm trapped?"

"You didn't make it onto the Council. What now? Raise a child? Raise the voice of pointless opposition to those in power? Stand beside Ahrik?"

"You still don't like him, do you?"

"You do?" Renla's face shifted from impulse to apology. "I'm sorry. That was too forward." She broke eye contact and gazed out the window once more.

Zharla followed her friend's gaze out the window. "Who am I to say what turns my life will take?" She sighed and locked eyes with Renla, thinking how much more work Nayr would be without someone to help. "I still believe we can change our future, Re'le." Zharla drew her friend into an embrace. "I release you from your oath. *En-li me'bood*," she said in the Old Tongue. "You fight your war. I'll fight mine."

Renla hugged Zharla and held her tight. "Thank you, Zhe'le."

Nayr tugged on Zharla's skirt. "Mama. Pay wid me?"

Zharla tousled Nayr's hair and squeezed Renla's shoulder as she pulled away. "There's just one thing I need you to help me with before you enlist as a hayla."

A short while later, a chime announced someone at the door. Zharla dissolved the door, then shivered. Leren stood on the top step, shrouded in a cloak, the bright scar on his cheek announcing him from under his hood. Zharla told herself she would check who it was before opening the door from now on.

"Mistress Tamer-li." He stood with military precision. "May I come in?"

She let him into the entryway, but no farther. They stood, stiff and distant. An awkward silence pervaded the space between them, but Zharla refused to break it, much less invite him to sit. Renla entered from the kitchen and stood in the doorway behind Zharla, maintaining the social propriety of the meeting and making sure he knew she was sizing him up.

Leren shifted his feet, then recovered some semblance of bearing. "I have a message from Father's supervisor, Aanin Shehur-li."

"Leren, as long as you're in my home, call him 'Ahrik,' not 'Father,' okay? And just so we're clear who it is we're talking about, Aanin Shehur-li is just 'Sheresh'."

"Yes, Mistress Tamer-li."

"Zharla. My name is Zharla," she said.

"Yes, Mistress Zharla."

"No, just 'Zharla'."

"Yes, ma'am. Zharla." He looked around in haste, as if to check that no one else had heard him use Zharla's first name.

Zharla drew a devilish pleasure from making him feel uncomfortable. Military discipline was the only life this man had known. She raised an eyebrow. "The message from Sheresh?"

"Yes, ma'am. It's right here." He pulled out a square of paper. Zharla took it and saw that it was formatted like the military orders that Ahrik received. Zharla creased her brow in annoyance.

> Mistress Zharla Tamer-li:
>
> Your son, Elef Me'yan Nayr Tamer-li, is to report for training in two weeks at the Ingress Center, Mekele. If taking him there yourself is inconvenient, transportation will be arranged for him.
>
> Aanin Sheresh Shehur-li

Zharla fought to control her emotions, mostly rage, mixed with fear. Trembling, she handed the note to Renla, who read it, shock spreading over her face.

"Tell me, Leren," Zharla articulated with delicate fury. "Do you know why they want to take my son from me three years early?"

"No, ma'am, but I understand that beginning the training is an honor. Aanin Shehur-li also mentioned that he would be willing to meet with you to discuss it."

Is he blithe, or oblivious?

"Get out," she ordered.

"Yes, ma'am," he said. He sniffed and wiped his upper lip with a finger. "Ma'am, is there some message you want me to give to Aanin Sheresh?"

She bore her eyes into him. "I'd tell you to tell him to go stare at the sun until his eyes burnt out of their sockets, but I'd much, much rather tell him that myself. Leave."

Renla slipped by them and palmed open the door.

"Yes, ma'am." Leren turned on his heel and departed.

Renla resolved the door and turned, her face deep with concern. "Are you okay?"

Zharla shook her head but refused to speak because it was the same as refusing to cry. Nayr came in from the next room and just held her hand. He said nothing. Zharla smiled, bent down, and gathered him up in a warm embrace.

"Zhe'le, are you really going to take him to Mekele for this?" Renla asked, incredulous.

Zharla drew in a deep composing breath, then responded with icy control. "Over. My. Dead. Body." She squeezed Nayr a little closer, and he did the same.

Zharla spent the rest of that day trying to figure out how to get a secure message to Ahrik. She tried sending a local, civilian message to Alrem, but she received no response. He was probably tied up in defending against the rebel invasion coming from Hof Chelek.

It would only take the rebel force a few days to arrive at Mekele, or so they said. Ahrik had said he was going to Mekele, but she had no idea where in Mekele he was. She tried going to the officer club, but she didn't see anyone she recognized. She was tempted to send Ahrik a message at his military account, but she was sure other eyes would read it. She even considered going to Mekele herself, but she decided that would draw too much attention.

Zharla chided herself for not setting up a danger code before he left.

As darkness settled over the city, she returned home, anxious to play with Nayr for a bit and then lay him down, the ultimate goal being to relax for a moment before catching a few hours' sleep. She ascended the front steps and palmed open the door.

When she entered, Nayr ran up. "Mama!" he exclaimed, throwing his arms around her neck. "Pay monster wid me?"

She thought what it would mean to say no. "Ooooh, I'd love to!" She forgot her exhaustion and stomped around with mock ferocity, gesticulating wildly and tickling him when she caught him, until he escaped and continued his flight, accompanied by squeals of unbridled glee. Zharla would catch him again, and the fits of laughter would return, aided of course by Zharla's fingers.

When it was time for bed, Zharla asked Renla, "Has he eaten?"

Renla stretched her shoulders and turned to Nayr. "Would you like a bedtime snack?" As Zharla expected, his answer was in the affirmative, and negotiations began over what that snack would be. Strawberries. Zharla sat, exhaled, and watched Nayr chomp away.

"I luh you," he said, with a matter-of-factness that only a child his age could muster.

"And I love you, Nayr," Zharla said, kissing his forehead. At moments like this, she forgot his provenance. He was his own person, innocent of the violent act that had brought him to her. He looked like Shahl, but it mattered so little. Nayr was who he was, Ahrik was who he was, and Zharla was who she was. And that was enough. She no longer pined for what she could not have. None of it was just.

That would never change. But she accepted it.

Done with his strawberries, Nayr asked, "Pay monster?"

"No, Nayr. It's time for bed." So a tantrum began, breaking Zharla's reverie and forcing her to pause in forming the fierce words she would have for Sheresh in the morning.

Owls hooted a slow and ominous dirge. They knew that death hung on the winter night. Anda's core shivered against the dank ground, not from the moisture but from the thought of the world he was about to enter, a world he'd always despised, a world he'd always told himself was beneath him.

Anda was about to become a soldier.

He and Esh'a lay on their stomachs. Their heads poked above a ridge in Meran's lee, scanning for movement. The outline of Meran Mountain stood faint against the predawn light, and Anda thought what it would be like to have his old life back, to turn back the calamity that befell him, and to enjoy the quiet luxury of books, peace, and learning.

A new shiver coursed down his spine. He shoved down thoughts of his erstwhile life. This was his new reality. The sooner he accepted that, the faster he could move on to something better. He feared, though, that life would get much worse before it got better.

He gave an uncertain hum. "You sure Ahrik's base is out there?"

"Positive." She nodded into the darkness below them. Her long braid swished behind her. "About fifteen degrees to the right. One thousand five hundred meters ahead. Two pines on a ridge running perpendicular to this one. That's the main base entrance. You'll enter at the grunt entrance, two hundred meters before that." She assessed him with piercing black eyes. "Someone will meet you."

"What'll you do if I fail?"

She chuckled. "Keep fighting the bastards until they leave us the sunfire alone."

He looked away, serious. "I could turn, tell them all your secrets."

Esh'a leaned into him. "Don't worry, you don't know enough to matter. If you do turn, don't let them see that rebel burn on the inside of your arm. They'll kill you."

He tried to smile, tried to return her devil-may-care gaze. "That may happen anyway."

Esh'a stuck out an assessing lower lip and gave her head a curt, vigorous shake. "Just keep your head down and meet me back here after you finish the job."

Anda backed off the lip of the ridge, then rolled onto his feet and ran through a quick precombat check of his equipment. He paused and glanced up the ridge at her. "I thought this was just another delivery for you."

She followed him back down and stood in front of him. "You're starting to grow on me. If you disappear, I'll come find you." She paused. "So come back, okay?"

Anda drew out the stare. It had been a long time since a woman looked at him like that, since that morning in the social hall, before the Matron Tamer-li and a rebel explosive tore his life to shreds.

She put a hand on his shoulder, raised her eyebrows. "Okay?"

He nodded something like assent, then looked down at the insignia on his uniform. "You sure these are genuine?"

She slugged his unit insignia. He stepped back from the force of the blow. He frowned at the dull pain blossoming over his left breast.

She smiled. "3d Hand, 3d Standard. You're a Marauder now." She pushed him back toward the lip of the ridge. "Go on, before I decide to desert with you and go hide where no one can find us."

Anda had a hard time shaking that thought from his mind as he trudged through the clingy underbrush on his first night as an assassin.

The day dawned dreary and dank, rare for Meran, but it matched how little Zharla wanted to face Sheresh. But face him she must, if she was to have any hope of swaying the decision on Nayr's education. Zharla's hope ran thin. Army decisions were rarely questioned, and war lurked on their doorstep. But she determined that she must succeed.

She entered the office of the newest Chief Elder and suppressed the bitterness of being passed over for the Council. She put on her most pleasing face and engaging demeanor. She suspected that Sheresh knew she disagreed with the decision to train Nayr so early, so why start off with hostility? Better to make him want to change his mind or, better yet, make him think that changing his mind was his idea.

"Good morning, Mistress Tamer-li," Sheresh said, his voice a bit too merry.

"Yes, it is good," she said, with just a little less brightness.

"So," Sheresh said, with a wary eye, "no hard feelings over my appointment?"

She broke eye contact with nonchalance and studied the handkerchief in her hands. "Who am I to question the wisdom of the Council of Elders? Why would I resent someone else being heaped with all this responsibility?"

He gave a plaintive shrug, as if he, of all people, could generate no answer to those questions.

She eased herself into a seat and found a matter-of-fact expression for her face. "Besides, there are a great many details to work out for Nayr, aren't there?"

Sheresh smiled, as if to conceal surprise that he had gained such an easy victory. "Yes, there are."

"Very well, then I suggest we begin with what exactly you'll teach Nayr."

His face fell into genuine confusion. He shifted in his seat and cast a sidelong glance at the wall.

Someone was listening in.

Sheresh considered her. "It's quite involved, but the short answer is that he'll be learning the same things that any ketel commander learns at this age."

"And what is that?"

"Surely you're not interested in so obtuse a topic? For most civilians, the military curriculum is boring."

"Oh?" She had him on the defensive. Surely he realized that she was no mere army spouse, waiting with eager anticipation for her opportunity to sacrifice something, or someone. The army existed to serve the nation of the Eshel, not the other way around. She was part of that nation, so she held her ground, mixing the pleasantness on her face with the expectation that she would soon receive the answers she deserved. She folded her hands in her lap in a gesture of resolution.

Sheresh stammered, then formed his words on the fly. "It's... rather..." He cleared his throat. "New ketel commanders learn to work as one with their ketela, to lead their men in battle..."

"Chief Elder Shehur-li, war should be a long way off. You do know how old my son is, right?"

"Old enough to begin his military education," Sheresh said with little conviction. "Nayr will of course learn everything that other school children learn: history, mathematics, language, humanism, science. With a ketel of one hundred thousand, we need more time to make sure he learns the intricacies of leadership."

"Ah, that is a big number." Zharla feigned conceding the point, then paused for effect. "I wonder, what does it take to lead one hundred thousand soldiers?"

"There will be many adults to help Nayr grow into his duty," Sheresh said.

Zharla bore her gaze into Sheresh. "Including his mother."

If this took him aback, he did not show it, but Zharla pressed on, heedless.

"I lead a mining conglomerate with at least as many individuals in it"—this was a useful exaggeration, since she had not yet inher-

298

ited her mother's position—"so surely I could teach him something meaningful about leading large groups of people."

Sheresh held up a hand, a gesture that verged on insult. "With all due respect, Mistress Tamer-li, I'm sure you have much to teach him, and you may do so when Nayr is at home, but as a matter of state security we cannot have civilians involved in training. Certainly you understand that—"

"I understand that you want to tear a child from his mother's bosom."

"Don't you think that's going a bit far? The boy will be three in a little over a year, which is when all children in the Eshel enter school."

"Very well, then we will wait a year to begin his training. Certainly you understand the need for my child to have a childhood as similar as possible to that of other Esheli children, right, the very people he will be defending?"

"Well..."

Zharla pounced on his hesitation. "How can he defend the people of the Eshel if he does not know and understand them? If he can't make the decision whether to be a soldier or not, at least let him develop, on his own, what kind of soldier he wants to be."

She smiled. "I'm sure the full Council of Chief Elders would understand this reasoning if an appeal made its way there." Zharla had no idea if such an appeal would get anywhere. It was a monumental bluff, but she got up as if to leave all the same. "Shall I wait while you draw up new training orders, or shall I await their arrival at my home?"

Sheresh exhibited a stunned look, but he rallied quickly. "No, wait. Please sit down. You haven't even had anything to drink. Tea? Juice?"

"Aren't we agreed that Nayr will begin his military training at the age of three, the same age that every Esheli child enters school?" She considered staying on her feet but thought better of it. No need to be rude. She sat once again, reveling in the discomfort this inflicted on Sheresh, obviously a neophyte at the political game.

"It has been a very, very long time since we've had a ketel of a hundred thousand, so there's no one in the army who's experienced it. We want to be sure that the Ketel of Nayr is never misused."

When he said this, Zharla realized, finally and with horrible understanding, what leverage she had over Sheresh and everyone else who wanted to control her son and his ketel. Until that moment, she had relied only on a bluff to bargain, but she realized then that she had much more power than that. She now knew that, more than anything else, Sheresh and his ilk had to prevent the true nature of the ketel system from coming to light: the clones, their training, and most importantly their true purpose. If she could threaten that, and do it subtly, without revealing that she knew their secret already, then she could get anything she wanted from them.

"Misused?" Zharla asked. "What purpose could one hundred thousand men have to follow my son to war?" She made it sound as innocent as possible.

The response was flat, immediate, and direct. "That is a matter of state security, Mistress Tamer-li."

The face of Sheresh Shehur-li read like a boring book, but Zharla could see that his neck was just a shade redder than it had been. She was not sure if he realized it yet or not, but he had just admitted, beyond a doubt, that the Ketel of Nayr did in fact have a clear purpose. It chilled her spine to speculate on what that purpose might be.

"I see," she said. "What are we to do, then? It seems you'd prefer that I not raise the issue of Nayr's education with the Chief Elders, but..."

She knew Sheresh would see this for what it was: a veiled threat to take the government to court. This would be truly unprecedented, especially in time of war. It would risk making the entire ketel system public.

She held her breath and rested her clammy hands in her lap. Sweat beaded on the back of her neck.

"Hmmm." Sheresh stroked his chin, in what were painfully slow movements for Zharla. "I think it would be better if we didn't get the full Council involved for now. Of course, that is your right as a woman of the Eshel, but why don't you let me see if I can get a delay in your son's training? Shall we say, six months?"

So Sheresh was willing to deal. Zharla relaxed, and she hoped he didn't notice.

"Six months? Why not ask for a year or more? The location is also an issue, as training Nayr in Mekele would force me to change my residence to another city. You could also request a change in location. Why not have him trained here in Meran?" Zharla would never be in a better position than she was now. She might as well ask for the world.

Sheresh considered this, his face a mask of thought. "I believe I could arrange a change to Meran, but my superiors would be more willing to accept this if the training began earlier. How about two months?"

Zharla took a turn to feign thought. She really only wanted to get a change in location to Meran and an extension of a few weeks over the two weeks they'd already given her. She had everything she needed now, but there was no reason not to ask for a bit more. "Three months," she countered.

He sighed. "Three months, with a change to Meran. I'll submit the request today and let you know as soon as I hear back."

She hurried home. Zharla barged in and Renla looked up in surprise, still on her knees, scrubbing walls that Nayr had scribbled on.

Zharla knelt down beside her and picked up a damp cloth to help scrub. "We're moving back to my mother's house," she said. "You need to be able to leave with Nayr at a moment's notice. Do you remember the secret tunnel? At any point from two weeks and beyond, people may come to take Nayr, and we must not, I repeat not, let him fall into their hands."

She rested her hands on Renla's shoulders. "You must be ready to take Nayr to Meran Mountain until Ahrik's men can protect you. Is that clear?"

"Yes, Zhe'le." Renla probed her with searching eyes. "Stop scaring me."

Two days after the decision to move back to the Tameri compound, Zharla and Nayr were building towers out of blocks, seated on the floor of the parlor, when the door chime announced a visitor. Zharla moved to get it herself. She kissed Nayr and said, "Stay right here. Don't get into anything." *Yeah, right. Don't breathe, Nayr.*

She straightened her clothes and peered through the viewer to see who was outside. For a second she thought it was Ahrik, returning from Mekele for a short visit, but then she realized that was what she wanted, not what really was. The army wouldn't release its commanders on home leave right after calling all ketela to the colors, not while Esheli land was under enemy occupation. No, this was just one of Ahrik's men, his features shrouded enough by a hood to be mistaken for him. It was probably Leren or one of his group. Their protection was thorough, even though they rarely came into the house.

She reached to palm open the door, but then, in the instant between reaching for the door control and pressing her palm to open it, Zharla's memory injected a cruel, sickening association into her consciousness. The video file from the dying judge. The judge who was probably was dead already. Zharla had assumed that the video showed Ahrik and Shahl together when they were younger, but then she saw, in her mind's eye, as vividly as if he were standing there with her, the Ahrik look-alike bring his hand up to his nose in a motion that, she realized as her heart plummeted to her stomach, she had seen when Leren delivered his message just three days earlier: it was a tic that belonged to Leren.

She knew, with absolute certainty, that Shahl had never known or been a part of the secret of the ketel. He had never been near Leren, had not even known he existed. The Shahl look-alike in the video must have been someone close to Leren, someone connected with her case. Why else would the judge give it to her? The Shahl look-alike in the video was her rapist.

"Dear, sweet Lady, the judge knew all along," she said. Her hand hovered over the palm reader. Her legs grew weak. Her head swam. The moment ushered a bewildering truth. It was the only thing, in that moment of sickening, reckless association, that was in fact true at all. Nothing else mattered a whit.

She drew her hand back from the palm reader. She wanted to crumple to the floor, racked with uncontrolled sobs, to tear pictures from the wall and destroy the entryway. She wanted to run far away from that place and never, ever come back.

But she knew that none of that would do any good. She knew, because some deep well of courage told her so, that the time had come to claim her personal victory, to win her war.

A muffled voice sounded from the other side of the door. "Mistress Tamer-li?"

Zharla looked through the viewer. Leren. She saw the scar.

Eyes fixed on the door, she reached into her tunic and removed the heat knife, sheath and all. She set the knife on the side table, drew in a tremulous breath, and pressed her palm to open the door. Leren materialized before her.

"Mistress Tamer-li, may I come in?"

"No." He stood before her, confused, but she did not give him a chance to speak. "You are a soldier, and yet you know nothing of honor. You fight our wars, yet our trust in you is forfeit."

"Mistress Tamer-li, wha—"

"I don't know how, and I certainly don't know why, but you had something to do with my rape, and I will have no part of you or any of your men in my home. So, no, you may not come in. Not now, not ever. Go away, and do not ever, ever come back." Before he could respond or move, she resolved the door.

Through the viewer, she saw Leren stand there, dumbfounded. He turned and walked off. Zharla had won.

"Who was at the door?" Renla asked behind her.

Zharla eased herself around and faced her friend, smiling with relief. Zharla hugged her. "Re'le, I am free."

Ahrik sat at his desk and answered mail at his command center in Mekele, where they were preparing to defend the eastern approaches to the city. "That's odd," he said.

Ayen looked up from his desk, on the opposite side of the office. "Father? Everything okay?"

"No," Ahrik said. "My wife just sent me a message saying that everything is okay."

"So..."

"She's never done that before. Ever."

"Shall I send for your shuttle, Father?"

"No, no. That's okay. Leren and his men are there to protect her."

> LEREN: She knows.
> SHERESH SHEHUR-LI: How?
> LEREN: She was never supposed to know. Now what?
> SHERESH: Hmmm. This changes everything.
>
> ---
>
> Voice recording from the archives of the Ketel of Ahrik,
> 20 Kenen Sheni RY 2500

18 | Convincing the Pira

QUESTIONER: Did you have a keteli name before Ahrik came to power?
KETELI (ANONYMOUS): Yes, it was—
QUESTIONER: No, no. I don't want you to say it. I just need to know whether you had one or not.
KETELI: That's stupid.
QUESTIONER: Mind your tone, keteli.
KETELI: My name is Thorn. If you're going to call me anything, call me that.
QUESTIONER: Do you realize that you're no longer anonymous?
KETELI: I'm not an idiot. What good is a name if you don't use it?

Exchange during the inquest into the rise of Ahrik,
RY 2519

AHRIK blinked back a yawn. He'd only slept a few hours in the three days since the muster. If he stopped moving, he would simply drift into unconsciousness. The expectations of his men kept him moving. The knowledge that his nation was in peril kept him moving. His duty kept him moving.

Ayen entered his office with a tray of steaming tea, dark and rich.

"Ah, just what I needed."

Ayen nodded smartly. "Father, briefing in three."

Ahrik grunted in response and sipped his tea. He pondered

the weight his duty had become. "Ayen, why would the army use light-attack shock troops in static defense?"

Except for the handful of men he'd tasked with securing Zharla and Nayr, back in Meran, he and his ketel were entrenched along the eastern approaches to the capital, Mekele Eshel. Some two thousand kilometers separated them from the rebel beachhead at Hof Chelek.

"Father, shall I add this to the agenda for the briefing?"

Ahrik made an unpleasant sound. "Evasive, are we?"

Ayen gave a weary smile, his exhaustion just as deep. "They say a berzerker attack is imminent, Father."

Ahrik stood and took another sip of the rich tea, letting the liquid slide down his throat with a burning, sweet awareness. Ahrik scowled. "This is too easy."

"Shall I issue new orders, Father?"

Ahrik set down his tea and rubbed his temples. If he changed his orders, someone at higher might notice. This endangered the Ahit and everything they'd built up over the last two years. If he followed these orders blindly, however, he endangered his men's lives. His ketel had dug and reinforced their defensive positions in two days. And now they were just supposed to wait to be attacked?

He had to find a way to disobey.

Zharla's message squirmed at the back of his mind, like the key piece in a house made of toy blocks, inconsequential until it moved just so and the whole structure came tumbling down. But he was caught up in briefings and meetings and reports after she sent it, and could only send her a quick reply. Afterwards, in the wee hours of the morning, he caught an hour or two of sleep. When his alarm woke him, he jumped to his desk to see if she'd responded. Nothing.

It probably meant little, but it could mean everything. Ahrik was glad Leren was there.

Ahrik worked his tongue across the back of his teeth, unsure what the right decision was here. "Hold on new orders, Ayen."

Ayen sighed at his handheld. "The engineers are ready for you, Father."

Ahrik scratched his chin. "Remind me what briefing this is."

"Father, status report on defensive preparations."

Ahrik nodded, dragged himself down the hall, and straightened up before entering the briefing room.

"Father," the briefer began, stabbing at a graphic model with a pointer, "we have lines dug here, here, and here, with positions for operational reserves in the rear. Crew-served gun emplacements are spaced every two hundred meters along the line, with interlocking fields of view and communication trenches reaching all the way to the rear. The ketel has also dug and begun improving shelters all along the front. When the enemy comes, we will be sufficiently protected from their exploding metal shells to turn back any assault on the capital."

"Is aerial reconnaissance in place? Is it active?" Ahrik asked. "What about ground reconnaissance teams?"

"Check, Father. Based on the enemy's expected rate of movement, we'll have at least two days' advance notice before they come in range of our lines. Ground reconnaissance has begun emplacing low yield tectonics along a minor fault we found about five hundred kilometers out. Right here on the map, Father. We didn't want to chance using the higher yield weapons. Aerial reconnaissance has also seeded atmospherics. We'll be able to slow the enemy's approach, perhaps even stop it."

Ahrik was skeptical. He didn't show it. "Good. How long before the enemy shows up?"

The briefer looked at his colleagues in a way that said he didn't want to answer. "Hard to say, Father. Higher has kept us in the dark on their intelligence assets. Based on distance and terrain, though, we estimate four days."

Ahrik scrunched up his mouth and leaned forward in his seat. It was like the army was trying to lose. Somewhere in the system, nonchalance had turned to laziness, and laziness to decay, and decay to rot, till the system was nothing like it was originally intended. Ahrik breathed in to focus on the task at hand. "What's your name, keteli?"

"My name, Father?" He blinked. "They call me Goggles, but my number is—"

"No, no," Ahrik said. He held up a hand. "Just your name. Goggles. Thank you." A stunned silence hung over the room. Ahrik hadn't done this before, kept a briefer from giving his number. Protocol demanded that numbers be used. Ahrik raised an eyebrow. Change was hard, but necessary. "First."

"To the fight," they answered.

After they filed out, Ahrik turned to Ayen. "Get me Hawk."

"Zero-zero-two-one reporting as requested, Father." Ahrik's aerial recon commander gave a crisp salute. Not twenty minutes had passed since the briefing.

"Hello, Hawk," said Ahrik. He returned the salute. "How are your boys?"

"Ready for a fight, Father. Things have been slow since that one-month stint over the Emerald Moon."

Pain stabbed Ahrik's mind. "We lost a lot of good men that day."

"We fight to preserve their memory, Father."

Ahrik saw perfect conviction on Hawk's face, and he wished that he saw that same faith within himself. But Ahrik knew too much. The keteli system was not sustainable.

Shahl was right to rail against the military, even if he did not know the whole sordid story. An army of clones, raised in ironclad devotion to a few commanders, made it easy for a small group of powerful people to control how and where violence was used to enforce rules. In time of war, this level of control belied the subtle veneer of freedom that people thought they enjoyed. Now, another small group of powerful people, maybe even the same people, supported the rebel side in this war, ensuring that a state of war endured indefinitely.

Life was a fable. Women's rule could not remain as it was.

When enough people realized that clone soldiers underpinned it all, they'd be repulsed, just like Zharla was when she saw Ahrik's sons. Things would get very difficult for his sons, clones like Hawk who knew nothing but war and fighting and intense personal loyalty to one man and to the aging ideal of people ruling the world because of their gender.

"You're right, Hawk. That is the best way to preserve their memory." Ahrik swallowed and took a slow breath. "I have a mission for you. Very close hold."

"Check, Father."

"The ten thousand of Daf'e were supposed to be taking back Hof Chelek. Do you remember that ketel? We trained with them about four years ago, right after they gave us live distillers."

Hawk nodded with an air of fond remembrance, of a simpler time.

"I want to find out what happened," said Ahrik. His heart sank at the far-off look on Hawk's face. "I want to know why they didn't retake Hof Chelek from the rebel berzerkers, and I want to know where those berzerkers are now. What state are they in?"

"Check, Father."

"No one finds out about this mission outside the ketel, and as few men as possible within it. Am I clear?"

"Perfectly, Father. I'll conduct the mission myself."

Ahrik narrowed his eyes. "I need you to come back."

Hawk nodded, deep in thought. "I'll follow the lines of the transporter system to make it look like I'm a civilian transporter."

Ahrik nodded his assent. "I need an answer by dawn."

"Understood, Father. Report by dawn. Friendly and enemy disposition vicinity Hof Chelek. Check."

"First."

"To the fight."

After Hawk saluted and left, Ahrik called in his aide.

"Father?"

"Sit down, Ayen. What if I stopped calling you my sons and you stopped calling me Father?"

Ayen caught his breath and grew solemn. "That's all we know, Father."

"Could you do it?"

"We can do anything you ask, Father, but what's the point?"

"To prepare for the day when you're just like anyone else, subservient to no one."

"Our subservience is willing, Father. We are not citizens."

Ahrik rose and jabbed at his punching bag. "True, but if that changes... can a person learn freedom?"

Ayen thought on this for a moment. "Father, can anyone know the answer to that before it happens?"

Ahrik stopped and put his hand out to bring his punching bag to rest. "That makes me wonder, Ayen, if anyone is truly free."

"Father, you, of all people, would know that."

Ahrik stared at Ayen for a beat, unwilling to disabuse him of the fantasy. Maybe the farce was a useful one, at some level.

Ayen cleared his voice with a note of apology. "What would you call us, Father? We don't all have names."

Ahrik gestured ignorance with a shrug and a frown. "I'll be away until tomorrow morning. Contact me over the tendril link only if you hear from Hawk or Leren."

"Of course, Father."

Ahrik turned to leave, but Ayen raised a trembling hand. "Father," he said. "Please don't."

"Don't?"

"Don't stop calling us your sons. Please, Father."

Ahrik did not know what expression crossed his face then, but it was not one he had ever known before—a mix of sadness, pity, contemplation, and pain.

"I won't. Not now I won't."

Anda was grateful for two things. Before he infiltrated the Ketel of Ahrik, 3–3 Marauders, 1st Company, Two Squad, the rebels trained his body without mercy on the Emerald Moon. The rebels also taught him to clean a distiller and sharpen a qasfin. For two days after they shipped out to Mekele, all he did was dig trenches using his distiller with the vacuum tube attached, to expel the refuse to the rear. When he wasn't doing that, he disassembled and cleaned his weapon or sharpened his blade. That, and listened. He said as little as possible, which he found to be much easier than he'd expected it to be. "No, sir" and "Yes, sir" were all he needed. The life of a grunt might be dull and exhausting, but it was easy on the brain.

It gave Anda time to dwell on revenge, on whether he should even try to return to Esh'a. He'd always thought of this as a one-way trip. What would she care if he didn't come back? Then he thought of the burn on the inside of his arm, and what it meant to her. She'd made him promise to come back. He'd said he would, but doubted it would happen. No one kills a ketel commander and lives.

"Yuh dun't say much, do yuh?" one of his squad mates asked him on day three of their deployment. The rasping keen of the squad sharpening their qasfina punctuated the question like a descant. Or a dirge. Anda couldn't tell which.

Anda looked at him and made his eyes as dead as possible, then shook his head. The keteli shrugged, angled his body away from Anda, and went back to sharpening. Like Anda wasn't even there.

Which was exactly what Anda wanted. At times like these, the squad spoke freely. And Anda listened. He already learned that about half of the units in the Army of the Eshel were made up of clones, not just the Ketel of Ahrik. He gathered that they weren't happy about the war. He learned that Ahrik circulated down to the companies only rarely, so Anda would have to find some way to slip away, to take a message to command. For revenge.

Now, Anda stayed alert and made his whetstone sing along with the rest of the squad.

"Rumor has't wu'll be shuppin' out soon t'cutch us some 'zerkers," said one of his squad mates.

"We's here till we ain't, an' yuh'll like it," answered the squad leader, adding a scowl for emphasis.

Another keteli grunted in the squad leader's direction. "I heard wu'll fullow Cummand'r Leren back t'Meran."

"Ya," chimed in another, "t'guard Father's wife."

Anda sharpened a little more slowly. If the hand commander was away from his command on the eve of battle, it must be important. Did Zharla need protection, or was she a prisoner?

The squad commander growled. "We's here till we ain't."

The first keteli chuckled. "Father didn't guv th'bust urders, sendin' Cummand'r Leren."

Anda slowed his whetstone a bit more.

The second keteli answered with a chuckle of his own. "Check, ya. Poke over'n Three Squad says—"

The squad leader slammed his qasfin onto his cot with a sharp clang. "'Nough." He cast a wary glance in Anda's direction. "We dun't need more stories 'bout whut Poke did."

Anda froze, then recovered and pretended to check how sharp his edge was. He struggled to keep his breathing regular. This Poke, in the next squad over, did something. maybe to Zharla. And the squad leader didn't deny it happened, only that he didn't want to hear about it.

Could Poke be the rapist?

Only a mighty force of will kept his hand steady as he restarted his whetstone. It'd be a shame to slice a finger off now, with revenge so close. Ignoring the rapist in his own ketel for all these years was justification enough for what Ahrik had coming.

Anda paused in his sharpening once again, to ask himself what it would mean if the rapist really was so close. Anda had to find a way to get over the Three Squad. He had to determine, somehow, whether Poke was the rapist.

Ahrik ascended the steps to the central temple in Mekele, site of the confrontation between Shahl and Zharla a lifetime ago, when Ahrik was locked in a battle with the rebels at the transit station in the Kereu. With each step, Ahrik asked himself what could have been. What if Zharla had chosen Shahl instead of Ahrik? Would someone in his own ketel still have attacked her? Would someone still have concealed the clones of Shahl?

Would Ahrik still consider starting a civil war to reform women's rule?

He entered the temple and turned to hug the wall, shadowed from the dim light of the Emerald Moon, away from prying eyes. The days of the ketel system were numbered.

No more clones. The Ketel of Nayr would be the last.

If civil war broke out, many Eshela would die, and for what? The Esheli Republic had brought life. Many Eshela had more or less than they deserved, but who was Ahrik to say that they deserved death? But if Ahrik didn't start a civil war, it might happen anyway. If it would happen anyway, then Ahrik might as well launch it on his terms.

Ahrik sat and leaned his head and hands against the stone pew in front of him, an act of false supplication that any pir'e or confessant would construe as a desire for solitude. Ahrik had no place to say that his sons, his men, deserved anything more than nameless servitude to women's rule. Even if women's rule was rotten, and Ahrik wasn't convinced it was, he wasn't sure he could carry more innocent lives on his conscience.

Ahrik risked giving up the only life he'd ever known, his first oath of loyalty. Women's rule had drawn lines across society, with the men's rights movement and people like Shahl on one side, and those like Sheresh, supposedly fervent defenders of women's rule, on the other. Whatever action Ahrik and the Ahit took would certainly be interpreted in this context. Even if the Ahit desired only to reform the government, not remove women from power and make a man just as worthy for high office as a woman, it would still be difficult to keep the men's rights movement from mobilizing even more.

The only way that a military government, even a caretaker government, could maintain security would be to align with the men's rights movement. Concentrating power along any other lines would mean years trying to extricate the military from rule. Even if Ahrik and most of the Ahit were actually committed to women's rule, there would be no going back to it if they moved against the government. Women's rule might not be the cause of society's ills, but it would be the culprit.

Ahrik stared in despair at the stone temple floor, tinted green by the moon. The consequences of doing nothing looked just as dire. Men had begun The War, and they had nearly destroyed all human life on the planet, but bringing men into government might be better than the alternative. Ahrik shuddered. If this government remained in power, unaccountable as it was to so many, it would continue to prosecute a reckless war until the Esheli people stood on the knife's edge of existence. This government had not devised a response to the berzerkers, nor to the enemy's use of atomics. The army had the new tectonic and atmospheric weapons, but as a cure for atomics, they were no better than the disease. If Ahrik did nothing, the destruction would be immense.

The reason for this inaction was clear. The government wanted to perpetuate the rebellion. The root problem was not in the rebels' methods, which were grotesque, but in those people within Esheli society who benefitted from the kall–drugs–slaves–weapons nexus centered on the White Planet. The solution to this war lay somewhere in that nexus, a nexus that this government was either unable or unwilling to disentangle.

Ahrik kneaded his temples. As he did, the cold, stone pews rubbed against his forearms. He had to know what the government intended for the hundred thousand of Nayr. In about fifteen years, it would be the most powerful force on the planet. Unstoppable. The group of individuals that oversaw their education and training would rule the planet by force of will. In a system of reliable, accountable government and stable women's rule, this was not a problem, but under the current conditions, the prospect terrified Ahrik. If the conflict with the Kereu was not resolved by the time the Ketel of Nayr came online, it would be resolved afterward, and the conflict would depopulate the Kereu and sully the Eshel. The face of the planet might not be scoured by radiation, as in The War, but most of the people on the planet would be just as dead, killed off one by one at the hand of the hundred thousand, not by the millions because of atomics.

The only way to avoid another cataclysm was to subject the Ketel of Nayr to accountable civilian control. To Ahrik, this meant female civilian control, which was the purpose of the whole ketel system. The ketel system brought fighting men up in the tradition of peaceful women's rule, a deadly but precise weapon in the hands of wise rulers. Saving the planet from the scourge of Nayr required preserving women's rule and the ketel system that underpinned it.

So Ahrik reasoned, but war was the province of passion, chance, and reason. War guaranteed nothing. Men clamored now for what they called rights. Reform to women's rule was coming. Reforms could come through peaceful discussion or through violence. If the Ahit chose violence, the ketel system would be exposed to society as a whole. If the Ahit left the system to peaceful discussion, it might erupt into violence anyway.

Ahrik had sent Hawk to find the ground truth about the enemy, but he wasn't sure now, in the moonlit temple, whether knowing any truth would help at all. In the moment of decision, when Ahrik was forced to choose between stepping into or staying out of the political crisis, how could he say what the right decision would be?

He brought his hands to his forehead, as if in supplication. Perhaps the best he could do was to do right by his men, those people closest to him. Maybe that now included Zharla, or even Nayr. The boy represented the hundred thousand, the power to determine the fate of millions. If Ahrik was to act in the crisis, whether to take over the government or let politics play out, he would let his love for his men, and his regard for Zharla and Nayr, be his guide.

If the government sent the ketela into the streets to defend a-
gainst the men's rights movement, then the Eshel would be best
served by the Ahit turning on the government, not by attacking
unarmed protesters in the streets. If the ketela spilled the blood of
protesters, the people of the Eshel would never forgive them, and
the men's rights movement might destroy the government anyway,
leaving the Ahit and the ketela out in the cold. If the Ahit turned
on the government and worked with the men's rights movement to
reform women's rule, then the ketela would be seen as saviors of
the Eshel, which would allow them to win the war and integrate the
clones into Esheli society. Women's rule and the keteli clone system,
as currently constituted, operated on borrowed time.

Ahrik stopped his false prayer and raised his head, as if in supplication to the sliver of moon above. He hoped the Ahit would never
have to act. He needed to speak to the other members of his Ahit cell.
He needed to speak with Zharla. The predawn light crept over the
temple wall. Hawk would be back soon with his report. His fingers
gripped the pew in front of him and he readied to pull himself up.

He was grateful for this moment of solace, even though it meant
the sacrifice of much-needed sleep. His path was clearer now, despite the groggy fog that even now pushed its way back into his
fatigued mind. He paused after standing to pull in a deep breath,
but then hesitated, holding it in, because he heard as he did so the
subtle yet unique rhythm of the Ahit code being tapped out on a pew
behind him.

He could ignore it and walk out. The only members of the Ahit
he wanted to talk to now were in his own cell. He turned toward the
exit, but out of the corner of his eye he caught a glimpse of a red
robe. The only other person in the whole temple, the only one that
could have tapped out the Ahit rhythm, was not a military officer at
all, but a pir'e.

He paused, just long enough to show he'd heard.

"So," the pir'e said, his voice deep and soft, "my suspicions were correct." He motioned to the space beside him in the pew.

Ahrik sat and rubbed his chin. "You must be Analt."

Analt nodded.

"How are you—"

"A member of the Ahit?" said Analt. "I was a company commander in a ketel of one thousand, but the ketel commander and most of the ketel were killed or lost in the Kereu, at the beginning of this war."

"You don't look familiar. Whose ketel?" asked Ahrik.

Analt shrugged. "I escaped, or they let me go. I'm not sure which. The best place to hide was the presbytery. If they're trying to kill me, they haven't found me yet."

"How many of you are there?"

"Former ketelis in the presbytery, or Ahit members in the presbytery?"

"Yes."

"Out of the thousand or so former ketelis who are pira now, only about twenty are in the Ahit, at least that we know about. If a keteli wasn't a company commander or higher in his ketel, he is unlikely to make a reliable Ahit member."

Ahrik processed the implications. If the Ahit had spread to the pira, then they were even more well-positioned to take over the government, if it came to that. Ahrik shuddered and cocked his head. "You pira who are Ahit members, what do you want?"

"The justice that we never got. We want you to know that we are here."

"What would you do in the event of a..."

"A coup?" Pir'e Analt asked.

Ahrik winced. Hearing it out loud made it seem wrong. "I prefer to think of it as a transitional arrangement. A transition would be smoother without any surprises from the pira, if it comes to that."

A deep and unsettling chuckle issued from the pir'e's throat, darker than a moonless night, coupled with a face as happy as a nightingale. "My friend, it will definitely come to that, and it will not be your choice. Prepare for your transitional arrangement, as you call it"—he chuckled again—"because before long the people will clamor for change and you will have to step in, just to keep the streets from running red with blood. Even now, the government is lying through its teeth. The rebel berzerkers are nowhere near Mekele. They haven't even broken out of the beachhead."

"I'll verify that soon."

"Verify away. It won't change much. We will never meet again, you and I, but you will know when the pira act. We will bring tens of thousands into the streets, maybe hundreds of thousands."

"It might not come to that."

"When your man Hawk comes back from Hof Chelek, you will know I am right."

Ahrik drew himself back in shock. He could not know about Hawk's secret mission.

"Don't act so surprised. I'm in the business of knowing, Shadhir Jeber-li. Goodbye, and mark my words: your clones will be in the streets, out in the open, before the new moon."

Ahrik sat in disbelief. That gave him less than a day to prepare.

> SHERESH SHEHUR-LI: I'm not sure I can protect you anymore.
> MATRON TAMER-LI: You used me. You needed the weapons and drugs I brought you from off-planet to fight your phony little rebellion.
> SHERESH: [sighs] If you play with fire, sooner or later you'll get burned.
>
> ———
>
> Voice recording found in the Tameri clan archives during the inquest into the rise of Ahrik, RY 2519

19 | Uncertain Moment

Justice for all! Women's rule must fall!

The pira's call to revolution, 23 Kenen Sheni RY 2500

I N the settling gloam, Zharla's beloved city smoldered. The caller network said that men's rights protesters battled peace forces at the docks. Zharla went to her window to see for herself. The angry glow of burning warehouses down by the port made her mind imagine the furious chanting, wave after wave of the angry mob dashing themselves against the peace forces' shields and batons.

Who will die tonight?

Renla had lain Nayr down, then fallen asleep in his bed. Zharla crept into his room and reached a hand to Renla's shoulder. She remembered the night so many months ago when she had woken her friend to sneak out of the family compound to buy a heat knife in the bowels of Shtera Umqi. That was after the rape, when her world seemed a swirl of pain and sorrow, but now cynicism haunted her thoughts and showed her evil intent at every turn. Zharla enjoyed the bright spots in her life—Renla's friendship, Ahrik's loyalty, the hope that Nayr promised—but she spent most of her time now avoiding the script of some contrived theater, where morality was turned on its head.

"Re'le," she whispered, nudging her friend.

"Wha—?" Renla sat up and wiped a curly, reddish lock from her face, taking in a waking breath. "I fell asleep again, didn't I?"

"That's okay, my friend." Zharla tried to smile. She motioned for Renla to follow her out. As Renla rose, Zharla paused to consider the sleeping boy, so serene. If they could save Nayr from the swirling vortex that threatened him, then her life would be fulfilled. Zharla's coded plea to Ahrik, the all's well she knew he would disbelieve, had gone unrequited. She wanted to believe that Ahrik was truly unable to respond, that evil forces were intercepting his messages, that the murmurs of affection she sensed were real. But doubt crept in nonetheless. She steeled herself for the possibility that he would not come back in time to rescue Nayr from the grasp of evil men like Sheresh.

Zharla resolved the door and put herself within whispering distance of Renla, standing in the second floor corridor. The Tameri family mansion lay quiet, in a fitful sleep. "I need to leave," whispered Zharla. "You remember what I said about protecting Nayr?"

"What's going on?" Renla's face bore worry.

"It's better you not know, Re'le. If I'm not back by tomorrow morning, then you'll know I can no longer help you or Nayr. You must protect him."

"No, Zhe'le." A tear glinted in the pale starlight leaking through a window. The new moon gave off no light.

Zharla brushed away Renla's tear. "I'm doing this to give Nayr a better life." The fate of Nayr, of the world, trembled like a flower in her hands. She bore a visceral disdain for the rot, lies, and poison that fed the flames down by the docks, that curdled the anger upon which her people now choked. She dared not trust her determination to bear up this tender hope to some brighter future.

Ahrik strengthened her will. He might be unable to overcome the forces that threatened the peace of the Eshel, and less able still to rescue Nayr from the manipulation of scheming men and women, but he had become a man she could care for. That gave her strength.

Renla grasped Zharla's hand. "I won't ask what's going on, because you know I want to think your thoughts, to live your hurts."

"I know." Zharla hugged her friend, drank in the sweet scent of love. "Go find Ahjoz. Make sure that my mother does not see you exit the family compound. Remember the plan."

Renla shook her head, buried it in Zharla's tunic, moistened the soft fabric.

"Re'le," Zharla said, with what confidence she could muster, "Ahrik will come for you, and you must trust only him to protect our Nayr. Nayr is the hope for the future. He must be reared by those who want peace. Do you hear me? Peace. Ahrik will find you, and when he does, he will know what to do. He will protect our future."

"Why does that future not have you in it, Zhe'le?"

"I hope it will." She was not ready to die, but no one ever was. She left Renla, set her face against the unknown, and passed into the dark of night. As she slipped through the kitchen and out the back door, she remembered that she'd left her heat knife back at her old house.

Her war was already won. Now it was time to fight someone else's.

"Have they denounced the government yet?" Ahrik asked. The operations center simmered with tension.

"No, Father," said Brain, "but the callers report that the docks of Meran are on fire. The curfew here in Mekele is holding, but it is not clear how much longer that will be the case. If the pira denounce now, it will be a long night for the Eshel, especially if they report even half of what Hawk saw."

Ahrik nodded. "Are the interceptors of the 4th Hand in position to communicate with the ketel commanders I identified?"

"Check, Father."

"What of the 3d Hand?"

"Father, Leren and one of his standards—the 3-3 Marauders— are three kilometers from Mistress Zharla's residence in Meran, and the other standards in that hand are dispersed in static defense against the supposed rebel advance, here in Mekele."

"And the 2d and 5th Hands?" Ahrik didn't know which hand held the traitors, so he'd dispersed them all.

"Deployed covertly in Meran and Mekele city centers, Father, as you ordered." Brain shuffled his feet, and Ahrik saw his men exchange nervous glances. They did not like being so close to the public. They wanted to remain hidden from society. Ahrik wanted to tell them what was going on, to reveal his plan to save the Eshel from its government, but only if it was truly beyond the point of saving itself. If he told his men why he wanted them to deploy like they had, and if the coup failed, then the government could hunt his men down and ask them why, knowing what was going on, they still did nothing to stop it. Ahrik could not expose them to such a risk.

Instead, Ahrik simply confirmed what he already knew would be the case. "Have the ketel commanders I identified been asked if they can spare distiller packs?"

More nervous glances, but the lie held.

"Yes, Father," Brain said. Brain shot a questioning glance at his team, and some figures came up on the display. "Halsa and Kimen both replied that they have three thousand units each to spare, and that they could have them to us within four hours. Se'ed and Ghemid replied that they could send a full ketel's worth tomorrow morning, and Arnab replied that all of his distiller packs are tied up at the moment, but he will see what he can find at Eastern Command. The final commander, Alrem, Lady keep his ketel, responded that he might be able to scrounge up some packs at higher." Brain paused before continuing. "But Father, we would never need that many—"

Ahrik cut him off with a look. "Good. Now, we wait."

"Mistruss Tamer-li. Yuh'r out."

One of Ahrik's men blocked the alley. She moved to the right, and he moved with her. "Let me pass," she said.

"My urders say to keep yuh safe, and ut's nut safe t'leave home now."

His accent sounded just like that of the weapons dealer in Shtera Umqi, and she wondered if there was a connection between the ketela and the ah'sbi gangs.

Zharla planted her feet. "Who gave those orders? What unit are you with?"

"3–3 Marauders, 1st Company, Three Squad." He crouched into a fighting stance, hand at the blade on his hip. "I won't hurt yuh, but yuh don't hurt me."

"I'm not armed," said Zharla, showing her palms. The distant bark of night herons by the docks haunted and wheeled away on the air, and clouds shrouded the stars, as if they wanted no knowledge of what transpired in the alley. The night chill began to bite.

What few features of the keteli she could make out, she studied intently, sizing him up. She pondered her next move, then gave what she meant as a disarming smile. "I must leave, for the sake of those I love. My only chance at passing you is to overpower you with violence, but I trust your ability to make this impossible. We are at an impasse."

"How to sulve it?"

"First, you do not call your fellow ketelis."

"How do yuh know I 'aven't ulready called 'um?"

"Easy. In order to transmit over the tendril link, you need a moment of intense concentration, albeit a brief one. I've seen my husband do this, and I've been watching you since you stopped me. You have not yet transmitted. You want to gain favor with Leren by capturing me alone. Such a lack of loyalty is unworthy of a son of Ahrik, no?"

The soldier's eyes widened, and Zharla knew she had hit close to the mark. She pressed her initiative.

"Why do you defy my husband?"

The soldier drew himself up, looked her in the eye, and declared, "I'd die fur Father."

"Such strong words." Zharla moved forward, to emphasize the bluff. "Such frail conviction."

He backed up a step. "Yuh go back 'ome."

She drew close enough for him to know that she meant what she said. "You know that my husband never published an order to confine me to my home, and you know that some of your higher-ups are willing to defy Ahrik, even if you think you do not."

A glint of fear flashed across the soldier's face. Zharla could tell he wanted to deny her accusation, but could not. He backed up again. Zharla stepped toward him once again.

The keteli shook his head. "My... Cummand'r Leren's business is 'iz own."

"Is that how you think the world works? You're just a keteli, a clone soldier, taking orders and living and dying for a man you call 'father,' and what you do or don't do has no impact on the real world. You live a life of violent servitude, devoid of responsibility, divorced from consequence. Wake up! Wake up and look at the world around you. For centuries the keteli clones have been a closely-guarded secret, yet here you stand, supposedly protected by the cloak of darkness and your fancy uniform, but at any time some stranger could walk up and think, 'Why is Zharla Tamer-li having a conversation with her husband in the middle of an alley at night, only a half-kilometer from her home?' Now that would bring a lot of uncomfortable questions, wouldn't it?"

Zharla poked her finger in his chest.

The soldier looked around, as if expecting a stranger to emerge at just that instant. "I... I nuver thought about it like thut."

"No, of course you haven't, because this is a new world. The world you know is dying, and the one that's taking its place has real consequences for violence and for people that hurt others." A twinge of guilt twisted within her breast for preying on this lone soldier, but she reminded herself of her purpose. "As soon as the callers realize the extent of military cloning, your veil of anonymity will evaporate, and you'll have to find a way to become a part of society, and if society asks what you've done, you may have some explaining to do, because it won't be enough to say that Leren made you do it, or that you 'wuz jus' fullowin' urders.'"

"I nuver wanted t'hurt anyone."

"It's too late for that, keteli. Do you even have a name?"

He looked to the cobbled stones with a dejected face. "Seven-five-zero-three."

Zharla knew she had almost won, but her object was too important to let pity sway her now.

He furrowed his brow. "Why 'too late,' Mistruss Tamer-li?"

That question almost broke her, but her spirit held. If she didn't do this, the lives of millions might be on her conscience. She had to save Nayr. She had to get to Mekele to find Ahrik. She suppressed the tremor in her voice. "Tell me, seven-five-zero-three, what do you know about the night of my wedding?"

He squeezed his eyes shut and shook his head with surprising violence. "Nothin'. Nothin' t'all." He backed against the alley wall.

"You know what happened that night, don't you? At least you heard whispers and rumors, right? A small group from the 3d Hand infiltrated my family compound, didn't they? Was it the 1st Company? They found my room, didn't they? Was it Three Squad? Your squad? I've no idea how they got in. Then what happened?" The keteli crouched down, and she crouched down next to him, her eye level just above his, her breath at a whisper. "What happened, seven-five-zero-three?"

"No. No." He looked up, his eyes saucers of fear.

She glared straight into them. "They. Raped. Me."

Seven-five-zero-three covered his head with his hands. "I wunted no part of it."

"You were there, weren't you?"

He squeezed his close-cropped hair in his hands. "I wuz there."

She slipped his qasfin from its sheath and brandished it in front of the soldier's cowering form. It would be so easy to slip it through his face, or into his chest. It would gratify her, if only for a moment, to share her pain with this accomplice to her rape. Vengeance seethed inside her, looking for a way out, but in her mind she knew that if she was to rise to some higher purpose, she had to let this man live. She needed him now, in order to accomplish her plan.

She looked down and saw the soldier's eyes, no longer wide with fear or drawn into slits of anger or alert with a move to defeat an opponent in a position of advantage. His eyes were now calm, acceptant, resolute. Resolute in the knowledge of his guilt, and resolved to the consequences of his actions.

She cast away the qasfin. It clattered against the pavement, dull, gray, and cold. She could not destroy the nobility in those eyes.

Zharla reached a hand down to help seven-five-zero-three up from the alley floor. "I forgive you." She considered him. "I imagine it is not done this way in the ketel, but I will call you Risen, for you have risen from guilt to a higher purpose."

"I huvn't done anythin' good yet, Mistruss Tamer-li." He rose and turned to let her pass.

"Then start by coming with me to Mekele. I need to find Ahrik."

"I cun do that. I know where all th'checkpoints are." Risen knelt on the ground and bowed his head, palms on the pavement. "Mistruss Tamer-li, I wull help yuh. I die for Father. I die for yuh."

She stole a glance up and down the alley, uncomfortable that this man was kneeling to her, unsure what was expected in response to the situation. She tugged at one of his combat straps. "Get up, please."

He nodded, but kept his eyes low. "Yes, Mistruss Tamer-li."

She stooped down to retrieve his qasfin, struck by the fervency of his oath. He would not be deterred, and she hoped that his same courage and loyalty resided in the rest of Ahrik's men. They would need it before the night was done.

She handed him his qasfin. "I hope, my new friend, that your wish is not granted too soon."

Ayen appeared in the doorway, eyes breathless. He panted. "Father, the pira denounced."

They trotted to a stop in the operations center as the midnight sermon to the new moon played on a compiler display. "Father," said Brain, "he just accused the government of lying to the Esheli people." Pir'e Analt described the destruction at Hof Chelek in bombastic tones.

"Ayen," said Ahrik, "order the 2d and 5th Hand commanders to secure the temples in Mekele and Meran. They are to use the least violence possible to protect the pira and their temples from government retaliation."

Ayen focused on the tendril link.

Ahrik returned his attention to the pir'e. Analt mentioned how the rebels were nowhere near the capital, and how the rebel advance had actually stopped completely. The pir'e described the destruction just as Hawk had. Twenty thousand Esheli troops gone, and at least twice as many rebels. Hawk had seen what remained of logistics depots, defensive works, command posts, and thousands upon thousands of bodies, but no one alive, as far as he could tell. Hawk had been confident that the rebels were no longer consequential as an offensive force, assuming any were left alive.

But the keteli defenders were also dead, tens of thousands sacrificed for some vague purpose.

Pir'e Analt described the mountains of Hof Chelek, broken up and cast down, the buildings around the city nothing but rubble, plainly the effect of massive tectonic activity. The pir'e described how wind and rain had made the port area unrecognizable. Little trace remained of peaceful human habitation.

Ahrik's shoulders sank. "The army misjudged the strength of the tectonics and atmospherics, and now twenty thousand men and an entire city are gone. Send a message to the other ketela. We need those distiller packs. Now."

"Check."

"And get my shuttle ready. I'm going to lead the fight with the

5th Hand."

Zharla and Risen sped toward Mekele on the midnight transporter. The compiler display at the front of the transporter capsule ran Pir'e Analt's midnight sermon in honor of the new moon. The destruction at Hof Chelek horrified her, although her companion gave no sign of either reaction or understanding. He remained huddled in his seat with Zharla's cloak pulled over his head. She'd given him her cloak so as not to draw attention to the fact that he was a soldier. His plaintive reaction to the destruction in Hof Chelek unnerved her. Maybe war did that to you, allowed you to separate yourself from destruction and death. Some might call this courage, some fear.

Zharla gulped as she watched the sermon. She fought to control her breathing. She whispered, "Risen, the streets of Mekele might be enflamed when we arrive."

The Mekele transporter station was packed with irritable, pushy people clamoring to get on transporters to the rural areas. Peace forces crawled over the station. They didn't check their identities, so Zharla and Risen avoided explaining why he looked like her husband and shared neither his retinal scan nor his eloquence.

Once outside, the improbable duo kept to the shadows as they made their way east. Zharla heard chanting and drums on the night air as protesters gathered. She saw threatening groups of youngsters congregate on street corners. The smell of sweat, urine, and cheap hallucinogens crept after Zharla and Risen as they passed the pots of brewing discontent. Frequently, they saw smaller, but no less threatening, groups of peace forces on patrol. For the moment, everyone kept their distance from each other, regular streetgoers like Zharla and Risen walk-running to their destinations, keeping clear of both law and lawbreakers, and the peace forces and clutches of youth giving each other a wide berth.

The *pop* and *thunk* of distiller weapons sounded in the distance.

They passed a column of hayla—not peace forces, but soldiers—jogging towards the center of the city, distillers at the ready, faces fierce.

"Where are they going, Risen?" she hissed.

He squinted in their wake. "Prob'ly th'central temple, Mistruss Tamer-li."

"Take me to Ahrik."

They worked their way eastward, toward Ahrik's base. Zharla heard the sounds of large masses of people chanting, shouting, and marching toward the center of the city.

Risen gave a nervous groan. "Lotta people fightin' t'night."

As if to punctuate the thought, a pair of military aircraft hummed overhead. A second pair of craft slid in. Blue and red tracers lit up the sky as they darted and jerked among each other.

Zharla and Risen looked at each other and ran. A new kind of war had begun.

At the eastern edge of the city, Risen gasped and jumped toward a wall, yanking her back by the arm.

His chest heaved. "Sorry... 'bout yur arm... Mistruss Tamer-li." He nodded forward. "Bad things... HQ."

"How... can you see? There's... no moon... no lights." Zharla wiped her brow and opened her eyes wide to see if they would adjust to the intermittent starlight, but it was no use. She had no idea what to look for.

"I know... where... t'look." He pointed. "Militury road... three hills north... crawlin'... wuth peace forces... if Father's there... no use ... t'yuh 'ny more."

"I... I need to see... for myself."

"Can yuh... run s'more?"

She fixed him with a glare and steadied her breathing, for emphasis. "I ran this far."

He smiled. "We might need... t'run back... t'th'city centur... ten ur fifteen minutes... no long'r."

"I can do it." She couldn't help but notice that her breathing was returning to normal more quickly than his.

"Good...If I say...yuh run." He cocked his head and took a deep breath. "No stuppin'. Back to station." He peered at her. "Check?"

"Yes. Check." She had no business using that word.

By the time Zharla could see what Risen had seen, her clothes were full of stickers, her knee was bruised because she had tripped on a root. She saw the peace forces, though. They were milling about, apparently unsure of their next move. A few soldiers, probably Ahrik's, sat on the ground, bound together hand and foot, their heads hung low.

"Is Ahrik there?" she asked Risen.

"No, Mistruss Tamer-li, but—"

He did not finish, for just then a twig snapped behind them. Zharla whipped around to find herself looking at the wrong end of a distiller. The tingling buzz told her that it was primed to discharge.

"Don't move a muscle," a threatening voice warned in the darkness beyond the weapon.

"She dies. Yuh die." It was Risen. Somehow he had managed to bring his weapon to the ready in the fraction of a second it had taken her to turn around. Amazing.

"I don't think so," came another voice out of the darkness. The buzz of at least five other distillers priming followed. Risen did not lower his weapon.

"What are we supposed to do with these two?" asked the first voice.

"Anyone have a light—a very dim one? I think all our lookers are...otherwise engaged." Zharla heard some ominous chuckling in the dark. After a soft rustle, a dark shape moved toward her. Risen growled.

"Okay," one of their captors said. "Take it easy. I just need to see what we got." The shape moved a bit closer. "Look, friend, anyone with reflexes as fast as you has got to be keteli. In fact, it's a good bet you didn't need this light to see us. I can see my lamp reflected in the back of your cat eyes." The men paused. "Wait a second," he said, moving the light back and forth between Zharla and Risen. "What in the name of the Lady are you doing here?"

moving the light back and forth between Zharla and Risen. "What in the name of the Lady are you doing here?"

"Yuh. New Guy." The squad leader spat in Anda's direction. "Go up t'Three Squad an' fin' out whur th'healurs are."

At Anda's questioning glance, the squad leader sighed with exasperation. He dragged Anda to the opening of the alley they had occupied and pointed up the murky, cobbled street. "Tuh alleys up, on th'right, check?" He gave Anda a firm push in that direction. "An' hurry. We's joinin' up wuth cumpany'n ten, check?"

The streets in this part of Meran were deserted. Meranis were either rallying at the docks or at Shtera Umqi, in-mountain, or ensconced safely at home. He hoped Zharla was safe at home now.

He was almost to the second alley on the right when a forbidding realization assaulted him. He knew this street. The high wall across the street was the southern wall of the Tameri family compound. Down on the corner, past the second alley, was the tea shop where he waited in vain for Zharla a lifetime ago.

A hand reached out and grabbed a fistful of his cloak, then dragged him into the alley. The fist found the side of his head next, and Anda slammed into a stone wall. "What're yuh thinkin' trekkin'n th'open? Yuh furget we's in an urban 'vironmunt?" The fist yanked him up. "Wait'll I—"

The assailant sucked in his breath, and Anda tried to regain his footing as he was dragged forward and thrown to the ground.

"Ho, Poke. It's yer twin, check?"

Ketelis circled around him and chuckled low in the glowering dimness. Anda's senses returned. He scanned the faces and found the eyes that could have committed the evil Anda suspected him of. Anda stared into a face like his own. A needling ire crescendoed to a fire within his breast.

A hand thrust down to help Anda up. "Leave 'im 'lone, check?" A healer. "Yuh from Two Squad? We're dun 'ere."

Before he left with the healers to go back to his squad's hideout, Anda took one last look at Poke, at the rapist. If he could only kill one, he'd have to decide whether it should be Ahrik or Poke.

"Status report," said Ahrik.

"Father," said Goggles, from the intel shop in the 5th Hand. "2d Hand reports temples in Meran secured. 3d Hand earlier reported Ketel of Nayr secured, but then nothing for the past hour. 4th Hand reports movement by other ketela to secure Chief Elders and caller network stations. Stiff resistance in Mekele from the peace forces and some hayel forces backing them up. As you know, Father, Arnan and our 5th hand have secured the temples in central, south, and west Mekele, but we are facing resistance elsewhere."

"Any word from command company?"

"No, Father. They reported large numbers of peace forces approaching after you left. They may be engaged."

"Not likely. They'd know I wouldn't want them to spill blood just to defend the headquarters. They probably left a few prisoners and withdrew, to catch up with me later."

Goggles furrowed his brow. "Have you tried hailing Brain on the tendril link, Father?"

"No response. Did Leren and the 3d Hand give any news about Nayr and my wife before communications dropped?"

"No, Father."

Something needled him about how communications with Leren dropped. He didn't want to believe that his best hand commander could be the traitor.

Ahrik pressed his lips together and considered the situation. He'd made the central Mekele temple his forward base, so he walked away from the bustle around the altar area and through the pews. The early autumn night was chilly but not cold. The peace forces in this part of the city had given up quickly, so they stood around outside the temple, disarmed and sipping tea, Ahrik's men keeping a close watch. The operation wasn't over yet, but it had been fairly bloodless, and most of the organs of the state were in the hands of the Ahit. Navigating the politics tomorrow morning would be tricky, but for now Ahrik felt like they had won something.

One thing didn't sit right, though, and it centered on Meran, Zharla, and the 3d Hand. He sat and focused on this, but then a thought intruded on his mind: *Father.*

Brain? he cast back.

Sorry. No good... tendril... need... practice.

Brain couldn't keep the tendril link strong, even though they were fairly close. Ahrik would have to work with his command company on that.

What news, Brain?

HQ... taken... most... withdrew.

Ahrik sensed that Brain struggled to relay something important. *What else, Brain?*

We have your wife.

"Sweet Lady of the Emerald Moon." Ahrik rushed back to the altar area. "Goggles, find Bat. I need my shuttle. This is not over yet."

> SHERESH SHEHUR-LI: Prepare for your liberation, keteli.
> LEREN: What's your price?
> SHERESH: Kill Ahrik.
> LEREN: [scoffs] No liberation is worth that.
> SHERESH: [pause] Fine, then capture the boy. If you cannot capture him, then kill him, and his mother, too.
>
> ---
>
> Voice recording found in the archives of the Ketel of Ahrik during the inquest into the rise of Ahrik, RY 2519

20 | Battle for the Ketel of Nayr

Kill the woman. Kill the child.

Leren's order to his men before the Battle for the Ketel
of Nayr, Kenen Sheni 24 RY 2500

Z HARLA shivered against the cold, dark night on the Eshel's central plain, unsure if she was a captive or a guest in the very watchful company of Ahrik's men. Ahrik's shuttle landed, and the wind rustled through the long grass, whispering premonitions of the futures that could be. The shuttle's ramp extended, and Ahrik walked out, his boots swishing on the fitful prairie.

She eyed him with care. *What have we won tonight, and what have we lost?* Risen moved closer to Zharla, as if unsure where his loyalties lay.

Ahrik nodded to her, his form silhouetted against the shuttle's landing lights as he moved toward her. The breeze picked up when he stopped, and he did not smile. He stood farther away from her than a loving husband should. "Zharla."

So, he is just as unsure of us as I am. "Ahrik, I'm glad I found you." She took two quick steps toward him and made as if to embrace him. She relished his look of astonishment, but it did little to calm the squeamishness in her gut. She had to know where they stood, so she hugged him, light and chaste, but as she did so she drew her mouth close to his ear and whispered, "Which of these can I trust?"

She stepped back, hands clutched to his shoulders, and looked at him. "I thank the Lady that you have come back to me. Now take me home." The men chuckled as Zharla and Ahrik made their way to the shuttle, Risen in tow. She reached for Ahrik's arm, but his arm wasn't there. He had slipped his arm around her shoulder. He squeezed her to him and, as his men gave a chorus of support for their leader, he leaned down and whispered back, "Ayen and Brain and the pilot. In the cockpit, tell me your news."

Anda recoiled at the stench of blood and cauterized flesh.

"Goin' t'hurl, Anda?" one of his squad mates teased. The keteli sauntered over, a bandage pressed to the base of his neck.

Anda fought to control his breathing. The company's healers passed from one squad member to another, excising compilers. Anda didn't hear a single cry of pain, even though he saw no anesthesia administered.

The healers approached. Anda hoped they would buy his story about having his compiler excised earlier. That they'd believe the scar left by Zharla's heat knife. One keteli brought a scanner up to the back of his neck while the other readied a scalpel. "Thus'll be quick," said the one with the scalpel, in that way that healers do when a procedure will not feel quick at all. "Wait a sec..."

Anda tried to mimic the keteli dialect. "It stopped wurkin' tuh munths 'go. No ruplacement yet." He held his breath, even though he'd told himself over and over that he would not. No need to draw undue attention to himself.

"Huh," the second healer said. "That's a nusty scar. They 'lready caut'rized?"

The one with the scanner broke in. "C'mon. We gut fifty more 'f these t'do."

"Right," answered the one with the scalpel. "It's yur lucky day, keteli. Firs'."

"To th'fight," Anda answered, astonished that his little deception worked.

■

"Bat."

"Father?"

"Seal the cockpit."

"Father." The partition between the cockpit and the main cabin resolved, and the murmured conversations of the protection squad faded. Ayen plunked away on a handheld compiler, and Brain stared into the middle distance, in communication with his intelligence team over the tendril link. The scared keteli, Risen, cast his eyes this way and that like a frightened animal, and Zharla gave Ahrik her characteristic, expectant stare.

He would not get any more alone with his wife. "Why did you come, Zharla?"

"My rapist is one of Leren's men," she said. An ominous silence descended on the cabin.

"Did you confront Leren?"

"Of course."

"That explains why you and I haven't been able to communicate for the last few days." It also explained why Leren went dark tonight. There was no telling now if any of 3d Hand's initial reports were accurate.

Ahrik exchanged a knowing glance with Ayen and Brain. He didn't need the tendril link to know what they were thinking: the traitors were likely in the 3–3 Marauders. Ahrik groaned. Brain glared at the unit designation on Risen's uniform.

Bat glanced up from his piloting. Risen clamped his hands over his ears, eyes shut.

"Ahrik," said Zharla. "There's more." She told Ahrik about the judge and the video recording.

Ahrik buried his head in his hands while his regret mixed with dread. How he wanted to reach out to Zharla and show her, somehow, that he would always be by her side. "I missed something so simple, and it hurt you."

"Ahrik," she whispered.

"Had I only trusted you from the beginning. Had I only treated you as you deserved..."

"Ahrik," she whispered again. Her hand moved.

"...none of this would have happened. I should have understood things as clearly as I do now." He squeezed his scalp mercilessly.

"Ahrik." She grasped his arm.

He froze, unable to meet her gaze. "Had I been with you on our wedding night," he said, "you would not have been raped."

He looked up, itself a monumental chore, and studied his wife. Guilt threatened to burst from his eyes, and he felt himself brought low. "Zharla." He choked, squeezed his eyes shut, and focused on her again. A single, mournful tear slid down his cheek. "Please forgive me."

She sighed and moved her hand onto his. It did not ease the pain, but told him that she would always be with him. He wiped his eyes and looked at his wife again. She undid her restraints and knelt beside him. She slipped her arms around his shoulders, nestling her head in the crook of his neck. She pressed herself to him, and Ahrik believed there was an inkling of hope in the world.

As she drew away, after too short a time, Ahrik noticed that her wrists were bare. The necklaces that Shahl had given her were gone. She saw where he stared, saw the question in his face, and gazed at him with reassurance. Peace flooded her eyes. No trace of scorn, of remorse, of blame for what he'd done. Or not done. Just her and him.

"Zharla, I—" He wanted to say more after he said her name, but even those trusted few within earshot were too many to hear those words. Those words were ones that only one other set of ears should hear.

Zharla smiled, not with her mouth, but with her whole person. She smiled like he had never seen her smile, not in the years when they were children, and certainly not in the time since they were married. He smiled back and felt something new, something reflected in her face.

"Father." Bat, a whisper from far away. "Ten minutes from Meran." He needed orders, a plan. Ahrik's heart was about to beat out of his chest, and he still had one more battle to fight.

He turned to Zharla as she buckled back into her restraints. "Do you know if Nayr and Renla got away from Leren and his men?"

Her look of worry said everything.

He rubbed his chin. "If you're willing to take some risks, I have a plan that just might work."

The company commander stood on a box in the tea shop they occupied. Anda knew it well, because he spent his last evening in Meran here, before his life turned into a living hell. He looked out the window and across the street, at the high wall surrounding the Tameri family compound. He never thought he'd be back here. Not like this.

"Attention, 1st Company, 3–3 Marauders," said the 1st Company commander. "Orders are to occupy the roof of the Tameri house at the signal from the advance team. It'll get hot after that, but the rest of the standards in 3d Hand have some new weapons to help us out. They've left their positions on the outskirts of the city and are coming to support us here."

Someone whispered, just a bit too loud, "Izn't this contrury to urders?"

Anda looked over at Three Squad to locate Poke, the rapist, while the tea shop buzzed and the company commander whipped his head around, looking for the source of the question. "Yeah, it's contrary to orders, keteli, but so is everything else we're doing. Every one of us had a chance to beg out, just like they did before that op in the Kerewi village. You beggin' out, keteli?"

"No, sir."

"That's what I thought. We're fighting for a bigger cause than Ahrik, here, 1st Company. We're fighting for freedom. Move out."

Anda kept the rapist in his field of vision as the company filed into the night.

Zharla crouched in a dark alley across from her family's compound. She peered up and down the cobbled street, lit only by stars. The street sat empty, as if the city knew what horror threatened. The wall of the compound, three meters tall, loomed over them. Ayen tapped away at his handheld compiler while Brain covered the murky street with his distiller. Fog began to roll in from the bay. Risen crouched beside her, fingering his qasfin. Five of Ahrik's men, half of his protection squad, had just left to enter the compound by the front gate.

Ayen breathed out in frustration and set his compiler down on the pavement. He looked at Brain. "We've lost all contact with 3d Hand. The 3–3 is around here somewhere, I know it, and the rest of 3d Hand have abandoned their posts around Meran. The whole hand's probably converging here."

Brain swore under his breath. "We need to find Nayr and rendezvous with Father. Fast."

Zharla moved toward them. "I'm not leaving without Renla."

"Yes, ma'am," said Ayen. Worry crossed his face. He turned to Risen and pointed to the Tameri estate. "Reconnoiter."

"Check," whispered Risen. He turned to Zharla. "Mistruss Tamer-li, thuy'll keep yuh safe."

She nodded, and Risen slid through the shadows. He slipped across the street and slinked to the darkest part of the wall, where his figure became a shimmering silhouette that melted into the wall behind it. In one movement, he jumped halfway up the wall and scrambled up the rest of the way, pausing momentarily at the top before he shimmied over. Had she not known where to look, and been following him with her eyes, Zharla would not have seen him do it.

So that's how they got in that night. She turned to Ayen. "How did Risen do that?"

Ayen picked up his handheld compiler and stared at the middle distance, as if he had just been asked a stupid question. "Do you mean, Mistress Tamer-li, that you do not know about our genetic modifications?"

"I can tell you are modified. I don't know how."

"Many of us have larger, stronger hands with the ability to grasp sheer surfaces, although we have to train for months to be able to do it as well as Risen did. I cannot do it."

"I see."

"May I? Our reconnaissance patrol just entered the compound, and Risen is emplacing sensors around the building." He tapped at the compiler.

She nodded, then looked at Brain, who had stepped to the other side of the alley when Risen left. He scanned the street with piercing, alert eyes. Ayen worked fervently and displayed complete trust in his comrade to protect him while he was vulnerable. Every movement was practiced, comfortable, as if death and destruction were a game to them. Maybe killing and dying had to become a game at some point, so it didn't take over your mind.

They waited, but for what, Zharla feared to question. Brain covered the street with his distiller, and Ayen worked on his external compiler. Zharla memorized every building, every nook and cranny of the alleyway, which all her life had been marvelously insignificant until now, when there was nothing to do but learn it by heart. Her eyes drifted and wandered, exhausted but sleepless. She scanned the darkness of the alley, the pebbles on the ground. Her gaze rested on an odd-looking pebble, about the size of the end of her thumb, possessed of a dark, dull sheen. Curious, she reached out and picked it up. It was surprisingly heavy and a bit wet. She was revolted at first but managed to overcome it.

"What's this?" she asked, her voice perhaps a little too loud. Ayen and Brain turned, and their eyes grew as wide as the sky above. Ayen snatched it out of her hand, and Brain immediately cleaned her palm with disinfectant from his healing kit.

"This," said Ayen, raising the object up in his gloved hand, "is an internal compiler. It used to be in the neck of one of Leren's traitors."

"They took them out?" asked Zharla. Her stomach churned.

Ayen nodded, then paused, sending a tendril message to Ahrik.

Brain explained, "The compilers are for tactical communication, but also emit a faint signal to track position. Our equipment told us they'd be here, but they were not." He locked eyes with Ayen. "The game is changed. We thought they were trying to find us, but now we have to find them."

Ayen pursed his lips. "If they're inside, your family is in grave danger."

Brain shook his head. "The way through the main gate is compromised. They must be watching after the protection squad entered."

Zharla looked at the pavement. Should she break the oath she'd made to her grandmother? "There is another way," she whispered.

Perhaps they were all oathbreakers tonight.

"Wait," said Ayen. He paused to receive a message from Ahrik. Panic flashed in his eyes. "Father has found Nayr and Ahjoz on Meran Mountain, but Miss Renla is not with them."

Brain cast a nervous glance at Zharla. "We have to hurry. Without Nayr, they might not hesitate to kill your friend."

Ahrik scanned the bleak night, trudging up the familiar trail on Meran Mountain. It had to be a coincidence that Zharla told Renla to send Nayr here, to the same place where he and Shahl had hiked as boys.

The thought of Shahl made Ahrik wish he'd treated his brother better. Maybe the decision ceremony would have been different. Ahrik would have been a better brother, a better husband, a better man.

If he'd been a better man, Shahl would still be alive. If he had been a better man, he would have told Zharla to choose his brother instead, and then the vicious mire of war would not have sucked them in, along with Ahrik. It might have touched them in different ways, but in easier ways, ways that were not so final and unchangeable.

The eerie familiarity of the trail reminded him of all that could have been. He trudged on, stopping on occasion to listen for movement and peer into the stillness. At one such pause, he swept his gaze out to sea, where the faint light of predawn had begun to creep over the horizon. Every day dawned clean, but nothing could be done for the sins of yesterday.

The *zing* of a distiller charge sizzled by, yanking Ahrik back to the present. The contrail crackled orange, which meant it was one of the local security models, not a keteli weapon. He crouched and pointed his weapon toward the source of the contrail, but heard movement in the underbrush instead. He cursed his sloppiness.

"Drop it," yelled a voice out of the darkness. Ahrik reached out over the tendril link to the five members of his protection squad who were with him. He felt them there, in the darkness, slowly surrounding the source of the voice.

"Ahjoz, is that you? It's me, Ahrik." No answer. Another distiller charge came in—*zing*—and buried itself in the rock above Ahrik's head. The sharp smell of sulfur and ozone settled over him.

"I missed intentionally," came the voice again.

This time, Ahrik was sure it was Ahjoz. *Do not harm him*, he cast to his men.

"Ahjoz, listen. I'm Ahrik and I've come to help Renla and Nayr—"

"Quiet!" The forbidding silence accentuated the sound of a single distiller charging in the darkness. "Drop your weapon."

Ahrik unhooked his kall line and eased his distiller down, then began to creep forward. "Ahjoz, Renla and Nayr are in danger. We're here to protect them, just like you are."

"Come toward me slowly." The distiller went quiet, and Ahrik relaxed. He continued forward, but when he was only two meters from where Ahjoz's voice had come from, he stumbled and skinned his hand on a rock. Ignoring the pain, he continued on. When he arrived, Ahjoz was not there. Instead, he heard the sound of a distiller charging again, this time just over his right temple. Five other distillers sprang to life, making an ominous chorus.

"If you kill me, you'll be dead in an instant," Ahrik said. *Do not harm him unless he kills me*, Ahrik cast.

"I'll take that risk, boy. I am nobody, but if you are who you say you are, then you are very important. There are a lot of copies of Ahrik running around tonight, so I need to be sure it's you."

"Fine."

"Tell your men to charge down their weapons."

"Do as he says," he called, even though he knew it wasn't necessary to call out. His men would understand how to act.

"Tell me," said Ahjoz, "what was the last thing your wife said to you at the decision ceremony?"

"How do you—"

"Tell me!"

Ahrik remembered exactly what Zharla had told him before they exited the parlor, after they were supposed to have consummated their marriage. Her words convinced him to leave her as soon as he could, to give in to the hate he now regretted. He sighed with pursed lips. "Few marriages have such auspicious beginnings."

Immediately, the distiller charged down.

"Thank you for coming," said Ahjoz.

Ayen reached out over the tendril link, and Ahrik stopped cold. *Father*, cast Ayen, *Leren's traitors cut out their compilers.*

"Something wrong?" Ahjoz asked.

"We have to hurry," said Ahrik.

Ahjoz rubbed his chin. "I have Nayr, but they took Renla hostage. Nayr and I only barely escaped."

Ahrik paused to send this to Ayen.

"Father," one of his protection squad said, *Twenty men approaching from the north. Eight hundred meters out.*

Bat, Ahrik cast to his pilot. *Exfil.* He turned to Ahjoz. "When the shuttle comes, it won't be able to land, only hover, so you'll have to jump up into the bay doors. My men will help you, but keep Nayr close."

Ahjoz nodded. His white stubble glistened in the predawn light.

Ahrik measured the distance to the crest of the mountain. "Ahjoz, switch distillers with me. No need to make it easy for them to find Nayr with those orange contrails." The gentle hum of the shuttle rose toward them. "Men, this exfil is going to be hot. You know what to do." He paused. "First."

"To the fight," his men answered. They fanned out in a wide arc and dug in with their distillers. Five against twenty, and the twenty held the high ground.

So much death.

Bat came in fast, creating bosonic disturbance as he braked. Ahrik's stomach fluttered. When Bat hovered to a stop, the attackers opened up with their distillers, answered immediately by Ahrik's men. As soon as Ahjoz and Nayr were aboard, Ahrik followed, manning the distiller mounted in the shuttle bay, laying down cover for his men to follow. *Tha-wunk! Tha-wunk!*

Get up here, he cast. The predawn light filled with the *zing* and *thu-thu-thunk* of distillers. One charge slammed into the shuttle's hull, eating a hole next to Ahrik's hand. The attackers brought a crew-served weapon online from the top of the mountain. Ahrik's heart sank. His five men could probably prevent the small arms from overwhelming the shuttle, but once the crew-served weapon registered the distance and angle correctly, the shuttle would be turned to slime.

Father, Bat cast to him, *getting hot.*

Ahrik clenched his teeth and squeezed off a few more charges at the crest of the mountain.

Go! his men cast up from below.

Ahrik knew they were right. *Go, Bat.*

"What about the others?" yelled Ahjoz over the rising hum of the shuttle's boson drive.

"They'll conduct a fighting retreat down the mountain," Ahrik lied. The shuttle pulled away, and the angry contrail of a crew-served charge sailed through the spot where they'd been hovering just moments before. As they made their way toward the Tameri family compound, one by one, five tendril signals from Meran Mountain winked out in Ahrik's mind.

Zharla, Ayen, and Brain emerged from the tunnel. The glow of new morning smeared the lip of the compound wall with light. They hugged the shadow along the wall, and Zharla looked at the concern on Ayen and Brain's faces. "I'm sorry you must put yourselves in danger on my behalf, and for Renla. I can't repay you for that loyalty."

Brain checked his distiller, then drew his blade. "The opportunity to serve the Eshel is recompense enough, Mistress Tamer-li."

"Mistress Tamer-li," said Ayen, handing her his compiler, "you can see the progress of the recon team." A model of the compound sprang up, with five red points of light, representing the five members of Ahrik's protection squad that came with them. They drifted through the front door of the building. Another red dot, Risen, set sensors on the outside of all entrances and windows, scaling the building's walls as he went. Ayen cleared his throat and drew his own qasfin. "If someone moves inside a room, we'll see it in blue on the model."

"How long until Ahrik gets here?" she asked.

"Less than five minutes, Mistress Tamer-li, but he'll approach the compound from the southeast and make sure the main gate is secure before making the rendezvous."

Risen's dot circled the walls outside the building, and the five red dots from the protection squad circulated through the ground floor. They left the women's hall and formal dining room and circled back to the main entrance.

Ayen primed his distiller and looked over at the compiler. "The ground floor is clear."

The five red dots rose to the second floor. Zharla cocked her head. "I don't see any blue. No one is on the first two floors, then?"

"This feels too easy," Brain said. He scanned the building with a worried look.

Ayen leaned back with a sigh against the mountain, pensive. "Risen's sensors haven't reported anything yet, either, but he's not all the way around the building yet. No one is alive on the second floor."

"People are dead on the second floor?"

Ayen stopped to receive a message. "I'm afraid so, Mistress Tamer-li, but none of them match Miss Renla's description. Would you like to see a direct feed?"

She nodded, then bit her lip. A low resolution video appeared. Three corpses lay outside her chambers, wearing security guard uniforms. Zharla cringed, but sighed with relief at not recognizing them. "Maybe Mother brought them in temporarily." Her mother must have known that something like this would happen.

Brain nodded. "There are signs of a distiller fight in these rooms. See, look here and here. Who won? Where are they?"

Zharla returned a blank stare. Her mother probably conspired to be spirited away at the first sign of danger. Zharla said a little prayer for Renla's safety.

"Risen is done with his circuit, and he should return soon." Ayen groaned. The two soldiers narrowed their eyes and peered at the building.

"He's going for the roof," Brain said, grunting with approval. "We hadn't considered they'd hide hostages on the roof."

The dawn light illuminated Risen's lean figure as he slid up the wall on the side of the building nearest them. When he got to the top, he stopped just below the lip and bobbed his head up and down to peek over. He reached down to his waist and pulled something out.

"A sensor," said Brain.

Risen craned his head to look in their general direction. Another sensor came online on the model, and the roof went alive with blue.

Brain gasped. "There must be a whole company up there."

Ayen shook his head. "Some of those are civilian hostages. The sensors can only tell which are Ahrik's and which are not, and the traitors removed their compilers."

Zharla looked over at Risen again. He disappeared.

"He cloaked," said Ayen. "I hope he waits to make his move."

Brain stopped, then jerked his head toward the sky beyond the compound. "I have Father on approach."

Zharla followed his gaze and saw Ahrik's shuttle, trailing fumes and jerking through the sky. The shuttle descended to only a stone's throw from the compound gate when, to her horror, streams of tracers shot up and through it. The shuttle fell from a fearsome height, and the dull crunch of metal on stone bent over the compound wall, the reverberation pulsing under their feet.

Brain brought his weapons up, ready to leap into action, but Ayen put a hand on his arm. "Wait. Those distiller charges came from outside the compound, not inside the wall, and"—he paused to receive a tendril message—"Father, the guard, and the boy are alive and well. They'll enter the compound soon."

"The pilot?" asked Zharla.

Ayen shook his head, face grim.

Brain squinted. "I see Father and Nayr. The old man is limping. They've entered the compound and made for the far corner of the wall. How long before the 2–2 reserve arrives? What about the 4th Hand interceptors? We're going to need air support."

Zharla looked at the model. The five red dots were almost at the roof entrance.

"It'll be tight," said Ayen. "The whole 3d Hand is bearing down on us."

A dull boom echoed from inside the building, and two of the five red lights inside blinked out. The other three red lights staggered back from the roof entrance as blue lights from the roof poured into the stairwell. The three red lights retreated to create a new bottleneck at the doorway to the corridor, then began a leapfrogging retreat. Zharla saw that it couldn't last. Blue dots were already trying to flank the red ones using side corridors, or carving through room walls.

Brain's shoulders sank. "The traitors have seen Father and the boy. The only thing protecting them from that sea of blue are those three ketelis."

The three red dots went out. Ayen motioned for Zharla to carry the compiler, then readied his weapons. "We need to take and hold that roof if we're going to get out of this alive."

Risen slipped over the roof's edge and separated a knot of blue lights, then he moved and crouched behind cover. Half of the blue lights had already gone down the stairwell from the roof.

Brain, Ayen, and Zharla ran to the building, heedless of who might see. Zharla prayed, *Lady of the Emerald Moon, give us time.*

They slammed themselves against the rear wall of the house. Zharla nearly fumbled with the compiler. Ayen and Brain exchanged a glance. Zharla thought it was a comment on her flaccid grip, but then Ayen looked at the compiler display and tapped it once. A host of voices curdled inside the building, then cut off suddenly. Muffled cries of pain echoed throughout the ground floor. Something large crashed down, and once again the ground rumbled underneath them.

Ayen gave a wicked smile. "The recon team set a scrambler mine on the grand staircase. That helps our odds." He moved along the wall to the rear staircase enclosure, a convex structure that jutted out from the rest of the wall, near the entrance to the kitchen. Without hesitation, he and Brain raised their distillers and melted a woman-sized hole in the wall, revealing the staircase behind.

"Stack," ordered Ayen. Brain hugged the wall behind Ayen, ready to plunge through the new door. "Mistress Tamer-li, stay between us."

Zharla's mind was equal parts fear and focused energy. Frantic screams shrilled from the roof, along with the eerie sounds of a distiller fight.

Brain smiled. "Risen. Surprise, at the right time, is powerful."

"Go!" shouted Ayen. Ayen jumped through the rough opening and started left up the spiral staircase, taking two steps at a time. Brain followed and spun to the right, sending two or three distiller charges into the kitchen. Zharla heard cries of pain from that direction as she hurtled herself through and followed Ayen up the stairs. They got to the second floor doorway and Ayen stopped her with his hand. Ayen sprayed his distiller down the second floor hallway as Brain rushed up the stairs behind her.

"Go!" Ayen shouted again, and then Zharla leaped after Brain, with Ayen behind her this time, shouting and meting out death with his weapon.

Brain got to the top of the stairwell and covered the third-floor hallway, his distiller crackling with energy. Zharla reached him, the fear and adrenaline of battle brimming in her chest.

Brain heaved a breath. "The stairway to the roof is ahead. I can pretend to have you as a hostage, the slow approach, or we can just charge on through, weapons alight, nice and quick."

Ayen bounded up the stairs. "They're not far behind. Quick or slow?"

They looked at Zharla. "Quick," she said. Nayr, Ahrik, Renla, Ahjoz, and Risen needed them on that roof, and now.

"I hoped you'd say that," said Ayen. He launched forward.

Brain grabbed her arm. "Stay focused on the door to the roof. Do not look at the ground. It won't be pretty."

Brain and Ayen blasted the way ahead of her, and she slipped on unimaginable things, smelled and saw unimaginable things, and heard the unimaginable groans of the wounded and dying. She just held her mouth closed and burst through the door to the roof and retched, and then dry heaved, then pulled herself over to Risen by force of will, crawling over writhing bodies and stiffening bodies and puddles of blood.

By some miracle, Risen lived. The air was a lethal web of distiller charges, zinging back and forth. She stayed as flat as possible, curling up behind the power transformer that Risen used as cover. With so little room behind the transformer, she couldn't even crane her neck to see if Renla was okay.

"Brain!" Ayen screamed. "Take the edge of the roof! I'll cover the door!"

"Check!" Brain yelled, frantic.

Risen's breathing came shallow. One leg hung useless below his knee. "Missuss...Tamer..." he gasped. "I'm dyin'...for yuh." She couldn't imagine the pain he was in, but he still had his distiller out, shooting, eyes wild and desperate.

The distillers lulled, and she looked in the direction of the hostages. Renla, her mother, and most of the servants were there. Before the distillers could start up again, she lunged over to where they cowered behind a water tank, riddled with holes, their hands and feet tied and mouths gagged, bodies drenched with water draining from the tank. She worked at Renla's bindings with trembling fingers, but it was no use. The water had expanded and tightened the rope. She swore and cast about for something to cut through the bindings. Risen's qasfin. She looked over in time to see a volley of distiller charges slam into the transformer. He moved back, but too slowly. One charge disintegrated his exposed shoulder, and his arm with the distiller in it went limp. He slumped over, unconscious, his head and torso now exposed to the enemy. She lunged to pull him back behind cover, yanking on his good leg, but another charge found its mark and the side of Risen's head disappeared in a cloud of red and gray.

"Risen!" She grabbed the distiller on Risen's arm and tore it off. Stuffing her hand into the weapon, she felt around for what she hoped was a trigger. She fumbled with the pack, but it was taking too long to get off.

"Ayen and Brain, we lost Risen!" she yelled.

Tethered to Risen's lifeless form by the kall line, she peeked out from behind the now shapeless transformer. Three men were charging Brain's position, screaming something inchoate. Brain didn't see them. She brought Risen's distiller up and squeezed. *Thu-thu-thunk! Thu-thu-thunk! Thu-thu-thunk!* When she finally released the trigger, she saw that she'd cut the three men in half.

The elation sickened her. She worked her hand out of the grimy weapon and struggled with the clasp on Risen's qasfin. The distiller volleys paused again, and Brain sprang out from his position. The enemy went silent. Had they won?

No, Zharla sensed it was only temporary.

Zharla sawed the qasfin back and forth against Renla's bindings.

When her hands sprang free, Renla tore off her gag. "Zhe'le. Ahjoz took Nayr, but—"

"I know. They need our help." She cut off Renla's leg bindings, then turned the qasfin on her mother's wrist bindings. "Do something useful," Zharla said when her mother's hands were free. Zharla let the qasfin clatter to the roof.

Her mother ripped off her gag. She choked back a sob. "I'm so sorry. So sorry."

"Traitor," said Zharla, her glare wicked. "Now is not the time for apologies."

Her mother grabbed a fistful of Zharla's tunic, tears flowing. "I never knew they would hurt you."

Zharla gripped her mother's wrist and wrested her tunic free, then reached for the qasfin and placed it in her mother's hand. "Save your family now."

Zharla and Renla crawled toward the edge of the roof closest to Ahrik and Nayr, fearing the worst.

A gruff hand yanked her up by the arm. Ayen shouted, "Lay it down, Brain! Kill *anything* that moves toward Father's position."

He dragged Zharla the rest of the way to the wall at the edge of the roof. "You too!" he shouted at Renla. He turned back to Zharla. "Put your hand in here. Feel the trigger? Point and shoot. Got it? Do you see your husband and son over there in the corner of the compound? They must live!"

She nodded. He wrapped the cord around her upper arm and slipped the pack on her back with sickening efficiency. Her eyes grew wide with fear and self-loathing, but this was soon overcome by the pleasure of little people on the ground trying to pick her off the roof but missing by a wide margin while she cut them down like dry grass.

The shooting started. The dam of hell fury broke. The fury didn't just fill Anda's veins. It filled the air and made the hate palpable. Three Squad took it hard, going from the roof into the house. They eventually made it through. The mass of men pushed Anda toward the stairwell, and he heard shouts and distiller charges exchanged behind him.

"Move! Move!" his squad leader screamed. "Outta th'house! Take thut position by the wull! Kill Ahrik!"

Anda got to the second floor, then realized he'd lost track of the rapist. He cursed. The rapist should have been right in front of him, at the rear of Three Squad. Anda squeezed into a side corridor to think through his next move. He heard a popping like the sizzle of bacon, then a loud crash, then saw pieces of men fall as the main staircase to the ground floor melted away. Cries of surprise cut short. Anda assessed his options and made for the one place he knew the rapist would go.

Ahrik, Ahjoz, and Nayr stumbled through the main gate after the crash, then made their way to the nearest corner of the compound, where they could keep the high wall at their backs. Ahrik carved a hasty position in the soft earth, as far away from the building as possible, where they could pick off all who approached.

Traitorous members of his ketel poured from the main entrance to the Tameri mansion. Once, his attackers had been sons to him, but now they dropped like stalks of cane before a scythe. Ahjoz, eyes wild, squeezed off distiller charges beside him, to much less effect. Nayr wailed at the bottom of their hasty slit trench, not out of fear, but because he wanted to fight. The assault grew heavier and heavier, but then a curtain of distiller charges slammed into the assailants from the roof, tracers burning red as dawn crept over the wall on the opposite side of the compound.

Thanks for the respite, Ayen, he cast over the tendril link.

Father, your wife is with us. Will work our way down to you.

Check, he cast. How would they make it down from the roof? A company of traitors lay in wait between them. Ahrik had to trust his men.

He dropped two more attackers at fifty meters and scanned for more assailants. Nayr screamed and tried to scramble from their slit trench, but Ahrik yanked him back. Ahjoz, ever faithful, stood on his one good leg and shot at targets much too far away for him to hit.

Father, someone cast to him, *2–2 Reserve here*. All 2d Hand sub-commanders had been killed at Nejru Gulch, so his tendril link to this new subcommander was weak.

Ahrik gritted his teeth and squeezed off two more charges. He couldn't remember the subcommander's name. *Secure the building*, he cast. *Ayen and Brain on roof.*

Check, Father.

Ahrik looked to his left and felt the satisfaction of loyal men entering through the main gate of the compound.

Ayen? Ahrik cast.

Check, Father. Air support on target in two minutes, Ayen cast back.

First, Ahrik cast.

To the fight.

Ahrik looked at Ahjoz. "We might win this."

Ahjoz only nodded, panting. Sweat poured down his face.

A massive explosion tore through the far wall of the compound, over two hundred meters away. Half the wall disintegrated and blew toward the house, and fragments rained down around them. On instinct, all three ducked farther into the trench.

A fine dust settled and hung in the air, adding to the dawn fog like creeping death, and a thousand voices pierced that fog with a cry of battle: "Leren! Leren!" Angry blue tracers spilled from the gap, cutting into Ahrik's stunned reserve from the 2–2. An odd clanking sound issued from the gap as well, metal grating on metal, and two roving, metal hulks appeared out of the fog and mist, giant machines of death. The 2–2 discharged their distillers at the enemy, but one of the metal hulks fired its main gun, and an entire corner of the building collapsed. Its metal projectiles sliced through the 2–2, exposed on the open field between the compound entrance and the mansion.

Ahrik heard two dozen cries of shocked death in his mind, and he staggered back at the pain. Where he dared to hope before, now he fought despair. How quickly the winds of battle shifted.

Ayen, report.

Rest of 3d Hand, Father. Ahrik felt his aide's dejection. *Air support delayed by interceptors loyal to government.*

Ahrik had no other combat power. His hand was played. He should have known that the real fight would be here, in the Tameri compound.

Father, Ayen cast, *interceptors report two more units loyal to government on approach.*

Ahrik stole a quick breath. In war, the simplest thing is difficult.

Dazed, Zharla picked herself up off of the roof. That explosion was much more powerful than the one from the men's rights demonstration. Her ears rang. Her head hurt. She reached up and her hand came back bloody, but she didn't have time to inspect it because Ayen ran over to her, frantic, and shouted something she could not hear. He ran back to where the corner of the roof used to be and pointed down. She scrambled to him. The ringing in her ears began to subside.

"...ver there! Shoot there! Now!" Ayen screamed.

Brain shot his distiller from the rubbled edge of the roof, eyes drawn in fury, mouth open in a grim rictus. *Thu-thu-thunk! Thu-thu-thunk! Thu-thu-thunk!* She followed his tracers down and saw two huge things, doing the nefarious work of death among Ahrik's men. Fire spurted from their sides. She and Ayen joined Brain, and dozens of red tracers, from all directions, slammed into the first hulking beast. It stopped, sagged, melted, and went still.

Brain moved on to the other one, which had begun moving its long tube in their direction. "For Ahrik!" he screamed. Ayen stopped and looked at Zharla with fearful knowing and lunged at her, grabbing her and throwing her back. A ball of fire erupted behind them, cutting Brain's scream short in a piercing eruption of noise. Fragments rained around them. She looked back. Brain was gone, along with another section of the roof. She chanced a glance over the edge, but there were fewer red tracers going into the second machine than had gone into the first.

Ayen whipped out his compiler and turned wild eyes on her. "You have to get off this roof!"

She looked down at the model on the compiler and saw a few red dots on the ground floor and more outside, but there was a mass of blue coming up the stairwell at the back of the building, the ones they'd ascended, the only functioning stairs from the ground floor.

She shot a questioning glance at Ayen. He pointed his distiller down and started melting away the roof. She did likewise. It would hurt to get down this way, but it was preferable to going like Brain did.

A forbidding sound came from the entrance to the roof. She stole a glance in that direction. Renla and some servants had barricaded the door to the roof with the ruined water tank. Renla reached down to slip her hand into a discarded distiller. They might die here, like this. Ayen looked at her, then Zharla watched him stride off to meet his fate at the stairwell. *Lady*, Zharla prayed, *take this hate and this violence, that I may overcome.*

The gap in the roof widened. Another section of the roof exploded in a mass of fire, knocking Zharla over. Searing pain shot through the arm that was in the distiller. She winced and stuffed her feet into the hole she'd made. She had to get down. To Ahrik. She dropped down and twisted her ankle but gritted her teeth against the pain and set to melting the floor once again. Ayen shouted on the roof above her.

The distiller stopped. She pumped the trigger inside the weapon. Rattled it. Nothing. The hole to the next floor, to her chambers, was just big enough to wriggle through. The din of battle sounded around her, on the roof, elsewhere in the building, and outside. Footsteps sounded in the hallway. She ignored the pain in her arm and began to shake off the distiller and pack.

Suddenly, her mother was there, sliding the pack off and grabbing Zharla's good arm. She eased Zharla down through the floor, and Zharla cried out in pain as the jagged floor scraped her sides and she fell into her quarters below, or what had once been her quarters. Her mother followed, falling a meter or so after dangling from the ceiling. Zharla heard another explosion on the roof, and Ayen's shouts went silent.

Renla.

Men of Ahrik! Ahrik shouted over the tendril network. *On me!* He sprang from his trench and charged, the distiller fierce and warm on his arm. A hundred men sprang up with him and shortened the distance to the second machine. It sprayed wicked death from its smaller guns, but the massed distillers soon disabled them and finally destroyed the thing completely. Ahrik and his sons held no pity for the cries of men dying inside, scorched to death with melting metal, lungs burned from the inside out by the distillers' noxious after-fumes.

He turned toward the building once again and looked to the sky; interceptors hummed in from the north.

Air support here, Hawk cast to him over the tendril link.

You're late, cast Ahrik. *Secure the roof. Destroy anything coming from the stairwell or the far wall of the compound.* He cast Hawk visual coordinates through the tendril link.

Check, Father. Red tracers from a half-dozen interceptors poured into the stairwell opening and into the area beyond the steaming hulks of metal.

Ahrik pinged the 2–2 commander over the tendril link.

Father?

Secure the house, then the perimeter of the compound. More of them are coming.

Check.

Ahrik scanned the building and saw a figure dangle and drop into Zharla's room. He began to run, but then tracers slammed into the ground around him and he dove for cover. "Zharla!"

Anda crept along the wall, feeling for doorways in the dimness. The battle faded to a dull clamor behind him, still dominated by the screams of squad leaders urging their men down and out of the building. The light of day began to infiltrate the building. The company was bottled up. Some must have gotten out, but more were in the building than should have been.

A thunderous boom rocked the building and threw him forward.

A cheer went up from the men down the hall, behind him, and he looked up to see a figure emerge from a doorway in front of him. It was Zharla's room, at the corner of the building, on the second floor. The figure stopped in front of Anda. Poke. The rapist.

Poke's lip curled into a churlish sneer. "We're 'bout t'take Ahrik. Let's go!"

Anda moved to block his way. "Why were you in Zharla's room?"

"Zhar... Wait a minute, who're yuh?" His eyes narrowed to suspicious slits. Another explosion rocked the building, definitely closer. It knocked them both off balance.

Anda brought up his distiller, and the hum intensified. "Why did you rape Zharla?"

The rapist cackled. "Yuh mus' be th'real me! Should I call yuh 'father'?"

"Why?!" Anda shook the distiller, fury in his voice.

The rapist smiled a wicked smile. "Others fight fur men's rights an' women's rule, but who fights fur th'ketela?"

"You've ruined a lot of lives."

The rapist snarled. "An' I had a good time doin' it."

Anda squeezed the trigger. Instantly, he regretted it. The charge zipped by the rapist's head and sank harmlessly into the wall. A wave of relief flooded over Anda.

The rapist laughed. "Th'jilted lov'r comes back from th'dead t'defend his woman's honor, but he can't eve—"

A third explosion rocked the building, and Anda's finger squeezed the trigger as he fought to regain his balance. He looked up and saw the charge catch the rapist square in the throat, nearly severing his head. The rapist's face contorted in shock and pain. He stumbled toward Anda and fumbled for his weapon, then collapsed. Anda, shocked, squirmed out of the distiller and tossed it next to the rapist's gurgling form.

Anda stepped over bodies and ducked into Zharla's room just in time to see two female figures drop from the ceiling.

Zharla dropped into her chambers and knew that someone else was there. A presence, in the direction of the door. She knew this just like she had known, but denied, that someone had been in her room on the night she was raped. She grunted and hobbled on her twisted ankle over to her table, two meters away. Propping herself up, she asked, "Where are you?"

"Here." A familiar voice called from the doorway, ringing from the ages of her mind. She knew the face that materialized and began to move toward her. There, in the din and clamor of battle, the clarity of her memory surprised even her. The decision ceremony sprang to her mind as if it were yesterday.

"Shahl?" Her voice slipped.

He froze, avoided looking at her. "I haven't heard that name for a lifetime."

"Come back to us," she pleaded.

He swung his head in a slow arc. His gazed carried off into nothingness, then fixed on the east. "I'm not that man anymore." He made an agonizing pause, then looked her in the face, like he only just realized she was there. "Your rapist is dead. Your torment is over." Shahl tossed a data capsule, and it clattered to the floor. "I know how they did it."

It didn't matter anymore. She looked down at the data capsule but did not touch it. "My torment... my torment was not like you think, Shahl."

"Stop calling me that!"

Zharla's mother stumbled between them.

"Mother," Zharla said. "Let me handle this."

"No, Zharla," said her mother, staring down Shahl. Metal glinted in her hand. Risen's qasfin. "Get to the window, Zharla. The hedges will break your fall."

"Mother, don't do anything rash."

"It would be much less than I deserve, Zharla." She turned toward her daughter. "Go."

Zharla moved toward the window, steadying herself with one hand on the table.

"Whatever you do, do it quick," said Shahl, stepping toward the door and glancing at the qasfin with that distant, unnerving stare. "Reinforcements are coming."

A pack of men burst into the room. The light was just good enough to illuminate a scar running down the face of the leader. Zharla pushed off from the table and hopped backward toward the window, but stumbled and fell.

Leren leveled a fierce gaze at Shahl. "Keteli, what's going on here? Why is that man dead in the hall?"

Shahl, or the man once known as Shahl, responded with perfect military precision. "Sir, I duspatched th'man in th'hull fer runnin' from th'fight." He nodded in the direction of Zharla and her mother. "Found these tuh civulians. I bulieve they're the Matrun and Heiress Tamer-li."

A hole tore open in Zharla's heart. Tears welled in her eyes and she lifted herself up, one arm on the window sill. She gathered her strength for one final push to the window.

Leren glowered at the women, eyes bloodshot, and crept down the stairs. "I'll take care of this. Go kill Ahrik. Save the boy."

As suddenly as he had appeared, Shahl disappeared from Zharla's life, and her heart sank under the weight of what could have been.

"Advance no farther," Zharla's mother warned, her stance fragile, the blade trembling in her hand.

Leren chuckled and fumbled with something at his waist. "I am going to kill your daughter; then I'll kill her husband. You made a deal, so move out of the way."

"No!" her mother screeched. She lunged at Leren, Risen's blade brandished overhead.

Leren looked surprised, but not unprepared. He jerked his head to dodge the blade, but it bit into his shoulder. He cried out in pain, then flung her mother to the side with his good arm. Risen's blade skittered across the stone floor.

Her mother didn't give up. She clawed and scratched at him, then tugged and pulled on his bad arm, eliciting more cries of pain and an effluvium of cursing.

Zharla heaved herself the last distance to the window sill, looking to the hedges below while the struggle clamored behind her. With a deafening suddenness, the sounds of struggle ceased, her mother silenced forever, but Zharla was too scared to turn around, too scared to have that image etched on her mind. She focused all her energy, all her will, all her strength and pushed off with her good leg, reaching a sitting position on the window sill. One more push would send her to safety in the hedges below.

Behind her, Leren screamed, "For freedom!" She looked back. Leren knelt, blood streaming from his shoulder, eyes, and cheeks. His fingers closed in on something small at his waist, his calm eyes steeled against inevitable truth. Then, in that moment of terror, the world went white. Just as quickly, she was thrown like a rag doll through the air, in searing pain. Then blackness.

"No!" Ahrik screamed. From his position, he saw his wife flung to the ground with a sickening crunch. Heedless of the danger, he slid to the ground next to her. The battle around him faded to silence in his mind. He was too late. Had he just arrived moments earlier. *No, no, no!*

"Zharla," he pleaded. "Zharla." No other words came. No other thoughts came to his mind. Only one: *Zharla.* He dared not touch her, for fear of causing more damage. Her eyes fluttered briefly, but he dared not hope. *Zharla. Zharla.*

He screamed in his mind for the healers. Her eyes opened to slits. "Ah'ke." Her breath came shallow. "Hold. Me."

"Zhe'le," he said. He still knew no other thought, but he carefully, tenderly cradled her head and shoulders in his arms. He caressed her face. "Zhe'le." *No, no, no!*

"Ah'ke." Her eyes squeezed shut, then opened. "I would. Have. Borne." She breathed a few more shallow breaths. "Our children."

He shook his head. This was not happening. "And you will."

When she drifted off, he said her name over and over. He knew his tears were wasted tears, but he let them fall nonetheless, tears for futures lost, tears for hopes that were no more, tears for a world made new from sorrow, a world that he knew too well but liked much less than the world that had been. He saw a world without Zharla in it, a world he could not accept.

"Father," said a healer, eyes widening at what he saw.

"Fix her," Ahrik ordered.

"I'll try, Father." In the next moment, Renla ran over to him with Nayr. She sucked in her breath and bit her lip.

"Daddy," Nayr said.

For the first time in a new age, Ahrik looked at Nayr. "Yes," he said, "I suppose I am."

He found Hawk and the 2–2 commander on the tendril network. *We have a battle to win.* With that, Ahrik turned, Biriq and distiller in hand, and faced the demons of war.

TWO YEARS LATER.

THE day dawned abnormally brisk for the summer, but even that could not dampen Ahrik's spirits. He walked to receive the operations brief for the final offensives on the Emerald Moon. He and his aides strode across the parade at his global command center east of Meran. The original subterranean base had been transferred above ground. He returned subordinates' salutes as they passed.

"Good morning, sir," said one female officer, saluting smartly.

He stopped. "Good morning, Renla. I almost didn't recognize you in your uniform."

"Good to see you, sir."

"I see new first lieutenant's insignia. Congratulations."

"Thank you, sir."

"How is life in the Ketel of Ahrik? Where do they have you assigned?"

"The army takes good care of me, sir. I've been assigned to lead a squad in the moon op. I'm looking forward to the challenge."

Ahrik nodded his approval. "Space infantry."

Renla paused, hesitant. "Sir, permission to ask a personal question?"

"Granted."

"How is your wife, sir?"

Ahrik beamed and breathed in the fresh air. "Zharla is making good progress. They're going to lift her out of the induced coma today. There will probably be many months of physical therapy, but this is a very good day, Renla, as I'm sure you'll agree. A very good day. Thank you for asking."

"Thank you for the news, sir."

"Good day, lieutenant."

"Good day, sir."

Acknowledgments

I USUALLY take the time to read acknowledgments because they say
so much about the writer and the book. Before I wrote a novel, I
thought that only writers of those big, thick academic books incurred
the kinds of debts that require drawn out, thoughtful recognition
of everyone that contributes to a project. Academics spend years
researching and enlist the help of many others in the process, but
the novelist just writes. Right?

Nope. It turns out, writers of all types enter a sort of literary
debtors' prison, most with a life sentence. I am no different. My
paltry "thank yous" can in no way repay my debts, but I certainly
hope they lay bare the weaknesses that others have strengthened,
so that my benefactors and you, kind reader, find some measure of
satisfaction in the time and energy you've so generously given me.
Please know that any weaknesses remaining in this work are mine
and mine alone, although many have helped me avoid embarrassing
mistakes that readers will never see.

My first debt goes to the great minds who've gone before. Erich
Maria Remarque and Rick Atkinson helped me see the possibilities
in a book about war. Science fiction greats like Isaac Asimov, Robert
Heinlein, and Orson Scott Card captivated me with their sweeping
ideas. Jerry Pournelle answered my e-mail once, which was really
cool. Samuel Huntington and Sam Sarkesian made me think long
and hard about how a military officer relates to the society he defends.
I paraphrased or quoted Carl von Clausewitz, Frank Herbert, Adam
Smith, and Kenneth Waltz. The first reader to email me with all four

instances in *Rise of Ahrik* will get a signed copy of the printed book and dinner if we're ever in the same city.

I incurred a tremendous debt to those who suffered through this work in its various stages. Phillip Absher, Marie-Claire Antoine, Tom Bruscino, Linda Evans, Sam Green, Bill Shavce, Robert Stewart-Ingersoll, Aaron Toronto, Ben Toronto, Melissa Toronto, Sharman Toronto, and Tom Wingfield read and commented on the entire manuscript. Tom Wingfield read the manuscript twice, in fact, and caught some egregious errors in the final proof. My daughters read and commented on the book as well, even though science fiction wasn't "their thing," and Sharon Benjamin's effusive praise inspired me to keep moving this forward. Members of the Abu Dhabi Fiction Writers Group gave insightful comments on the first chapter. Forrest Cole, Angie Crowther, Abby Garrick, Kym Merrill, and Powl Smith also read chapters. I am especially grateful for Powl Smith's insights into technical military matters, and for explaining the intricacies of the Powl Doctrine. These readers' reactions and comments made this a better work, and if I have forgotten anyone who helped me along the way, please accept my sincere apology and remind me of my debt.

A number of professionals helped me, and I'm as indebted to them as the others. As an unrepentant empiricist, I disputed the evidentiary claims in C. S. Lakin's *12 Pillars of Novel Construction*, but this novel is better because I swallowed my pride and heeded her candid advice and incisive editorial observations. Rachel Paul edited the manuscript at an earlier stage, Aaron Toronto helped create the book trailer, and Nancy Wride designed the cover (twice), despite my penchant for indecision. Lyz Kelley encouraged me to self-publish my work and showed me that it is not only possible, but desirable. Judy Peterson, my high school English teacher, taught me the value of detail by presenting me with a list of "fatal errors" and failing one of my papers because I forgot to put a period at the end of a sentence

Not all my debts felt good in the acquiring, but they all did me well in the end.

My deepest and most lasting debt is to my dear wife and children, who believed in me and gave me the time to finish this. Thank you for letting me dream. May your personal sacrifice make a better world for us all.

Thank you, kind reader, for trusting me on our journey. Imagine the world we could create if everyone trusted each other so.

EXTRAS

Revenge of the Emerald Moon

Chapter 1
War Among the People

THE pitter-patter of feet stopped Anda, his hand poised to cycle the airlock. With a smile, he set down his helmet and knelt down to gather his daughter in an embrace. "Up already, Cera?"

She coughed, then hugged her stuffed *dubbi* tight. "I can't sleep, Abbi."

She hadn't slept well since falling ill, and Anda was not surprised to see her up before he headed out to the tanks.

"Can you go to Imma's bed?" He stroked Cera's long auburn hair and smiled, but inwardly he steeled himself for another fit of coughing.

He and Esh'a had tried everything they could to help Cera fight this mysterious illness, but weeks of healers and treatments had done nothing. Cera still suffered from coughing fits. Anda gritted his teeth. Every day she grew weaker, it seemed. *Why can't I help her?*

Cera shook her head and gave him a stern look. "Not back to bed. Story."

Anda sighed. "Quickly. I have to check the algae before Home-rise."

He sat on the heated stone floor and pulled Cera onto his lap. "Do you know the story of the *pter'a* flower?"

Cera shook her head, then yawned and cuddled into the crook of his arm.

Anda squeezed Cera close, and the little girl clutched her *dubbi* to her chest.

"Many thousands of years ago, before The War, the *pter'a* flower grew all over," he said.

"Was this on Moon, Abbi?"

"No, Cerit, this was on Home. Back then, there were no people on Moon."

Cera looked up at Anda with sleepy eyes. "I'll go Home someday."

Anda pursed his lips. "Home is not a good place now. Many people die there." He shifted Cera on his lap, with a pause to indicate that he would continue the story. "They said the *pter'a* flower had magical properties, that it could heal any wound."

"Could it cure me, Abbi?"

Anda stroked his chin, as if considering the possibility. "I bet it could, Cerit," he said, trying to build both myth and hope at once, "but it's been two thousand years since anyone has seen the flower on Home." He stroked her hair and squeezed her shoulder. "But I believe it's out there, somewhere."

"I'll find it." She coughed. "Then I'll get better."

All Anda could do was smile. He hadn't the heart for much else.

Footsteps shuffled towards them, and Esh'a leaned against the dome wall next to the airlock. Her bloodshot eyes told Anda that she, like Cera, had not slept well. Esh'a shivered and pulled her nightgown close, then glowered and shook her head in a slow arc of displeasure. The small wooden capsule of vanilla hanging from her neck swayed with the motion. Her hair cascaded over her shoulders, as if it too disagreed with what Anda was doing.

Her eyes narrowed with skepticism. "Telling her about the *pter'a* flower again?"

Anda pled with his eyes, but Esh'a met his gaze with cold despair. *Have hope*, he wanted to say, but he worried that they would lose Cera, and then afterwards Esh'a would succumb to the mercilessness of loss and fate. If Cera died, it would destroy them.

Anda gazed at his wife. He couldn't remember the last time they kissed each other good morning.

"I have to go check the tanks," he said, nudging Cera towards Esh'a and unfolding himself from the floor. *We have to pay for these treatments somehow.*

He stepped to the airlock once again, but Cera tugged on the thigh pocket of his exosuit. "Abbi, will I die and never be found, like that flower?"

A lump formed in Anda's throat. He bent down to look Cera in her pale eyes, red-rimmed and weary from pain and illness. Anda stroked her hair once again. "Not if I can help it, Cerit."

He didn't dare look at Esh'a before cycling out through the airlock. He knew he would see only scorn and bitterness in her face. He did not begrudge his wife her pain, her longing for what should have been, but Cera needed hope now more than ever.

The healer at the nearest outpost had told them yesterday that there was nothing more he could do. "They're starting a new trial this week at Kalevo," he'd said. "Treatments every month. I'll see if I can get her in." The healer had given them a grim look. "But even if she gets in, I don't know if it'll work."

Anda bounded out to the algae tanks in Moon's lowgrav. With every leap, he screamed into his helmet, frustration and anguish boiling over. *How can I pay to go to Kalevo every month? How can I give my wife hope? How can I save my daughter?*

The light of Homerise over the horizon fed his anger. On Home, Cera would be cured by now, he was sure of it. But he and Esh'a couldn't go Home. They were marked. They'd be hunted, probably executed if they went back. What good would it do Cera to have her health, but no parents?

The tanks came into view, seven squat cylinders of dull steel, each twenty meters across. The algae they cultivated served two purposes. The gasses the algae emitted made Moon's thin atmosphere more breathable, but, more important, the algae helped feed Moon's population, over two million now. They said the atmosphere would be breathable in less than twenty years, but Anda only cared about today. About getting his daughter better.

Homerise cast its blue-gray pall over the broken landscape. The moss grew thick on Moon's rocks and boulders. The wispy haze of clouds tinted Homerise a dozen shades of green.

Anda used to love this time of morning. No matter his problems, he could lope out here and find peace, peace of recognizing how small he was to the cosmos, and of sensing the presence of some greater plan.

But that was gone, faded into an unreachable past. Without his family, he was nothing. He wanted to believe that the universe had a plan for him and for Esh'a and for Cera, but now he felt like he stared into blackest night.

At least he had his algae crop. That was something.

He made one final leap and wrapped gloved fingers over the rim of the first tank, three meters from the base. His feet jammed into the footholds on the side of the tank with practiced skill. He pulled himself up and peered over the side.

He froze.

Instead of a deep green, the surface was pale, almost thin blue. Black rimmed the inside of the tank. He checked the water temperature reading on his helmet display. Normal. He synced his exosuit's compiler to the tank's system and checked bosonic heaters, acidity, gas proportions, radiation retention. All readings normal. Except biological activity, which sat at sixteen percent, too low to sustain life.

How? Algae production was the oldest form of agriculture on the Emerald Moon. Tanks didn't just fail like this.

He scrambled down from the rim. Nervousness climbed up his chest. If one tank failed, could the others? *Everything I own is here, in these tanks.*

Anda bounded to the next tank, leaped up, and pulled himself to the rim. His heart sank. The surface of the algae in the second tank was even paler than the first. Anda checked the readings. Bioactivity at nine percent.

Frantic, he leaped to the ground and bounded to the next tank, and the next, and the next. Every one, dead. At the last tank he crumpled to the ground, a vacant husk of despair.

What was I supposed to do differently?

Despair turned to agony, and agony to fury. He balled his fist and slammed it into the ground, over and over and over again, until his suit sounded the oxygen alarm. *Rupture in right glove*, the display read. *Oxygen levels at twenty-eight percent.*

Anda took in a deep breath. It wouldn't take that long. To die. To let the cold heart of space take him.

Twenty-seven percent.

He took in another breath and searched for a reason to smile.

Then Home cleared the horizon. Emerald light crawled over the ground.

Twenty-five percent.

He pushed himself off the moondirt and took a single bound towards home, then another, and another. He could almost feel the oxygen leaving his exosuit.

Fifteen percent.

Oxygen levels in his exosuit stood at zero as he cycled through the airlock. He tore his helmet off. The artigrav kicked in. When Cera ran up to throw her arms around him, he smiled.

He couldn't help it.

Ahrik tapped a finger on his desk and licked his swollen lip. He wondered how long the violence would last. Zharla woke up fourteen years ago, but gone now was the joy of being together. Of seeing each other's greatest hopes fulfilled. Their erstwhile joy did not bear up under the weight of childlessness and the burden of governing a planet. The violence she inflicted on him became more frequent when Nayr started asserting himself. Ahrik worried for the future.

He still loved his wife—that would never change—and she loved him, deep down, he was sure. After so much of life lived together, how could she not love him?

He stared down at the paper on his desk. He pondered the implications of signing it. His eyes wandered over the statuettes commemorating a career's worth of deployments, victories, and even one or two defeats, regimented on his desk as if at parade. His eyes flicked to the far corner of his desk, where his *qasfin*, his greatest fear, lay concealed. He knew the blade would still be sharp, even after all these years, but oh how Ahrik enjoyed its repose. He considered the paper Zharla wanted him to sign. Could he bear to unleash the demons of war once again?

Signing the paper would change everything with Nayr, his stepson. How many years did Ahrik work to build this relationship? Conceived in pain, Nayr was the only child Zharla ever had, and Ahrik raised Nayr like his own. Didn't she know what signing this order meant? Nayr was still their greatest hope for the future, but signing this order now was, for all intents and purposes, an invitation for Nayr to start a civil war.

Ahrik saw it. Zharla did not. Every day, Nayr consolidated his power, positioned his forces, and cultivated the favor of those on the Council of Elders. One of those Elders was particularly close to Nayr: Sheresh Shehur-li, Nayr's greatest champion.

Sheresh was the only person in the world Ahrik truly hated. He started the last war, seventeen years earlier, and in order to make the peace he and Zharla shuffled the truth of his role under the rug. Sheresh had the blood of hundreds of thousands on his hands, but Zharla didn't care, and Ahrik could do nothing about it.

Ahrik snapped the paper taut to take one more look at it. How it beggared belief. Ahrik wanted nothing more than to make Sheresh pay for his crimes, but to do so now would come at catastrophic cost.

Injustice was the cost of peace. Get along with the criminal who started the last war. Now, Sheresh was using his position on the Council to groom Nayr for power. If Sheresh and the Council put Nayr on the throne, Sheresh would control the world. Ahrik and Zharla needed more time. More time to teach Nayr wisdom. More time to prepare for the inevitable transition.

Sheresh was already an old man when the last war started. Ahrik and Zharla needed more time for Sheresh to die. But Sheresh needed to die naturally, not like this, under an executioner's blade.

Ahrik set the paper on the desk. He saw their dilemma, as plain as the full moon on a clear night. How could Zharla refuse to see it?

He pushed himself to a standing position and stepped over to the window. The stone buildings of Meran gleamed in the morning sun, reflecting off the bay. The glimmering light prompted memories of the battles he and his sons fought to protect this fair city.

The Emerald Moon stood high in the morning sky. How long

Ahrik fought to keep the moonie rebels at bay.

His wife, Queen Zharla, had been awake for fourteen years of peace, but was in a coma for the three years of the War for the Kereu before that, three years that saw the Ketel of Ahrik, his sons, spread over the planet and the moon, in an effort to preserve what remained of women's rule, fighting the forces of sedition, hate, and prejudice, those forces that Sheresh raised in secret so long ago.

She's coming, said a voice in his head. The voice cast into his mind over the tendril link, his connection to his sons, his clones. He grew up with them, fought with them, and bled with them. Of the ten thousand he started the war, only two thousand remained, 2,158, to be exact. What a price his sons paid to preserve women's rule. To defend Zharla's reign. And now she dared to trespass on his domain, to see if he did her bidding, to pursue that folly of statecraft, to thrust an entire planet into war once again.

Thank you, Hawk. Hawk was the only member of Ahrik's command group that remained from the halcyon days of first combat, during the War for the Kereu. The rest of the old command group were either broken and retired or rotting in the ground, their remains scattered throughout the worst places in the world, on the moon, and in space. He and his sons realized soon after the War for the Kereu began that combat held no glory, only pain and an unknown grave. What did Zharla give up to achieve her power? Little, by comparison to Ahrik and his sons. Her comfort and delusion blinded her to the horrors of war.

Footfalls sounded behind him. He did not acknowledge her, but he heard the paper rustle from his desk. He felt her hand on the small of his back. Almost, he wanted to believe they could have what they once did. Her touch surprised him, that she would dare after what she did just the day before, and because her touch still sent a jolt of excitement down his spine.

She leaned into him, ever so slightly. "Dear, don't we want to sign this order?"

How could her voice still electrify him, even though he knew what she really was, a half-crazed monarch who endangered her people with pointless obsessions? "You say 'we'," said Ahrik, "but we agreed on a division of labor: you rule, I govern."

She smiled and rubbed his back. "Ah'ke, I...Oh."

She stared at his lower lip and took out her handkerchief, but Ahrik jerked his head back. He moved away from her, his face incredulous. He nodded toward the paper in her hand. "Tell me what this is really about."

She played dumb—oh unbecoming charade—then dabbed her handkerchief at her forehead. "How do you mean?"

"I mean, why do we need to put Nayr's mentor on trial for crimes against the race?"

"He unleashed a bioweapon on the Emerald Moon three months ago, near some remote outpost called Kalevo." Zharla's face feigned disbelief. "He violated the treaty with the moonies. He endangered the peace. How can we ignore that?"

Ahrik knew she cared neither for moonies nor the peace. He stepped around the desk, ostensibly to view the holos on the wall, but also to put the desk between them. She tended to lash out whenever they discussed her obsession, Shahl, his long-dead brother, and Ahrik sensed that he was about to come up.

"This order endangers the peace," he said. "Ignoring the behavior of Sheresh keeps us safe, Zhe'le. You do know that he started the last war, right?" Ahrik paused to consider what he was about to say. His eyes half-closed with pain. "Some of us remember what the War for the Kereu was like."

Zharla glared at him. "You call this peace, Ah'ke? We rule all of Dom, an entire planet, but ghouls haunt our dreams."

Ahrik frowned. "He's dead, Zhe'le."

She looked out the window and into the morning sky and twisted her handkerchief in her hands. "We'll find him, Ah'ke. He's out there on the moon. Somewhere."

Ahrik padded over and worked the piece of paper out of Zharla's hand. "You're asking me to sign a declaration of war," said Ahrik. He steeled himself for the half-truth he was about to utter. "Nayr and his clones are coming of age, and he loves power too much. This trial is an attack on his mentor's honor. This is all the excuse Nayr will need to..."

Zharla shifted her weight and eyed a challenge in his direction. "To what, Ah'ke?"

"He's unstable, and Nayr and his clones are coming of age today." He paused for emphasis. "Nayr loves his mentor very much."

Zharla snorted. "Love, Ah'ke? He loves his mother." Her lower lip quivered. "He loves me more than anything."

Ahrik wondered if that was true, but he dared not try to disabuse her of the notion now, when she might strike again. "He's not..." Ahrik pursed his lips and shook his head. "He's not ready to rule."

"You have to give up power sooner or later, Ah'ke."

"He's using you, Zhe'le. Sheresh is using you."

She scoffed. "That's ridiculous. Sheresh is weak. He needed me to keep him on the Council of Elders."

"You did that against my advice."

"I have this under control. Sheresh overreached, and now we'll put him in his box, where he belongs."

"You're asking for war. Begging for it."

She gave him a condescending smile and stroked his shoulder. "I think power has gotten to your head, dear. Maybe we should start thinking about a transition."

Ahrik ripped his shoulder away, but his eyes flashed with the sting of her remark. "You know me better than that." She knew he wanted only to serve his people, but now she accused him of selfishness, when he was anything but. She couldn't see that, either.

He glared at her with finality. "War is nothing to be trifled with, Your Majesty."

A glazed look passed over her face, as if she heard none of what he said. She turned to look up into the sky. "If Shahl is up there on the moon, Sheresh may have killed him with his bioattack."

Ahrik threw up his hands. Blood pumped into his neck. "And

there we have it. Your obsession with my dead brother drives us into a war we can ill afford."

She stepped to him and caressed his face, but her eyes glinted like obsidian. Ahrik stiffened, but forced his body to welcome her advance. He needed her, if he was to succeed. The people loved her, almost worshipped her.

She leaned in and kissed him, and he was equal parts revulsion, submission, and exultation. "I'm sorry about your mouth, dear. It won't happen again."

She always said that, the day after.

She rubbed his arm, and a strange look whispered into her eyes. "If you don't want to sign the order—"

He narrowed his gaze. "You already signed it, didn't you?" He looked away. "I'm so sorry, for us all."

She froze at the accusation in his voice, then gave a slow nod and looked away. She stepped to the door, but paused before palming it open. Her hand hovered over the reader. "I...I told him."

Ahrik's eyes grew wide, and a chasm of fear opened in his gut. "You told Nayr?" Ahrik stumbled to his desk and slumped into his hoverchair, expression vacant, head light. "Zharla, what have you done? He doesn't need any more reason to hate me."

From his hoverchair he reached for the secret compartment set into the far corner of his desk, an intricate tremor in his hand. He pressed his fingertip onto the miniature reader next to it.

The compartment cover dissolved to reveal his *qasfin*, resting on soft velvet the color of blood. Face grim, heart longing not to do so, he lifted his cherished and reviled *qasfin* by its hilt and took in the gleam of its tight crescent blade, as sharp as the day it was forged. Biriq.

He tested its weight in his hand. Fourteen years since he hid Biriq in this place, and now he lifted it out once again, much earlier than he hoped he would. Its name meant Lightning, that it might fly with speed and power.

"Zhe'le," he said, still focused on his blade. "Do you know what this means? Zhe'le?" He looked up. She was gone.

Hawk, he cast over the tendril link, *mobilize the* ketel. *Quietly.* Maybe there was still a chance to avoid a war with Nayr and his one hundred thousand supersoldiers.

Nayr palmed open the cabinet to the sparring weapons and considered, for a moment, whether he'd be justified in using a sharpened *qasfin* instead. He was seventeen years old today, his *qer'ish* day, and for every single day of those seventeen years the person he called Father lied to him. And if Nayr was anything, he was honest, with himself and with others. He expected nothing less from those he loved.

Used to love.

He frowned and padded across the room. His soft-soled sparring boots gripped the glimmering wooden floor. Afternoon sunlight streamed through the window facing Meran Mountain and bounced off the floor, a king's ransom worth of wood here on Dom, this dry, rocky world.

He rested his palm on the reader next to the combat weapons cabinet, the one with the sharpened weapons, and asked himself if the world would notice if he incapacitated Ahrik, the man he once called Father.

No liar deserves to rule the world.

Nayr examined the gleaming combat *qasfina*. The morning light caught their curved steel blades, atomic-sharpened to wicked tips. He lifted one off its rack and hefted its familiar weight. The leather-bound hilt creaked in his grip. So many years of training, and now today, his *qer'ish* day, he finally contemplated using one for real, against an enemy he never knew he had.

Someone must protect Mother, and the world, from Ahrik's lies.

The door dissolved with a whoosh behind him, and he grabbed a cloth from the rack inside the cabinet.

"Hello, son."

Ahrik's voice raked his ears like teeth grinding ice. The word "son" stood in the air like a monument to Ahrik's disloyalty. How did Ahrik command his *ketel* all these years while lying like that?

Ahrik pulled off his combat boots. "Sorry I'm late."

Another lie. "No problem. I was just polishing the *qasfina*."

Ahrik grunted as he slipped on his own sparring boots. "You know, the palace has servants to polish those."

Nayr wondered what drove Ahrik to lie. The power to rule a planet was surely an intoxicating drug, but was it worth selling one's soul? Ahrik had to be stopped.

Nayr replaced the combat *qasfin*, but a twinge of doubt interrupted the action. Maybe now was the right time, after all. He could surprise Ahrik while he focused on his sparring boots. No, Nayr decided. He wasn't sure what Mother would think. No point in killing or maiming Ahrik unless he was sure the Queen wouldn't disagree.

Nayr walked back across the room, nodding to acknowledge Ahrik's comment about the servants. "A man dependent on others isn't free," said Nayr. "Isn't that what you always say?"

Ahrik raised an eyebrow and stood to choose his weapon from the sparring cabinet. "What's wrong, son? Is it what your mother said?" His shifted, like a weasel. "We can talk about it."

Nayr paused before reaching for his favorite sparring weapon, a *qasfin* with a heavy oak hilt and soft iron blade. The extra weight made him stronger, for when he'd need to wield a blade for real.

His thoughts wandered once again to the combat *qasfina*. He could switch one out for a sparring blade later. He and Ahrik sparred every week. Ahrik wouldn't notice the switch until it was too late.

Would Nayr regret his indecisiveness today? Nayr frowned. Ahrik would assume it was in response to his question.

"Son—"

"Don't call me 'son'," said Nayr, pulling on its sparring gloves.

Ahrik pulled on his own gloves, then looked away. He pretended like he was in the throes of some inner turmoil. "So, she really told you."

The old man was holding back. Nayr shook out his arms and legs, but narrowed his eyes in distrust. "What else are you keeping from me?"

Ahrik stood and pursed his lips, then bored his gaze into Nayr. Yet another lie hid behind his eyes. "Let's spar."

How long could the old man hide from the truth? Nayr's wrist compiler chimed. He frowned. He'd forgotten to remove it. He looked down, though, and his head swam.

A message scrolled up the tiny screen, from Sheresh, his closest mentor and friend:

> Just arrested. Accused of crimes against the race. Order came from the palace.

Ahrik. Who else would have signed the order, but Sheresh's oldest rival?

Nayr's blood boiled. He sensed this day would come. Long ago, Sheresh was Ahrik's first supervisor. In private, Ahrik accused Sheresh of starting the War for the Kereu seventeen years earlier, before Nayr was born, but Nayr spoke with Sheresh often about it. Nayr was sure: this was another one of Ahrik's lies. And now Ahrik had trumped up charges against Sheresh, the wisest man Nayr knew. His closest friend.

Nayr threw his wrist compiler into his bag, strapped on his arm guards, and picked up his sparring *qasfin*. "Yes," he said. "Let's spar."

No sooner had they crouched into their stances than Nayr flew at Ahrik with fury and motion. Ahrik dodged and parried. Sparks glanced off his arm guard when Nayr's blade struck. Ahrik grunted with the effort, and Nayr caught a satisfying sheen of worry on the old man's face.

They usually started slow, but Nayr was in no mood to go easy. Let the old man have a heart attack, for all he cared. It would save Nayr the trouble.

Ahrik regrouped and swung his blade. Nayr dodged and leaned back to cut Ahrik's legs out from under him with a kick to the back of the knees. Ahrik spun out of the way, but Nayr relished the look of surprise on Ahrik's face.

Nayr couldn't understand why Ahrik had done it. Why lie about being his father for all these years? Why invent charges against Sheresh? Why lie to Mother in order to consolidate his rule?

Ahrik launched another counterattack, but Nayr was smaller. And quicker. He used Ahrik's momentum against him. Nayr tucked into Ahrik's attack and slammed an arm guard into his ribs. Then, as Ahrik's blade rushed towards Nayr's head, he slid out of the way, spun, and brought his own blade onto the small of Ahrik's back.

Ahrik cried out in pain and crumpled into a roll away from Nayr. He gave a withered grunt. Bosonic springs under the floor cushioned most, but not all, of the fall. Their subatomic hum groaned under Ahrik's weight. Ahrik crouched on all fours, like a tiger ready to spring, but Nayr leaped first. Ahrik tried to dodge, but Nayr's knee connected with Ahrik's gut, along with a satisfying squelch and rush of air leaving Ahrik's body.

Ahrik slumped onto his back, the fight gone out of him. He lay still. His breath heaved, his eyes looked stern, and he examined the ceiling. "I...deserved...that."

Nayr scoffed and threw his practice *qasfin* to the ground. He was furious enough still to ignore the basics of blade safety. He just didn't care. One day his life was just like he wanted it, and the next he faced a different future, fraught with uncertainty and self-doubt. "Who decides what we deserve or don't deserve?" Nayr asked. "At least you had a choice."

Ahrik sat up. "Now wait a minute, so...Nayr."

Nayr ripped off his arm guards and gloves. "Why?"

Ahrik's shoulders sank towards the floor. "You sure you don't want to go another round? Settle your mind a bit?"

Nayr tore off his sparring boots. "Why didn't you tell me?"

"I wanted to..." Ahrik looked off. He avoided Nayr's piercing glare, then focused on the floor. "It doesn't change anything. People may say your military blood isn't pure, but you and I both know that doesn't mean a thing."

"You're not my father. By law, I shouldn't have one hundred thousand clones to command." Nayr slammed a fist into his bag. "My life is built on a lie. How can I lead my sons? I am a liar."

"No, Nayr. Your *keteli* clones are yours forever, because of your tendril link with them. No one can change that," said Ahrik. He slipped his own blade onto its rack and stretched his back. He sighed a look at Nayr. "You're the Queen's son. She has no daughters, nor will she. You're next in line for the throne. What worries you?"

Nayr guffawed, then shook his head. "You don't get it." He took his wrist compiler out of his bag and slapped it on his wrist. The wrist compiler reminded him why he was so furious. "Just because *you* are obsessed with power doesn't mean I am, too. I care about my sons and about serving Mother, not about ruling this desiccated rock."

Ahrik started to peel off his gloves. "Service and rule are one and the same, Nayr. We hoped you'd have learned that by now."

Nayr sealed his bag shut with a ferocious swipe. His thumb and forefinger pressed together like a vice as he ran them across the two sides of the biomesh seam. "Don't bring Mother into this." He drilled his glare into Ahrik and took a step forward. He thought about finishing what he'd started. "Your lust for power blinds you. You can't see the evil you sow."

Ahrik narrowed his eyes, but kept his demeanor calm. Nayr trusted him like a viper guarding a bird's nest.

Ahrik nodded in his direction. "I can help you, Nayr."

Nayr shouldered his bag. "Help me what? Betray Mother? Execute my mentor?"

"Ah," said Ahrik. He looked away with a hint of guilt. "So this is really about Sheresh."

Nayr stepped to within an arm's length of Ahrik, but Ahrik didn't move a muscle. So arrogant. Nayr poked a finger into the old man's chest. "I will expose your lies, Ahrik Jeber-li. Stay away from my friends and family."

Nayr shouldered his bag and stormed out. As he did, he accessed the internal compiler implanted in the base of his skull. This tech was the privilege of every *ketel* commander in the Army. The internal compiler gave him the tendril link to communicate with, command, and control his clones. His sons.

The internal compiler also let him store vast amounts of information, accessible only to him and encrypted to his unique genetic code. He created a new file, named it "Revenge", and put a single word in it: *Ahrik*.

Anda and his family trundled along in the hold of the farming co-op's cargo freighter, deep green blocks of freeze-dried algae jostling all around them. There were fewer blocks in this harvest than before the Black attacked Moon's algae tanks, so Anda drew comfort from the rich pungency of the cargo wafting around them. They bumped back and forth as the freighter navigated the uneven terrain on its antiquated hover system.

Anda and Esh'a were still in debt for their tanks and seed algae, and with the failure of their crop they couldn't afford to take the subtransporter to Kalevo, much less a shuttle. Anda wondered if he and Esh'a had made the right choice, all those years ago, to run from Home and live in self-imposed exile on Moon.

He looked down at Cera, sleeping peacefully despite the bumpy ride, nestled between him and Esh'a. He smiled. Without their choice to marry and live on the Emerald Moon, they would not have their beautiful daughter. Now, ten years after they chose exile, seven-year-old Cera was in a healing trial, so their trip to Kalevo would serve two purposes: start Cera's new treatment, and find a way to keep their farm afloat. They would make this work, just like they had every time before. Even after he discovered the dead tanks yesterday,

Anda felt hope.

Esh'a shifted her weight. She caught Anda looking at Cera. Her eyes softened and she smiled at him. He reached an arm around and squeezed her shoulders, but she didn't lean into him like he desperately wanted her to. Still, his heart sang at the smile he'd gotten out of her.

"I'm glad she finally got to sleep," he whispered.

Esh'a's eyes grew serious and studied the steel-grate floor of the freighter. "She'll need all her strength to fight this."

How does she always see challenge where I see opportunity? Even after all these years, it surprised Anda how different they could be. They loved each other. This was just a rough patch.

Anda shrugged to concede her point. "We'll go to the healing clinic first thing, then over to Yosi's place. He'll be able to help us with another loan."

Anda could tell by the way Esh'a looked back at him that she thought Yosi would be as much help as a meteorite shower. She fiddled with the vanilla charm at her neck and smiled again, but this time it wasn't deep and heartfelt, like before, but a brave face for an unwelcome future, like she didn't have a choice. "Cera," she said with a note of concession, "is the priority."

The freighter jerked up and then jolted forward, knocking Anda and Esh'a against the algae blocks. The blocks rattled violently inside their steel bindings, and Esh'a looked at Anda in alarm as she used her arms and body to stabilize Cera. The girl stirred, but remained asleep. The bindings held, and Anda and Esh'a both breathed a sigh of relief. "Sorry!" the pilot yelled from the front.

Anda cast a confident eye at his wife. "We can do this."

Esh'a's face tightened with worry, and her eyes welled a deep red. She breathed in, then let it out slowly, looking anywhere except at Anda. She patted his knee. "Sometimes, Anda, hope is not enough. Sometimes, we have to make hard choices."

Panic flushed through Anda as he realized what she was suggesting. "We already made the hardest choice. We're here on Moon as a family. Don't undo that."

She closed her eyes in frustration. "We can starve together, or I can do what we both know has to be done."

Anda just shook his head, not daring to speak or look at his wife. For a long while, they rode in silence, until the pilot called back, "Five minutes!"

Anda gave his wife a tender sigh. "Let's try with Yosi, but...if it comes to splitting up...let me go instead of you."

Cera began to stir, and Esh'a laughed off his request. "You know as well as I do that my chances of survival down there are much better than yours. Too many people know who you really are."

Cera yawned and rubbed her eyes. "Abbi and Imma, I'm hungry. Are we there yet?"

Anda squeezed Cera and smiled. "Almost there, Cerit."

Esh'a locked eyes with him again, and, as if in compromise, said to Cera, "We'll go to the healer first, so he can help you get better."

When they cycled through the airlock at the Kalevo clinic, the receptionist's face was grim and frazzled. The waiting room was packed. A deep sense of unease tunneled its way into Anda's chest. Kalevo was small, an outpost on the outskirts of a settlement, not even a town. Nothing like the city at Moon Station Prime. It was midmorning here, much too early for this many people to be at a healer's office.

"I didn't know Kalevo had this many people that could get sick," he whispered to Esh'a. They didn't even have an appointment. Their lives, this far out from Prime, didn't require that much planning.

The receptionist sighed when they told him they were there for the trial. "That's pretty important," he said, searching for something with bloodshot eyes as his fingers whisked over the compiler screen. "Let me check with the healer about getting you in."

He came back a minute later and motioned for them to follow him. "Shouldn't an orderly take us back?" whispered Esh'a to Anda.

Anda shrugged, but his worry deepened. He gripped Cera by the hand and followed the receptionist to an examination room.

After too long a wait, the healer entered and motioned for them to sit. He remained standing, a mask of exhaustion on his face, and leaned against a counter. He showed his palms in exasperation. "I'm sorry, but I'm not the healer running the trial. Can you come back tomorrow? Get here just after Homerise?"

"What's going on?" asked Esh'a, her brow furrowed, her voice wary.

Beside them, Cera fidgeted.

The healer pursed his lips. "The healer who was leading the trial and two of the orderlies left this morning, without warning. You know how it is when people leave."

Anda, wondering why this should matter, leaned forward and rested his elbows on his knees. "They left Kalevo?"

The healer avoided eye contact, then paused. "They left Moon."

Anda's breath caught in his throat. No one ever left Moon. Those that left were sellouts. "They went to Home?"

The healer nodded.

Esh'a shifted uncomfortably in her chair, her demeanor incredulous. "What the sunfire for?"

"Asylum," said the healer, his tone measured and uncertain, as if he wasn't sure they could handle this information.

Anda looked at him, confused. "Why would anyone want asylum there? People come here to escape Home, not the other way around."

The healer looked at them like they'd been hiding under a rock for the last ten years, which was, in a way, true. He sighed like he would have to explain something to a child. "Most of the people out there in the front waiting room have symptoms like your daughter's, but your daughter was one of the first reported cases. That's why she qualified for the trial."

Cera cleared her throat and smiled at the healer. "Thank you," she said, hugging her *dubbi* tight.

The healer cocked his head. A smile broke on his face as he looked down at her. "For what...uh...Cera?"

"For helping me get better."

He pushed himself away from the counter and crouched down so his eyes were on a level with Cera's. His eyes conveyed a barely disguised wonder. "Promise me something, Cera. Always be this positive, okay? No matter what."

She nodded like she'd never consider anything else. "Sure."

The healer looked up at Anda and Esh'a, and his brow furrowed with concern. "I have to be honest. In the last two weeks, this illness has begun draining Moon of its population. There are reports of crop failures in the outlying districts, and just today even rumors of failures closer to Prime, and some people say they're connected to this Moonlung or Creeping Cough or whatever it is they call it."

"The Black." Anda's shoulders slumped.

The healer rolled his head with uncertainty. "No one really understands it, but one thing's for sure: Prime is a sweltering hive of despair right now, since there are a lot more people who want to leave than can."

Esh'a stood and squeezed her hands with impatience. "So, you'll be here tomorrow when we come to start the trial?"

The healer gave them a sheepish smile. "Maybe. Maybe not. I put in an application, too."

The air seemed to rush from the room, and an empty, woozy feeling opened up in Anda's mind, as if the artigrav had shut off all of a sudden. They'd come to Moon ten years ago to get off the grid, for peace and safety, for a better life, but could they really live here if everyone else simply left?

Esh'a muttered a curse and sliced out of the door. She was in the airlock before Anda even thanked the healer and prepped Cera's helmet.

They bounded towards Yosi's place, the three of them hand-in-hand. Esh'a commed Anda on their private channel, the one they used when they didn't want Cera to hear. "It's started again, hasn't it? We won our independence, and we're winning the peace, so they want to cut us back down to size with another war."

Anda frowned at the prospect. "Let's not jump to conclusions."

She hissed in annoyance. "Don't be naïve."

Anda couldn't meet her eye. "A war would be so pointless."

"I'd rather fight a pointless war and survive than give in and die anyway, Anda. If they can do this to Moon, then they'll stop at nothing."

An uncomfortable moment passed. Anda could tell Esh'a had something else to say, but didn't know how to say it. He almost agreed with her about fighting. When it came to the goodwill of the people on Home, Anda's reserve of hope ran precious thin.

Yosi's place came into view, three small domes peaking over the horizon. Home was about to set, and Anda was glad they would spend the night with Yosi and his family. It would do them good to be with friends again. Yosi was the closest thing Anda and Esh'a had to family.

Cera, between them, squeezed their hands and commed over the general channel, "I'm hungry."

"Almost there," Anda and Esh'a said in unison.

When Yosi's place was only a few bounds off, Esh'a commed Anda over their private channel again. "Do you think your brother had anything to do with this?"

Her question stopped his blood cold. He didn't want to believe it could be possible, but he knew if Home had anything to do with the illnesses and the crop failures and the mayhem at Prime, then there was a good chance that Ahrik knew about it, at least, even if he may not have ordered it done.

Anda knew his brother and his rash, impulsive heart. He could have ordered this. Anda frowned back at Esh'a. "Let's see if Yosi has any answers."

Yosi received them like old friends always do, with food and a warm embrace, his eyes sharp and discerning, but his face otherwise armed only with a gregarious smile, expected of someone who made his living convincing people to give him money. His gaggle of kids swarmed around them, and Cera, hunger forgotten, blended right into the mix, frolicking and running from one dome to the next, which were connected by a bewildering circuit of tunnels. Yosi's wife, fecund, plump, with her head shaved like most people from Moon, admonished the children as they bolted past, time after time.

After they ate a simple meal, the children's ruckus reignited, but Yosi and his wife laughed it off as the four adults sat around the table. "So, Esh'a and Anda," asked Yosi, scratching his bald pate, "how's the farming?"

Esh'a looked at Anda and pursed her lips. Cera coughed as she ran by, and Esh'a called, "Cerit, why don't you take a break?"

Anda shifted in his seat and drew in a breath to buy time, unsure how to broach what was coming. "That's one reason we're here, Yosi."

"Oh?" asked Yosi, his eyes narrowing and head leaning to one side in a gesture of mild curiosity.

Anda's shoulders and eyes fell. There was no mincing words. "The crop failed."

Yosi shared a sharp glance with his wife, then laughed, nervous. Yosi had lent them the money for their farm, and the loan was still years away from being paid off. A crop failure would sting Yosi, too. "Ah, you mean that one of your seven tanks failed, right?"

Esh'a got up and ran after Cera as she flew by. Anda sighed and shook his head slowly in Yosi's direction. "The whole crop."

"All seven tanks?"

"All seven tanks."

Yosi slumped back in his chair and examined the ceiling. "Anda, I—"

Anda waved a hand to cut off what Yosi was about to say, words Anda suspected he didn't want to hear. "We have a plan, Yosi. Just float us for one more cycle, then we'll be in a position to—"

Yosi stood, cutting him off in turn, and cast a desperate look at his wife, then back at Anda. Anda's breath caught in his throat. Esh'a returned and stood in the doorway to the dining dome, Cera clutched by the hand, huffing from the exertion of play, on the verge of another coughing fit. They always started when Cera ran around too much.

"We can't give you any more money," said Yosi, with forbidding finality. "You both did great things for independence. You fought bravely in the war, and we know that Home wants nothing more than for you to walk out the wrong end of an airlock. I know how important the farm is to your lives." He stared at the floor. "But the markets are wild now. The exodus from Moon is making demand for algae erratic. We've lost"—he looked at his wife again—"a lot."

"I...I know," said Anda. "You've done what you could."

"The truth is," said Yosi's wife, huffing and working herself out of her seat, "we applied for asylum. Yosi here didn't have the heart to tell you." She frowned and looked from Anda to Esh'a and back. "He knows what Moon's independence means to you."

Anda exchanged a knowing glance with Esh'a, still standing in the doorway. She fingered the canister of vanilla at her breast, then looked away, worry lining her face.

Cera walked over to Anda, glided it seemed to him, and took his hand in her frail fingers. She coughed, and her body convulsed with the effort. Anda winced and rubbed her back, helplessness coursing through him.

The coughing continued, and Cera climbed into his lap. After the coughing had subsided and her body had gone flaccid from the effort, she took a few breaths and gave him a weak smile. "Abbi," she said, "are we going to Home now?"

Anda didn't dare look at Esh'a, for fear that emotion would overcome him. In his mind's eye, she was covering her nose and mouth with her hands and turning away from the door so that Cera could not see her tears or hear her sobs. The image alone nearly sent Anda over the edge.

"No, Cerit," said Anda, clinching the lump in his throat with force of will. "Just Imma. You and I will stay here."

Made in the USA
Middletown, DE
23 November 2021